With Wine Comes Wellness

Book 3 of the With Wine Series

JE Johnson

JE JOHNSON AUTHOR LLC

ISBN: 979-8-9901462-5-9 (Paperback)

ISBN: 979-8-9901462-6-6 (Ebook)

Contents

For the ones who learned to love themselves after the fall.
For the ones who came back home — to their bodies,
to their breath,
to the quiet strength they didn't know was theirs.
For every soul who's been cracked open
and still chose softness.
This is for your healing.
Your hope.
Your return to the light.
— JJ

Trigger Warnings

This novel contains themes of addiction recovery, emotional trauma, and mental health struggles. It includes references to substance use, grief, and emotional manipulation, as well as moments of danger and psychological tension.
Reader discretion is advised.

Chapter 1

ALEX

I woke up gasping for air. It felt like an elephant was sitting on my chest. Sweat drenched my clothes, and my hair clung to my head. My pulse was racing so hard I wondered if I should call for a nurse, but there was no call button. I reached over to the nightstand for my cell, but that was missing as well, and the anxiousness increased. As my eyes adjusted to my surroundings, nothing looked familiar—I had no idea where I was. My chest was tightening the more I panicked, cutting off my airway further. I jumped out of the bed, trying to get a better look around because I knew I had had nothing to drink last night, so this wasn't some drunken excursion I couldn't remember. My hands shook uncontrollably as I ran them along the wall, searching frantically for a light switch to illuminate this blinding fear. The sound of waves subtly invaded the quiet darkness in the not too far distance.

Where the hell are the lights? Where the hell am I?

Overwrought with horror, I frantically searched the wall for anything to calm myself down.

I stopped searching and placed both hands firmly against the wall, noticing its smooth and damp texture—unfamiliar but familiar as well. I closed my eyes, taking several deep breaths. The air felt humid and smelled salty. In the distance, the sound of crashing waves enlightened me. The last thing I remembered was being in the hospital hooked up to machines beeping and humming, not whatever was going on here. As my breathing regulated and my heartbeat slowed, the memories became clearer. "Breathe in through your nose and out through your mouth," I instructed myself, remembering the hospital's instructions for managing panic attacks. The doctor told me it was PTSD from the assault and the fight. Slowly, I opened my eyes and took one last deep breath, turning around slowly to face the direction the unexpected sound was coming from. Despite the anxiety, the waves were calming me, and my heartbeat was syncing up with the rhythm of the ocean. I cautiously made my way to the edge of the room where I saw the moon in the distance—my eyes adjusted to the sliver of light it was giving off, barely illuminating my feet. That's when I realized there wasn't a wall in front of me. I was standing there open to the outside world with nothing to protect me and no phone to call for help. Clenching and unclenching my fists until my nails dug into my skin, I closed my eyes, desperate to figure out why I was here. I was here for a reason, but what reason was that?

Ah, yes. Rehab. I was here for rehab.

I lowered my head in shame as the tears slid down my face.

Lisette and I got here last night on Roman's private jet. I was in Bali, hopefully getting the help I needed to recover from the events of these past few months. This is the first night of a forty-five-day stay at an exclusive rehab center in Indonesia that specializes in addiction.

Addiction.

And here I thought I was nothing like my mother. Turns out that wasn't true after all, but I was damn sure not going to follow in her footsteps. Instead, I stepped out onto the covered deck then farther to the edge, wrapping my arms tightly around me, inhaling the warm salty air, swaying to the musical waves. My face was still sore, and I reached up, touching my cheek, placing the other hand over my ribs, which were still tender to the touch, feeling the remnants of the bruises left by Tanner. I tried my best to rub the memories of that night from those particular wounds, but it only ended up making it worse by flooding my mind with crystal clear details of what happened that night. My eyes stung with tears again as I remembered the sounds and sights of cameras clicking and flashing. Then I locked eyes with Roman just as he witnessed my second assault. My body trembled, wracked with silent sobs I stubbornly clung to, each shudder a testament to my unspoken grief. On the edge of the deck, I sat and wept silently until my tears were gone, the creak of the wood a constant reminder of my misery. I returned to bed; the sheets tangled and hot, tossing and turning until the sun finally rose.

**

"I don't know if I can go back after this." I looked at Lisette, as we stood on the beach staring out into the vast ocean on a clear warm night with a billion stars lighting up the sky. The moon was so big and bright—but all I could think was, "

I wonder if Roman is seeing what I'm seeing."

His mother, who is my therapist, smiled but didn't say a word. Reaching over, she took my hand in hers. She understood completely what I was going through. She was kind enough to sit in on my first counseling session, earlier that day, to make sure that the counselor I would have for the duration of my stay was up on the events that brought me here—and that I could trust them in such a short amount of time. I was still having trouble admitting to myself, much less to anyone else, that I truly had a problem.

"How did you do it?" I asked, taking in the fresh briny breeze and gazing up at the sky.

This was her last night staying at the rehab center, "Wisdom by the Water Wellness Retreat" where she encouraged me to go after the fight.

She stayed three days with me to take a little R&R for herself while helping me get settled in. She knew about this place because she stayed here once after too many of her patients took up residence in her head.

"Alex, when I returned home after treatment, I had to completely change my life. My profession, among other things, brought me here. I didn't go back to work when I went home."

I'm so confused. What does she mean she didn't go back to work?

"But I thought I was your patient? You've seen me in a professional manner." I swallowed the lump in my throat, hoping her answer differed from the thoughts in my head.

"I still have my license, but I retired from my practice. Roman asked me to help you. He knew you were like us. He thought you were special."

I doubled over in laughter, thinking about the word *special*.

"Oh boy, was he right! A special kind of crazy." I said more to myself than her, since I didn't mean for that to come out of my mouth.

She laughed with me and gingerly put her arm around me.

"No, you're not crazy. A little intense, maybe, but not crazy. I've never met an empath like you before. You absorb and radiate so much emotion it really is like a superpower. You just didn't seem to have control over what you absorbed and what you emitted. Some of the rougher stuff got the best of you for a time." I put my hand over my mouth and tears fell, replacing the laughter.

"You stayed because of me, didn't you? This hurt you again, didn't it?" The realization hit me hard that I was the reason she needed a break. My hands hit my knees as I sucked in a gulp of air trying to catch my breath as the splashing of tears at my feet held my attention. She put her arm back around me and helped me stand back up.

"Yes, Alex, what happened to you affected me. You affected many people. I'm mostly here for you, not because of you. I needed a break after everything that happened, but I wanted to make sure you were going to be okay. You're going to have to find a way to forgive yourself. You're going to have to come to terms with the consequences of your actions and decide what your life needs to look like for you when you get back. My guess is you won't be the same person you were before you left..." She gently turned my face to look at her. "...even before any of the bad stuff happened. Try to find the very best version of Alex, for yourself. And remember, nobody's perfect." I was so glad she didn't sugar coat that for me. Her honesty is what truly resonated with me.

"Roman prayed for me before I left, and I felt it. Can you pray for me and ask him to keep praying? In fact, let everyone know that's all I need and the only thing I ask of them." I sniffled and wiped my cheek with the back of my hand as I decided calling out to that higher power may have actually been my saving grace that day, and if prayers worked then, I hoped they worked now.

I stood up taller, taking a deep breath as I shook off the self-pity and reached out to give Lisette a hug.

"Of course, sweet girl, of course."

"And please tell them I'm sorry." I am so, so sorry. I thought about my best friends, Abby and Maggie, and wondered if being sorry would be enough for what I put them through, not to mention my family.

"I think I'll let you do that yourself."

I took a deep breath, smiling off into the distance, but wondered how anyone was ever going to forgive me.

Lisette went home the next morning. In the three days she was here with me, she helped me navigate the retreat. I had to pick three extracurricular activities on top of the group counseling sessions to take. I chose meditation as one. It sounds easy enough, but so far, it's been the hardest. It's not a lot of fun sifting through the garbage in my head.

Then there's the Ayurvedic class. This is the most fascinating to me. I'm going to learn how to make different herbal teas and tinctures that helped with all kinds of ailments—mental, physical, and emotional. The curriculum teaches everything from how to grow them to how to make medicine with them.

The last thing I signed up for was a community outreach program that helped build homes and play with kids and read to them. Hopefully, it will keep my mind focused on the project I still needed to finish at home.

And finally, one last thing Lisette said to me before she went home was, "Yes, you are worthy of love and that's going to be a struggle for you to believe. But while you're here, you'll have time to work on that." I felt like that was the most important bit of information she could've left me with, and the one that was going to torture me the most.

***

ROMAN

When the plane landed, I got off to help mom get her luggage on board. It was weird being here knowing Alex was so close, but I wouldn't be able to see her. I gave my mom a hug. I couldn't shake the thought this was all my fault. Returning to the beginning is something I wished I could do, but would it really change anything?

"How are you?" I asked cautiously, raising an eyebrow. She looked rested, thankfully.

She smiled and said, "I'm great, honey."

I'm not going to pretend I don't want to know how Alex is, but I have to be prepared for the doctor patient privilege response.

"How is she?" I inquired, looking off into the distance as if it were directly where she was. I was hoping she would tell me that Alex was good and that she still loved me. That there was still a chance for us. My mother just smiled, looping her arm around my waist.

"Let's talk on the plane."

It didn't sound like I was going to get the answer I was looking for.

As soon as we were in the air, the flight attendant brought us breakfast and mom proceeded to tell me about Alex.

"Alex has settled in. She only had one thing for me to ask everyone, and that was to pray for her. She knows the damage she caused and she's carrying that weight right now."

I nodded my head, feeling the giant gaping hole she left in my heart.

"She needs to forgive herself," my mom said with compassion.

I thought about how scared I was for Alex prior to the fight, and how there was nothing I could do to help her. She seemed so out of control. I also knew all the good she was doing before the fight, as well.

"You know, despite the destruction left by hurricane Alex, she made a lot of positive progress. The project she was working on was in capable hands. She started a non-profit that will hopefully be up and running while she's away, despite a few snags that's delayed its start. It's going to be used to renovate or restore other neighborhoods like the one she was doing before she left."

"Roman, I have an idea. Let's talk about it when we get back. I'll need you to call a meeting." Mom seemed really excited about something.

"Sounds like a plan. Gimme a hint?" I kind of knew she wouldn't, but it was worth a try.

"When we get home."

Mom doesn't play the same games Alex does. I should be thankful, but I missed those games—mostly because I missed her.

When the plane landed it was late, so I drove mom home and went back to the penthouse. It was quiet here, but peaceful now. I used the quiet to pray for Alex, like she requested. I kept the pictures of her with her family and friends on the bookshelf. My prayers felt more effective when I focused my attention on a tangible item.

I listened to our favorite classical music and thought about all the good times we spent in this room, wondering if we'd ever have another moment together, happy or otherwise. The phone was ringing, with Amelia's name flashing across the screen.

"Hey Amelia." I leaned back on the sofa and pushed my hair away from my forehead, noticing I needed a haircut and since Amelia's on the phone, maybe she could schedule that for me.

"Sorry to disappoint, it's just me." Harrison sounded frustrated.

"Oh. Why are you calling from Amelia's phone?"

I guess I'll have to schedule my own hair appointment.

"Mine's in a bowl of rice. I dropped it in the toilet."

I chuckled, "That's fantastic, but I'm assuming you're going to buy another one, right?"

"Yes, but I can't obviously do that right now since it's 10 pm on a Sunday and I'm hoping...never mind...who cares about my stupid phone, how's mom? Thought I'd call and ask you first, just in case." I laughed again because Harrison hated female drama, including our mother's.

"She's good. I dropped her off a little while ago. She wants to call a meeting. She has an idea about something."

"About what?"

"I don't know. I was telling her what Alex had done before she left, and she said she had an idea that she would share when we were back. Said she wanted to call a meeting to do it."

"Gotcha. How's Alex? Did you get to see her?"

"Mom said she's doing well. Says she has a lot weighing on her and she wants us all to pray for her. No, I didn't see her." I gazed over at the picture of her on the shelf and smiled.

Harrison said, "Man, I'm sorry. Are you okay? We'll definitely be praying for you both."

Lots of praying going on.

I hope it helps.

"Thanks. I guess that's all any of us can do for her."

"If you need me, let me know. I'm serious." Usually if my brother said you could count on him you couldn't, but this time seemed different.

"Thanks. I'll talk to you tomorrow." I'm glad I have the support system I do. It hasn't been as hard as it was the last time. I still have the friends I met through Alex— Matt and Maggie, Abby and Jack and their kids. It's good to have people to talk to that know her so well.

Chapter 2

ROMAN

M onday morning felt like a fresh start.

For the first time in what felt like forever, I walked into King Construction without carrying the weight of a dozen problems on my shoulders. Projects were moving the way they were supposed to move. Crews were where they needed to be. Timelines were holding steady. Even the atmosphere inside the office felt lighter than it had in months.

Sunlight spilled through the windows behind my desk, stretching across blueprints spread over the conference table while the quiet rhythm of another workday moved through the building around me. Phones rang in nearby offices. Printers hummed. Conversations carried faintly through the hallway.

Normal.

God, I had missed normal.

The court mess was over. The chaos surrounding Burrow Township had finally settled down, and for the first time in months, it felt like everyone could breathe again. More importantly, Marcus Ellington was gone. I leaned back in my chair, slowly turning it toward the windows overlooking downtown Cincinnati while my mind drifted back over everything that had happened.

The fight. Hell. I still couldn't believe any of it had actually happened. I'd made Marcus a deal that night. If Alex won, he retired and left Cincinnati. At the time, it felt simple enough. Now, looking back, I wasn't entirely sure I'd call what happened winning.

Alex damn near started a war. Still, she beat the hell out of Tanner, and somehow that entire ridiculous chain of events had exposed things bigger than any of us realized at the time.

Now Tanner sat in jail; Alex had been shipped halfway across the world to rehab; and Marcus Ellington, the corrupt politician with an equally corrupt family, had vanished without so much as a press conference or public statement—Gone.

Just like that.

For months it felt like his fingerprints had been all over everything surrounding Alex. Burrow Township. Permits. Zoning approvals. Money changing hands where it shouldn't. Entire neighborhoods paying the price while people like Marcus lined their pockets pretending they were helping. Alex saw it. She'd stood in front of a judge and told him exactly what she believed was happening—that Marcus had manipulated permits and accepted kickbacks while people suffered because of it.

Thankfully the judge listened but more importantly, he investigated and once someone started pulling at the threads, the entire thing unraveled faster than anyone expected. Marcus disappeared and left everyone else standing in the wreckage—A couple police officers. A property inspector. An appraiser. Someone inside permits. A clerk.

People who thought power protected them...who thought no one would ever question what they were doing.

My jaw tightened when I thought about the officers—those scumbags.

Every time Alex stepped foot into that neighborhood trying to help people who needed it, they treated her like she was the enemy. They harassed her. Questioned her motives. Made things harder simply because she refused to ignore what everyone else pretended not to see.

Meanwhile she kept showing up without hesitation, without expecting anything in return. Because that was Alex. She walked straight into difficult places when everyone else walked away.

For every terrible thing that had happened to her, Alex had quietly left something good behind. Ella, Burrow Township, families who finally had someone willing to fight for them. People who mattered enough for her to keep showing up when it would have been easier not to.

Even me, especially me. At first, I thought Alex was reckless. Then stubborn. Complicated. Good—truly good.

The kind that kept believing people deserved better no matter how many times the world proved otherwise.

I leaned farther back into my chair as something unfamiliar settled through my chest. Relief. Peace. Maybe gratitude. For the first time in months, everything felt still.

No crisis. No emergency. No disaster waiting around the corner. Just one ordinary Monday morning. My hand rested against the arm of my chair while my thoughts drifted somewhere they always seemed to find their way back to.

Alex.

I wondered what she was doing right now.

***

ALEX

This place really is amazing.

There are no electrical fixtures in the bungalows. At night, we have to use candlelight, and every candle is housed inside a hurricane lamp. I found myself wondering if there was a reason for that as I wandered around my room searching for any sign of electricity.

I opened drawers and cabinets, eventually finding a couple of flashlights for use after dark, but there were no outlets anywhere. No lamps. No plugs. Nothing.

The first night I was here, I went straight to bed, completely overwhelmed by the trip and the reasons behind it. I hadn't yet realized I would need the candles because there was no electricity in the rooms.

It's wild.

And, if I'm being honest, a little nerve-racking.

Now I keep a flashlight on the nightstand beside my bed in case I need it during the night, or in case another panic attack leaves me discombobulated—which would be putting it mildly.

Outside, fairy lights are strung throughout the trees lining the walkways. The tiny lights branch off in different directions, leading to each area of the retreat. It's not as though the entire property is without electricity. Apparently, we're just not meant to use it while we're in our rooms.

This place gives new meaning to the term unplugged.

I also spent a lot of time thinking about the walls after Lisette told me there really weren't many of them. The rooms are mostly open. Each bungalow has three walls, while the fourth is made up almost entirely of giant sliding glass doors that most people leave open because it's warm year-round. According to Lisette, the doors are only closed during storms—not ordinary rainstorms, but the kind of weather that makes people pay attention. So far, I haven't seen one.

The covered porches keep the rain out anyway.

We each have our own private bathroom, and every detail has been thoughtfully designed to feel peaceful and welcoming.

Honestly, if you ask me, this place feels more like a luxury spa retreat than a rehabilitation center.

My phone is locked away in the main building with all the other electronics. They're under the impression that most of us are here because of social media addiction, which seems to be the running joke around the retreat.

Apparently, they've had several people in the past week desperately trying to get their phones back because they just had to see if they had a text message, a notification, a like, or some other social media update waiting for them. According to the staff, a few even tried bribing them.

The thought made me cringe.

Then again, the thought of what was probably happening on social media when I left made me nauseous.

If I never have access to it again, it will be too soon.

I still don't know how I let someone make me feel so unhinged, but if I'm being honest, it wasn't just one person. There were several people involved, including myself. At some point, I'm going to have to find a way to make peace with all of it. I need to make amends where I can, let go of what I can't change, and learn how to forgive.

Our group counseling sessions always begin with prayer.

One of the first things they asked us to do was pray for the people we've hurt and the people who've hurt us. The first day, it took me nearly twenty minutes to get through my list. The majority of the names belonged to people I had hurt rather than people who had hurt me.

Eventually, they suggested I pray for a few people each day so I wouldn't miss most of the group discussions.

They had a point.

Over the last few weeks, I've gotten a lot off my chest. More importantly, I've gotten to know myself better than I ever have before.

It's been almost three weeks since I've had a drink, and to be honest, I don't miss it.

Not even a little.

As I was walking out of the counseling session today, the therapist stopped me and asked, "Alex, how are you today?" She's a very sweet Indonesian woman with the cutest accent. Her name was Melati. I smiled and slowed down to wait for her to catch up.

"Today, I'm doing pretty well. Headed to my herbal lesson and then meditation on the beach." I pointed towards the walkway that led to the beach where the meditation took place.

"How is the herbal class going for you?"

"I love it. Trying to figure out why I'm so obsessed with the herbs, though. I mean, I know there's medicinal uses for them and I can make teas, but I feel like there's something I'm missing." She smiled as she put both hands on my shoulders and looked me straight in the eye.

"Just ask the right question. Are you coming to our little get-together tonight in the main building? We've missed you at the last two." I shrugged.

"Maybe. I still struggle to decide whether I should have fun."

What does that mean, ask the right question?

Melati grabbed my hands and looked at me thoughtfully. "Who are you worried about?"

"Not sure what you mean?" I squinted, wondering who she might be talking about as I simultaneously wondered what the right question meant.

"Is someone going to scold you for having fun?" I laughed at myself but then a sadness swept over me, thinking about all the people I've disappointed.

"Huh, I don't know. I guess I just kinda feel bad or guilty about having fun when I've left so much pain behind me." She rubbed my arm and was full of that sympathetic expression but for some reason it felt safe instead of irritating the way it used to.

"When is your herbal class?" she asked as she slipped her arm through mine.

"In about an hour, I was going to go for a walk."

"Good, so was I. I'll walk with you." She kept her arm through mine and talked to me about releasing guilt. She told me that everyone back home was going to have to deal with their own pain and all I could do was work on mine. That other people's thoughts, feelings and emotions were not my responsibility. It sounded an awful lot like a conversation I've had with Dr. King. I wondered if this is where she learned it. So, I guess, tonight I'm going to a party and I'm going to try to have fun.

In my herbal class today, we made tinctures, and I learned about anti-anxiety herbs and antidepressant herbs. We had already learned about the herbs that give you energy and relaxed you and helped you sleep. We made some tea with them, and they turned out to be very relaxing and calming. I didn't love the taste, so I needed to talk to someone about that and see if adding flavor to them would hurt the efficacy. Afterwards, I went to the main house to get a quick snack before meditation on the beach.

When I arrived, I munched mindlessly on fruit and crackers while sipping tea. I stared off into space, trying to think of a question to meditate on, but I was getting nowhere. Oh well, since that wasn't helping, I walked down to the beach early to get a good spot instead.

I picked a place off to the side right in front of the water. I sat down and leaned back on my hands, lifting my head towards the sky. It looked cloudy today and the breeze from the water was cooler without the sun beaming down. The meditation leader approached me with a coconut to hold. Every day, she gave us something different to keep our focus. The coconut brought back memories of before I left when Roman told me to have fun with the coconuts. I laughed out loud, startling myself, then opened my eyes and looked around at everyone looking at me and I whispered, "Sorry." They smiled and giggled, then we went back to eyes closed and thinking inwardly.

I concentrated on the herbs and what questions I could ask.

"What can I do with herbs?" came to mind and I asked it over and over. I got nothing, so I guessed that was the wrong question. "What herbs are important?" again I asked, over and over...nothing. I was getting frustrated when finally, I gave up and thought, "

"God or whoever, I need your help with this one. I'm here, I'm reaching out. What have you got for me?" I pleaded internally.

I dropped the coconut and aggressively grabbed sand in both hands, then released it, watching the granules fall back to the beach on either side of me. It was very calm and silent, and a question popped into my head...

What can the herbs do for my mom?

Well, now that's a weird question, considering my mom is dead. Someone up there likes jokes, I see. That question really irritated me. I clutched the sand with both hands, squeezing as much of it as I could, then threw it back toward the water.

I was about to give up and spew obscenities at the sky when I opened my eyes and yelled, "That's it!!!"

Then the skies opened, revealing the reason for the hurricane lamps.

Chapter 3

ROMAN

Amelia stepped into my office Monday morning with a smile on her face.

"Your mother's on line one," she said.

"Mom, why didn't you call my cell?" I asked as soon as I picked up.

She laughed softly. "I told you this was business and I was going to ask for a meeting."

"Okay, did you set that up with Amelia?"

"No, I wasn't sure what I needed to do. I've never asked for a meeting before."

A smile pulled at the corner of my mouth as I leaned back slightly in my chair. "I guess the first thing we need to do is identify the purpose of the meeting."

"Yes, of course," she said quickly. "Would you like to have lunch and discuss it?"

Of course I was going to say yes. Life had moved at a relentless pace lately, and somewhere between Burrow Township, construction schedules, court issues, architects, budgets, and everything else that had consumed the last several months, lunch with my mother had quietly become one of those things we kept meaning to do and never seemed to make happen.

"I would love to. Do you want me to pick you up?"

"No. I thought I could meet you at your office and bring everyone lunch."

A small smile settled onto my face. I never turned down food, especially food from Mom.

"Perfect. How about noon?"

"I'll see you then, honey."

After the call disconnected, I set my phone down and shifted my attention to the conference room where Shay and Darius had practically established permanent residency this week. Blueprints, renovation plans, contractor estimates, and paperwork covered nearly every inch of available table space while meetings rotated in and out throughout the day with architects and residents who had already purchased homes through the Burrow Township redevelopment project.

The focus right now centered around renovation allocation. Residents received funding based on income levels to make necessary improvements to their homes, and if money remained afterward, they could use the balance toward additional renovations or improvements that better suited their needs. The process sounded straightforward until real life entered the equation. Budgets stretched thin. Unexpected repairs surfaced. Costs climbed. They always climbed.

Right now, we operated within limitations because the nonprofit still hadn't officially been established, and without Alex here, we'd reached something of a standstill. We knew pieces of what she envisioned. We knew enough to keep moving forward, but Alex had always carried larger ideas than the rest of us could immediately see. She thought three steps ahead while everyone else tried to catch up, and now we were left trying to build something important while missing the person who understood the full blueprint.

The five hundred twenty thousand dollars returned from Texas thanks to Grant and his previous life had given us breathing room, but projects like this consumed resources quickly. There was always another expense. Another family needing help. Another unexpected complication waiting around the corner.

Fortunately, Darius had become one of the strongest assets we had.

The man understood budgets in a way most people never would, and I suspected part of that came from growing up differently than the rest of us. Resourcefulness looked different when money hadn't always been there to cushion mistakes. His grandmother, Ella Jackson, brought lunch nearly every day they worked in the office and somehow always managed to pack enough extra food for Harrison, Amelia, and me. Ella prayed harder for Alex than almost anybody because she understood exactly what Alex had done for Burrow Township, for her family, and for people who had spent most of their lives believing no one important noticed whether they struggled or succeeded.

Watching Darius build something meaningful after the way he treated Alex when they first met still felt remarkable to me. The woman never held grudges the way most people did. She challenged people. Forced them to look at themselves. Refused to give up on them.

Guess he was thankful for that "uppity bitch" now.

The thought nearly pulled a smile out of me.

Alex never gave up on people. She never gave up on communities. She never gave up when everyone around her decided something couldn't be fixed. I only wished she could learn to offer herself the same grace and opportunity she gave so freely to everyone else.

My eyes drifted back toward the conference room before settling on project files scattered across my desk, and somewhere in the middle of budgets, housing plans, nonprofit discussions, and redevelopment efforts, I realized Alex had somehow managed to leave fingerprints on nearly everything happening around us. Even halfway across the world, she still felt woven into the foundation of what we were building.

I had a few minutes before meeting Mom, so I escaped to the employee green space I'd built, hoping to find some peace and quiet amidst the plants and soft sounds of the water fountain. With the sight of a cascading waterfall, the feel of the cool, smooth bench beneath me, and the sound of gently flowing streams; I was reminded of our walks along the river. I settled onto the bench overlooking the waterfall, putting in my earbuds. As I listened to classical music, I felt her presence beside me and wondered what she was doing. Although I struggled with the negative impact of her experiences, I tried to objectively list the pros and cons. While there were some definite downsides, the positives greatly outnumbered them. Did she even realize how much good she accomplished? I wondered if they'd let me write her a letter and tell her what's going on here–what she started. That would be a good question for my mother when she gets here. At the very least, she can explain the preferred method of contact.

I got up to get in the elevator and there was mom, right on time.

"Hi Mom," I said as I gave her a hug and we rode the elevator up together. We walked past Amelia, who came out from behind the desk and said, "Hi Mrs. King" throwing her arms around her.

"Hi Amelia, and you know it's Lisette."

"Sorry, it's a habit. I'm at work." I rolled my eyes.

"It's really annoying too."

"Stop it." Mom shoved my arm.

"You don't mind if Harrison and Amelia join us, do you?"

"Of course, that would be perfect." We had lunch in my office and mom got to tell us what her big plans were.

She excitedly began, "Okay, so after spending a few days with Alex at the retreat, I learned some things. One, she thinks she needs to do everything herself. She was just starting to trust people when all of this craziness happened. After reaching out to Burrow Township community members, she began establishing a nonprofit to serve them, as you all know. She fell in love again, which she never thought she'd do."

She glanced over at me and smiled before continuing.

"But it was all too much for her, so she closed herself off. She thought the court case and everything she had planned were going to become a burden, and she knew she couldn't take anyone on that journey with her. She asked me to tell all of you this because she didn't want anyone thinking she was abandoning the project, and that's why she trained Shay and Darius so thoroughly."

I stood and walked toward the window, shoving my hands into my pockets.

Hearing my mother say Alex fell in love again felt like getting punched square in the gut. I'd wanted that with her so badly that somewhere along the way, I think I stopped paying attention to whether she was ready for it too.

After her mother's accident, I pushed dinner when I knew she wasn't ready. When the police told her she needed somewhere safer to stay, I pushed her to move in with me when she wasn't ready for that either. Even when she told me she wasn't ready, I kept moving forward anyway because I convinced myself I was helping. Protecting her. Giving her stability. Giving her space to breathe.

In fairness to me, she always said there was an out clause.

But standing there looking out through the windows, my hands buried in my pockets while the city moved beyond the glass, I couldn't ignore the uncomfortable truth settling into my chest. Even Mom told me to slow down. To be patient. To leave the girl alone for a while. I couldn't. Maybe because once Alex got under your skin, logic stopped carrying the same weight it used to. Or maybe because some part of me knew exactly what I wanted long before she was ready to figure out what she wanted. Either way, this wasn't entirely her fault. Part of it belonged to me too.

Harrison brought my thoughts back to the room. "Ok, so what is it you want to do for Alex? I feel like that's where this is going."

I smiled, knowing my mom's heart was always in the right place.

"I want to get this non-profit in motion for her. We can at least get it started, and she can adjust it the way she wants it when she gets back. We know she already has the basic premise for it and got the paperwork finished for it to file. And Harrison, you've already talked to some investors, correct? What's their position?" I looked to Harrison for the answers to these questions since I was avoiding Alex as much as I could while she was setting this up. I made sure she focused on the investors, which is Harrison's department.

"They said they're waiting for Alex since it's hers."

"Well, is anyone else on the paperwork as a partner or anything?" I was hoping she didn't really think she could do all this by herself and that she was planning to take on a partner or something. Geez what an asshole I am for not being more supportive in this endeavor for her. I know nothing that's going on with it because I was too busy being a jerk.

"Oh damn. Yeah, I totally forgot. The clause states that if anything happens to Alex, preventing her from performing her duties temporarily or permanently, Darius Jackson will fill in." I would've thought she'd have chosen Harrison maybe, or Grant even—I wonder if Darius knew.

"I'll be right back." That girl and her clauses, I should've known. Time to put this plan of hers into action.

***

ALEX

I jumped up from my mat and took off running toward the herbal building. Torrential rain soaked me within seconds, drenching my clothes and plastering my hair to my face, but I barely noticed. Why had it taken me so long to think of this?

I'd been working with these herbs for three weeks now. Three weeks of learning combinations, studying properties, understanding uses, and somehow all I'd managed to focus on until now was treating things like cold symptoms and minor ailments. The realization hit me so hard I couldn't sit still another second.

By the time I reached the building, I was soaked, breathless, and practically slipping across the floor trying to get inside before they left for the day.

Mr. Tanjung immediately looked alarmed.

"Alex, are you okay?"

Bent over with my hands braced against my knees while I fought to catch my breath, I noticed Amat standing nearby looking far less concerned and far more entertained. Actually, entertained wasn't strong enough. He looked like he was actively trying not to laugh at me.

"Sorry," I managed between breaths. "I just needed to catch you before you left for the day and it's pouring out there."

Mr. Tanjung stepped closer.

"Alex, what can we do for you?"

I pushed wet hair back from my face and wiped rainwater from my eyes. "I have a question about the herbs."

My brain immediately answered itself. Of course it's about the herbs. What else would it be about?

"What might that be, Ms. Kennedy?" Mr. Tanjung asked.

His patience with me was honestly astounding.

"Is there a way to combine herbs to create the same effect as alcohol without the repercussions?" I blurted out.

I paused. My brain immediately replayed the sentence. Was there a better way to say it? The thought moved through my head so fast I stood there processing my own words for a second before finally nodding.

Yep, that's what I meant. I admitted to myself then straightened quickly and planted my hands on my hips.

"You mean drunk without the hangover?" Amat asked with a laugh.

I laughed at the absurdity of the question myself.

"Kind of?" I continued, "More like satisfy the addiction without the hangover or the inebriation?" I tilted my head and bit my lip, waiting for my answer.

Mr. Tanjung smiled.

"Would you like to take my advanced Ayurvedic class?" He said as if he'd been waiting for me to have this aha moment. I knew this was the answer to my prayers.

"Yes!" I shouted, then gave both of them a hug, bouncing up and down. They gave me the new schedule and I headed back to my room to change for the party. I was definitely in the mood for fun now.

I threw on a cute white cotton dress with thin shoulder straps, slipped into my brown woven flip-flops, and made my way toward the main house for the get-together. Thankfully, the rains came and went quickly here. One minute the sky would open and dump buckets of water like the clouds had finally given up holding it all in, and the next minute everything would settle back into stillness again, leaving behind damp earth, heavy humidity, and the clean smell of rain clinging to everything around you.

The storms did come with drawbacks though.

The power went out often here, especially when those fast-moving downpours rolled through, which explained why every room used hurricane lamps with candles instead of traditional electric lamps. Part of it was practical. The electricity wasn't exactly reliable. The other part was intentional. No electronics. No charging devices. No easy way to stay connected to the outside world even if someone wanted to. At first, I thought it felt excessive. Now I understood it. It forced you to be present. Thankfully, they supplied flashlights, so when the lights disappeared for a while, we never found ourselves sitting completely in the dark.

By the time I reached the main house, the storm had already passed, leaving behind damp sand and warm air that wrapped around my skin like a blanket. Twinkle lights glowed softly overhead while every glass wall surrounding the gathering space had been opened, allowing the sounds of the ocean and evening wildlife to drift inside. The dance floor had been set up directly in the sand, and a two-man band played Jimmy Buffett songs that somehow felt perfectly suited for a place where people came to heal pieces of themselves.

The buffet table stretched along one side of the space filled with local cuisines whose scents blended together beneath the salty ocean air, while a non-alcoholic bar sat nearby where I found Melati already waiting.

"What are you drinking?" I asked as she held a coconut, its husk fresh, topped with a bright, miniature umbrella.

"Tea." She answered.

I looked at the bartender and nodded.

"I'll have the same, please." I turned towards Melati after placing my order and wondered if she had somehow known what I needed to ask during my meditation class.

"Did you, by any chance, know what I was looking for with the herbs?" She laughed her sweet, melodic laugh.

"No, but you were so excited about the herbs all the time. Something was there. I was just helping you stay focused."

"Well, thank you." I bowed my head respectfully and leaned against the back of the stool next to her.

"Mr. Tanjung told me you decided to take his advanced class after seeing him. Said you came to him with a brilliant idea?"

Brilliant was the last compliment I would ever give myself after all the stupid crap I've done.

"Brilliant? Me? I don't know about that. I think my mom sent me the question and ya know what? She was brilliant, she just lost a battle she didn't think she could ever win, and I want to see if I can help people win the battle she lost." She didn't give me too much of the sympathetic eyes, knowing it would probably make me cry.

"Lisette told me about you. She said you were special. She said you spend a lot of your time helping others but not helping yourself much. Don't get me wrong, we love all the help you've given us in the community and the children love you. But sometimes we need to think of ourselves so we can be more help to others. If your energy reserves are depleted, how will you be able to help anyone?" I never thought of helping in that way before.

"That's probably true and a really good question. This is the most I've ever really done for myself. I enjoy helping build stuff and I love real estate. I haven't been to the gym since I got here, so that's an excellent substitute and, of course, hanging out with the kids is a total joy. Kids are so calming to me."

"Well, this is a pretty great place to take care of yourself. How about you take a seat and join me."

I realized I'd been standing there the whole time.

"Thank you, I'd love that." I quickly sat down and wanted to hear anything she could teach me after that.

Melati and I talked for a long time and sipped on our tea. She only asked me questions about myself so I could take inventory. This was the thing I was having trouble with. in our counseling sessions. I hated talking about myself. This is the most selfish conversation I've ever had, but I learned a lot about myself that I never really paid much attention to.

Meditation is something I like to do—Lookout Park comes to mind. I enjoy solitude, but I dislike loneliness—might be the reason I collected so many cell numbers—just in case. I love animals and children, but the reality of my work schedule means I'm rarely at home, and it would be irresponsible for me to take on the responsibility of a pet or child. I fear getting hurt because I use pain as protection instead of using good things to shield myself from pain.

She opened my eyes to the fact that the universe, God, whatever, is where we all get our strength. All this time, I've been doing everything on my own. I was making my own path when there was a unique path being paved for me.

"Next time you meditate, I want you to listen to what this new path is showing you. When you get on that path, no matter how difficult it may be, you'll know it's the right one when all the pieces fall into place. In the everyday, and even amidst struggles, you will discover joy. You will also learn when to rest. You're in this place because you finally heard the call to rest. That part of your journey was complete, and it was time for a new one." I couldn't help the tears that fell, but thankfully it wasn't a lot. If I never met Roman, who knows where I'd be right now.

"Melati, am I allowed to write a letter home?"

"Of course you are." She added, "Alex, I haven't seen you at church yet. Do you think maybe it's time? Everyone's beliefs are individual here. It's letting you know you're never alone and you are loved." I smiled and nodded, thinking how difficult it was for me to believe anyone could love me after what I put them through, much less God. After that talk, we discussed nothing else heavy. We mingled and danced under the stars.

Chapter 4

ROMAN

Standing at the conference room door, I quietly watched Darius standing at the front of the room confidently walking the architects through the initial ideas for the project. Budget reports, renovation estimates, and architectural drawings covered nearly every inch of the conference table while Shay sat nearby listening as discussions moved between timelines, projections, and development plans. Watching him now, it was difficult not to think back to the first time Alex suggested giving him a job here.

At the time, I thought she'd completely lost her mind.

The police painted a picture of Darius early on, and if I was being honest with myself, I accepted it far easier than I should have. Alex didn't. She pushed back immediately. She saw something in him long before the rest of us understood what was actually happening in Burrow Township.

Where I saw complications and liability, she saw intelligence, capability, and someone worth believing in.

The truth turned out to be uglier than any of us realized back then. Darius wasn't a problem to solve or some young man headed nowhere. He was intelligent. Driven. Capable. The corrupt police officers used him as a scapegoat while helping clear people out of that neighborhood for a crooked politician who cared more about profit than the people living there. Alex recognized it almost immediately because she always had a way of seeing through noise and distraction and finding the truth sitting underneath it.

I leaned quietly against the doorway while Darius passed budget projections around the room and answered questions from the architects with a level of confidence that impressed even me. His ideas were thoughtful, practical, and smart enough that I found myself mentally taking notes while he spoke.

"This is good work, Darius. As soon as my committee gets a chance to go over these numbers, we'll be in touch." Roland, who was one of the investors, said before standing up and shaking Darius's hand.

"Yes sir, thank you for your time. I look forward to working with you and your team." I don't know how Alex saw what she saw in this young man, but she has a gift.

"Hey there Roman. I didn't think you were coming to this meeting." Roland patted me on the shoulder as he and his associate walked past me in the doorway, was headed out of the meeting, leaving them with the rest of the committee.

"I'm just looking for Darius." As soon as Darius saw me, he lost his concentration. I'm absolutely going to dedicate Burrow Township to Darius and his family.

"Hello, Mr. King." I laughed because he always seemed so nervous and intimidated around me—Alex gave me plenty of shit for that.

"Hey Darius, can I talk to you for a minute?" I looked over to Shay apologetically for interrupting. "Can you handle the rest of the meeting?" She nodded and smiled. Another prodigy of Alex's with leadership skills. She always seemed kind of flighty to me, but I wouldn't try to take her on in a board room, the girl has no fear. I'm sure she learned that from Alex.

Darius rushed out of the room, asking, "Is everything ok?" I clapt him on the shoulder.

"Darius, everything's great. We just found some new information that we need your help with."

He shook his head, confusion etched all over his face. "Why would you need my help? You're way smarter than me." I laughed.

"First off, neither of us knows that; I've just been in the business longer. Second, someone left you in charge while she's away." His eyes grew enormous along with the smile that spread across his face.

"Alex? Have you talked to her? Wait, did you say in charge" He asked excitedly and with a look of nerves all over his face. I acknowledged him and we walked into my office.

"Darius, my man." Harrison chimed, pulling the terms of the non-profit up on his computer right to the clause as I started the introductions between Darius and my mom.

"Darius, this is my mother, Lisette King." He walked over to shake her hand, and she stood up and hugged him. I thought she had tears in her eyes, but she held them back thank goodness.

"Darius, it's so nice to meet you. Alex told me so much about you and your grandmother. Your family is very special to her."

He nodded and quietly reciprocated the feelings. "Same." Ok, mom, this is a business meeting. We need to keep the kid's head in the game.

Harrison interrupted the sentiment, "Ok, great, Alex is awesome, moving on."

"Harrison, could you please tell Darius what's going on here?" I motioned my hand in his direction. Harrison smacked his hands together and clicked his tongue with excitement.

"So, Mrs. King, over there..." He winked at our mother, "...spent some time with Ms. Kennedy recently. After that brief stint, she decided we should move forward with the non-profit without Ms. Kennedy on her behalf; only until she returns home, of course. This clause, right here..." He points the cursor to the clause, and it illuminates on the big screen. "...says we can do that because you're now in charge until she gets back." Harrison said, whipping his head in Darius's direction. Darius' mouth hit the floor.

"She told me there was something she needed to tell me before she left, but she must've forgotten." He was staring right at the screen. "Do you think I can really do this?" He looked around at all of us as he honestly asked, looking terrified or maybe excited.

"If Alex thinks you can, then so do we. We'll help you every step of the way." He nodded absentmindedly, looking really nervous.

"I don't want to mess this up for her." I smiled thinking of how intimidated people were by her.

"What do you think Alex would do if you messed it up?"

He laughed and his eyes went wide as saucers when he said, "Kick my ass!" The room erupted in laughter, but Darius locked eyes with our mother.

"Sorry, Mrs. King." He looked embarrassed but what he said sent shivers down my spine, because he wasn't wrong.

"Oh lord, not you too!" We laughed again and then Amelia set up a meeting for all of us to get this non-profit up and running for Alex before she came home.

I talked to my mom about writing a letter to Alex and she let me know that letters were an acceptable means of communication for the patients at the rehab.

When I got back to the penthouse, I sat at the island with a pen and paper and stared at it, not even knowing where to start. As much as I wanted to write her a personal one just from me, I thought maybe it would be better if I just told her what all her hard work had accomplished and have everyone sign it. I got up and poured myself a bourbon, but before I took a sip, I asked myself why I poured it.

Did I do it to relax? Did I need it?

Ok, the answer to both those questions, thankfully, is no. I poured it because I like the taste, and it reminds me of hanging out with my dad when he first handed the business over to me. Pretty scary, though, that I felt I had to ask myself that after everything I saw Alex go through with her mother's alcoholism and potentially her own.

I filled the letter with Darius and Shay's accomplishments with the non-profit and how well they're doing on the relocation and how excited everyone is to help them. Matt's contribution to the election of Marcus's replacement, I informed her, was significant. I explained to her that her information to the judge about Marcus directly caused his downfall and the corruption in Burrow Township. I told her how her love for a community and her willingness to fight, even by herself, moved mountains. I told her about how I went to see Bruce, to basically tell him how pissed I was at him for what he did, only to find out that hundreds of women have reached out to him to sign up for self-defense classes. Some instructors go to the local women's shelters to talk to them and teach basic classes to give them hope and a sense of self confidence and protection. Then I put that letter in a drawer. I decided it would be best if everyone got to tell her themselves when she got home.

After I got everyone to write a little something to her, I had Amelia mail it. Since doing that, I didn't look at her return next week as her coming back to me. I was only hoping she was returning in one piece. She left shattered. In fact, I think this time away was good for me as well. I didn't feel so obsessed with her or with our connection and the anger seemed to have dissipated.

I had wanted to be there to pick her up when she got home, but after talking to my mom, we both decided that her family should be the ones there to get her. Her dad, aunt and brothers were planning to pick her up at the airport next Friday. I also found out she had made Grant her power of attorney while she was away, and she bought a house away from the city. He said it was a little farmhouse on about five acres of land. He said she was planning to grow a garden. There was also a greenhouse on the property. I remember when my mom came home the first time from the retreat. She had the whole backyard practically replicated to what she loved about the retreat. I wonder if this was Alex's way of replicating what she loved about the retreat, too.

Who would've thought the woman I met in the bar that night, sitting there by herself, was carrying so much. I knew she was special, I just never would've imagined, that night, what she was capable of—good and bad. "Don't judge a book by its cover, is all I'm sayin'."

***

ALEX

As I walked into the church, I looked around and saw people of all different nationalities, wondering if it was a Christian church, or what kind of church it actually was. I didn't have to hear or see anything for the tears to start falling, though. I felt the love surrounding me, a feeling so strong it made my heart swell and brought tears to my eyes. The weight of it all crashed down, and I sat in the back, tears streaming down my face as I silently wept. After a little while, when the tears had finally stopped, only then did I notice there was someone next to me—comforting me.

Melati was smiling and holding a box of tissues in front of me. I sniffled and mumbled, "Thank you." As I took one and blotted my face dry.

"You're welcome." She waved her hand around her head through the church and added, "You're always welcome here."

I listened and paid attention to the rest of the service. Afterwards she brought me up to meet the pastor and he told me about a wellness pool that everyone goes to after service for healing.

"It's a healing pool, but sometimes we just go down there to swim." and he winked, as if that was supposed to mean something to me. I decided to visit the pool to see what everyone was talking about. Ocean laps were my usual routine, but a pool might be preferable. I walked through the tropical jungle with Melati and the pastor down a dirt path lined with the most amazing, colorful foliage and flowers. We chatted as we strolled and I asked about the denomination of the church and they said it was nondenominational because there were people of all faiths that came to the retreat and the purpose of the church was to find the higher power you felt most comfortable releasing your burdens to.—like the twelve-step program my mother was in once.

We walked what seemed like forever in a dense covering of thick palm trees and colorful flowers carpeting the jungle floor. When we finally came to an opening—I stopped dead in my tracks, in awe, my mouth slightly parted as I stared at the sight in front of me. It was a sanctuary hidden in the forest. Memories of Roman's parent's house popped into my head. I thought of it as a tropical retreat in the middle of the city. Now I know where it came from. Lisette brought her healing place home with her. I smiled as I watched people swimming in the crystal clear pond with the waterfall and the little cave behind the cascading water. It was so serene, I immediately felt at ease.

The Pastor bellowed out, "Ok, who's ready?" I looked around.

Ready for what?

Melati put her hand gently on my cheek and asked, "Are you ready to give your burdens to God?" I looked around at everyone. They seemed so peaceful and happy—I wanted that too. As the tears fell, I nodded my head and walked into the crystal-clear water with the pastor. It was warm and inviting. I took a deep breath and closed my eyes as I lifted my head to the sky.

"Give your life to Jesus and this water becomes your wellness." As the pastor said the words, they flowed straight into my heart.

"Just let go." I heard the voice say as if it were coming from somewhere inside of me. I took one last breath before being submerged underwater to wash away my past.

The torture of writing so many letters to everyone vanished at that moment. When I emerged from the water, I knew exactly what I needed to say and who I needed to say it to.

Chapter 5

ROMAN

The rest of the week flew by. Friday morning was here before I knew it. I ached to share the incredible things that had happened while she was away, but my primary concern was her well-being and seeing her smile again. Amelia was smiling when I walked past her desk. I loved we were all happy she was coming home. It seems like an eternity since the fight and all the things leading up to it that caused so much strain and anxiety in everyone's lives. Not that I will ever forget what happened, but I hope to God, it's really over for her sake.

Mom was calling, so I answered, waiting to get confirmation of her arrival.

"Hi honey. Just wanted to let you know she's home. She's going to be staying at her dads for a couple of days."

I smiled, and a wave of relief washed over me.

Mom had flown back with her, and Dad picked Mom up from the airport instead of having me do it this time. At least that spared me from accidentally running into Alex and ruining her reunion with her family.

The truth was, I had no idea where I stood with her.

For weeks, all I'd thought about was getting her home safely. Now that she was finally back, I realized I didn't know what came next. Part of me wanted to call her immediately. Another part thought she probably needed time to reconnect with the people who loved her and had missed her while she was gone.

I couldn't blame them.

I'd missed her too.

More than I cared to admit.

So for now, I was content knowing she was home, surrounded by family, and exactly where she was supposed to be. Whether there was still a place for me in her life was a question for another day.

"Really? I'm happy to hear that. How is she?"

Alex told me she was never going to be able to stay at her parents' house after her mother died, so I'm glad to hear she's trying to get past that for her father's sake at least. I know he misses her, too.

"She's good. She's fantastic, in fact." My mother confirmed.

"That's a relief."

We said goodbye and I put my head back and let out the breath I felt like I'd been holding since she left.

Amelia walked into my office and handed me an envelope. "This just came in the mail. It's a letter from your mom." That's weird.

"Why did my mom mail me a letter?"

"It's addressed to King Construction care of Roman King" then she smiled and walked out. I opened the letter, not knowing what to expect. All I could do was smile when I saw her name. It was a letter from Alex to "Everyone." I wondered if I was supposed to know who everyone was.

Amelia knocked on the door and said, "Hey, I got one too." She must've had mom copy them and send them individually.

"Come on in. Let's read this together. I'm guessing we all got the same letter." Harrison came in and was about to say something while holding his up and I pointed to the seat next to Amelia as she was about to read.

"Should we check and see if anyone else got a letter before we start?" I asked, knowing Darius and Shay were somewhere in the building.

Amelia said, "Nah, I feel like this is our little Alex bubble. Let everyone else have their Alex bubble." I smiled, then nodded and she began.

"Dear Well, Everyone,
I'd like to start by saying thank you. Thank you for all your love and friendship. I couldn't have survived this without you. I know I caused a lot of pain and hurt and for that I am deeply sorry, and I hope you can forgive me. It was everything I could do to forgive myself. This time away has shown me I can't do everything myself. I can't be everything to everyone, and I can't be anything to anyone without first figuring out who I need to be for me. 45 days seems like a long enough time to figure that out, but a wise man once told me it took a lifetime to create this mess and it's not going to get fixed overnight. LOL! I'm a work in progress and I'm working really hard to progress in a positive direction. Not only for me but all of you as well.
With Love,
ALEX"

The room was quiet with as sense of peace, with the feeling that Alex was finally healing.

***

ALEX

Goodbyes are never easy, and this group was especially hard to let go of. They saw me through mental and emotional pain that I've never even allowed my friends to see. I set my luggage down on the front step and hugged everyone and made sure to say that I would be in touch. There were still things I needed, that I couldn't get anywhere else—like knowledge of how to grow and cultivate these herbs. Lisette's car pulled up and I took a deep breath realizing that meant I was truly leaving the security of this special place and reentering the real world. Seeing Lisette, again, however, made me so happy and the thought of seeing Roman again sent butterflies to my stomach and a smile I couldn't hide to my face. I still hadn't opened his letter yet. I planned to do that on the flight home. Once we got on the plane, I took a deep breath and said, "Here we go." Lisette smiled as she squeezed my hand.

"How do you feel about going home?"

"I expect things to be different. I'll be staying with my dad for a few days. Wasn't sure I'd ever be able to do that again." I swallowed hard at the memories of waking up in the hospital being told my mother was killed in a drunk driving accident while she was on her way to be with me. "I think mom was with me at the retreat—kind of the only capacity she's been capable of, I guess. When she told me everything was going to be ok, while I was unconscious, I don't think she meant after the accident, I think she meant right now. Grant bought a house, for me, in the country that I haven't seen yet" I chuckled a little, "but I know Grant wouldn't put me in something horrible so I'm excited to see it. It has a greenhouse. I'm planning to grow the herbs I learned about in there, maybe get a dog..." I was wringing my hands in my lap, staring at them as I spoke. "...I've got to get a little distance from my old life, ya know?" She was smiling, and I wondered if she thought I meant Roman. I wish I knew if he wanted to see me.

"I'm excited to see your new place. Would you mind if I come out and bring you a housewarming gift?" Lisette, thankfully, got me out of my head. I nodded excitedly.

"Of course. I want to have a housewarming get together and invite everyone. Not until I get settled in, though." I slumped back in the seat feeling a little overwhelmed with mental to do lists.

"I'd be happy to help you with anything you need." She offered.

"Thank you." I looked down at the letter that was sitting patiently in my lap, waiting for some attention.

"Do you want me to give you some privacy to read that?" I shook my head.

"No, I may need you after I read it." I opened the letter, scanning it real quick in case it wasn't something I should be reading in front of his mother. As soon as I was sure it would be ok, I began to read it out loud.

"Dear Alex,
We hope you're doing well. By we, I mean everyone at King Con-
struction, Johnson Realtors, your friends and family. We wanted
to tell you we're thinking of you and that you haven't been forgot-
ten. Everything that's happened in the past few months has your

signature on it, literally and figuratively. When you get home, we would like to show you how much you have influenced, for the better, every life you've touched since the day you ran out of gas. Probably even before that. We send you our best wishes for a homecoming filled with love and joy.

With Love,
ALL of US!!!"

There was a brief message from everyone. Even Abby and Maggie's kids signed their names.

Thank you, Roman.

The relief that letter brought was as cleansing as the wellness pool and I knew at that moment coming home was where I needed to be now. My eyes welled up with tears and for the first time I couldn't be happier they were there.

When the plane landed, I ran straight over to my dad and my aunt, hugging them both tight. I looked up at my brothers and yelled, "What are you two waiting for, an invitation? Get over here." It was the best group hug ever. Lisette came over and talked for a second with everyone then she headed over to the car where Mr. King was leaning waiting for her. I glanced over to see if Roman had come, but he wasn't there. I didn't know if I had expected to see him or not, but my heart sank a little with his absence. I smiled weakly at Mr. King and waved as he returned my smile and nodded.

We went back to dads, and I got situated in my old room. I hadn't even looked at my phone yet. It was somewhere at the bottom of my suitcase. What I needed to do was relax and get settled in before thinking about this giant list of things I knew were waiting for me. Talking to my family about what I had gone through to get well was going to be first on the list.

"I think I'll just make myself a tea." I said, as I followed my aunt into the kitchen after she offered to get everyone a drink.

As I grabbed a mug from the cabinet, and stared blankly out of the window, my aunt walked over and gently rubbed her hand up and down my back.

"Everything ok?" I nodded but held back the tears that threatened to fall thinking about how something as simple as having a drink turned so dark and tragic.

"This was a lot easier at the retreat." I admitted.

"What was?" She looked confused.

"Being around alcohol." I filled the mug with water and put it in the microwave. *"Not just a drink"* the thought weaseled its way in, but several, on multiple occasions that seemed to be more important than any other thing that I could've been doing, like taking better care of myself instead of bitching about my mother as I turned into her.

"What's the difference between being around it here and being around it there?"

"There was none." I looked at her with eyes wide and tried not to laugh, but I couldn't help it. I burst out laughing and she did, too.

After we regained our composure, she asked, "Do you need us to put it away?" I shook my head.

"No, I don't think so. What am I gonna do, lock myself away from the world? Have everyone walk on eggshells and change their lives so they don't make my life difficult?" I just kept laughing as I remembered the fight before I left. "I literally kicked someone's ass twice my size. Why shouldn't I be able to kick alcohol's ass?" I didn't want to upset her when I said that, but she didn't have the reaction I thought she'd have either.

"Atta Girl" she exclaimed and wrapped her arm around me.

"I'll be out in a minute; I'm going to make some tea." She kissed my cheek. That's when the thoughts of what I was planning to do popped back up in my head and I couldn't wait to call the Santoros and go see them solidifying everything I had done was truly for the best.

Chapter 6

ROMAN

"Hey Roman, you going to mom and dad's for dinner tonight?" Harrison asked the second I picked up his call while I was skimming through the finance section of the paper. Saturday night dinners with the family used to be just the four of us. Mom, dad, Harrison and myself. It was uncomplicated and relaxing. That was until I brought Alex with me and before Harrison surprised us when he finally told us (I mean me since everyone else already knew) he and Amelia were dating, and he brought her.

"I'll be there. I see you got a new phone."

He laughed. "I did." He proudly acknowledged.

"Did you get water wings for this one?" I teased.

There was silence before he sneered, "Ha!Ha!" and hung up.

My routine of no working on the weekends was prioritized once more, along with going to the gym and walking by the river—a scheduled daily activity as well. It was a cool fall morning the trees were just starting to change colors, and the air seemed to always smell cleaner in the cooler months. I put my earbuds in, taking in the scenery as I made my way to the banks. I stopped at the coffee shop "Brew Ha Ha" that Alex introduced me to and had my usual—coffee and a bagel. As I reminisced about Alex, I never noticed someone was trying to get my attention. I looked up, pulled from my daze and said, "I'm sorry, were you talking to me?" The young lady giggled and blushed. Her cheeks glowing a bright pink and I sighed deeply preparing myself for the swooning.

"Yeah, sorry, did I interrupt something? It's just really crowded, and I was wondering if you were by yourself?" I looked around and it didn't look all that crowded to me, but she seemed pleasant enough and I was just about finished, anyway.

"Um, no, please have a seat..." *I'm sitting at a table for four—I guess I can share.* "...I was just thinking about anything except work." I don't have to be a dick just because I'm not interested, and her laughter seemed so carefree like Alex's once did. She seemed younger than Alex, with shoulder-length brown hair and pretty blue eyes. She had a friendly smile, too. It was weird that I hadn't even thought about talking to another woman after I met Alex, but I had to be realistic that Alex may not be coming back to me.

"Thanks, I just have some work to finish for school." She must be quite a bit younger than Alex then.

"Where do you go to school?" Small talk really isn't my thing, unless of course it was with Alex. Then I wanted to know everything I could about her.

"Xavier University, Grad school. It feels endless." I remembered those days when I thought I would never make it to graduation.

"Roman King." I offered my hand out of politeness, but I really needed to leave before I gave her the wrong impression.

"Hi, Lacy Davenport." She grabbed my hand as she bit her bottom lip with a starry look in her eyes. I retracted my hand casually, getting the feeling this might be a mistake.

I asked the obvious question to remove the awkwardness. "What are you in school for?"

"I'm finishing up my MBA."   She held her drink up to her lips and hesitated before taking a sip and looking at me one more time through her lashes.

"Well, I don't want to distract you, so you finish that up and I'll get out of your hair." She smacked her hand down on top of mine, then pulled it away quickly with a surprised look on her face.

"Oh, don't worry about it. I was really just getting out of my house. My roommate is kind of a pain and wanted to do something today, but she's so annoying. I used it as an excuse to get out of there. I know, kind of a jerk move, but I didn't feel like hanging out with her." Her babbling felt uncomfortable, and I wasn't in the mood for the star struck looks or the aggressiveness. I needed to end this ASAP.

"Well Lacy, it was really nice to meet you, but I have to get going. I have a full schedule today." Her face tensed up and her brows furrowed before she quickly replaced the irritated look with a fake smile as she flipped her hair.

"That's ok. What's your number? I'll plug it in and text you really quick, so you'll have mine too. Maybe we can get together some other time." She reached her hand out, wiggling her fingers, like I would just give it to her because of that. I smiled, thinking about the time I did that with Alex, and it actually worked. Not this time, however.

"I don't think that's such a good idea..." She didn't give me time to finish.

"What? Do you have a girlfriend or something? You're not wearing a ring, so I'm guessing you're not married."

Do I have a girlfriend?

That's a good question and I'd rather find out the answer to that with Alex than this chic.

"Lacey, I'm not sure where you thought this was going for you, but for me, it's going nowhere. Please excuse me." I quickly collected my belongings before this conversation escalated. I wasn't getting a good vibe from her at all.

Is this what's out there if Alex and I are over?

The thought made me sick to my stomach.

When I got back to the penthouse, I threw my wallet and phone on the counter. My wallet flipped open to reveal quite a mess of business cards and receipts that I needed to get under control and clean out and my phone lit up with an unknown number text message.

Unknown Number: "It was really nice meeting you. I guess you changed your mind. Hope to see you again soon." I spun around, freaked out there might be someone in my apartment. Who the hell is this? Is it Lacey? I didn't give her my number. There was a kissy face emoji at the end. Should I ignore it and just block the number or see who the hell this is and how they got my number?

My phone buzzed on the table with another text before I even decided what I wanted to say to the first one.

UNKNOWN NUMBER: *"Did you get my last text?"*

UNKNOWN NUMBER: *"Just wanted to make sure you're getting my messages."*

Great, a freaking stalker in the making.

ME: *"Who is this? I think you have the wrong number."* That's probably the best explanation for this.

UNKNOWN NUMBER: *"It's Lacy, silly. We just had coffee together."*

Are you f'ing serious? I thought I was clear I wasn't interested.

ME: *"How did you get my number?"* This chic is nuts.

LACY: *"You gave it to me. Your business card was lying on the table. I figured that was your subtle way of giving me your number. Thought you might have a girlfriend or something and didn't want anyone to overhear."*

What the hell is wrong with this woman?

She thinks I want to cheat on my *"girlfriend"* with her and she's ok with that?

ME: *"Look, Lacy. I'm sorry you thought that's what happened, but I didn't mean to leave my business card on the table. Please don't contact me again. I am not interested."*

I hope that was enough to stop the text messages and I threw my phone on the counter as I headed back to take a shower.

***

I pulled up to my parents' house for dinner and parked next to Harrison's jacked up custom chrome Ford pickup. Ostentatious has always been my little brother's way.

"Hey everybody."

My day had gone smoothly after the meeting with Lacy, who never texted again, and I walked over to the bar where dad made me a bourbon neat just the way I like it.

"Who the heck is blowing up your phone like that? Is it Alex?" Amelia asked as I looked at my phone and saw message after message roll on the screen. I shook my head because I know Alex would never behave like that. I should have blocked her number this morning, but felt it was a waste of my time and figured she'd get the hint.

"No, it's none of your business Is who it is." I gave her the same response she gave me once. She laughed.

"Is it a chic?" Harrison inquired.

"Nope." It's embarrassing it what it is.

"Did you meet someone you need to block?"

I smiled because she knew that's exactly what it was.

"Oh, lord." She whined. "I'm not going to have to run interference at the office, am I? I'm really not in the mood for your drama queens. Please, just block her. Does she know who you are and where you work?"

Sadly, she does, but it wasn't exactly my fault.

"Seriously, you're being overdramatic." I countered.

Harrison backed his girlfriend. "I don't think she is. I've seen a girl or two in that building hunting you down as you've gone into hiding while Amelia does your dirty work."

This was true but not recently, and I doubt this girl would do that. At least I hope she wouldn't.

"Ok, she knows my name and I didn't hand her a business card. It accidentally fell out of my wallet, and she picked it up. Actually, thought I was trying to cheat on a girlfriend with her."

"And she texted you anyway?" Amelia asked with raised eyebrows and a disgusted look on her face.

"Sure did. That takes balls."

Before I could say or do anything else. They both said simultaneously, "BLOCK HER!" I laughed as I took my phone out of my pocket and Amelia grabbed it and threw it at Harrison. I just sat there watching them act immature. It felt good to have fun for once. It had definitely been a while.

"Real cute. Very mature." I snickered, but silently hoped Harrison would mess with her. On second thought, she really could be a psycho and that's the last thing I needed.

Harrison read the texts as we laughed until he abruptly paused, walking back over with a smile on his face, handing me back my phone.

"Thanks. Are you all finished?"

He nodded and sat back down, winking at Amelia. I looked at him curiously.

"What? Did she send a nude?" Amelia rolled her eyes and Harrison shook his head. Glancing at my phone, I couldn't resist a smile.

"I'll look at it later."

It was a text from Alex.

***

ALEX

It's been a nice relaxing day with the family. I took Sadie on a long walk. She was getting a little slow in her old age, but my dad's elderly lab was the perfect pace for me right now. I needed to slow down and take in all the scenery. Having my aunt with me for the weekend was just what the doctor ordered. I wanted the complete truth, no sugarcoating, and she was the one to give it to me. In fact, I was doing great. I considered this solitude, and solitude was what I needed to replenish myself, not to avoid people. I wanted to make sure I had enough in the tank for everyone else when I was ready to reach out. Lots of text messages came in letting me know they were all glad I was home. My plan was to get back to everyone tomorrow and this week. I still had a lot to do before returning to work.

I needed one more week to move into my new place, which Grant had hired a moving company to move everything from my apartment to the new house, but he didn't know where I wanted anything. Shay and the boys were sent over to do the decorating. I'm sure that meant Shay did the decorating and the boys moved the furniture where she told them to. The one person I hadn't heard from was Roman. I guess that shouldn't surprise me.

"He may have moved on for all I know." I thought as I walked Sadie back towards the house.

Maybe it's time for me to think about moving on as well.

After dinner I made a tincture tea for calming. I was wearing my coziest sweats and took my phone out on the back patio, sitting on the sofa by the firepit, then wrapped myself in a fluffy blanket. Sadie climbed up slowly and curled up next to me. This was the perfect time to finish this thrilling trilogy I started before I went on my extended vacation. I kept looking at my phone between chapters, but I didn't want to stress about getting a message. It's not like he's reached out the entire time I've been gone, or even since I've gotten back. Maybe he was waiting for me to reach out first. The anxiety from this mental volleyball game was getting to be too much, so I took it upon myself to send him a quick text, with no expectations.

ME: *"I just wanted to say hi and let you know I'm back. I'm sure you already know that. I hope you're doing well."*

I re-read the text a few times to make sure I was ok with it. When I was sure it would suffice, I hit send and laid the phone down.

The rest of the family came out with a drink and we talked, we laughed and we reminisced about the good times we had with mom. It felt good to talk about her and make her memories loving and positive. After everyone went to bed, I stayed out a while longer, just relaxing in the quiet and finally there was a text from Roman as a sense of relief and dread washed over me at the same time.

ROMAN: *"I'm doing well. How are you?"*

Thank God it was relief I was left with. Just seeing a text from him gives me butterflies. Another text came through.

ROMAN: *"Can I just call you?"*

I think that would be alright. In fact, I think I would love that. Even if he's calling to tell me he's moved on, I just want to hear his voice.

ME: *"Yes."*

I took a deep breath when I saw his name scroll across the screen.

"Hello." I answered with a huge grin on my face.

"Hi." His voice sounded almost chipper.

"Is it stupid that I don't know what to say?" He asked, and I started laughing. I felt like a schoolgirl with a crush.

"No, I feel the same way." I'm glad it wasn't just me feeling this way.

"I'm really happy you're home."

"You are? Did you hear I moved?" His response surprised me. I haven't seen or heard from him in over a month, leaving me with no way to know what he was truly feeling.

"I am happy you're home. Yes, I heard you moved—Grant told me. I know you're at your dad's as well." He chuckled.

"Did you actually link us on life 360?" I laughed just thinking about the day he told me he had lo jacked me to keep an eye on me. I was glad he was joking about that.

"No, mom told me..." he said through his own laughter. "...I think she's happy you're at your dad's, so I don't stalk you."

I couldn't help but wonder if he had waited for me after all.

"Yeah, I decided the first place I needed to go wasn't my new place since I haven't even seen it yet. I really needed to be with my dad and my aunt."

"I think it's great. Glad you felt you could do that. I know it was hard after your mom's accident." I liked that it's easier for me to talk about my mom now and not break down crying at every mention.

"I think my mom's spirit was with me at the retreat. I think where she is now is the place she needs to be in order to help me and watch over me, if that makes sense."

"I'm sure she was. That's a great way to think of her." This is one of the easiest conversations he and I have ever had. No games, just a natural flow.

"I'll be back in the office in about a week. I need to get moved into my new place and I have another business idea I'm going to speak to the Santoros about." There was a deafening silence on the other end of the line.

Did he just hang up on me?

Uh oh, what did I say? Did I just mess up the flow? I was getting a little anxious.

"Roman, did you fall asleep?" I asked timidly, hoping for a response, and he chuckled.

"No, sorry, I just thought I heard you say you had another business idea." I smiled, patting Sadie mindlessly on the head, thinking about adding more to my already saturated to do list.

"You heard correctly." This was worried, protective, Roman.

"Do you think it's a good idea..." He paused and I heard him sigh. "...I'm sorry, it's none of my business."

I forgot about this side of him but I didn't really hate it like I thought I had previously.

"Roman, it's ok to be concerned that I'm adding another thing to my plate."

I heard another enormous sigh on the other end of the line.

"Yeah, but it's none of my business. You know what's best for you."

"I do now, maybe."

I wanted him to know that I had worked on things while I was away.

"Oh yeah. Can you share?" He asked—hopeful.

"Maybe not tonight, but I will. Oh, yeah, I'm having a housewarming party. I mean, when I get moved in and settled. Do you think you'll be able to make it?"

His voice, now a low rumble, was smooth and relaxed.

"I wouldn't miss it."

I wanted to finish on a pleasant note tonight.

"Thank you for chatting with me. I'm gonna call it a night." A wave of anxiety washed over me, and I held my breath, anticipating his reaction.

"It was nice talking with you, Alex. I'm glad you're home."

As I ended the call, a sigh escaped my lips, a mixture of relief and exhaustion. That was a good call. Totally painless, not what I was expecting at all. Something was still there between us, I could tell. But I'll have to be careful; I haven't quite figured things out yet. One more text and I'm good for the night...

Chapter 7

ROMAN

Nothing but good relaxing sleep last night. No dreams of any kind. I checked my phone to see what the weather was doing; sunny and sixty-five, my favorite. I walked to the coffee shop for my usual coffee and bagel, then sat out on the patio while listening to classical music on my earbuds. My conversation with Alex occupied all my thoughts, bringing a smile to my face.

The smell of freshly brewed coffee and freshly baked bread was just what the doctor ordered until it ended abruptly when someone sat down at the table. I smiled as I took one earbud out and said, "Hi, Lacey, right?" She just cocked her head to the side.

"Yes, it is. I'm surprised you remembered since you haven't responded to any of my texts." And here it is, the reason I have to block contacts.

"Lacey, look, I think I was clear when I said I wasn't interested and asked you to please stop texting."

Besides the fact that Amelia blocked and then deleted you from my phone.
She gave me such a dirty look.

"You didn't even try to get to know me." She whined loudly; her brow was so scrunched I was worried it would stay that way. I rolled my eyes, thinking about how much it used to piss me off when Alex would do it to me. I'm sure that did nothing to calm her down.

"Plain and simple, I'm just not interested."

She squinted her eyes so hard, not trying to cover up the facade of the girl from yesterday. The sweet act had to be a front for whatever this is coming out now.

"You think you can just talk to people like this because you look like you do and own a big company? You're just a big rude jerk!" She yelled, and the surrounding patrons turned to look. First time I ever thought being a jerk was a good thing.

"What you're doing right now is very unattractive." I should really shut my mouth and let her leave, but I don't like being yelled at. "I sat here to have coffee in peace and listen to music and this is the second time you've interrupted that. So, if anything, you're actually the rude one."

Thankfully, she didn't make a scene after her little hysterics and just huffed off.

I looked up to the sky and mouthed, "Thank you."

After the coffee shop, I got ready for church and headed over. Harrison and Amelia were waiting at the bottom of the steps.

"Hey. Mom and dad here yet?" I asked as I glanced behind me.

"No. Mom just texted. They're on their way."

I nodded and looked around nervously and at my phone, thinking she may have somehow managed to find another phone and start texting me again.

"What's up with you?" Harrison asked.

"What do you mean?"

"What happened?" Amelia pried as she curled her lips, trying not to laugh. I shook my head, embarrassed by the whole thing.

"She popped up, miraculously, at the coffee shop again and went off on me. It was stalkerish, to be honest."

Harrison laughed and slapped me on the shoulder.

"You're an idiot. Surely you know better than to engage those kinds of women. Did you think you were getting a one and done out of it or something?"

We laughed as someone cleared their throat behind me.

"Nice conversation to have on the steps of the church, boys." When we turned around, mom and dad were right behind us with Alex. Amelia broke the silence and hurried over, hugging her aggressively.

"Oh my God, you look amazing. How are you?" Amelia squealed. Her face lit up.

"Thank you. I'm doing great." She sounded amazing and healthy. Her face was glowing. Harrison was next and pushed me out of the way. He picked her up, swinging her around.

"Harrison, I'm happy to see you, too."

When he put her down, she was laughing. Mom, dad, Harrison and Amelia left us to finally say hello.

"Sorry, if you heard that conversation." My cheeks burned as I shoved my hands in my pockets.

"Don't worry about it. You're pretty irresistible. You'd definitely make a girl go crazy."

A playful wink from her as my hands left my pockets and reached out, pulling her close in a tight hug. I closed my eyes, taking a deep breath, inhaling the intoxicating scent of vanilla and lavender that I never wanted to forget.

I whispered, "I've missed you, but I'm so happy you prioritized yourself and are here with us today."

I felt a searing heat as her grip tightened, our souls merging into one.

"I feel the same way." She replied.

Holding hands, we entered the church and joined the family, feeling once again optimistic about our future.

***

ALEX

After church, I opted to ride with Roman back to the house for brunch. I couldn't stop thinking about my new place and all the things I needed to do to it and for it. What I really needed to do was go see it first and foremost.

"Could we go to the house after brunch?" I asked hopefully.

"Sure, I'd love that. Do you want me to take you home first to get your car, or can I drive you?"

"We can ride together. I mean, you'll have to bring me back, too, if that's ok with you. I just want to check it out." Was this feeling of nervousness ever going to relent? Thankfully, pulling up to the house redirected some of my anxiety.

Roman walked around the car and opened the door for me, like the gentleman he's always been, then walked me through the house, holding my hand, to the back patio.

He leaned in and whispered, "Does everyone's drinking bother you?" I was wondering how long it would take for people to get over the fact I was sober now. I know how much I hated walking on eggshells around Roman when things were bad—this was no different.

"Not at all. Does it bother you?" I nudged his side, trying to lighten the mood a bit as he rolled his eyes.

"Ok, I'll shut up." He said, trying to reign in his overprotective nature.

I giggled, then whispered back, "I personally think eye rolling is sexy. Do it again for me?" His face suddenly got serious. It might be too soon for this. I didn't know how he felt about me yet, either.

"That's it, come with me." Maybe I lightened things up a little too much. As we walked to the swings, he grabbed my hand, and I laughed nervously. He sat on one and I sat on the other. He turned to look at me with smoldering eyes.

"You're killing me..." He took a deep breath with nostrils flared and a tick of his jaw. "...I've thought about you every minute of every day since you left." As surprised as I was, it was also a huge relief. It made me smile even though I wanted to cry. The emotion I felt behind what he was saying was powerful, seeping into my pores like a drug.

"That makes me so happy, Roman. You have no idea. I thought I lost you. I thought I lost everyone, and I carried that with me for so long at the retreat." My hands had a white-knuckled grip around the ropes holding up the swing. "To hear you say that means everything..." Tears fell down my cheeks and he reached over, wiping them away as he patiently waited for me to finish. "...I feel light, like a weight's been lifted. I've been working on my stressors, and nothing has bothered me lately."

A wave of calm seemed to settle over him, his shoulders slumped, and a peaceful expression replacing his previously strained one. With a sigh, his arms fell limply to his sides. His eyes clouded with uncertainty, peering at me, their expression a mixture of apprehension and curiosity.

Carefully, he tipped closer and softly asked. "Can I work on these things with you?" I remember pushing him away when he tried to help me work through my issues, but now, his presence in my life is indispensable; I can't imagine my life without him.

"I would love that."

The swing creaked as he pulled it close, then his lips were on mine. A fresh start filled with the promise of new beginnings.

***

ROMAN

We went to Alex's new house to meet Grant for the key following brunch. I trusted Grant's judgment, so I was looking forward to seeing the house. We drove about fifteen minutes north of the city, then headed east for another fifteen minutes. He chose a house about ten minutes from the Santoros, apparently on purpose. The farmhouse was a pretty nice size, white, two stories, with a wrap-around front porch. It had large porch swings at both ends. Mature trees shaded the secluded house's front yard, and no neighbors near enough to see. I looked over to see her eyes were wide with surprise as we pulled up the gravel drive to the house, tires crunching and the scent of freshly cut grass filling the air as I lowered the car window.

"What do you think?" I asked. She was excitedly biting her bottom lip. I affectionately patted her knee. She looked a bit nervous.

"It's perfect. This is exactly what I was hoping for."

Hoping for, for what exactly?

We walked hand in hand around the back of the house; the afternoon air filled with the scent of honeysuckle. The back was a vast, empty yard, stretching out behind the house like an empty canvas under a pale sky. To either side of the path were trees, their leaves rustling in the breeze.

"I wonder where her property line is." I thought as I scanned the area.

There was a big greenhouse about fifty yards from the main house. We strolled back to check it out. The greenhouse looked unused, but it was nice and clean. The gears were visibly turning in her head; a look of deep contemplation was on her face, so I broke in on her thoughts.

"Well, are you going to share?" The soft strands of her hair felt delicate as I kissed the top of her head. A puzzled expression fell on her beautiful face.

"Share what?" Lost in her own thoughts, she barely registered anything when she was introduced to a new place. She was fully immersed in her environment.

"Whatever you're thinking?"

She giggled. "Oh, I was just thinking about where to start. I was picturing this place full." She threw her arms wide as she gestured to the inside of the greenhouse. She had the look of a child on Christmas morning all over her face.

"Full of what?" I was hoping for a glimpse into her creative mind, some inkling of what she was thinking.

"Herbs and flowers." *Hmm.* I was thinking vegetables and fruit, but she's definitely thinking something else. I mean, she has been pretty mellow. Maybe she's thinking of growing pot. Perhaps grow medicinal marijuana and that's her new business.

Walking back to the house, I spotted Grant coming around the side. Releasing my hand, she ran and leaped into his arms, a joyous laugh escaping her as she landed. There was definitely a special bond between those two. The question of whether he should confess his past to her lingered, but I sensed the secret wouldn't stay hidden forever—it felt like a ticking time bomb. Truth always finds a way to be revealed. I shook Grant's hand and we followed a very excited Alex through the back door.

Chapter 8

ALEX

I don't even remember letting go of Roman's hand. Overwhelmed with emotion, I ran straight into his arms, the smell of his cologne filling my senses. I loved having one dad, but having two felt like having a built-in support system—two sets of hands to hold, and two hearts full of love. Though I fought back the tears, the strength of his hug was overwhelming, a much-needed source of comfort.

"It's so good to see you, baby girl," he said, his voice warm and tender. Tears threatened to spill over.

"It's good to be home."

He kissed my cheek, a quick peck that smelled faintly of coffee, then handed me the keys, and I ran up the wooden deck stairs to the back door. Just inside the door was a spotless mudroom; the floor was gleaming, and new hooks hung on the walls. A dog bath and a custom-built dog crate were among the gorgeous features of the house—maybe a sign I should get a dog. Shay and the boys had finished arranging the furniture, and the room almost felt complete—the air smelling faintly of polish and wood. New appliances and modern furnishings showed that this place had undergone a full renovation. Though much of the original wood remained, adding character to the colossal kitchen, the space was undeniably modern, with high-end appliances. I loved the new kitchen and couldn't wait to cook in it, imagining the delicious smells that would fill the air.

Four bedrooms and three and a half bathrooms seemed excessive, but I figured I could make it work somehow. Getting one or two roommates might help with the gardening at least. I glanced into an empty room with bookshelves; I concluded it was definitely going to be my office. I took a quick look in every door to familiarize myself with the surroundings.

I loved the big wide wooden staircase; the scent of aged wood filled the air as I ran my fingers along the polished banister. Most of the house was painted a stark white, offset by the rich, dark wood trim. I flew up the stairs two at a time, the rhythmic thud of my feet echoing in the stairwell.

Okay, I see now.

There are only three bedrooms, not four, as I had initially thought. Two bedrooms were combined to create a master suite with a spacious walk-in closet and a luxurious, spa-like bathroom, complete with a soaking tub and rainfall showerhead, which I planned to use frequently. That was clever. Having seen many older homes, I recognized the pattern of small bathrooms, closets, and bedrooms—a consequence of design choices from a different era where space was used differently.

"Hey Grant? Is there a basement? I can't remember." I shouted, the sound bouncing off the walls as it traveled down the hall and stairs, hoping to reach them. Older homes like this used storm cellars in place of basements. I really hoped this place had a dry, clean basement.

"Yes. It's finished too." He answered.

Oh, thank goodness, I don't know if I could handle an old dirty basement that looked like a scene from a scary movie. I couldn't wait to see it. Before I got to the bottom of the stairs, I stopped.

"How do I get there?" My eyebrows shot up—maybe I should have accepted his tour offer, but my excitement got the better of me.

He laughed, pointing down the hall. "There's a door on the back side of the stairs."

I hurried down to the bottom of the stairs, where I found a large, old wooden door with an antique handle. I braced myself for the sight of a dusty, spider-infested basement, the phantom musty smell already filling my nostrils. Panic set in before I even opened the door. Instead, what I found was quite the opposite. Flipping the light switch revealed carpeted stairs, sheetrock walls, and wall-to-wall carpeting. On one side of a large bar stood a gigantic projection screen TV—comfortable, reclining movie theater seats faced the screen. On the other side of the bar was a big, dark brown leather sectional—the worn cushion hinting at many hours spent lounging. The space, more of an entertainment area than anything else, gave me some great ideas.

"Who set this place up? I mean the basement. Whose stuff is this?" I looked over at the both of them, hoping they didn't go out and buy me anything.

"This actually came with the place. I had all the furniture cleaned and the walls painted, though." Grant said.

I stood there in awe, completely overwhelmed by the area before me. I loved everything about this place. The sheer amount of effort and time Grant must have invested in this place for me is incredible—I can feel the love in every detail.

"This is amazing. This will be the perfect place to have sleepovers with the kids." The words left my lips, and instantly, hot tears streamed down my face. I missed their small hands in mine—I missed them. Not knowing when I'd see them again really hit hard. I inhaled sharply, the air catching in my throat, and pressed my palms to my tear-streaked face, weeping silently.

***

ROMAN

We followed her into the house, letting her explore. She didn't seem to need us to show her around.

"How's our girl?" Grant thoughtfully asked. It was a little easier to be around him after the nightmarish news about who he really was. I mean, I guess I should be glad he's on our side if we're going to be around an ex-mob hitman.

"Amazing. I've never seen her so at peace. She seems to have worked out a lot of whatever was torturing her."

"I'm sure a lot of that has to do with you." He smiled and put his hand on my shoulder.

"I don't think so. This was how she was when she got home. I just feel thankful she's letting me be a part of it."

I hope that I have something to do with it but I truly think she did the work for herself this time.

"Do you know what she wanted this place for?" Grant asked, as confused as I was, it seemed. I would've thought he knew since he bought the place for her.

"No, do you?"

"No, I have no idea. She said she has a business idea."

"Huh, that's the same thing she told me. She wants to grow herbs and flowers in the greenhouse. Do you think she wants to open a flower/herb shop or something? Maybe a dispensary?"

"I don't know, but whatever it is, she needs the Santoros' help, so I doubt it." He seemed just as intrigued as I was to get to the bottom of this business idea she needed the mafia winemakers for.

"Yeah, what would she need them for? She's staying away from alcohol."

"I'm not sure, but you know our special girl. She's always got something up her sleeve. Let's hope it doesn't cause us all another heart attack."

The memory of the last secret she held was seared into our minds—the brutal sounds of the fight, the musty odor of the boxing ring, and the sight of her facing a monstrous rapist twice her size. She blew past us down to the basement and we followed.

"This place is amazing. The perfect place for a pizza party sleepover." She exclaimed as tears sprang free from her eyes.

She must have been thinking about the kids. That was difficult for her, so I took her in my arms and held her until she got her composure back.

"Next on the agenda today will be to visit the girls...sound good?"

She shook the tears from her eyes, the single nod firm and resolute. Now was as good a time as any to begin the long process of healing. They can avoid her if they choose, but I understand how much they rely on one another.

I called Matt while she explored the rest of the house. He's married to Maggie, one of Alex's best friends. He also acted as one of her lawyers in her case against Tanner.

He answered, "Hey Roman."

"Hey Matt. I'm with Alex." There was a second of silence before he responded.

"How is she?" He sounded sincere. I know she put them all through a lot and they were still guarded.

"She's really great, actually. We're at her new house." Though I wasn't sure they knew she'd bought another house, I suspected someone would have let them know somehow.

"Yeah, what's it like?" Now it felt like filling the void with mundane questions.

"It's pretty amazing. A nice farmhouse out in the country with a lot of yard. Has a really cool basement with a theater for movie and pizza nights."

I was reluctant at first, but because they were my friends, I felt comfortable going ahead. I just wanted to see where we're at here. It seems things are alright, judging by his laughter.

"I know where you're going with this, but I don't think it's a good idea for the kids to have sleepovers with Aunt Ali yet." I laughed, thinking that's not really where I was going, but why not poke the bear anyway.

"I'm pretty sure she'd agree with you, but she'd like to see all of you today if it's ok."

"Hang on, Maggie's right here, talk to her. If she's okay with it, I'm cool." And poke the bear we have.

"Hello Roman." I understand her feelings, even if she seemed slightly reserved. Alex made a huge gamble with their friendship.

"Hi Maggie. How are you?" She snorted.

"I'm doing good. What's up? What does she want?" Although not furious, she was aware of my conversation with Matt regarding Alex.

"I'd like to bring Alex to see you all today."

She hesitated, then snapped, "I haven't spoken to her in over a month. I know she wrote to us, but she's been back and hasn't bothered to reach out."

"I know. This isn't easy for her." She sounded more annoyed with each response.

"She obviously found it easy enough to talk to you."

"My mom had more to do with that than I did, I think. She went to church with us this morning and I drove her out here to see her new house. I was the one who suggested we see you all today. She misses the kids, Maggie. Your family to her and she let you down. I don't think you understand how hard this is for her. She's not drinking anymore either."

I heard Maggie sniffling—she was clearly upset. I hadn't meant for that to happen, but I wanted her to see Alex—to understand what I saw in her. Losing each other is the last thing they need.

She calmly responded in a much warmer tone, "Fine, you can bring her. Do you want me to call Abby for you?" I released my breath. Abby was Alex's other best friend. They were practically inseparable until the shit hit the fan.

"No, that's ok, I'll call Jack." When we hung up, I had the same conversation with Jack, but Abby was a little different. Jack was Abby's much more mild husband. He was also one of Alex's attorneys that helped her secure the fight to end all fights.

"Yes, bring her. I need my friend back. Is she still my friend?" Her tone was cheery and hopeful, not like Maggie at all.

"I think you're going to like this friend a lot." I said with a smile on my face.

"Thank you, Roman." She sounded grateful. Then I heard a big scream come from the front of the house.

***

ALEX

I sat on the front porch with Grant while Roman called Maggie and Abby. I was so worried about what they were going to say. Things didn't end well before I left. They've never been afraid of me being around their kids. I must've really done a number on them and everyone, probably. How could I have been so careless with those relationships? I feel like such a failure and a complete asshole. I tried so many times to pick up the phone and call them or just text them since I've gotten back, but I didn't have the words and sorry just didn't seem like enough. The thought of Roman calling to invite me to their house left me feeling utterly gutless and ashamed. If they say no, it's my own damn fault.

"Grant, how's the office? I mean, how're Shay and the boys?" I asked as a distraction, to get the head chatter quieted.

"Everyone's fine. Of course, we all miss you, but Shay has really taken Darius under her wing and guided him...honestly, that kid's been amazing—he's a natural. You really hit the bullseye with him. Ryan and Landon are doing just fine. Oh, by the way, you'll be getting a wedding invite to Landon and Piper's wedding at the office. It's this weekend and he didn't know where to send the invite."

"Oh my gosh, already? Was I gone that long?"

"Yes, for us you were gone way too long. For them, you were gone long enough for a shotgun wedding." I screamed.

"Oh my God, are they pregnant?" A wide grin stretched across his face as he nodded.

"That's so exciting. I'll get to the office tomorrow and get my invite." Hugging him, I bounced up and down.

"Is everything okay?" Roman sat down next to me with concern etched all over his face.

Still very much excited, I announced, "Yes, it's better than ok. Landon and Piper are getting married this weekend. They're having a baby!" He smiled, his eyes crinkling at the corners, pulling me into a warm, tight hug, then we said goodbye to Grant.

Roman said, "Honey, everyone wants to see you. Maggie's still a little upset, but I know she misses you. I don't know if the kids are going to be around, though. They didn't say and I didn't ask." A tight smile touched my lips, my throat constricting with unshed tears, as he opened my car door, the engine's hum a dull background noise to the lump in my throat on the way to Maggie's.

My hands were clammy as we pulled up to Maggie's house—the sight of her imposingly large white home, usually so charming, now felt menacing. I sat there for a minute and took in a few deep breaths. Despite my uncertainty, I know we'll face this together—these are my best friends, and I have complete faith in our friendship.

With a furious burst, Maggie came out, and Roman immediately stepped in front of me, causing me to shake my head and gently push him aside. I had to handle this on my own. She stood toe-to-toe, her voice a furious growl inches from my face as she spat, "I am so mad at you right now!" I took a few more deep breaths, trying to quell the rising tide of anxiety, the smell of pine needles and fall, doing little to calm my racing heart.

"I know. You should be," I agreed with her gently to calm the atmosphere.

With tears on her cheeks, she embraced me in a crushing hug, and I returned it, wanting the moment to last. We hugged and sobbed together for a moment before I broke free to breathe.

"Maggie, could you ease up, you're crushing me." We both fell into a fit of laughter.

"This is your fault. I still go to those damn kickboxing classes."

Tear stained but arm in arm, we walked into the house laughing the entire way. Behind me, I heard Abby screaming. I spun around to see a huge Abby charging towards me.

"Oh my God, Abby, look at this baby bump. It's the most beautiful thing I've ever seen."

I went straight to her belly before I hugged her. She was both laughing and crying. I hugged her the best I could with that belly, trying to keep us apart. Matt and Jack hugged me, asked how I was, and we continued our conversation on the back patio. I checked in with the girls to see if they still had Sunday brunch. They said they weren't. Instead, they were going on Saturday in order to attend church and brunch with their families. I smiled, remembering I had done exactly that earlier this morning.

Suddenly, I heard someone yell, "Hold on!" No running." Next thing I know, there's three very excited little people screaming for their Aunt Ali. I glanced around, and Matt winked. I was sobbing uncontrollably, but holding my three little angels, feeling their warmth and innocence, washing away all my worries.

Chapter 9

ALEX

I walked Roman to his car, after dinner, the cool evening air soothing against my skin, and leaned into him.

"Thank you for today. I know we haven't had a genuine conversation yet, but I wanted to express my gratitude for your help today. I needed all of it."

The touch of his hands was feather-light yet firm as he tilted his head, his lips brushing against mine in a kiss that stole my breath and made my knees buckle.

"We have plenty of time. I'll see you in the morning at the new place."

Mhmm.

Damn, the man's patience was the stuff of legends—it was a tangible thing, a quiet force.

Returning to the house, I sank into the soft cushions of the couch next to my aunt, and we talked for a couple of hours, the quiet hum of the house, with dad asleep, a backdrop to our conversation, before heading to bed ourselves.

"So, you and Roman are back together?"

I waited for the punchline. Usually, she has something more to say about his appearance. This time, there was nothing.

"I'm not really sure what's going on. We haven't talked about it, but I think it's moving in the right direction." She looked at me skeptically. "Slowly." I insisted.

Quickly making sure she didn't think I was jumping back into something too soon.

"I'm sure you'll make the right decision, whatever that is. Now, when are you coming to visit me in North Carolina?"

The weight of my neglect pressed down on me as my aunt's words, though loving, carried the expectation of a long-overdue visit.

With each passing second, I savored the precious minutes before she left. Her absence would be heavy on my heart with my mother gone, but thinking of the warm Southern hospitality and delicious barbecue, I made a mental note to get down to North Carolina for a visit.

***

In the morning, I said goodbye to my aunt before packing my things into the car and having breakfast with my dad.

"Ali Marie..." Dad says like I'm fragile, but who could blame him. "...you seem like you're doing good. I'm sorry I had such a hard time being there for you. I'll do better."

My dad wasn't much of a talker before, but I think after everything that's happened, I may not get him to stop talking. I hugged him tight.

"Honestly, if I were in your shoes, I doubt I would have chosen any other path. I wouldn't wish that experience on my child. I'm sure it was painful to watch. I don't really know what happened to me. The situation felt completely out of my hands, but now I'm much calmer and I'm determined to avoid anything that might have caused that chaos."

A single nod, the way his eyes glistened—revealed a grief I had never seen him express before Mom's death this year.

Dad and I said our goodbyes, his hand warm on my shoulder as he promised to visit the house soon.

I slid into the driver's seat, pushing the ignition and the engine roared to life. Immediately, I punched in Roman's number. "Good morning," he greeted, his voice warm and familiar.

"I'm headed to the house now if you want to meet me over there."

"Already on the way. I should be there in about fifteen minutes."

A smile touched my lips, thinking about his excitement to see me. A warmth spread through my chest to the heart, once broken and shattered, now on the mend.

"I think you're going to beat me there, but I'll see you soon." The phone call ended, and I immediately cranked up the radio, feeling the bass vibrate through the car as I hit cruise control on the highway, enjoying the ride towards my new beginning.

***

ROMAN

I'm sure she's awake, but she's spending precious time saying goodbye to her aunt this morning, so I won't disturb her with a text. I picked up some strong, dark coffee *(her favorite)* from our favorite place and some African daisies for her new home. Thinking about the first time I brought her flowers was pretty humorous. She asked me if I got them for her grave. I may have been right about her suicidal thoughts, but it seems she's moved past that. I certainly hope she has.

Pulling up to the house, with the windows down, the fallen leaves paving the drive, crunched under the tires as I breathed in the fresh, cool autumn air. She told me it was one of the things she loved about the country. As I came to a stop, I heard the gentle sway of the porch swings. The rhythmic creak was a familiar comfort, thinking about the swings behind my parents' house. I scanned the front porch, noticing how empty it seemed, then I remembered the cheerful display of flowers at the nursery I had passed.

"Perhaps we should get some plants for the porch?" The thought came and went, since I didn't quite know where we stood. As I imagined our life together in this place, the sound of tires on gravel announced her arrival. I put the flowers and the coffee down and stood at the bottom of the stairs. The urge to rush over and scoop her into my arms was overwhelming, but

I was patient—watching as she slowly exited the car and approached. A serene smile played on her lips, and her eyes held a newfound tranquility. Gone were the rigid shoulders, replaced with a confident stride and a bright, healthy glow. She looked like a completely different person.

She was waving and smiling.

"Good morning." She said cheerfully.

I smiled back, gazing at her. I genuinely thought I wouldn't get this chance again. I shook off the unwanted thoughts and wrapped my arms around her as soon as she was close enough.

"Good morning. I brought you coffee and flowers to help with the unpacking and decorating."

"That sounds like a good start," she said, a smile playing on her lips.

I held the door for her and the soft click of each light switch echoing as she turned them on, room by room, on our way to the kitchen.

"Looks like it's time for me to stock up on groceries." I didn't even know where the grocery was around here. "I don't know where anything is around here," she said with a bit more than a chuckle.

"That's what google is for." I casually mentioned.

Her reaction seemed like anxiety to me, and although it was unexpected coming from her, I understood it.

She excitedly grabbed my hands, saying, "Let's get everything unpacked, and then I want to talk."

Getting reacquainted felt like starting from scratch; I didn't know how to navigate this new Alex.

"Okay." I agreed.

I'll just go with the flow and let her guide us until we're comfortable enough to be ourselves.

The better part of the morning was dedicated to unpacking and putting away her knick-knacks and pictures. The moment I brought up the porch plants, she sprang up from unpacking a box and clutched my biceps.

"I saw a nursery on the way over. Thought we might buy some plants for the front porch, if you'd like." I offered.

"Yes, can we please do that?" I found her enthusiasm refreshing and it made me laugh.

"Whenever you're ready." I suggested.

She practically ran to the car, grabbing her purse from the coat rack by the door. Then we sped off to the nursery. We still had things to discuss, but it could definitely wait.

In the large nursery, she showed the woman a picture of the porch and asked her opinion. The woman selected several easy-care plants, which we then arranged on her front porch.

***

ALEX

After Decorating the front porch, thoughts of my previous life ran through my mind. Here's where I would sit at the kitchen island or the sofa with a glass of wine, just enjoying some classical music and a quiet evening. *Was I really turning into an alcoholic?* Who am I kidding? I wouldn't have had one glass of wine, I would've drunk the bottle, maybe more. The thought of it brought tears to my eyes. My chest ached with a heavy tightness, a suffocating pressure, until the embrace of calming arms eased the pain.

Roman's voice, a low murmur, tickled my ear as he whispered, "Penny for your thoughts?"

I spun around when I heard his voice.

"Oh, considering inflation, it's probably worth at least a dollar now, wouldn't you say?" We laughed and he reached his hand out for me to hop off the stool.

He softly pulled my hand, nodding toward the sofa. "Let's talk for a minute," he suggested, but the idea made me nervous.

"Any plans for cooking dinner tonight?" I attempted to shift the focus.

"We'll get to that, but I can tell you have something on your mind, and you should probably get it off your chest."

It was actually good that he realized I was anxious and helped me to calm down.

"You know, you're right. Holding onto things has only caused me more stress and anxiety." I swallowed the lump in my throat before I confessed. "The idea of a glass of wine crossed my mind. Not actually pouring one and drinking it, but how I used to have a glass of wine...or a bottle..." I mumbled "...whenever I wanted."

"And that has you wanting a glass now?" He spoke quietly, his voice low and measured as he cautiously inquired.

I adjusted my position uncomfortably, trying to think about how I should say this without freaking him out.

"It's clear to me I shouldn't drink. I have quit and I plan to stay that way, but I'm still battling cravings. I need to steer clear for a bit until I have a better handle on things."

Once more, his reassuring embrace enveloped me as he said, "I'll support you in whatever you want. I can quit with you."

I sank into his side, the gentle rhythm of his breathing a calming presence against my ear as all the tension melted away.

"I appreciate the offer, but I wouldn't want you to alter your life to fit mine." He gently sat me up, his gaze intense as he looked directly into my eyes.

"I'm absolutely changing my life for you. I'm willing to quit drinking if that's what it takes to have you in my life. Seems like a small sacrifice to me."

I'm really hoping this is for real. I don't want to wake up if this is just a dream.

Following a fun dinner where we cooked together, the clatter of his packing echoing in the quiet kitchen snapped me out of my quiet calm—he was packing up to leave. Uh oh, here's that damn anxiety again, the cold sweat prickling my skin and a sense of impending doom settling in.

"Shoot, did I forget to ask if you could stay tonight? My mind is a mess. I hope you can forgive my absentmindedness."

My eyes fluttered shut and then open, a silent plea to appear calm as the impending panic attack threatened to overwhelm me.

"Maybe," he said, a playful glint in his eye as he winked.

"Did you bring clothes?"

With a flirtatious smile, he gave a small nod of his head.

"Just in case, yeah, wishful thinking, I guess. They're out in the car. I'll be right back."

"Thank God I wasn't going to have to spend the night in this house by myself," I thought as a profound sense of relief settled over me, erasing the earlier unease but now it was being replaced with the chilling memories of Tanner's relentless pursuit and the brutal attack, leaving my mind racing, every nerve on high alert.

"Oh no, how am I going to live out here by myself?" I groaned, the noise a low, guttural rumble in the back of my throat—a full-blown panic attack took over.

***

ROMAN

I was hesitant to offer to stay over, so I was relieved when she invited me. As I entered the house from getting my bag from the car, I found Alex doubled over, gasping for breath.

My bag hit the ground as I raced towards her, my heart pounding. "Alex, what's wrong?!" What happened?" She heaved, her chest rising and falling rapidly. I quickly got her some water. When she sat up to drink, her face was an angry purple, tears streaming down her body shaking. She finally started to relax after taking several deep breaths.

"I can't do this." She whispered through the tears.

Oh great, have we broken up again already?

Calmly I asked, "Can't do what, honey?"

Between gasps she said, "Live... Out... Here..." I paused, taking a slow relaxing breath myself.

Not about us, that's good to know.

"Right now, you should just breathe, then let's talk about this for a minute."

Several minutes passed before she was calm enough to speak.

"I'm in the middle of nowhere. Alone. By myself. What the hell was I thinking?"

Her expression looked terrified. This was definitely new. The Alex I knew wasn't afraid of shit. A small chuckle escaped me as I attempted to understand this new information. My brave girl is no longer brave. I liked it less than I anticipated. I gently wrapped my arm around her shoulder, hoping the warmth would comfort her.

"Since when are you afraid of the dark?"

Being taken to deserted Lookout Park at night terrified me, but she frequently visited on her own. I had no idea what was happening. She stared at me, her trembling lips and wide, frightened eyes giving in to her fears.

"I guess it was when the harsh reality of the world outside hit me. My PTSD diagnosis came from the hospital doctors. It was confirmed at the retreat."

The memories of that awful night—the drugs, the assault—were surfacing, and the feelings that flooded back were unbearable. I could only imagine the weight of her experience and the emotions it must have evoked. The fight, a brutal display of aggression and fear that lingers in my memory. I doubt I will ever forget it.

I pulled her into my arms, her heart beating fast against mine. "Tell me, what can I do to help?"

I had no intention of suggesting she do anything. I only wanted what was best for her in the present moment.

"Could you stay with me this week? I'm feeling a little overwhelmed by the quiet and the emptiness. I adore it here, honestly, but I'm not ready to face this challenge alone." She spoke so low I could barely hear her.

She preferred to struggle alone rather than admit she needed help—it wasn't in her nature to ask. With a sigh, she nuzzled her face in my chest, the warmth of her body radiating against me, and I wrapped my arms around her, my face nestled in her soft hair.

"I'm happy to stay as long as you'd like me to. Staying with me at the penthouse from time to time is also an option." I suggested.

She nodded and drew nearer, my grip tightening around her.

"I'm here for you for whatever you need."

She nodded slowly, her head bobbing gently.

With a sudden push, she moved quickly to the kitchen. Frantically, she rummaged through the bag on the kitchen counter. I didn't know what she was doing—her behavior seemed completely erratic.

"Is there anything I can help you with?"

She shook her head, and I joined her in the kitchen, pulling up a stool at the island. She was obviously focused on something. Her hands moved with practiced ease as she brewed tea, then a tiny vial emerged—several drops, iridescent in the light, were added to the cup. The whole thing had a mad scientist vibe.

"What was that, if you don't mind me asking?" Her head shot up in surprise, a peal of laughter along with it.

"I didn't even know you were there. Sorry. It's something I learned to make at the retreat. It's a tincture made from herbs that has a calming effect. A sort of anti-anxiety drug without the drugs or the side effects."

"Is this part of what you weren't ready to tell me about?" She nodded excitedly. "Would you like to talk about it now?" I asked, my eyebrows raised, hoping she was ready to share this new venture.

"Yes, but give me a minute to have this tea. The anxiety is a little rough on me sometimes."

So, all this time, this is what's been masked by the tough exterior, huh?

"Of course. Take all the time you need." Keeping my gaze fixed on her, I tried to understand her internal state by observing her every move and facial expression, noting even the smallest details. Her anxiety was palpable—a suffocating wave of heat and rapid pulse. I could almost feel it. Simultaneously, I sensed her fierce struggle for control. I didn't want to intrude on her quiet contemplation, so I stayed at a distance, watching as she delicately poured the steaming tea.

She took a delicate sip; her lashes fluttering as she looked at me over the rim of the cup and asked sweetly. "Can we grab some blankets and go sit out on the porch, on the swing?"

"Sure." I pulled a pair of thick, wool blankets off the couch and we settled onto the gently swaying porch swing. With each sip of her warm tea, a peaceful serenity spread across her features, calming even me. Her slow, deep breathing, faded everything into the background as she smiled, relaxing her face.

"Ugh, that's better. Sorry about that."

She experienced a rollercoaster of emotions in a short period. I perceived a conflict playing out in her fluctuating emotions. Though unusual, it wasn't out of character for her. I've seen her go from anxious to calm in a matter of seconds. I've just never seen her go through more than a couple at a time.

"Nothing to be sorry about. This I understand."

While I don't experience it to the same extent, I'm familiar with anxiety.

"So, during my time away, I unexpectedly found myself immersed in the world of chemistry, experimenting with various herbs and their uses. I was consumed by the idea of finding a viable alternative to alcohol for alcoholics—a solution that could truly help them. I must have been in the early stages of it, or maybe even fully experiencing it myself. I'm not really sure."

Now I was utterly captivated, my curiosity piqued.

"Tell me all about it."

"I'm not sure, or perhaps I am, why I decided to take an Ayurvedic medicine course. Maybe I tried it because the title included the word "medicine". I was looking for a way to help myself. I realized after several weeks that this class offered something more significant than just cold remedies or better sleep. Although, getting a good night's sleep was also crucial for me." My fingers ghosted across her hand as I hung on every word.

"To understand why it mattered so much, my counselor recommended I ask myself the right questions. In one of my meditation sessions, I asked all kinds of questions but got nothing. A joke I'd initially disregarded unexpectedly occurred to me. 'What can these herbs do for my mother?' was the question that changed everything."

"I guess I can see why you may have thought that was a joke, given the reality of the situation."

"Oh, for sure. I rushed to the herbalist and asked if herbs could be combined to mimic alcohol's effects on an alcoholic without the negative consequences. He suggested I join his advanced class, and now here I am." She inhaled deeply as I watched her take another large gulp of the fragrant, soothing tea.

"When did you make up your mind about returning to church?" I was reluctant to ask. She seemed so mad at God.

"At a party I'd been avoiding for weeks, actually. I struggled with self-forgiveness, believing I didn't deserve to have fun while everyone at home suffered because of me. My counselor convinced me to go. It was a necessary step in my recovery. I cried throughout the entire service, but a visit to the wellness pool afterward brought a profound sense of peace. Oh, and I was baptized," she said, waving her hand dismissively, as if it were a commonplace event. I drew her near, wanting to reassure her she could confide in me. "It's not a secret or anything—what I'm doing with the herbs. I'd been waiting for the right time to explain." She seemed to know what I was thinking.

"Alex, that's an amazing idea! I apologize for being a jerk when I asked about starting another business." I steered the conversation away from the church, back to her new business idea, her eyes lighting up with renewed enthusiasm.

"No, you were right. I don't know how I'm going to do the non-profit and this business and the real estate. I'm getting anxious just thinking about it. That's one reason I'm taking so much time before I get back to the office. I need to really evaluate this and see what's most important to me."

I could tell the stress was definitely trying to throw her off balance—her shoulders were tense, and her breathing was shallow.

"I'm pretty sure I have a solution."

I desperately wanted to offer some comfort, and I would've said anything, but this time, I genuinely possessed a solution.

"What is it?" She asked with extreme urgency.

The thought of figuring this out right now seemed paramount to her, but it could wait.

"Can you come to the office with me tomorrow?"

Her brow furrowed.

"Which office?" She asked.

"Sorry, mine. Others besides myself have input and solutions to share."

"I have to swing by the real estate office to pick up the wedding invitation," she reminded herself.

"You're coming with me, right?" She said hurriedly.

A fresh wave of anxiety washed over her.

"Of course. I was hoping you were going to ask."

"I could've been a little more polite about that. I didn't mean to imply you had to go if you don't want to..."

I had to stop her from going off the rails with this simple invitation, so I softly touched her shoulders, turning her to face me.

"That's not how I meant that. It makes me happy that you want me to join you, that's all."

"You must think I'm a bigger basket case than before."

I laughed, and the rest of the night was a breeze.

Chapter 10

ALEX

The shrill ring of Roman's alarm sliced through the silence of the morning. I hadn't set my alarm for over a month; the quiet mornings felt strangely peaceful, as I thought of all the things I used to get up for—such as working out.

"Where am I going to work out all the way out here?"

It hit me I didn't even know if there were any gyms nearby.

The sound of sizzling bacon filled the kitchen as I made breakfast while he got ready for work, then I showered and got ready for my day. I grabbed my trusty jeans, a simple white t-shirt, and draped a comforting brown, fluffy cardigan over my shoulders; the cardigan smelled faintly of lavender from my hair. I quickly twisted it into a messy bun and slipped on my worn brown leather boots. Roman walked me to my car, his touch gentle as he opened the door and helped me into the driver's seat. Listening to the quiet hum of the engine as I followed him to the office, was an act of staying in the moment. With a few deep breaths and the slightly bitter taste of the anti-anxiety tea lingering, I exited the car after we parked in the familiar location in the building's garage.

Roman opened the door and I quickly grabbed my purse and my almost-cold tea, then we rode the smooth, silent elevator up to the fifteenth floor. Aware of my aversion to large crowds, he quietly guided me around the busy, noisy lobby. As the elevator ascended, he held me tightly against the glass wall, the building's waterfall feature visible but obstructed by his embrace. I could feel the slight vibration of the elevator against my feet. I should probably tell him about my fear of heights—the dizzying sensation, the overwhelming urge to pass out—but it could wait.

The final stretch felt hushed and expectant; then a breathy whisper brushed my ear. "Wait until you hear the amazing things that have happened while you were gone."

A lightness filled me as I turned, the anticipated kiss a burst of sunshine before we stepped off the elevator. Roman released me and I immediately went over to Amelia's desk, hugging her tightly. I blinked back the tears, and she bit her lip to stifle her squeal.

Harrison was leaning next to her desk and said, "Hey, don't I get one too?"

"Of course." I exclaimed as I hugged Harrison, his embrace a comfort, before Roman ushered me into his office—the hurried pace quickening my heartbeat as he revealed our next destination while shifting into professional mode.

"Ok, we have a meeting this morning in the conference room."

Wait, what? Who's we?

"We?" My hands clenched and unclenched, the rhythm matching the relentless beating in my chest.

"Yes, I did, so let's go before we're late."

My shoulders slumped, the weight of my improper attire matching the disappointment and regret that settled in my gut. He wore a perfectly tailored gray suit, a crisp white shirt giving off a slight starch smell, his attire impeccably pressed was preferred. I desperately scanned the room, my eyes darting between strangers, searching for a single friendly face in the sea of people. Harrison was inside with several unfamiliar people. I gave Roman a confused look. Clearly, he caught my dismay, tucking myself deeper into the cardigan.

"It's ok, the rest of the team are on their way. They were stuck in traffic."

"What do you mean *'the rest of the team?'* Who's team? I don't know anyone in here now. Do I know the ones on the way?"

He let out a nonchalant chuckle.

"You will, it's fine. Let's go in and I'll introduce you."

Roman introduced me to investors, architects, and builders—all seemingly acquainted with me. Hopefully not from social media or the news. Their eagerness to meet me made it seem like I'd arranged the meeting myself. I needed a moment, and a peaceful corner, with my steaming cup of tea, offering the perfect respite. This was sensory overload.

Harrison sidled up to me while Roman was talking to everyone. His elbows bumped the table playfully as he plopped his face into his hands. His grin radiating pure mischief.

"Hey, you feeling ok?"

I couldn't help but glance at him; a full look would've sent me into a fit of laughter. I bet I look pretty stressed. I certainly felt it.

"Yeah, just wasn't ready for whatever this is. Do you know what's happening right now?"

Nope, not okay at all. I thought as tremors tried to overtake me. I squeezed the mug of tea tighter.

He simply admitted, "Yes." of course he did.

"Is this some kind of surprise, or what? I'm not sure what's going on, but it feels like it's centered around me."

The nervousness trying to return while every sip of tea held it at bay.

"This meeting has everything to do with you in the best way possible." Harrison whispered in a voice so low it was for my ears only.

At that moment two of my favorite people walked through the door, I smiled, their familiar faces replacing the nerves with joy. I leaped from my seat, narrowly avoiding a collision with Harrison as I raced towards them. Shay and Darius's eyes widened in surprise—it was clear they hadn't expected to see me either. I wrapped them both in a tight hug, my own tears threatening to spill as I held them close. Perhaps one or two tears escaped, which I hastily brushed away. Our reunion was abruptly halted; a sharp, percussive sound from Roman's throat pulled everyone's focus back to the subject at hand, whatever that was.

"Now that everyone's here, we can get started."

Shay and Darius sat beside me, with Harrison opposite, while Roman led the meeting from the head of the table. Switching off the lights, he started a video presentation on the large screen. My jaw dropped at the title on the monitor; Shay reached over and grasped my hand. It said, "The Kennedy-Jackson Foundation." I scanned the room, the silence punctuated only by the rapid beating of my heart as I met the eyes of everyone looking at me.

We turned our attention back to the front of the room when Roman said, "This is a surprise for Alex, so let me fill her in on what happened while she was gone."

A blissful smile bloomed as I dabbed away happy tears. The retreat seems to have left me feeling very emotional—I needed to manage this. Shay rested her head on my shoulder briefly, then sat up straight as Roman continued.

"As we all know, Alex started a non-profit before she took some time off. She also added a clause in that contract that said if she was unable to perform her duties permanently or for a period of time that Darius Jackson was to be left in charge. The news was undiscovered, initially—however, once revealed, we swiftly assigned Darius the task, and the operation began without delay."

Reaching over, I squeezed Darius's hand.

"Given his integral role, we support him staying on as CEO while Alex shifts to a more consultative role and explores business ventures both within and outside the organization."

I heard a lot of whispers, but I couldn't tell if they were positive or negative.

"Now, this is merely a suggestion, of course, and the final decision rests with Alex. I'll hand it over to her now to outline her plans for the company."

A surprising sense of calm settled where rage once would have burned; I felt an ease—a sense of peace I hadn't expected. I'd personally added that clause to the contract, and I was keen to understand his plan for making everything work. The weight of the contract was a physical reminder of my responsibility. One I took seriously.

I inhaled deeply, a lightness filling my chest as I stood tall—the words tumbled out. "Wow, Hi. That was definitely more information than I expected. Yeah, um, thank you all for attending and taking on this project in my absence, particularly Darius." Turning, I saw him—all dressed up in a sharp suit and tie, exuding professionalism.

"This project is very special to us both, and your efforts have gone above and beyond what I could have ever expected. I just want to thank you for that. With that said," I emphasized, a slight edge to my voice to make sure everyone knew I was serious.

"I included that clause because Darius was undoubtedly my top choice. I intended to make him a partner regardless of the recent turmoil. I owe a huge debt of gratitude to whoever let Darius know about the clause—my to-do list was so long before I left that I'd forgotten. I completely concur that Darius has the skills and vision to successfully run this company, and I will be there to offer my guidance and support. Shay Pierce," I directed everyone's attention to Shay with a pointed look and gesture of my hand, "possesses real estate skills that rival my own; her expertise is truly exceptional. Therefore, I'd like to offer her the head Realtor position for this project, entailing property acquisition and assessment for our renovation business..."

My breath hitched in my throat thinking about the next part of this speech as I scanned the crowd—their faces blurred, a desperate plea for connection lost in the noise of my own thoughts. A profound silence hung in the air as everyone seemed to be listening intently. My heart pounded and I proceeded with my senses on high alert—I was about to divulge demons.

"You're aware that the name of this company is The Kennedy-Jackson Foundation. It makes sense, my name being Kennedy, but it in fact honors my mother. But to build this foundation properly, I've decided to share leadership, accepting I'll have less direct control. The Jackson side involves real estate development and renovation, while the Kennedy side is a unique venture that I believe aligns well with this non-profit and demands my direct and immediate attention. This week, I have a meeting with a winery to explore the creation of a sophisticated, non-alcoholic wine, hoping to capture the full-bodied experience without alcohol. I'm not sure how well you know me or my mother, but she tragically lost her life in a drunk driving accident. She was an alcoholic and the drunk driver. After her accident, and probably before, I may or may not have been drinking too much myself..."

The words hung in the air, heavy with guilt, as I glanced at Roman. He stood silently against the wall, arms crossed, his eyes watchful. His smile was tight, a thin line stretched across his face, yet it held a flicker of sympathy. I'm sure the events were etched in his mind, as they were my own.

"...After forty-five days of intensive therapy and introspection at a rehab center, the answer became clear: my drinking was excessive and fueled by underlying problems." I heard a few people whispering before I said, "I understand the silence; people are scared of others' opinions. But I did this for me, and no one else. If my actions alleviate the suffering of others facing similar circumstances to mine or my mother's, that would be incredibly fulfilling. I intend to present my product at AA meetings and various healthcare facilities, including rehab centers and hospitals, targeting those who might find it beneficial. It's more than grape juice; it's a complex concoction of medicinal herbs, each with their own distinct earthy aroma and subtle taste that will pair well with wine, we think. I discovered them in Indonesia. When mixed correctly, these ingredients can fool an addict's brain into believing their addiction is satisfied without the morning-after consequences of a hangover or intoxication."

As the noise level in the room escalated, by excited chatter, Roman cleared his throat, bringing everyone back to topic.

One investor asked, "Do you really think something like that is going to work for people with alcoholism? Don't you think they like the drunkenness?"

I know I sure did.

"I'm sure there are people out there who enjoy being drunk, I'm not gonna lie, but this product wouldn't be for them. I'm not doing this to help everyone and I'm not doing it to eradicate alcohol. The point is to help people who want help. People who want to find some other way to get through the day or help them relax other than drugs and alcohol."

Another investor also asked, "Do you have any idea if it works?"

The words, "Yes, I do," were a heavy weight, each syllable a painful reminder. "At this time, I've only tested it on myself and not in the wine form. I've tested it as a tincture in tea. My research shows tincture potency is unaffected by flavoring, and since I, like many others, appreciate the taste of wine, I plan to discuss with a winery the possibility of creating a delicious, non-alcoholic wine base for my tinctures, which should complement the subtle tannins in the wine. I'll need a dedicated research and development team, plus a group of enthusiastic volunteers, to test the feasibility of this project. I know I can't solve every problem or make this universally accessible, it's simply not realistic. My idea is firmly rooted in practicality, not some flights of fancy. I'm hoping to help families who feel hopeless, just like mine did, to find a path forward."

Roman came over and interjected before emotion took over—which was definitely bubbling below the surface.

"Currently, the only aspect of this organization that concerns any of you in this room is the Jackson side. We're contacting different investors for this project." With a wave of their hand, an investor cut him off.

"What if we want to be a part of this, too? This is an amazing concept, presenting a great chance to make a difference in people's lives. I'd be happy to help in any way I can. My wife will be interested to hear this, given her father's struggles with alcoholism and many attempts at rehabilitation."

I felt a surge of motivation to continue, thanks to the promising possibilities. Now, I need to make that phone call to the Santoros—I can practically feel the gears grinding.

***

ROMAN

As the final words of the meeting faded, she discreetly pulled me aside, her expression serious. "I need to call the Santoros," she said, the urgency evident in her voice. "Your behavior around them seems off, but I'd really like you there when I speak with them, especially since you're handling their winery renovations. There could be a solution, if they're willing to help; for me to find a dedicated area to house the necessary tools and equipment."

"I feel fine around them, I promise." That was a lie. "I'd be happy to go with you and talk to them..." I forced a smile, hoping it masked the knot of anxiety in my stomach; happy wasn't the word I'd use to describe how I felt. "...If I do some additional work there for you, will you accept it as a token of my appreciation?"

Her eyes narrowed in thought, a slight frown etching itself onto her face.

"I'm trying to be more grateful, not taking things for granted, so presenting it as a gift is fine by me. We both know I can easily afford your fee."

I hugged her, feeling the soft fabric of her sweater against my arms as I smiled at this willingness to accept help. She'd always been resistant to it. I released her and rested my hands lightly on her shoulders.

"Do you mind if I ask something?"

"Of course." She had her hands casually resting on my forearms.

"Why do you analyze everything before you answer? Is this something you learned while you were away?"

A soft snort of amusement left her.

"Do I do that? I didn't notice." She mused while scrunching her brows "I guess I'm just trying to be mindful of what I say. You know, filter a little— think of the consequences. Guess I'm doing it out loud."

"So, does that mean no more sarcastic quips?"

The smile lit up her face. Then a conspiratorial wink followed.

"I'll save you some."

"Please do." I whispered.

"I need to go to Johnson Realty to pick up the wedding invite and then I'll be home." With a soft sigh, she whispered over my lips, just before kissing me.

"Ok, I'll see you at home, be careful."

"Home"—the very word sparked a vibrant warmth in my heart—piercing the clouds of doubt.

Chapter 11

ALEX

I reached out to the Santoros while driving to the office.

A cheerful "Hello, Alex" greeted me as Mr. Santoro answered the phone.

I'm just captivated by his warm, rich Italian accent; it's so charming.

"Hi Alessandro, how are you?"

"My dear it is so good to hear from you. I am doing well. What can I do for you?"

"I'd appreciate the opportunity to chat about a new business venture I'm working on and ask for your guidance."

"That's wonderful, my dear, would you like to come for dinner tonight? Lucia would love to see you. In fact, we would all love to see you."

"Perfect. Can I bring Roman? He's going to be involved in this as well."

"Of course. How about 6:00 pm?"

"Great, I'll let him know. Thank you. I look forward to seeing all of you, too."

I pulled into a parking space at Johnson Realtors; the sun gleaming off my freshly washed black SUV, practically blinding me. I excitedly called Roman to share the meeting time with the Santoros tonight.

"Hi honey, what's up? Everything alright?"

A sharp laugh escaped my lips at his disbelief; I couldn't tell if he genuinely doubted my well-being or if it had just become a conditioned response.

"You don't have to ask me that all the time. Seeing you so worried makes my own anxieties spike."

The faint sound of a sigh followed his chuckle—I could almost see him shaking his head, chastising himself under his breath.

"I'm sorry." Old habits die hard, it seemed. "I'll do better," he vowed.

"I called the Santoros. We're having dinner with them tonight at six. Is that going to be okay with you? I should've asked first, I know," I said, my heart pounding in my chest, "but I really want to find out right away if this will happen."

"Hey, just relax," He whispered, the words soft as a feather—a tone only reserved for me. "I understand your eagerness to launch this, but it's a process that requires patience; don't let anxiety get the best of you. Yes, dinner at six is fine," He replied.

"I know, you're right." I conceded. We said goodbye as I walked into the brightly lit office.

From behind her large desk, Felicity said hello, her voice calm and friendly. She avoided eye contact, a clear sign of her nervousness, which I was determined to alleviate.

"I'm a hugger, so if we're on the same team, I'd love a hug when I come in instead of just a hello—if you're okay with that."

The words felt a little awkward coming out, but I meant them.

"That's awesome. I've wanted to join your group for a while. You all seem so positive."

With a playful wink, I revealed, "Little secret, you already are. I'm sorry we haven't had more time to get to know each other better, but I truly hope we can remedy that soon. In the future, I hope to learn more about what you're working toward. Let's plan to have lunch as soon as I get back to the office and talk about that."

"That would be amazing," she breathed, a smile spreading across her face.

As I headed toward Grant's office, Landon suddenly appeared, his booming laugh echoing before his bear hug squeezed the air from my lungs.

Overwhelmed with emotion, I grabbed his face, tears welling in my eyes, and exclaimed, "Oh my God, Landon, I'm so happy for you! Grant told me the news. I came to get my invite and to personally congratulate you!"

"I know, right!! Being a dad and a husband feels surreal; I can hardly believe it's happening. I always wanted these things, but it's all happening so fast."

"You know Aunt Ali is available to babysit anytime, and I know you'll be a wonderful husband and father," I said, smiling warmly.

"I'm sure there's going to come a time, thank you."

"Make sure Piper lets me know when the baby shower is too and what the little nugget is going to need."

He looked worried all of a sudden.

"You're coming to the wedding, aren't you?" He asked anxiously.

"Landon, do you have baby brain too? I came to the office to pick up my invite. Roman and I will be there."

Relief washed over his face.

"Where the heck is your best man at?" I searched for Ryan, but he was nowhere in sight.

He had such a straight face when he said, "He's in your office redecorating."

"Wait, what? He took over my office. Did someone kill Grant?" We both started laughing and I realized I hadn't seen Grant around either.

"Landon, is Grant here?"

Something fishy's going on. My eyes narrowed as I looked towards my closed office door.

"I haven't seen him today."

I looked at Landon as if he were up to something. He was playing it way too cool, even for him. I headed toward my office.

I opened the door, but it was dark, and all the shades were pulled.

Ryan was not redecorating.

I turned on the lights, and everyone jumped out and yelled, **"SUR-PRISE!"**

Small heart attack, check.

"How did you and Darius beat me over here?" I was looking right at Shay, who looked terribly guilty. Her big bright eyes only told me she was really proud of herself for not letting it slip.

"We had Roman distract you for a few minutes after the meeting."

"Sneaky."

Grant came over and hugged me tightly, the scent of his familiar expensive Italian cologne filling me with pleasant memories and an urge to come back to work.

"You look so happy, baby girl," he said.

"I am, but how did you get this set up so fast?"

A chuckle rumbled in his chest as he shook his head, a wry smile playing on his lips.

"This has been up for about a week, and I'm surprised it's lasted this long. This morning gave us the perfect opportunity we'd been waiting for."

"We've missed you so much." Ryan chimed in without warning, "This place is a mess without you. Everything is running poorly and inefficiently."

Even if he was a big player, he was quite the real estate agent, and I didn't believe what he was saying for one minute.

"You're lying." I retorted playfully, my voice barely cutting through his laughter.

"You're right. We didn't even know you were gone." He joked, but that I believed.

"Thank God. Y'all probably got some work done around here without my drama." Relief flooded through me.

Grant's face was serious, almost stern, as he pulled me aside, his voice low. "Speaking of running this place, there's something that I'd like to talk to you about."

"Do you really want to talk about it today?" A ghost of a smile touched my lips—fragile and fleeting.

"No, it can wait until you're back in the office," he replied, the smell of stale bourbon clinging to the air as he spoke, making me wonder if there was something serious going on.

"I'm not in the mood for too many business discussions today," I replied. "This morning, we met at King Construction to discuss the non-profit, and this evening we're having dinner at the Santoros' to talk about my new business. You're more than welcome to join us." I waited, anticipating he would say yes.

"I have some things to do tonight, otherwise I would love to join you. Let's get together sometime next week and talk about your new venture."

I felt a wave of sadness wash over me.

"Of course, that would be wonderful. How about dinner at your restaurant, my treat?" His restaurant, Giovanni's Trattoria, was the only restaurant in Cincinnati that had more than a month-long wait list for reservations.

"Absolutely," he said, "but you'll never pay in my restaurant."

I was left wondering about what Grant wanted to tell me, a nagging feeling that he was keeping secrets gnawing at me.

***

ROMAN

After several conversations with investors about the new projects, I finally had a moment to myself. The quiet hum of the office a welcome change from their voices. The scent of garlic and herbs preceded Amelia as she walked into my office, a bag from Benita's Bistro in hand. That was my go-to lunch spot.

"Hey boss, I thought you might be hungry, so I wanted to check if you've eaten. You know, anticipate your needs."

"Have I given you that raise yet?"

"Of course. I mixed it in with some paperwork you had to sign. It was a big one."

A shared joke erupted into laughter.

"Seriously, I owe you a raise and I'm going to take care of that with HR today."

"I appreciate it, Roman. I can see you're busy, so I'll let you get back to work. Let me know if you need anything else."

She's my brother's girlfriend, yes, but she's the most incredible assistant I've ever worked with; if Harrison does anything to jeopardize that, I swear I'll kill him. The pressure of the new business deals consumed me, and lunch was the last thing on my mind; the tension was a headache waiting to happen. She had perfect timing.

As I was finally putting away my things for the day, Harrison strolled in with a grin, asking, "Hey man, wanna celebrate Alex's return with a drink?""

"I can't. I'm having dinner with Alex at the Santoros to talk to them about the new business."

"Damn, that girl is determined, isn't she?"

"I need to try to get her to relax a bit. She thinks this all needs to get done right now."

A curt nod, his eyes conveying a silent, "Good luck," filled with a mix of apprehension and hope.

I gave him a hopeful smile in return and a silent wish for similar fortune.

"How's her new house?"

"It's far and secluded." I said without hesitation. "Don't get me wrong, it's beautiful, but she's feeling a little scared being there alone, so I'm staying with her for a week, then see if she's okay on her own after that."

"And if she's not? Are you planning to move out there?"

I dismissed it with a shrug; I hadn't thought about it, given how little we'd seen each other since her return. No need to hurry.

"I doubt she wants that, but I told her I'd wait however long it takes for her to adjust; we'll see what happens."

With a shake of his head, Harrison's face showed clear signs of concern, his lips pressed into a thin line.

"She's definitely done a 180, hasn't she?"

I nodded, thinking about how vulnerable this Alex is.

"You have no idea. I barely recognize her. It's nice though. I'm wondering if this is how she was before her marriage/divorce, like Grant said."

"More relaxed version of the girl we knew? Is there such a thing?"

I shrugged. *Good question*, I thought.

"More vulnerable, trusting and sweet, I'd say. She's a bit tense, but she's improving."

I called Alex on my way to her house around 4:00 pm to make sure she was there.

"Hey babe. How was your day?" Her tone mellow and soothing to the ear, a sound that eased the usual tension.

I smiled, listening to her engage with nothing peculiar behind it.

"I had a great day. I hope you did as well." I responded.

"I had the best day I've had in a long time...." she sounded excited to tell me. "...I was so amped up from the day I felt the need to go home and soak in a hot bath to relax; I'm getting ready to run the bath water now. Of course, I had some more tea, too. I'm not trying to drink too much of it though because I don't want it to lose its potency." She was practically vibrating with energy—we should find a constructive outlet for that.

"So, are you in the bath now?" Her laughter, a bubbly sound, filled the cabin of my Mercedes.

"As a matter of fact, I was just getting in. Would you like me to save some room for you? There's plenty of room for two."

I was hoping she'd give me a blow-by-blow account of her activities, maybe with a little playful commentary. I hadn't expected an invitation this soon; it truly took me by surprise.

"You sure about that?" I carefully controlled my voice to mask my excitement, so she wouldn't hear how much I really wanted it.

"Mhm," she hummed.

"Ok, I'll be there in about twenty minutes. Do you think the water will still be warm?"

"Just hurry." It was a command, sharp and resonant, that I couldn't refuse.

Chapter 12

ALEX

As warm water filled the tub, steam slowly curled upward, softening the edges of the room while the calming scent of lavender drifted through the air, easing tension I hadn't realized I was still carrying. The quiet wrapped around me for all of a few seconds before a loud door slam downstairs shattered the peace, followed almost immediately by Roman's anguished cry echoing up from below.

My heart jumped before the sound of pounding footsteps taking the stairs two at a time reached me. Fast. Determined. Not dying. Relief settled in almost as quickly as the panic arrived, and I laughed softly under my breath. Apparently whatever happened downstairs hadn't injured him badly enough to slow him down.

Standing there in my silk robe, I crossed my arms loosely over my chest. The cool material skimmed against skin still warmed by steam, and suddenly a wave of self-consciousness settled over me despite everything we'd already been through together. Then he appeared, slightly breathless and completely Roman, and the look on his face hit me harder than I expected. He smiled—not the guarded smile or the careful one he wore when he was holding too much inside—but the real one. Bright enough it felt like it changed the entire room.

"Made it. Hi," he said between breaths.

Something nervous and unsteady bubbled up inside me and escaped as a laugh I couldn't seem to stop. It sounded softer than normal. More vulnerable.

"Yes, you did." I smiled back, warmth spreading slowly through my chest. "Hi there, baby."

The nervousness that had wrapped itself around me all evening slowly loosened its grip, and my arms naturally fell back to my sides while calm settled over me in steady waves I hadn't felt in a very long time.

"I love you," he whispered as he stepped closer.

The words brushed against my ear with warmth that somehow carried more weight than volume ever could. His arms folded around me carefully, gently, with the kind of tenderness that understood healing wasn't linear and some parts of me were still learning how to trust solid ground beneath my feet again. When his lips found mine, everything else slowly dissolved around us. The running water faded into the background. The noise inside my head disappeared. The weight I'd carried for so long loosened its grip until for one suspended moment there was only warmth, safety, and him.

Emotion rose so quickly it caught me off guard.

Tears blurred my vision as I slowly pulled back, our eyes finding each other immediately.

"I love you too," I whispered.

The words felt fragile. Sacred. Earned.

Water continued flowing softly behind us while lavender lingered in the air around me, and somewhere between recovery, heartbreak, healing, and learning how to stand back up after falling apart, I realized something I never thought I'd say again.

I was finally home.

***

ROMAN

Her desperate kiss, a last gasp of hope in the suffocating darkness that was finally clearing from a time long forgotten, clung to me like a lifeline—her "I love you," a prayer I couldn't deny.

That's it, I'm picking out a ring tomorrow.

The silken robe slipped effortlessly from her shoulders, the warm water promising soothing comfort and shared intimacy I did not take lightly or want to hurry. An exhilarating thrill shot through me as each layer revealed new beauty, a breathtaking sight, one that was still strong but void of bruises. I desperately needed more space than a cramped bath tub. I reached out and turned off the water.

A fiery spark ignited in her eyes as she glanced up, her stare burning into my soul. Her normally aggressive spirit had broken, and a desperate vulnerability that left me feeling grateful by her silent plea for guidance had taken its place.

"Why did you do that?" She asked. Her voice was husky, echoing in the vast ensuite.

"We're not doing this in the tub." A breathless sigh, thick with anticipation, vibrated through my voice, the sound of longing and desperation—desperate for her.

Her delighted giggle slipped free as I effortlessly lifted her, her arms wrapping around my neck while she held onto me tighter than before, and something about that simple gesture settled deep inside my chest. There was trust in it. Vulnerability. Need. The kind neither of us had been very good at admitting for a long time.

I buried my face briefly against her shoulder, breathing her in while laughter and nervous energy swirled between us, and slowly carried her back toward the bedroom. The look in her eyes when I laid her gently onto the bed nearly unraveled me. Beautiful didn't even begin to cover it. There was happiness there. Relief. Hope. A softness I'd missed more than I realized.

My pulse hammered harder against my ribs as I stepped back slightly, my fingers moving slowly over the buttons of my shirt while her eyes followed every movement with an intensity that made time feel slower somehow. The anticipation stretched between us, warm and electric, and for the first time in my life, I didn't want to rush through a single second of it.

"Roman, please," she whispered softly, her voice carrying enough emotion to nearly break me.

"I've waited a long time for you, honey," I said quietly, my heart pounding harder with every second that passed. "I don't intend to rush through it."

The smile that touched her lips settled something restless inside me. We'd fought hard to find our way here. Through fear. Through mistakes. Through timing that never seemed right and feelings that never stopped growing.

I moved closer again, taking my time, wanting her to feel every ounce of what words sometimes failed to say. The room felt smaller somehow. Filled with nervous laughter, unspoken promises, and something deeper than desire alone.

Her fingers curled around my hand. Mine held hers tighter. For so long it felt like life kept pulling us in opposite directions. Now there was only this. Only her. Only us.

"Oh my God, Roman. That was incredible," she panted.

"My love," I said softly, still trying to steady my own breathing, "that was only a small glimpse of what's to come."

My heart pounded hard against my ribs as I pulled her closer, kissing her with an urgency that had very little to do with desire and everything to do with relief. Gratitude. The overwhelming reality that she was here. Safe. Healing. Home.

For weeks I'd carried things I didn't know how to put down. Fear. Anger. Guilt.

The helplessness of watching someone you love hurt, while knowing there are some battles you can't fight for them.

I buried my face against her shoulder for a moment and closed my eyes, trying to quiet the noise in my own head while holding onto the peace of this one. The room around us slowly faded beneath the steady rhythm of breathing settling back into normal and the quiet comfort that came from simply existing beside someone who mattered this much.

"Roman," she said softly.

I lifted my head.

"You okay?"

Such a simple question. One I wasn't entirely sure how to answer. The past still played too loudly sometimes. The things we'd lost. The things she endured. The moments I couldn't protect her from no matter how badly I wanted to.

"Yeah," I finally said quietly. "I'm okay."

Her fingers brushed lightly across my face.

"You sure?"

No. But better. Better than before.

Her smile bloomed slowly, warmth filling her eyes. Peace settled between us quietly, not because life had suddenly become easy, but because somehow, we'd survived difficult things without losing each other in the process.

I wrapped my arms around her and rolled carefully onto my back, bringing her with me until her weight rested lightly against my chest.

"I guess we could use that bath now," I said quietly.

She smiled.

And for the first time in a very long time, everything felt still, like peace.

"Yes, please!" she exclaimed. Her playful shove against my chest felt like a spark of life from better days, and I pulled her close for one more kiss, stirring my soul, promising an eternity of love.

***

An ominous feeling settled in my chest as we pulled up to the ostentatious Italian villa sitting in the middle of nowhere Ohio, looking wildly out of place against the surrounding landscape. The sprawling stone exterior, towering windows, and excessive grandeur felt less like a home and more like someone's monument to appearances, and honestly that only tightened the knot sitting heavily in my stomach. Alex sat beside me with no idea who these people were, and that reality made things even harder.

Secrets.

Normally, I could walk into difficult situations and handle them. Negotiations. Conflict. Business problems. Bad news. I knew how to manage pressure. I knew how to compartmentalize. I built an entire career on keeping emotions where they belonged and handling problems as they came. But sitting here beside her, knowing I was carrying information she didn't have—information that directly involved her—left me unsettled in ways I didn't particularly like. I hated keeping secrets from her. Especially this one.

Because if there was one thing I'd learned about Alex, it was that trust mattered more to her than comfort. More than convenience. More than protecting feelings. Trust mattered because trust had been broken too many times in her life by too many people who convinced themselves they had good reasons.

And here I was doing it anyway. Protecting her. Or maybe protecting myself. Truthfully, I wasn't entirely sure anymore.

What I did know was that I couldn't lose her again. Not after everything we'd survived to find our way back to each other. Not after watching her fight so hard to come back to herself. And not after watching her rebuild pieces of herself she never should have had to rebuild in the first place.

I killed the engine and forced my expression into something steadier than what I felt before stepping out into the cool Ohio air. Gravel shifted beneath my shoes as I moved around the front of the vehicle and opened her door, extending my hand automatically while simultaneously preparing myself for whichever version of Alex Kennedy decided to greet me today.

Because depending on the day, offering assistance earned appreciation. Other days it earned a lecture on feminism. Sometimes both.

"You know you don't have to open the door for me every time." She chided.

I tried to hide the slight roll of my eyes.

"I know, honey, and someday you're just going to let me do it without reminding me." Leaning in, I gave her a peck on the nose. It almost felt like she was starting to appreciate it.

"Roman, Alex. How are you? So glad you were both able to make it on such short notice." Alessandro shouted from the top of the enormous stone stairs leading to his castle doors.

"*I wonder if they're planning to dig a mote.*" I thought as I gripped Alex's hand tight, not liking the fact that I have her anywhere near this or that she wants to become business partners with them.

They led us into the familiar sitting room where we first met when they asked me to renovate their property. Alex had sold them the property to open another vineyard to go with the one in California and North Carolina.

"Hello Roman, Alex." Lucia came over, offering a hug and kiss to both cheeks. It seemed almost normal except for the fact they may have been murderers at some point in their life.

"Lucia, it's so good to see you again." Alex genuinely cared for this family and Grant.

But would she still feel that way after she finds out who they are?

***

ALEX

"So, that's my idea. What do you think?" I asked, waiting patiently after walking them through the same presentation I'd gone over at the office.

More than anything, I wanted them to understand that while I absolutely needed this venture to be profitable in order to repay investors and make venture capital funding worthwhile, money wasn't the thing driving me. It never had been. I wanted to create something that genuinely helped people and gave them another option, another path forward when alcohol felt like the only answer. If this worked the way I hoped it would, the profits wouldn't simply build a company—they would build something bigger by cycling back into the nonprofit and creating opportunities for people who needed them.

"Alex, that's a wonderful idea. We absolutely love it," Mr. Santoro said warmly. "Let's plan to get together, talk through a business plan, and go from there."

For a moment, I simply blinked at him. That was it? No resistance. No skepticism. No immediate reasons explaining why it wouldn't work or all the ways it could fail before it ever got off the ground. Just support. Excitement. Belief. More belief than I ever imagined walking into tonight.

I never thought my life would take me down a path like this. Somewhere between loss, heartbreak, healing, sobriety, and learning how to rebuild myself from the inside out, I had somehow stumbled into purpose. Building this business and creating something that gave people an alternative to alcohol had already changed my life in ways I never expected, and suddenly the possibility that it could become real felt close enough to touch.

After saying goodnight to the Santoros, we climbed back into the car and started the drive toward the farmhouse. Darkness settled around us while headlights stretched long beams of light over quiet roads, and my brain immediately began moving faster than the car itself.

"Do you think it's going to take long to draw up a business plan and start implementing it?" I asked, unable to hide my excitement.

I had absolutely no desire to wait. My mind was already building timelines, lists, ideas, next steps, and possibilities before we had even pulled away from the house.

"My gut says we're looking at a few more days than you anticipated."

I sighed softly and leaned my head back against the seat. He was probably right. That didn't mean I had to like it.

The possibility of success buzzed through my chest with a kind of excitement that felt almost dangerous—not dangerous in the old way, not reckless or destructive, but hopeful. Driven. Alive. For the first time in a long time, I felt intoxicated by possibility instead of escaping into something that numbed me.

"I'm excited," I admitted quietly. "That's all. Making this a reality is so important."

"I have no doubts you'll make it happen."

The confidence in his voice swept over me more gently than reassurance usually did. Roman believed in me with a certainty I still struggled to find in myself sometimes, and that kind of faith carried weight.

By the time we pulled into the farmhouse driveway, a quiet sigh slipped from my lungs without permission. Porch lights cast a warm glow over the gravel while crickets hummed softly in the distance beneath the night sky. I sat waiting while Roman came around to open my door, and for once, I didn't protest. His hand settled lightly against mine and then my waist as he helped me out before leading me toward the quiet stillness waiting inside.

This really wasn't so bad.

Chapter 13

ROMAN

Saturday arrived before we knew it, bringing wedding preparations with it. I stopped by the penthouse earlier to pick up the blue suit she told me I needed to wear because apparently her navy-blue dress required coordination and I'd been given very specific instructions to match. As usual, I was going to look pretty basic. Navy suit. White button-up. Navy tie, even though I hated ties and found them borderline suffocating. I'd tolerate it for the wedding. Brown belt. Brown dress shoes. No socks. Some things in life were simply non-negotiable.

I adjusted the cuff of my jacket while sitting at the kitchen island when movement near the staircase pulled my attention away completely.

Alex.

She seemed to float down the stairs. The fabric of her navy-blue dress moved softly around her calves with each careful step while her heels clicked lightly against the wood beneath her feet. Her hair was pulled back, away from her face and shoulders. It swayed gently behind her as she kept her eyes lowered, cautiously watching each step. The graceful line of her exposed neck immediately became a problem I knew wasn't going away anytime soon. Not tonight—Possibly not ever.

I sat there watching her every step of the way.

"What?" she asked innocently, though the slight curve of her mouth told me she already knew exactly what she was doing. A blush settled softly across her cheeks beneath my attention.

"Yeah," I said quietly, standing from the stool. "We better get out of here before we ain't goin' anywhere."

Our favorite classical station played softly through the car speakers while darkness slowly settled outside around us. I glanced over at her again and realized I'd been smiling more lately than I had in years.

"You look incredible."

I reached over and intertwined our fingers, giving her hand a gentle squeeze.

"Thank you." She smiled softly. "You always look incredible."

I looked back toward the road before she caught what was happening inside my head.

I couldn't wait to make this woman my wife.

***

ALEX

Oh, thank God, I caught myself. I almost fell down the damn stairs gawking at him.

Who the hell looks like that?

That's a freaking gift from God. I hope he says thank you every night for all of that—I know I do.

I hadn't been to a wedding since Abby's over five years ago, and somehow, I'd forgotten how weddings carried a feeling all their own. The church was breathtaking. The last bit of sunlight streamed through stained glass windows, spilling soft colors across polished wood pews while fresh flowers filled the air with a subtle sweetness that mixed with expensive perfumes and the faint scent of candle wax. The quiet murmur of conversation drifted around us as people settled into their seats dressed in perfectly pressed suits and beautiful dresses that somehow made the entire room feel more elegant.

I spotted Grant immediately. He was standing with Shay and Owen, and Roman guided us over beside them where we exchanged quiet hellos before taking a seat next to them.

Landon stood at the altar looking handsome enough to make half the women in the room question their life choices, though beneath the polished appearance there was definitely a little nervous energy sitting behind his smile. Ryan, meanwhile, appeared to be scanning the room like a man conducting interviews for his next failed relationship, which honestly felt far more on brand for him.

The minute the music began, though, everything shifted. Conversations faded. Movement stopped. The room collectively turned in quiet anticipation.

Piper floated down the aisle on her father's arm, and Landon's entire face changed when he saw her. Pride. Love. Complete awe. It settled over him so naturally it almost made my chest hurt.

In a dress that shimmered softly beneath the church lighting with every careful step she took, Piper looked like something straight out of a fairytale. The delicate fabric moved around her effortlessly while emotion quietly settled over the room in that strange way weddings always seem to create.

Oh no. No. Absolutely not. I blinked hard. I put entirely too much effort into my makeup this morning to sit here looking like a woman filming a military reunion video on social media.

Not happening.

Throughout the ceremony, Roman held my hand securely, his thumb brushing lightly across my skin every now and then in ways that somehow grounded me without him even trying. Every once in a while, I'd catch him looking over at me with that expression.

That look.

What exactly was happening behind those eyes? Because if this man had suddenly decided to become wildly matrimonial after one wedding ceremony, we were absolutely going to need to have a conversation.

I slowly narrowed my eyes at him, hoping it was something harmless. Maybe something mildly inappropriate. Anything other than *that*.

I made it through the wedding without one tear.

Victory. I told myself.

A small one, maybe, but considering the amount of time I spent on my makeup this morning and the emotional landmines weddings tended to create, I was counting it.

Onward to the reception.

White and silver draped the space beautifully, accented with emerald green woven throughout the floral arrangements and table décor in a way that somehow managed to feel elegant without being overdone. Crystal caught warm lighting from chandeliers overhead, scattering soft reflections across polished floors while conversation, laughter, and the clinking of glasses blended into the kind of comforting noise that always followed moments worth celebrating.

Grant, Shay, Owen, Felicity, Roman, and I settled around our table while servers moved between guests carrying drinks and trays of appetizers. Music floated softly through the room while people laughed louder as nerves settled and celebrations officially began.

The only disruption to an otherwise perfect evening came from people apologizing profusely every time they accidentally offered me a drink.

"Oh my gosh, I'm sorry."

"I forgot."

"I shouldn't have asked."

At first, I smiled politely.

Then awkwardly.

Then somewhere around apology number six, I found myself quietly wondering if people thought sobriety came with a fragile warning label printed across my forehead.

I stopped drinking, that was it. The world kept turning. Music still played. Life still happened. It wasn't some devastating tragedy I needed everyone tiptoeing around. It wasn't even hard anymore.

Apparently, Roman noticed my growing frustration before I said a word because without warning, he stood beside me and extended his hand.

"Come on."

"Roman—"

"Nope."

"Roman—"

"Not negotiable."

I narrowed my eyes. He ignored me, naturally. A few seconds later he was pulling me onto the dance floor while music drifted around us in layered melodies and familiar sounds that somehow managed to quiet the noise in my head. His hand settled comfortably at my waist while mine rested against him automatically, muscle memory taking over before my overthinking brain could interfere.

"You know," I said quietly while looking up at him, "you're very bossy."

"You love it."

"I tolerate it."

"You definitely love it."

"Roman."

"Alex."

I fought the smile and lost as usual. And somewhere between the music, the warmth of his hand resting against me, and the way he somehow always knew exactly when to pull me out of my own head, the frustration slowly disappeared. For tonight—I was okay.

"Alright everyone, time for the garter and bouquet!" Landon announced with a mischievous glint in his eyes as the crowd gathered.

Does it really mean whoever catches the bouquet is the next to walk down the aisle? I seriously doubt it.

All the guys lined up and I swear I saw something between Roman and Landon as the garter practically fell right in Roman's hand.

"Ladies, you're next." Piper chimed in.

I did my best to find a place towards the back of the crowd. No way was I going to be knocked down and trampled for something I was definitely not interested in.

I watched in what felt like slow motion as the entire crowd parted with suspicious precision, creating a perfectly clear path for the bouquet to fly directly toward me. It hit the floor right at my feet.

Of course it did.

I stared down at it, then slowly lifted my eyes toward the crowd before looking back down at the bouquet again. Absolutely not. There was no way this happened naturally. Before I could even think about making a strategic retreat, Shay swooped in, picked it up, and shoved it directly into my hands.

Definitely a setup.

I narrowed my eyes immediately while laughter and whistles erupted around me. There was entirely too much satisfaction on far too many faces for this to have happened organically. No chance. Not buying it. Bouquet in hand like evidence from an active crime scene, I shook my head and made my way back toward Roman.

Traitor. He was trying to hide his smile. Trying being the key word and failing miserably.

I knew that look. The slightly lowered head. The amusement sitting quietly behind his eyes. That bottom lip pulled between his teeth in what I was sure he believed was a convincing attempt to appear innocent. It wasn't. Oh no. I knew exactly what lived behind that expression. And if this man thought I wasn't going to investigate his involvement in this suspicious bouquet conspiracy, he had clearly learned absolutely nothing about me.

"How in the world did you make that happen?"

"Make what happen? I did no such thing." He swept us onto the dance floor, the music swirling around us for one last dance tonight.

It was a beautiful wedding filled with heartfelt vows, joyful tears, and a palpable sense of love that seemed to make its way into every corner of the room, and I couldn't help feeling genuinely happy for them. Watching Landon and Piper together brought back memories of my own wedding, though if I was being honest, I didn't remember having nearly this much fun at mine.

Either way, tonight felt special. The kind of special you hoped people carried with them long after the flowers faded, the music stopped, and life settled back into ordinary routines. I wished them a lifetime of love, laughter, and happiness.

I must have fallen asleep on the ride home because I woke to Roman's face hovering only a couple inches from mine, his quiet whisper startling me awake.

"We're home."

Disoriented, I blinked a few times trying to gather myself while the soft glow from the farmhouse lights blurred through sleepy eyes.

"Need a hand?" he asked.

"No," I mumbled automatically, fighting the urge to say yes while my legs felt like jelly from sleep and an entire night spent in heels. Independence sat so deeply rooted inside me at this point that accepting help still felt unnatural sometimes, even when I probably should have.

I wrapped my hand around the door handle and pushed it open. Cool night air brushed against my skin as I stepped down from the vehicle. The door swung a little wider than I expected, and I hurried to shift my weight onto my foot.

Bad decision.

My heel caught against a jagged rock.

Pain shot sharply through my ankle so fast my brain barely processed what happened before my balance disappeared beneath me.

"Oh shit!" I yelled. "Ow! That fucking hurt!"

My knees buckled instantly and I bit my lip in pain and by the guilt of the words I allowed to escape. But thankfully, Roman still had hold of my hand. His grip tightened hard enough to stop what would have been an ugly fall while my other hand grabbed instinctively for the side of the vehicle. The laugh that had been sitting on his face disappeared so quickly it almost would have been funny if my ankle didn't feel like someone had taken a baseball bat to it.

"Alex?"

The nervousness in his voice immediately replaced whatever amusement he found in my stubborn independence a few seconds ago. Because judging by the look on his face—He knew this wasn't good.

"I haven't heard you use words like that since before you left." Unfortunately, I was in too much pain to laugh, or I would've joined in. I'm pretty sure I never said those words at rehab. It just didn't seem appropriate.

Okay, he was going to get his wish of carrying me.

"Roman, I can't walk. I have a bad feeling about my ankle." My gaze dropped to my ankle; the throbbing and the swelling was alarming, spreading rapidly and changing colors in a terrifying display of purple and red.

"Geez, babe. Do you need me to take you to the hospital?"

"I really hope not," I mumbled through the pain.

"Let's take a minute so I can get changed and take these shoes off before we decide on that. It might be nothing."

Although I knew it wasn't nothing, I could barely breathe it hurt so bad.

"I'm sorry to break it to you, but it's definitely something. It's swelling up like a balloon."

Great, just my freaking luck.

***

ROMAN

After carrying her upstairs, I called the local hospital to tell them we were on our way. I shrugged off my suit jacket before undoing the buttons on my shirt sleeves, feeling the fabric loosen around my forearms and neck was a relief. The bench was overflowing with the discarded clothes from our afternoon activities—jeans, t-shirts, a sweater—so I moved them to a basket and settled onto the bench to wait for Alex. Pain contorted her face, turning it bright red, as she stood in the bathroom doorway, her injured leg bent, hopping precariously to stay upright. The sounds of her labored breaths were all I could concentrate on.

"Come on, I got you."

With a surge of adrenaline, I scooped her into my arms and brought her swiftly as I could to the car, easing her into the passenger seat.

"I can't believe this happened. It's like I'm not allowed to have one peaceful moment in my life."

She had tears streaming down her face, staring straight through the windshield.

"Alex, honey, it's going to be alright. These things happen."

"If I had just let you carry me into the house, it wouldn't have happened, though. Why do I do this to myself? What the hell is wrong with me?"

"Would you stop it. Nothing is wrong with you. You're a strong woman. You twisted your ankle on a rock. One has nothing to do with the other."

I don't know the extent of what she went through at the rehab center, but I'm sure they tried to help her with the self-deprecating behavior. I won't placate her, but I will not let her ruin all her progress, either.

The world outside the car window was just a smear of gray, mirroring the pain I felt for her as I peered sideways at her silent tears falling. The ER entrance blazed with fluorescent lights, casting a harsh glow on the nearly empty parking lot. Despite its quiet charm, I hoped this small town had a competent doctor; otherwise, we'd be making the drive back to the city. I carried her inside, the antiseptic smell of the hospital hitting me with memories of Alex after her attack and that insane fight, as a wave of nausea hit me along with it. Thankfully, a nurse's quick arrival with a wheelchair banished the horrible thought. I pushed her to the desk, the monotonous squeak of the wheels agitating me, and helped her complete the admission forms to have something to take my mind off where we were. While everyone was helpful, I desperately needed to speed up the process; I wanted an x-ray, a diagnosis, and to get her home to bed as soon as possible—and the hell out of here.

"Thanks, doctor." I shook his hand and nodded as he dealt the blow.

She had a fractured ankle that would need six to eight weeks to heal.

She let out a sigh, not saying a word or shedding another tear. They put her foot in a stabilizing boot after wrapping it up tight. The doctor handed Alex a prescription for pain medication, and I watched as she closed her eyes tight, not even looking at the piece of paper he gave her. She reached out reluctantly and handed it to me.

"Can we fill this tonight?" I asked the nurse, who was finishing up with Alex, giving her all the instructions on how to take care of her injured ankle.

"Yes, the hospital pharmacy offers 24-hour service." She smiled sympathetically at me and then Alex, who looked exhausted and defeated, again.

"Thank you. Is it alright if I wheel her down there myself and get this? Are we all set?"

"You're all set. Be safe and have a good night."

With the prescription in hand, we hurried home, arriving at 2:30 AM, the house dark and quiet. Alex was unconscious from the pain medication they'd given her at the hospital, so I carried her into the house, her limp body heavy in my arms. To make her more comfortable, I carefully removed her clothes, being as gentle as possible, before tucking her in. I removed the rest of my suit and eased in next to her, being extra cautious not to injure her further. As I laid on my back, the events of the evening replayed in my mind, thinking how perfect it was up until we got home. The sounds of silence fading as exhaustion finally overtook me and I drifted off to sleep.

Chapter 14

ROMAN

The morning sun streamed through the window as I rose and as quiet as possible went downstairs to start the coffee and make breakfast. With a sigh, I rang my mom's number to inform her we'd be missing church today.

"Hey mom."

"Hi honey. Is Alex joining us for church and brunch again today?"

"Mom, sorry to say but neither of us will be at church or brunch this morning." Suddenly, a sharp, high-pitched scream sent chills down my spine. "Mom, can I call you back?"

"Yes, please. You'll have to explain to me what that was."

"I'll call you after church."

In a panic, I fumbled my phone, letting it fall to the ground, and ran upstairs to find Alex sitting on the floor—staring at the ceiling.

"I thought I had a nightmare about this. I just stepped out of the bed."

I walked over and slumped down next to her.

"Afraid not, babe. How're you feeling?" She leaned her head on my shoulder, looking up at me. Her eyes were really glossy.

"Like a freaking zombie. Do you think I can get through this without taking that stuff?"

I wish she could, but I don't see how that's going to be possible, even though I didn't like how they made her look or feel.

"I don't know. You can try. I'll be here to help you. I'm happy to stay another week to help you out."

"What about all the meetings I have this week? What am I going to do?"

"You can do zoom meetings. I'll get that all set up for you."

"What about you? Are you going to miss work?" Her panic increased.

"Alex, I can work from here and do zoom calls too, if I have to. I can do most of my work remotely." I offered a comforting smile and a reassuring touch to her shoulder, then leaned down for a gentle kiss on her head.

"This is embarrassing, but I need help getting to the bathroom. Did they give me crutches? I can't remember much from last night after we got to the ER." I nodded, helping her to the bathroom then put the crutches inside the door and let her be.

"I'll be right downstairs. Yell if you need me." I said through the door. This was going to be a challenge for her, but it seemed like maybe the universe was sending her another lesson on letting people help.

***

ALEX

I somehow managed to use the crutches to get downstairs. It wasn't without difficulty. What I found when I got there...Roman had created a cozy spot for me on the couch, facing the TV, and fashioned a makeshift office nearby, complete with my laptop. I flopped onto the couch tossing the crutches nearby and propped my booted foot up on a nearby pillow. A concerned Shay called me after I sent her a quick text; I could hear the worry in her voice. Although she wanted to help, there was nothing any-one else could do, so she offered to handle all the scheduling changes. For that I was grateful.

"Hey babe, do you need anything? I need to make some calls and get things moved around for the week. Are you okay for a few?"

Though he was the sweetest, I had a feeling he might make a bigger deal over this than necessary.

"All good. Do what you need to do." I tried to convince myself, but the pain in my foot was a relentless, throbbing fire that sent searing waves up my leg.

Nausea washed over me as I stared at the pills, the bitter taste already in my mouth. I wondered if this was really my only choice—a suffocating pressure bore down on me. I picked up my phone and called Roman's mom.

"Alex, I was just on the phone with Roman. He told me what happened. How are you?"

"Lisette, I feel like an idiot, but other than that, I'll live. I called because they gave me pain medication. They gave me a shot at the hospital last night, but I feel like garbage today. Do you think I should take it?"

"How does your ankle feel if you don't take it?"

Ugh, I did not want to answer that.

"It's not good..." I admitted. "...The pain is radiating all the way up to my hip. I'm just scared that I got rid of one vice and could get hooked on this stuff next."

"Alex, why don't you let Roman handle the medication? He can regulate it for you."

"Will you tell him he has to stand up to me, then?"

She burst out laughing.

"I'll talk to him and explain that you need his help to manage your medication. We can tell him the medication is causing strange side effects like forgetfulness, making you afraid of taking too much unintentionally, rather than focusing on the possibility of addiction."

I sighed, knowing she was the perfect person to call, but I wondered if I should just start being honest with him instead of telling little white lies.

"Lisette, you are a lifesaver. Maybe I'll just end up sleeping a lot."

With a sigh, we ended the call, and then the door opened, and Roman walked in, confidently, his desire to be here for me meant so much but I wondered if that would be enough.

***

ROMAN

"Hey Harr...I mean Harrison." I forget how sensitive he can be about calling him Harry.

"Hey asshole. I mean Roman."

I laughed—I had it coming.

"Sorry. How was church this morning?"

"Church was good. Where the hell were you two? I should say, what the hell were you two doing?"

"Popping pills and screaming."

It would have been more fun with a different meaning. Once more, there was silence on the line.

"What the...? Are you serious right now?"

"Harrison, is it ever just a normal boring night with Alex?"

He laughed.

"Ok, so you're going to tell me what that meant, right?"

"Sure. It was a fantastic wedding, and she was absolutely beautiful. She abstained from alcohol entirely. Sound asleep in the car when we got home, and I offered to help her to bed, but naturally she refused." I leaned back against the kitchen counter, shaking my head despite the smile trying to creep onto my face. "She fell out of the car; we ended up in the emergency room—her ankle is broken. She'll be in a boot for six weeks or more."

I could practically hear the reaction waiting on the other end of the phone.

"Yeah, it gets better," I continued. "They gave her pain medication she doesn't want to take, and this morning she stepped out of bed and completely forgot she had a broken ankle. That's where the screaming came in."

A laugh escaped before I could stop it.

"Pretty fun story, huh?" I chided.

Truthfully, it hadn't felt very funny last night.

Watching her go down after twisting her ankle took years off my life. Seeing pain hit her face like that after everything she'd already been through lately nearly sent me into panic mode before we even made it to the emergency room.

But this morning? This morning was at least a little funny. Not funny enough to tell her that. Not if I valued my life, anyway.

"Damn, is she ever gonna catch a break? I mean, she just got off the booze and now she's on the opiates. What the heck?" I nodded, then got a text from Mom saying I should talk to Alex.

"Sorry, gotta go, man. I'll talk to you later." I hung up and hurried into the living room.

"Hey babe, what's up?"

She looked at me with tears in her eyes and reached out with the pills in her hand.

"Please take these from me." She sniffled, her head hung low.

"Does that mean you're not going to take them at all?" Now I was worried.

She was staring at her hands while clenching them together so hard her knuckles were white.

"I called your mom to talk to her about what I should do." Her voice fell away as she looked up at me, her lashes shielding her eyes, a pained expression etched on her face.

"Okay, and what did she say? Did you decide something?"

"We agreed that having you keep track of the medications was the most responsible course of action. I only need those pills," she said, "either as prescribed, or if the pain gets too bad." She burst into tears.

"Honey, I have no problem doing that for you."

Interrupting, she sobbed, "We decided it's because I might forget the dose and take too much," before adding, "but I truly believe it's my fear of getting hooked, like I did on alcohol. Why am I being tested like this again? What did I do to deserve this?"

I sat next to her, gently pulling her into my arms, feeling her fragility.

"Alex, I'm here to help you. I know this isn't an ideal situation, but you aren't going to get through the pain without help. I'll monitor the meds for you and when you don't need them anymore, you won't take them. We'll make sure you get through this. We'll do it together. If you need my mom to come out and help, she will."

She continued to sob.

"Did you know she had to stay a few days at the rehab center because of me? I can't ask her to come near me right now. She doesn't deserve this either."

I knew why my mom stayed with Alex, but this is different, and she would absolutely come help her if she needed it—and she would be fine. At least I hope she would.

"Alex, let's not stress over this today, please. Do you need some meds right now?" She nodded. "I thought you might. Wasn't sure if you were in pain or just upset until I noticed your face turning bright red. I'm going to get you another water. Do you need any food?"

She shook her head no.

Thankfully, the medicine knocked her out. I made sure her foot was elevated, like the doctor said. I wrapped an ice pack around it while she slept. After placing a blanket over her, I stepped outside to survey the property and consider what to do next.

***

ALEX

I was wrong if I thought this would be easy. I'm now using my living room as both my office and bedroom. My inability to manage stairs meant I slept on the couch. I offered Roman the bed, but he preferred to stay close by, just in case, so he slept on the other couch. However, one week of makeshift life in the living room and kitchen, sleeping on the couch, and I'd reached my limit.

"Roman, I can't do this anymore. My back is killing me, and I don't want you to have to carry me up the stairs every day just to take a shower..."

There was worry etched on his face when he interrupted me.

"You can't possibly think I'd leave you to deal with this by yourself? Or climb those stairs without help."

I shook my head, showing my disapproval.

"I wasn't finished, babe. I won't be mobile for another couple of weeks, so I was wondering if we could stay at your place? Everything I need is all on one floor and has an elevator." Ignoring my words, he dashed over, his lips brushing mine before he began to frantically gather his things.

A booming "YES!!!" fractured the room's quiet as he yelled the word to me from across the space.

"Do you think I can use your office to have meetings as well? Zoom meetings aren't ideal." I said.

He was nodding and smiling as he packed up.

"Honey, could you pack a bag for me?"

He stopped dead in his tracks, turning slowly to confirm what I already knew the answer to.

"Umm, probably not. How about if I carry you upstairs and you can point out everything you want to bring, and I'll pack it for you?"

Clearly that was what I was hoping for.

He said he'd arrange for someone to check on the house as we locked the last lock on the front door. I sent my dad a text, making him aware I'd be staying at Roman's place for a while. Shay moved all our meetings to the conference room at King Construction, coordinating with Amelia to ensure the conference room's availability. It was much easier than expected to agree to this arrangement, even though I was a little nervous about being back downtown so soon. I figured I'd get there eventually, but this was much sooner than I expected.

I limped into the penthouse on my crutches, following Roman to where took my things to his room. Returning felt odd, but the two pictures I'd brought from when we moved in together were a comforting sight. I can't believe he kept them. A photo, taken by the Santoro's son, showed the two of us at their Italian villa style house, the sunset casting a warm glow behind us. A sudden rush of emotion brought a prickling sensation to my eyes.

He came out to the living room, his voice calm and gentle, "Sorry, I couldn't bring myself to part with them."

My nose scrunched up to hide the tears, a mask of composure over my once broken heart.

"Would it be alright if I kept these here? They'll make this place feel so much more like I belong here!" A wave of warmth and security enveloped me as he wrapped me in his arms.

"Yes, and this is always your home whenever you want it."

Two weeks—a mere blip on the radar of time, I figured.

***

ROMAN

Two weeks passed, and she was getting around much better on crutches. Further X-rays showed she didn't need a plaster cast or surgery and was ready for a walking boot.

As we left the doctor's office and got in the car, she inquired, "Although I'm allowed to walk on it, would it be alright if I stayed until it's completely removed? It's easier to manage everything through your office right now."

Her babbling felt like a smokescreen, a way to avoid a straightforward request for help or an open declaration of wanting to move in.

I broke in on her this time.

"You're always welcome to stay at my home, you know that. Tell me what's going on with you?"

I waited patiently for her to answer. She looked at me with a confused expression, her brows scrunched and lips pinched.

"What do you mean?" She asked.

"You don't have to explain anything to me. I want you to be here, you have to know that by now. I'd love for you to move in, but there's no rush. Keep your things here for as long as you need them and take your time deciding."

With a dramatic sigh, she threw herself onto the nearest chair.

"What the heck. I'm thinking of moving in permanently—it would make life much easier, wouldn't it? Like, that would be the smart move, rather than going back and forth all the time. Let me mull this over for a couple of weeks until this thing is off my foot."

My jaw dropped. *Did she seriously just say what I think she said?*

"Babe, are you saying you want to move in?"

She looked at the floor, shaking her head and smiling.

"Let's play it by ear for now because I did just buy a house and there is a reason for that."

"I understand. So, what is the purpose of the house?"

I already had her moving out of that place.

She patted the seat beside her, and I sat down, pulling her close while she explained everything she'd been working out in that mind of hers that never seemed to stop moving. She planned to grow herbs there for the non-alcoholic wine, and listening to her piece the vision together felt a lot like watching someone slowly bring a blueprint to life before the first foundation had even been poured. The greenhouse itself was a key part of the plan, but so was proximity to the Santoros. Location mattered. Logistics mattered. More importantly, building relationships with people who believed in what she was trying to accomplish mattered.

She explained that during her time in Indonesia, she discussed the idea extensively with both her teacher and her counselor, Melati. Apparently,

Melati knew a local farming family that would be happy to help grow the herbs if additional support was needed. Alex planned to discuss hiring that family during an upcoming meeting, and hearing the excitement in her voice while she talked through the details made it impossible not to smile.

Some people chased money. Some chased success. Alex chased purpose.

Even after everything she'd been through, she still somehow managed to build things that centered around helping people, and I wasn't sure she fully realized how rare that actually was.

Chapter 15

ALEX

Four weeks in this damn boot was testing my patience in ways I didn't know were possible. Roman refused to touch me for fear of somehow breaking me, which I found utterly ridiculous. Apparently, twisting one ankle transformed me into delicate porcelain in his mind, and no amount of explaining otherwise seemed capable of changing that.

I finally managed to get myself over to Bruce's studio. The second he spotted the boot, he lost it. Completely. Boisterous, unapologetic laughter filled the space while I narrowed my eyes at him.

"Ok," he said, trying and failing to regain composure. "I'm betting there's a good story behind that."

I scrunched up my face and shook my head while he walked over and pulled me into a hug.

"Bruce, there is no interesting plot to this story at all. I literally stepped out of the car and somehow this happened."

That only made him laugh harder.

Traitor.

Once he finally pulled himself together, we headed back to his office to talk. He filled me in on everything happening at the MMA studio after the publicity surrounding the fight and hearing how much momentum they'd gained from it honestly surprised me. Somewhere during the conversation, he asked if I'd consider teaching a weekly self-defense class.

I didn't even hesitate. I told him I'd love to. I just needed to sort a few other things out first. He understood, and I promised him I'd be back to kickboxing classes with the girls the second my doctor cleared me. It was also my first Saturday lunch with the girls since coming back.

We sat at our usual table at Sunny Side Up downtown and somehow keeping that tradition intact felt important. Necessary. Life changed. People changed. Circumstances changed. But some things deserved protecting. Since we moved lunch to Saturdays, everyone went back to church on Sundays and spent time with their families afterward. Looking back now, I realized how much I'd pushed God away during everything that happened and how wrapped up in my own struggles I became without fully considering the impact on people around me. The realization sat heavier than I expected. My friends loved me enough to prioritize me. To show up. To rearrange pieces of their lives around my pain. And while I'd been grateful for it, I hadn't fully realized what they were sacrificing to do it.

Church. Family time. Traditions that mattered. Perspective has a funny way of showing up when you finally still long enough to hear it.

I felt terrible knowing they placed our friendship ahead of things that mattered deeply to them, and somewhere between healing, slowing down, and learning hard lessons I never wanted to learn, I realized I needed to make amends.

This morning, I used my crutches because my foot was still too swollen and tender to put much weight on it, even with the walking boot. As frustrating as it was, I was finally giving myself permission to heal instead of trying to push through pain and pretend I was somehow immune to basic human limitations. Turns out healing required a level of patience I wasn't naturally equipped for. I hated every second of it. The slowed pace.

The dependence. The feeling that life kept moving while I sat waiting for my body to catch up. Still, I was trying.

By the time I made my way to the table, carefully maneuvering my crutches around chairs and people moving through the restaurant, both girls looked up at me and immediately shook their heads.

Maggie said, "You're late!"

I rolled my eyes and nodded.

"What else is new?"

The girls hugged me and said they ordered me a virgin Bloody Mary. I had had no pain meds in a few days, and though the throbbing was still present, it was becoming less intense. Every time I winced, Roman would ask if I needed my medication. I think it was bothering him more than me.

Abby, looking very pregnant now, said, "So, you've moved in with Roman again? How's that going?"

"Well, it's not as challenging as I thought it would be. I mean, being waited on hand and foot..." I pointed to the booted monstrosity. "... has its perks."

"Especially if the poor sucker looks like him."

Abby was always open about her opinion of Roman's appearance.

Maggie asked, "Yeah, so how does Roman feel about your hopeless ass?"

"Are you kidding me..." A laugh escaped my lips, "...if I didn't know what happened, I would've thought he did this on purpose. He loves it. Gives him a reason to do everything and anything for me and I can't do a thing about it."

I'm the one who couldn't stand being helpless.

"What about your new house? You didn't even get to live in it for a week." Abby exclaimed, her eyes widening in surprise.

"I know. We're still working out the details on that. It was just a temporary residence while I got my business off the ground, anyway."

A look of pure bewilderment crossed both girls' faces as they stared at me. You know, that look, the one that says, *You better start talking, or else.*

"What business?" they both expressed in unison.

"Ok, don't get mad at me for not telling you. I just forgot. I've been kind of overwhelmed since I got home."

Abby acknowledged, "I'm sure you have. That was a lot that went down before you left and since you've been gone, you've completely changed and started a new business on top of that?"

I gently wrapped my arm around Abby's shoulder, her head resting lightly against me.

"I've only changed the bad stuff, I hope. The new business is going to be fun. It's a non-alcoholic wine with a twist...fun without the repercussions."

"Omg, are you serious? Is that really a thing?" Maggie freaked.

"While I was in Indonesia, I studied herbs and learned how to create tinctures that would trick the mind. I mean that's all alcohol does, it just leaves you feeling like crap the next day and kills brain cells and shuts down organs. I just wanted to omit the negatives."

"Does it make you feel drunk?" Abby added.

I shook my head.

"No, there is no inebriation which I understand to some people that's kind of the point of alcohol, but it's not what this is for. This is literally for people like my mother who drank because they were tormented by something. I use the tinctures in tea right now for the anxiety I have from everything that happened."

"Do you have some of that now? Can we try it too?" Maggie inquired as Abby nodded in agreement.

"Of course. I'm planning to use the house I bought to grow the herbs that I'm using. I have five acres and a greenhouse. I've never grown anything in my life but the people I met at the retreat not only keep in touch with me, but it just so happens that a family from Indonesia lives close by and they know all about how to grow these herbs—so I'm going to hire them to help."

Maggie was so intrigued she kept asking questions that I was more than happy to elaborate on.

"So how are you going to make the wine? Is it going to taste like wine or will it be more like juice?"

"Well, I'm partnering with Santoro Winery."

Maggie exclaimed, "Oh, I love their wine. Are you using their California winery or their North Carolina winery?"

I laughed.

"They actually have a winery opening soon in Ohio. It's about ten minutes from my house. I sold them the property and they've become very good friends."

"How did I not know about this?" Maggie asked, so surprised.

"I have no idea. I guess I didn't know you knew anything about their wine since I didn't know about their other wineries until I sold them the property. I was pretty much consumed with myself if you hadn't noticed."

"Oh, we noticed alright." Abby pointed out as she rolled her eyes then huffed out a laugh.

"They were at the hearing, then came to the penthouse for a little while after."

"Alessandro and Lucia? That was them? They even brought their wine." Maggie exclaimed.

We laughed and continued to talk about anything and everything that had nothing to do with what happened. I told them I'd be inviting them for dinner to the new house as soon as the boot came off and had things started with the business. I mean, the house was something out of a Norman Rockwell painting. I loved it.

Other than going to see Bruce and having lunch with the girls, I'd never felt this helpless in my life. Sitting still wasn't something I did well on a normal day, but sitting still while watching everyone else move projects forward around me felt like torture. My brain wanted lists. Movement. Progress. Something productive. Anything productive.

Thank God Darius and Shay wanted another set of eyes walking through the neighborhood, looking for possible locations for the park and community garden. The second they asked, I was in.

It was early December now, and cold had finally settled over the neighborhood in a way that made everything feel quieter. Bare branches stretched toward gray skies while crisp air carried that familiar winter smell of earth, leaves, and fireplaces burning somewhere in the distance. The timing actually felt perfect.

We finally had funding for the community project with substantial backing and possibility.

Maybe this was exactly when we needed to start figuring out placement. Walking the land. Looking at accessibility. Figuring out where children could play. Where families could gather. Where vegetables and flowers and fresh food could grow in a neighborhood that deserved beautiful things too.

Maybe if everything lined up right, we could even start talking about a groundbreaking.

The thought alone filled me with enough energy to forget my frustration for a while.

I went to work with Roman and had Darius and Shay pick me up from the office later that afternoon. While I waited for them to arrive, Roman and I sat in his office discussing the next steps for the nonprofit and everything that still needed to fall into place to keep the project moving forward.

"I know we have investors for all parts of the business now, but what about a fundraiser? I would love to do something fun for the community and raise money for little extra things and maybe scholarships. We could donate some of the money to AA and special programs to help under-privileged communities. Give people hope. We're, seriously, lacking in generosity and hope."

Roman just sat there, listening. He didn't interrupt or interject his opinion, which isn't normal.

"Why are you looking at me like that?"

I always get worried when I have an idea and share it with Roman. The first time in his office, he shot the idea down, that was most important to me, because he was the one that was destroying the community.

"Just listening and admiring you, is all. I think it's a great idea. What do you have in mind?"

I took a deep breath.

"Well, I'd like to have a gala, you know, a fundraiser. I think we could actually have it here."

He scrunched up his face with uncertainty.

"Where, in here, would we have it?" He seemed totally at a loss, and I felt like I was overstepping my bounds now.

"The first-floor lobby and green space?" I asked, hoping I could explain more. "...This place is huge and the first floor is wide open."

Before I could elaborate more, there was a knock on the door. Amelia popped her head in.

"Darius and Shay are here to pick up Alex," she announced.

"Thanks Amelia." I said, as I forced a smile.

Roman said, "Have fun and we can talk more about this at home."

I smiled because home, coming from his lips, sounded amazing and I couldn't wait to get *"Home."*

I nodded, then walked over, giving him a peck on the lips.

"Thank you." I watched him all the way as I left.

Chapter 16

ALEX

I t was freezing today, so we were bundled up from head to toe. Even with the cold, the neighborhood was beginning to take shape as the cleanup efforts continued. Everywhere I looked, I could see signs of progress, and for the first time in a long while, it felt like the community was moving in the right direction.

We stopped by to see Ella's new house, where she and her grandsons would be moving soon. The renovations were absolutely stunning. Every room felt warm, inviting, and full of possibility. I couldn't wait to help her move in.

Hopefully, this freaking boot would be off by then.

As we were wandering around some pretty run-down houses, we heard whimpering.

"Did you guys hear that, or is it my imagination?"

They agreed they heard something and we went towards the noise and moved some wood that was piled up. Underneath the heap of junk there was a mama dog and her puppies; except none of them were alive except the one whimpering. I immediately picked it up without hesitation.

"Ok, do you think we can agree on the area that we should put the park and the garden?" They both nodded their heads and I asked them to take me to the nearest veterinary clinic I found on Google. This little guy or girl was emaciated and very little. Couldn't possibly be old enough to be away from its mama.

I called the clinic on the way there and they told us to bring the little one in and they would take care of it. Before we got out of the car, Shay said she needed to get back for a client and take Darius home. I told her not to worry, that I would call Roman and have him pick me up.

"I want to stay with the pup and make sure everything is okay."

Shay looked at me skeptically and said, "I feel like you want to do more than make sure the pup is okay. Do you think Roman will be okay with you keeping it?"

I laughed kind of in a joking way. I didn't even think about keeping him, just getting him to the vet. But ya know what? I think I will keep it. It's a survivor, just like me.

"If he's not, I have my own place out in the country that the pup and I will absolutely love." I said with a chuckle.

I really do have a great place to have a dog. She laughed and I hugged the both of them, telling them to make sure they took really good notes about today. I let them know to bring the notes to the next meeting, along with sending them to the other interested parties via email.

While I was waiting for information about the puppy, I texted Roman to tell him where I was and that I would need to be picked up, then called Ella. She answered on the first ring.

"Hello Alex. How are you, honey?"

She coughed a lot after that greeting.

"Hi Ella, are you feeling unwell?"

"Nothing to worry about, just a cold maybe." She didn't sound like her usual self, but I wanted to brag some about Darius.

"So, Ella, Darius is a CEO now. Did he tell you?"

She laughed. I couldn't help but smile, thinking about how far this relationship had come from running out of gas basically in her front yard.

"I cried for a half hour after he came home and told me the news and then I cried for another half hour when he told me you broke your ankle. You poor sweet girl."

I laughed again.

"Ya know something, Miss Ella, it wouldn't be me if something tragic didn't happen, apparently."

She didn't say anything as she fell into another coughing fit.

"Ella, are you sure everything is fine?"

"Alex, I'm good today." Her voice sounded hoarse and I felt something ominous in my gut.

"Ella, what do you mean by today? What's going on Big Mama?"

She started to cry—I felt my heart being squeezed in my chest.

"I went to the doctor recently and they found some things in my blood work, but they wanted to run some more tests to be sure."

"What kind of tests?" I asked. My stomach sank.

"The cancer kind." She hurried out.

I didn't want to fall apart on the phone, so I took a couple of deep breaths.

"Does Darius know?" I asked, as she sniffled.

"No, not yet." She sounded so calm.

"When are you due to get the results of these tests?" I felt myself slipping, but I had to hang on for her.

"When they call, they're going to make an appointment for me to come to the office."

"Do you want me to come with you when they give you the news?"

I somehow managed to find enough strength to try to be there for her.

She said, "Would you do that for me, Alex? I don't want Darius to hear it at the doctor's office. If it's cancer, I want you to be there with me to tell him. I'm going to need someone like you in my boy's life to help him, and you're the only one I trust."

I had tears streaming down my face, but I kept from crying while I was on the phone with her. As soon as I agreed to do that, we hung up and I broke down.

***

ROMAN

God, I'm starving. I wondered what we were having for dinner tonight, and the thought brought a quiet sense of satisfaction I wasn't used to feeling before Alex. There was a time when the penthouse felt more like a place to sleep than a place to live, but somewhere along the way that changed.

Now dinner at home meant something.

The thought of spending another ordinary night together inside *our* house carried a sense of contentment that once felt completely out of reach. Funny how the things I used to overlook somehow became the things that mattered most.

ALEX: *"Hey, I'm at the vet. We found a puppy. Shay and Darius had to leave. Can you pick me up? I'll ping you my location."*

ME: *"A puppy? Yes, I can pick you up. What do you want for dinner?"*

After waiting several minutes with no reply, I figured she was probably talking to the vet, and I quit looking at the phone.

Harrison and Amelia walked in into my office looking like they were ready to leave. It was already four, but I hadn't heard from Alex yet about the puppy other than getting her location ping. I glanced at the phone, but nothing.

Harrison said, "Hey, we're getting out of here. You and Alex wanna have a mocktail before we go out tonight, at your place?"

"What the hell is a mocktail?" I snickered.

"A faux cocktail." He said, like it was something we said every day.

"Why would I drink a fake cocktail?"

He looked at me like I was an idiot.

"ALEX?" He threw his hands on his hips, trying to figure out why I wasn't getting this extra stupid conversation. I couldn't help but laugh.

"She would think you're an idiot for drinking a fake one just because she doesn't want one. Plus, she hates everyone making concessions for her. She would rather you lived your life. You do you and all."

Amelia laughed.

"That sounds like our girl." Amelia looked at me, then turned to Harrison and said, "I told you that was a stupid offer."

Harrison brushed us both off and turned his attention back towards me. "So, what's the verdict?"

"Oh, um, no can do. Alex found a puppy at the site and took it to the vet. I have to go pick her up. She's stranded there, but she hasn't called me back to let me know if she's ready so I'm just going to head over there now."

"Is she going to keep the puppy?" Amelia asked, wide eyed.

"Sure, if it's a purebred Labrador or Golden Retriever and not some mangy junkyard dog."

Harrison laughed so hard I thought he was going to cry.

"Have you met your girlfriend? Do you really think she would ever buy a dog?"

Damn, he was right. I had a feeling we were about to bring home some mangy junkyard dog.

"I guess Mary'll be getting a raise." They both laughed and I headed out to the car.

My housekeeper has had it easy just having me to contend with. Now Alex and a mutt. She'll probably quit.

I tried to call Alex a few times and even texted her on my way there, but I got no response. I wonder if her phone died. This just isn't like her not to respond. I pulled up to the vet and headed in.

I walked in to find her hunched over, crying.

Oh no, did the puppy die?

I hurried over to her and put my arms around her.

"Hey babe. What happened? The puppy?"

She just shook her head and buried her face in my chest, wrapping her arms securely around my waist. I held her tight, letting her finish.

"If it's not about the puppy, what happened?"

I got up, prying myself from her grip to grab a tissue off the counter. She dried her face as she took a couple of deep breaths.

"It's Ella. She's having some tests run to find out if she has cancer."

Well, that sucks. I grabbed her and hugged her; not just for her, but also for me. I knew what a wonderful person Ella was. This was heartbreaking.

"So, they don't know anything yet though, right?"

"No, but I could feel something was wrong even before she said anything. They got some test results they didn't like and now they want to run more. She asked me to go with her when they call her to come in and read the results. If it's cancer, she wants me to be there when she tells Darius and the boys."

I kissed the top of her head.

"Damn, babe. I'm so sorry."

The vet came out and called, "Ms. Kennedy?"

I helped her get up and we walked over to the counter. She smiled through the tears and sniffled.

"Hi, I'm Dr. Grantham." I shook his hand and introduced myself because Alex was still processing the information about Ella.

"Was the puppy alone because this is a very young dog. Only a few weeks old."

She sniffled more, shaking her head.

"No, there was a mama and other puppies, but they were all dead and I couldn't bear to leave the poor thing to die."

She sounded so sad. I couldn't tell if it was from Ella or the puppy at this point since it was all sad information.

"Well, that was sweet of you because this little guy is pretty malnourished, and it wasn't looking good."

The doctor seemed very appreciative of her kindness towards this puppy.

"So how is he? Is it a he?"

She seemed to be getting her mental and emotional strength back as she started to concentrate on the dog instead of her news.

He smiled and said, "It is a he and we put him on a feeding tube and an IV to rehydrate him. Are you going to need some instructions on how to take care of him?"

She looked at me surprised by the question.

"Uh, what should I do?"

I shook my head and shrugged. I hadn't really thought we would take it home, but it seems to be lighting her up.

"Doc, what kind of dog is this?"

I think that's the first bit of information I need.

He smiled and raised his eyebrows while looking at me. "It's definitely a Pitbull variety, possibly mixed, but it looks full pit. We can do a DNA test if you'd like."

I looked at Alex and sighed. Of course it's a freaking Pitbull. I mean, Alex is a freaking Pitbull honestly.

"I don't know, honey. I'm not familiar with the breed other than the stereotypical stuff. Doc, what can you tell me about this dog to make me feel better?"

The vet looked at me, probably trying to assess if I'm man enough to take on this dog or if I'm just a big wuss afraid of a little puppy.

"Dogs are an extension of their owners. They tend to take on that personality. If you train them and treat them right, you'll have man's best friend. If you do the opposite, you'll have man's worst nightmare regardless of the breed. I've seen aggressive poodles and docile pits. There's always going to be some kind of natural instinct because it's an animal, but these dogs are not inherently bad."

Alex looked at me, smiled and said, "Don't judge a book by its cover seems to be the story of our life, don't you think?"

Right then, I knew I was adopting a dog. A Pitbull, to be exact.

The doctor gave us instructions on how to take care of the puppy and how to feed it since it was so young. It was going to need to be bottle fed for the next few weeks and basically treated like a baby. We stopped at the pet store on the way home and Alex looked like a completely different person. She had this helpless little puppy in her arms. You would've thought it was her child. We walked around the store and bought shirts, food, bottles, beds, a crate and toys galore. This was going to be the most spoiled dog on the planet.

On the ride back to the penthouse, I said, "Are you going to want to go back to the farmhouse so the dog has a place to run around?"

Her eyes got wide.

"That's a great idea. I can use the property as his playground. Do you think I'm a bad person keeping him at the penthouse?"

"Not at all. We can walk him down to the river. We can get him trained, he'll be great. What do you think you want to name him?"

He better be great. The stories I've heard about Pitbulls scare the crap out of me.

***

ALEX

What do you think you want to name him?" Roman asked as he reached over and gently pet the puppy's head.

I kept hearing I needed to find the way while I was at the retreat. *Hmmm, the way? I wonder what "The Way" is in Hindu or Buddhism?* I thought.

I spent a lot of time studying eastern medicines and became very fond of the culture. I grabbed my phone and googled 'The Way' in eastern religions and it came up with Tao.

I smiled as we pulled into the parking garage, "Tao. it means the way or the path. I feel like he and I are going on a journey together now. This is our path."

"Nice to meet you Tao. I love it. It's perfect. You're going to make an incredible dog, mom." He scratched under Tao's chin with one finger.

I let out a deep breath, thinking about what a huge responsibility this was going to be on top of everything else.

"Well, he's super little, and this is going to be challenging. Do you mind if I bring him to meetings in the little carry bag I bought? It's not like I can take him on walks, and I don't want to leave him in the crate. He's just too tiny."

He laughed.

"You can do whatever you think is best for him. I don't think anyone will even notice he's there. You're going to let him sleep in the crate at night, though, right?"

"Of course. He can't sleep in the bed, he's too little."

I smirked at him knowingly.

He looked at me and said, "Ever, right?"

I smiled and shrugged, giving him my own puppy dog eyes.

"Maybe, we'll see."

"Oh lord," He mumbled, grabbing as much stuff as he could out of the car, and I carried Tao.

We set everything up and I gave Tao a little bath in the sink and fed him with the bottle while Roman made dinner. I carried him back to the room so I could change. As of right now, he didn't do much other than eat and sleep and I'm sure, use the potty, so we lined his crate with puppy pads. The vet said he was only about three weeks old. His eyes were barely open at this point. He was freaking adorable, though. He was mostly white, with a few black and brown spots on him. I'm sure he had a lot of changing to do and who knows how big he'll get. I read on the ride home Pitbulls can get quite large, especially the males. He hadn't whimpered since we took him home. I'm thinking he was calling for help out there and now he feels safe.

Roman kept looking between me and the puppy.

"Are you going to put him down so you can eat?" He sounded rather annoyed.

I giggled.

"I don't know if I ever want to put him down. He's so sweet."

He laughed at me.

"Are you going to let me hold him, ever?"

Oh, so that's what this is about. He is annoyed because he wants a turn.

"Maybe. I mean, at some point, I might need to take a shower or use the restroom, but I could just take him with me."

I was just messing with him. He leaned over and kissed my head.

"I love this side of you. I know how you are with the kids, but this is really something special to witness."

"I'm a total sucker for animals." I admitted.

He smiled and scooted closer.

"Me too. Now give me that puppy."

I reluctantly handed Tao over to Roman and that was it. He was hooked. This little guy was our first official baby together. I don't know how a broken ankle and a puppy turned my entire world upside down, but I was in love with it all and knew this was going to be my life from now on except for the broken ankle.

Chapter 17

ROMAN

Oh, nice. This dream is spot on. Exactly what I needed.

Soft hands moved slowly across my chest, warmth lingering be-hind every touch in a way that felt so real I wasn't entirely convinced I was asleep. As much as I didn't want to open my eyes and ruin whatever my subconscious had generously decided to give me this morning, I could hear my alarm going off somewhere nearby.

Reality was calling—Unfortunately.

It had been weeks since Alex and I'd had made love, and if I was being honest, my patience was wearing thin and I felt like a complete douchebag because of it.

I finally forced my eyes open. Turns out I wasn't dreaming. There really were soft hands caressing me and attached to those hands was a beautiful woman looking entirely too pleased with herself. I smiled immediately...Yeah, I definitely couldn't have asked for a better way to wake up.

She said, "I didn't want to wake you, but when I tried to turn off your alarm you grabbed my hand and put it on your chest so I thought I should just try and wake you like this." Okay, so I created that dream myself. Good for me. I reached over and shut off the alarm, rolling back over to Alex.

"Good morning." I reached my arm around her waist, tugging her flush with my body. "You know you're supposed to be given the okay today to not have to wear that boot anymore. What are you going to do to celebrate?" I'm hoping from the lack of clothing she's wearing that we might be celebrating sooner than tonight.

She arched an eyebrow at me and said, "I don't think I'm going to wait for the okay. I think I'm going to celebrate now."

I moaned when her lips met mine and wrapped my arms around her. Okay, well if this is going down now, I'm not going to let her do anything to put that ankle back in jeopardy without the okay from the doctor. I rolled her onto her back, making sure her ankle was nice and safe over my shoulder where I could keep an eye on it. I rubbed my hand up and down the soft skin of her leg, planting a protective kiss on her ankle to let her know I got this. My eyes closed as my head fell back. She feels like silk and heaven. God, I hope I don't hurt her.

We took the day off from work so I could take her to the doctor and get her scheduled for physical therapy to strengthen her ankle and lower leg. When she told me she was going to see if Bruce could help her get it strong again, I cringed at the thought of what he would train her to do this time. I know he didn't mean any harm or have any intentions of what happened to have actually happened, but he did help her make it a reality. He trained her to actually hurt someone, even though he said it was just self defense. That still weighs heavy on my mind from time to time. I raked my hands through my hair at the memories of seeing her get punched in the face and kicked in the ribs. It was making me nauseous. The visions that I still have of her losing control and hitting the guy so hard in the face after he went unconscious and seeing the blood..."*Stop it.*" I told myself. I shook the thoughts to the back of my mind. I knew they would never truly be gone but I needed to bury them as far down as I could. It was hard to picture this beautiful, sweet woman that I love, losing control the way she did and becoming so violent. It was more something I pictured myself doing. I wondered if she was feeding off of my energy back then and that's what triggered the anger.

I needed to let it go.

After taking care of the puppy and getting ready, we headed to the doctor's office. She had more x-rays taken and a new set of instructions on how to care for her ankle now that she didn't need to wear the boot anymore. They gave her a brace in case it felt unstable and the name of a physical therapist near her house.

"Is it possible to get one closer to my downtown home instead?" She asked quietly while scanning between me and the doctor.

My heart practically jumped out of my chest when I heard her say it was her home, too. The doctor gave her the name of another physical therapist near the penthouse.

In the car I said, "So, are you going to go back to the farmhouse at all?"

I didn't want to bring up the fact she called the penthouse hers and freak her out. I wanted her to be comfortable calling it hers.

She nodded and said, "I have an idea about that. I need to spend time there getting it ready for the business, but I really don't want to live there. I'm not all that fond of living downtown either but I love living with you."

I smiled and patiently waited for her to finish saying what she needed to say.

"I think for now I just want to use the house for the "non-wine" business and do holidays there. I think it's the perfect Hallmark card, don't you?"

"You bought a house to spend the holidays in to take nice pictures and decorate?"

Honestly, I don't care what she wanted to do with it as long as she wanted to be with me. She scrunched up her face then started laughing and I couldn't help but join her.

"I think I did. I love those Hallmark movies so much and the house reminds me of them. I only watch them during the holidays, so I guess I'm only using my house for the holidays."

We both cracked up and I pulled her in close for a nice, long kiss.

"I can't wait to help you celebrate..." I said as I pulled away from the kiss reluctantly and got serious for a minute. "...It looks like Christmas is coming up soon." Speaking of Hallmark Christmases. "I know we didn't do anything for Thanksgiving because of your ankle, but I'd be more than happy to help you decorate the farmhouse for Christmas. We could have a Christmas party for friends and family, if you'd like, and that can be your housewarming party? I mean, if you still want to have a housewarming party since you aren't planning to actually live there now."

Her eyes were the size of saucers and she practically screamed, making the puppy bark. We were both surprised because that's the first time since we brought the little guy home that he's made any noise at all.

I guess he was excited too.

***

ALEX

It was still early when we got back to the penthouse, so I went downstairs to the fifteenth floor to Roman's office and called Amelia into the conference room.

"You okay?" She asked with a look of simple concern on her face. I was frazzled and panicked now. Compartmentalize all these other things with only two weeks to plan a party? How is that not overwhelming?

"No, I have two weeks to throw a Christmas party, and I need your help?"

She looked excited, thank God.

"If I help you, I better be invited."

"Are you serious? Of course you're invited."

"Is it here at the office?" She gestured around the room.

"No, it's going to be at the new house. I need to decorate the inside and the outside and have it catered for at least fifty people." I said, exasperated and slid down in my chair.

"How big is your house?"

"Much bigger than I thought it was when Grant told me it was a small farmhouse."

I leaned my head back and placed my hands over my face, letting out a big breath.

She laughed.

"What is your expertise as far as party planning goes?" I asked her through my fingers.

She looked like she was going to recite her resume to me when she sat up straight, leaning her elbows on the table, clasping her hands together.

"Well, I know a lot of caterers and people who put up and take down decorations, but it's kinda late for a Christmas party, so I'm not sure if anyone is going to be available on such short notice. You just have to decide how you want it to look, and I'd be more than happy to help you get the decorations and decorate." Then, before I could think about what she just said, she changed the subject, "By the way, where the heck is the puppy? Roman said you don't let him out of your sight and here you are with no puppy."

"He's with dad. He had a phone call to make. Said it was his turn to be a dog parent."

We laughed before I got back to the subject at hand.

"I have a huge storage room, so whatever decorations I get, I'll just buy them and store them in there. I could use some help decorating, though."

She reminded me also, "You'll need to send out invites too, I'm sure. Do you want to just give me a list of who you want to invite, and I can create a really festive email then Harrison and I will help you decorate. We can probably knock it out in one weekend. We'll do it the weekend before the party."

I managed a muted scream and hugged her—she was a godsend.

"Okay, great, let's have the party on the Saturday before Christmas. I'll get you the list by the end of the day. Are you doing anything after work today?"

She shook her head and said, "Do you want to go shopping?"

Not tonight. I think my foot has had enough. I moaned internally as my foot pulsed with what seemed to be a never-ending ache.

"I do, but what if you and Harrison come over tonight for dinner instead? You can meet Tao, and we can go through Pinterest and see what we can do, as far as decorations go, and then we can plan a shopping trip in the next couple of days."

"That sounds great. I'll let Harrison know. He's been trying to get together with you and Roman for weeks now and Roman keeps blowing him off."

My face fell, knowing that he was pushing his brother away because of me.

"It's my fault, and I'll apologize to Harrison as soon as I see him."

"Did I hear you need to apologize to me for something?"

Harrison was standing in the doorway, arms crossed, with a huge smile on his face waggling his eyebrows. I got up and walked over but he stopped me by the shoulders with a look of utter confusion on his face.

"Something looks different about you." As he was looking me up and down and then staring at my foot, he said, "Hmmm, you're missing your puppy purse." Then he pulled me in for a hug. "I'm just kidding. Roman told me you got that damn boot off finally. But I am concerned about where the puppy is. I heard you don't go anywhere without him."

"Yes, finally the boot came off. Pretty embarrassing how I broke my foot after everything I'd gone through before I left." Harrison seemed to cringe at the thought but stayed silent and I continued "Roman has Tao. He has to bribe me. I told Amelia I need her tonight and I want you to come."

He looked at Amelia curiously.

"We're going to plan a Christmas party together at Alex's farmhouse, so we're having dinner with them tonight upstairs."

"Well, it's about freaking time you two made some time for us." I shook my head while looking down, feeling terribly guilty.

"Harrison, I'm sorry. I feel like my drama has come between you and your brother, and I never wanted that."

"You should be. Now don't let it happen again."

Then he burst out laughing and hugged me.

***

ROMAN

Ok, I feel ridiculous carrying this purse around even though I know the puppy's in it. I pushed call on my phone.

"Hello Roman."

"Hey Grant. How are you?"

"I'm super, what's going on?" He said casually. "Is Alex alright?"

He seemed concerned now. I laughed into the phone. I'm glad I'm not the only one who asks that automatically.

"Yeah, for once she's fine." Now we were both laughing. "So, our girl wants to have a Christmas party at her new house. It really is a great house, by the way, even though she's decided not to make that her permanent residence."

There was silence for a moment from Grant's end, and I worried he might be upset and blame that on me somehow.

"She's not?" Grant questioned, a bit surprised, tinged with disappointment threaded through. "...What's she going to do with it, then?"

"She's using it for her wine business. Or should I say, non-wine business." I figured I'd tread lightly here but tell him the truth. "She also wants to have holiday parties there. She absolutely loves the place, but she said she just can't live out there by herself."

He sighed, what sounded a lot like relief.

"Thank God. I was feeling uneasy about her being alone out there. So, where is she living then?"

I smiled, thinking how glad I am that he agreed. Don't need *mafia man* pissed at me.

"She moved into the penthouse with me."

"Roman, that's the best news I've heard in a long time. How's her ankle doing?"

"She got the boot off today. She doesn't seem to be bothered by it and she starts PT next week."

"So, was this call to invite me to the party, or did you need something else?"

"Oh yeah, well, you're definitely invited, but something else too. This party she wants to have, it's kind of last minute and I know she's going to be inviting all her friends and family, but we really don't have the time to make everything ourselves. This is a stretch, but do you think Giovanni's could cater it?"

"Coincidentally, I also own a catering company, and they can cater just about anything you want, and we're always ready for last-minute parties."

"Grant, you're a lifesaver. Can you send me their information, and I'll find out what Alex wants to do for food? How many people she's planning to have, and we can go from there."

"It will be on me, okay?"

I hate that he wants to pay for everything. It makes me feel like I'm going to owe him something at some point. And I damn sure don't want to owe a hitman anything.

"Well, can I at least tip the staff?"

"Of course."

The penthouse doors opened as I was laying down my phone and getting ready to take the puppy out of the carrier and give him a little bath.

I heard loud laughter and then Harrison mumbled, "Nice purse."

"Shut up, Harry."

Alex came over to help me with the puppy and I pushed her away.

"No, you always have him. It's still my turn."

"Oh, this is good," Amelia snickered.

I got the puppy out of the carrier.

"Alex, will you please get me the puppy shampoo and a towel?"

I pushed her lightly out of the kitchen, and she ran down the hall to our room where we keep the puppy's supplies.

"This is..." Harrison started, but then he stopped when he saw what I was holding. "...Damn, no wonder you guys are so nutty. He's fresh from the mama. How old is he?"

"He's only four weeks old. They aren't supposed to be away from their mothers for eight weeks, at least according to the vet. Alex found him with his mother and siblings, but they were all dead."

Alex handed me the towel and shampoo, and I put the puppy in the sink as I trickled water out of the faucet. I gave Tao a little shower, then wrapped him up in the blanket, handing him to Amelia, who was hovering over me the entire time.

"I thought you guys were just being over the top about him. I really had no idea he was so little. What kind of dog is he? I know you thought you were bringing home a mangy junkyard dog that day, but he's beautiful."

Amelia threw me under the bus before I realized I hadn't told them what he was yet.

"A what? When did he say this?"

Alex was staring me down like how dare I call our baby a mangy junkyard dog. I grabbed her into a hug before she could actually get mad.

"When you called to tell me, you found a puppy in that neighborhood, obviously, my mind went to something a little less cute than this."

Alex smiled and turned around and said, "Amelia, clearly our baby isn't some high dollar dog, like Roman once suggested, but he definitely gave Roman the same reaction he had to me once." I was shaking my head and Harrison laughed.

"You're saying he was scared? Is that a Pitbull?" He inquired with a smirk.

I shook my head, smacking his shoulder, and Alex laughed.

"Yep. The vet had to convince him Tao was not a monster because he was a Pitbull."

Harrison was still laughing.

"You know Roman is like your typical CEO type." He stepped away as I was moving towards him, giving him the warning glare. He continued,

"He thinks his life has to be perfect. Perfect wife, perfect kids, perfect house and perfect dog. Meaning the ones from the Eddie Bauer ads."

I grabbed him, smacking the back of his head playfully.

"You are so full of it." I argued.

He pushed my hand away.

"Oh yeah. Why don't you tell Alex about the "In five Years" where do you want to be letter you wrote to yourself once?" Alex looked at me wide eyed with curiosity and I knew I was going to have to tell her about it or she would nag me until I did.

"Doesn't matter because clearly it's not what happened, so I must've been wrong."

Everyone's mouth gaped open, gasping at those words.

"Shut up."

I flipped Harrison the bird.

As the girl's went to plan decor and what not for the party Harrison pulled me over to the couch after pouring us a couple bourbons.

"Ok, man, spill it?" He said, taking a large pull of his bourbon.

Harrison's eyebrows were raised, and he wasn't going to buy any bullshit by the look on his face.

"What?"

"I know that look. Did you already buy the ring or something?"

I shook my head then leaned back on the couch and took a sip of my drink.

"Please don't let her hear you say anything like that. It freaks her out."

"I doubt it would freak her out now. She seems pretty freaking happy with this setup and your 'baby boy'."

I had the goofiest grin on my face watching her and Amelia work together to get the party planned as Harrison held the puppy, looking down at him as he talked to me in private, now with a faraway look in his eyes.

"It's been on my mind, but she hasn't been back long, and I don't want to stress her out."

I reached over, petting the puppy gently on the head.

He quietly blurted out in a hushed whisper, "I'm gonna ask Amelia!"

Now that surprised me. My head popped up and eyes opened wide, but no words came out. He looked up at me, and I thought I saw sweat forming on his forehead.

Before I said anything, he whispered, "I'm nervous as hell. I bought the ring already. I'm keeping it at mom and dads, so she doesn't accidentally find it, but I'm having trouble deciding how to do it."

"What about doing it at the party? Everyone will be there, and she definitely wouldn't suspect a thing, especially since she's so deep in the planning process of it."

"Let's get with mom. While Amelia and Alex plan the party, you and mom help me plan the proposal. How does that sound?"

I patted him on the back.

Oh shit, my little playboy brother is going to settle down.

Before me.

***

ALEX

After the initial meeting of the puppy, he got passed around from person to person while Amelia and I sat at the kitchen island, getting ideas for the party off Pinterest. The boys were in the living room drinking bourbon and entertaining the dog.

Amelia asked sincerely, "I'm sure you're sick of hearing this, but does it bother you to smell alcohol?"

"Honestly, at first, yes. I thought one sip of wine wasn't going to hurt, right? Then I thought about all the time I spent at the retreat without any, and I was fine. I just drank a lot of tea. Now, I can associate my tea with cocktails or happy hour. I have these cool tinctures that I can add too, and they have the same effect as alcohol or whatever I need them to have. I just don't feel like garbage after or lose any motor functions, ya know?"

"That's really cool. I don't drink much anyway, maybe a glass of wine or a cocktail once in a while. Do you think I could try your tincture and see what it's like? I wouldn't mind not drinking at all, either."

"Sure. Do you want to try it with tea?"

She nodded.

I made Amelia some tea and asked her which tincture she'd like.

"I have calming, antianxiety, antidepressant, one for sleep, one for relaxation, one for energy and a combination to mimic the effects of alcohol."

"The one that mimics alcohol. I'm so curious."

She had some plain decaf green tea, and I put three drops of the mixture in.

About fifteen minutes later, she said, "Wow, Alex, I feel super chill; like I've had a couple glasses of wine."

I find that I'm more excited when other people feel the effects than I do because it's doing what it was intended for.

"Yep. That's exactly what it's supposed to feel like. Once we work out how to stop the wine-making process, so there's no alcohol content but still tastes like wine, we'll be testing it out that way too. I still don't know how long it can be stored without losing its efficacy, but that's what the research and development teams are for. Clearly it won't be finished in the next month or two, but I'm super excited to get working on this right after the holidays."

We got all of our plans together for the party and I made a list of people to invite and sent that over to Amelia's email. We sat in the living room with the boys and I realized, "Oh crap, I got all the decoration ideas and the invites but what about the food? What the heck are we going to do about food? Amelia said everyone's already booked up for the holidays. How are we going to cook food for fifty plus people?"

I'm totally freaking out now.

"I can decorate and shop, but I can't cook that much food." Amelia informed us.

Harrison threw his hands up. "Don't look at me. I'll help put up decorations as long as you tell me where and how you want it. Other than that, I'll be the guy at the party eating and drinking."

"It's handled." Roman interrupted. "I just need to know what kind of food you want and how many people," Roman's reply landed all eyes abruptly towards him.

"What do you mean it's handled? By who?" I asked.

He smiled as he leaned over and kissed my cheek.

"Who do you know who owns a lot of businesses? One being a restaurant." He reminded me.

My mouth fell open in awe.

"Giovanni's is going to cater?"

Harrison and Amelia said at the same time, "What?" Harrison continued, "Um, how the hell are you going to get Giovanni's to cater last minute when you can't even get a reservation to eat there for months?"

"Alex, do you want to tell them or should I? Plus, Giovanni's will not be doing the catering. GIGI's is."

I said, "Did you talk to Grant today?"

He nodded.

"Ok, spill it." I demanded.

I sat back, crossing my arms.

"He apparently also owns a catering company and said they make sure to have extra time for last-minute holiday parties, so he needs to know ASAP what kind of food you want at the party and how many people are going to be there."

"Ok, I feel like Grant is just hiding a bunch of stuff from me. But since this is kinda perfect, Amelia, let's go back to our spot at the island and decide on some food for this party. Oh, and Grant owns Giovanni's if you didn't catch that."

We finished up getting the party organized, then Amelia and Harrison left and I plopped down on the sofa next to Roman.

"You seem to know Grant better than I do. What's going on?"

"Alex, I really don't." He said. "I called him to see if Giovanni's could cater last minute because it was you and he said no, but that he also owned a catering business that could."

It didn't seem like he was hiding anything from me. I may just be paranoid, honestly.

"I don't know. It just seems like he's so guarded with me about his life. He's like a father figure, only Batman style."

He laughed.

"Not sure what that means, but I'm never going to look at Grant the same."

"You know, mysterious. No one knows who he really is. No one knows where he lives. I certainly didn't know he owned a catering company."

"Well, maybe you should ask him."

"You know what? He did say he wanted to talk to me about the business. I wonder if he's going to retire?"

"I don't know. Like I said, I don't know much more than you do. I haven't heard anything about him retiring."

Chapter 18

ALEX

I can't believe I forgot to talk to Grant about the business conversation he wanted to have with me. I wondered why he hadn't called about it yet. Oh yeah. Broken ankle. Fragile Alex.

Geez, when were things going to feel normal again?

I finished my morning routine with the puppy and headed toward the kitchen, mentally sorting through everything I needed to accomplish today. I needed to stop by the real estate office and talk to Grant first thing. Then I needed to check in with Ella about her appointment and call Amelia about the party. I also needed to go shopping with Amelia.

Wait. We haven't even planned that yet, have we? My brain felt like ten tabs were open at once and somehow all of them were playing music. I sidled up to the kitchen island and eased onto the stool with the overwhelming feeling that I was forgetting something important on my to-do list. Which probably meant I was.

"Hey babe, I thought you were going to work this morning?"

I looked at him, confused.

"I am. Why?"

He looked at me a little quirky.

"No reason, I guess, except you've got your shirt on inside out and I'm pretty sure it's my shirt and I'm not sure what's all over your face."

His eyebrows were bunched as he pointed his finger towards his own face in a circle. I reached up only to find a hard substance all over mine, realizing I still had a mud mask on. I slowly looked down. I had on yoga pants and one of Roman's shirts and yes, it was on inside out. *Wow! Can you say preoccupied?!* His lip quirked up at the corners as he scanned me from head to toe. He touched his lips carefully against mine, so he didn't get the green substance on him.

"Do you need me to take the puppy with me today?"

"Definitely. I have no idea what's come over me. I just have a laundry list of things in my head that need to get done before the party, and clearly they've taken over to the point I didn't even realize I hadn't washed my face or actually gotten dressed."

The rambling was concerning as well.

"You know you don't have to stress over this stuff. We're all going to help you."

"I know, but there are some habits that are harder to break than others. Being a control freak seems to be one of them."

"I can tell. Don't worry about Tao, just go wash your face, get dressed, eat some breakfast and do what you gotta do."

I nodded and headed back to get ready for work for real this time. There was something I'd been planning to do that made me a little nervous—something I hadn't talked to anyone about, including Roman—and maybe that was where the brain fog was coming from. The thought sat quietly in the background, lingering just enough to distract me without fully demanding my attention.

I threw on something comfortable but put together. A soft black cashmere turtleneck with high-waisted black wide-leg pants that felt a little more fitted than I remembered, likely thanks to not stepping foot in a gym for months. Since my ankle was still healing, I paired it with black booties with no heel. A camel-colored wool trench coat pulled everything together, and after grabbing my purse, I headed to the office.

I called Grant on the drive over to see if he planned to be in today. He confirmed he would. And apparently, he was fully prepared for this mysterious business conversation. I nervously laughed to myself while driving, immediately allowing my mind to jump to ridiculous conclusions. What if he was retiring? Leaving the office to me? Absolutely not. Hard pass. That was responsibility I had no interest in inheriting.

By the time I pulled into the parking lot, I took a long breath and sat quietly for a second with my hands resting on the steering wheel. Oddly enough, despite whatever nervous energy had followed me all morning, I felt at peace with the conversation I was about to have with Grant.

As I pushed through the glass doors to the office, paying special attention to the name displayed across them, I drew in another steady breath.

I can do this.

Before I could think too much harder about it, Felicity stepped out from behind the desk and immediately wrapped me in a hug.

I whispered, "Thank you." She smiled, cheeks glowing pink over her alabaster skin.

"Is Grant in his office?" I asked as I swung my head in that direction, then back to her for confirmation.

"He is, and he's expecting you."

I caught a glimpse of everyone down the hall and waved, heading straight into Grant's office. I didn't want anyone to sidetrack me since I was not good. My focus was off today for some reason.

Oh lord, I hope it wasn't the herbs.

What if this was a side effect? No, I never considered that since they were natural. I abruptly brought myself back to the matter at hand when I was face to face with Grant's door.

I cracked the door to his office as he was hanging up the phone. He waved me in the second he saw me. I rounded his desk for another hug, that I knew would either create more anxiety or quell it altogether.

"Hello baby girl. You look wonderful. How are you feeling? I should say, how's the ankle feeling?"

I was flooded with embarrassment over the dumb way I broke my ankle to begin with, but the hug was warm and inviting—no anxiety at all.

"I'm good. The ankle's a little sore but just kind of feels like a bruise. That could just be from being in that damn boot for so long."

As usual, he sat us in the plush leather chairs to talk and not at the desk. Felicity brought us water and some cookies.

I asked a little nervously because cookies were usually brought out when we lost a sale. "Are you buttering me up for something?"

He laughed.

"Yes." He admitted.

My stomach was rolling now, wondering if this was the right time to tell him I was *quitting*.

"I guess we both have something we need to talk about. Why don't you go first." I said cautiously.

"Alex, I know your heart's not in real estate anymore. I've felt it since your mom died." Tears were building behind my eyes, but I wasn't going to let them fall as I listened, memories rising to the surface fast and furious. "At least not in the buying and selling of houses. What you're doing with the non-profit is much more suited to you at this time." Oh my God, he's firing me! Sort of. "I also know that you'll need a broker to keep your license with and of course, you're more than welcome to use this broker, you know that, but It's time you gave up your office, don't you think?"

I smiled, holding in the laugh as long as I could before I burst out in a fit.

"Oh my God Grant, I was so stressed out about telling you I was quitting."

I was laughing but his eyes popped open as if he couldn't imagine me ever doing such a thing, but he joined in the humor of the situation.

"Grant, there's something else. Why don't I know where you live and about all of these businesses you own?"

I couldn't hold it in any longer and blurted it out before I was too nervous to ask. He stopped laughing and a hush came over the room and his face seemed forlorn.

"I don't know, it didn't seem important I guess."

Not important? I thought we were close.

"Grant, you must know that I consider you to be like a second father to me."

He nodded, then looked away.

"I know baby girl. I wish I could tell you more but it's too painful—It's complicated."

I could see the hurt in his eyes about whatever it was that he didn't think he could tell me. I had no idea Grant was keeping something like this to himself. I hugged him tight, knowing how painful it can be to keep secrets.

"I hope someday you'll share it with me."

"I'm sure I will...someday." he hesitated.

"Ok, so who gets my office?" I said, throwing my hands in the air, lightheartedly, to change the subject back to the original nature of the visit.

The smile on his face returned.

"Shay and Darius are going to take over your office, for now. I'm actually going to pay more attention to my other businesses and make Ryan the BIC at this office. Train him up to take over when I sell someday. I'll officially just own it for now."

My mouth hit the floor. He *was* retiring.

"Wait, what other businesses besides the restaurant and the catering company? Yes, I know about that through Roman I might add?"

"The restaurant is definitely my favorite. The catering business is another lucrative favorite of mine. I named it after my grandmother GIGI." I smiled watching his eyes sparkle when he talked about his grandmother and then he continued, "I also invest a bit. In fact, I'm one of the majority investors in a little non-profit by the name of "The Kennedy-Jackson Foundation" I heard they're starting a non-wine company with some friends of mine." I guess I shouldn't be so surprised, but I was none the less.

"Are you serious? I'm planning to have a gala after the holidays to raise money for the projects I'm planning to implement through the foundation."

"I've heard. Roman and I talk a little here and there. He's excited about your projects."

"He is? I worry every time I bring something up to him that he's going to shoot it down."

He squinted, scrunching up his brows.

"Why's that?" He asked.

"Well, remember Burrow Township? I went to him to ask him for his advice on fixing it up. You know what it was? Don't bother lady, I'm tearing that down."

It's funny now, but definitely not at the time.

"Well, it looks like everything turned out the way it was supposed to in the end. It may have been one helluva bumpy road but we all made it."

Right as he said that I thought of Ella and how untrue that statement was.

***

ROMAN

Tao waddled around my office as soon as I released him from his carrier. I put puppy pads all over the floor in case of accidents, but I had no idea what I was supposed to do with him while I went to meetings.

"What the heck is going on in here?" Amelia exclaimed as she entered my office.

I laughed, pointing to the little man on a mission. She squealed—problem solved. She was clapping her hands and heading enthusiastically in the puppy's direction.

"Yes, you can take him and play with him and do whatever except feed him things. He still has to take a bottle but if you want to give him that when it's time, I'm fine with that too. I don't know how Alex did this all day?" I answered before she even had a chance to ask.

She laughed and ran over, scooping him off the floor.

"Where's his bottle and bag and stuff? What time does he eat next?"

I looked at the schedule on my phone that Alex put there.

"It says noon."

She said to the puppy, in a funny little high-pitched voice, "Ok, little Tao, you and me are going to have lunch together." then grabbed his bags and a puppy pad off the floor and left. I guess she didn't need anything.

Just as she shut the door my cell rang. It was Grant. I knew Alex was on her way over there to talk business with him, but I didn't think she would be there yet. I wonder if this has something to do with the party.

"Hi Grant."

I'm always weary about getting calls from him now.

"Hey Roman."

He didn't sound as upbeat as I'd like. This better not be more mafia crap.

"Everything okay? Did you get the menu for the caterer? Will that work?"

"Yeah, it's good no problem with any of that. I have a meeting with Alex this morning and I wanted to let you know, as a heads up, what it's about. Just in case."

Oh no, what was he planning to tell her?

"Grant, are you telling her what I think you're telling her?"

He laughed. Yeah, not funny.

"No, I'm firing her."

"What...what are you doing? How could you do that to her?" I practically yelled into the phone. Why does this guy's news always have detrimental implications for me?

"Calm down. Roman, she hasn't been to the office in months. I'm letting her off the hook. I feel like she's wanted to quit for a while now and hasn't had the heart to tell me. She's got so much going on with the new company there's no way she can keep this up too. She doesn't need it either. I'm going to tell you a secret..."

I interrupted and said, "Grant if you make me keep one more secret from her so help me God..."

He started laughing. I asked myself if I hung up on him, what could possibly happen? Yeah, death could happen. How did I get embroiled in this mess?

"Roman, you're the only person I trust to take care of my girl. This is something I need you to know in case something happens to me."

I don't care what it is. I was starting to breathe heavily and tapping my pen on the desk which was a clear sign or distress for me.

"No, you can't put this on me, Grant." I threw the pen across the desk, and it skittered to the floor. "You need to tell her."

"I can't Roman. But someday she'll find out and I probably won't be around when she does. Hopefully. In the meantime, I'm going to send you the name of my attorney in charge of my will."

Is he sick? Why am I the lead on this? Isn't he friends with the Santoros? Shit. I pushed away from my desk and shoved my chair, getting up to pace the floor.

"Grant, what's in that will?" Why did I even ask?

"Everything I own."

"And who's the beneficiary?"

He paused for a minute before he let out a long breath.

"Alex." he calmly stated then hung up.

She's going to kill me if she finds out I knew about all this and didn't tell her. I went to throw my phone across the room but stopped midway and gained some composure. She's already pissed I knew about his restaurant and catering business and she didn't. Now, he's about to fire her. Oh, but that's ok because when he dies, he's leaving her all his money and businesses, and God knows where that money came from. Screw him for putting me in this position. I texted Harrison to come to my office immediately. He's the only person I've ever told any of this to and I need to get the rest of it off my chest. I walked back to my desk, trying not to smash anything as I grabbed the chair and sat down with a little more force than intended.

"Hey what's going on?" Harrison said as he looked down like he just stepped in something. "What the hell is all this? He didn't piss or crap all over these did he because I just stepped on one."

I chuckled lightly and shook my head.

"No, I was just taking precautions. He's out there with your better half."

"She didn't even look up and say hi to me. We are not babysitting by the way. I'm not sharing attention with that mutt."

I chuckled. Hearing him be so into a woman is still new to me and I like the fact that it's calming me down and taking my mind off of Grant firing Alex, for the moment anyway.

"No worries, you'd have to pry Alex's dead fingers off of him to allow that. And don't let Alex hear you call Tao a mutt."

"Okay so what's up? Your text seemed kind of urgent."

"Well, Grant called me because he has a meeting with Alex this morning about something and he wanted to give me a heads up about it."

His shocked look definitely resembled my own at the time.

"Nooooo!"

I shook my head.

"Yep, same reaction I had but he assured me it wasn't that. He said he was firing her."

Harrison's eyes got wide. He gripped the arms of the chair and leaned forward in his chair.

"Wait. What? Is that supposed to be better news than the other?"

"Right? Well, he thinks she's been trying to quit."

"I mean he does know her pretty well, so that could be true, I guess. Are you worried about how she's going to react?"

I shook my head again. Well, maybe, but definitely not the only thing I'm worried about.

"He asked me to keep another secret."

Harrison's face fell down into his hands as he doubled over with laughter. When he came back up his face was red, and he had tears in his eyes.

"I told him not to tell me and he laughed it off and told me, anyway. He's sending me the contact info for his attorney in charge of his will. I don't know if he's sick or what's going on, but he left everything to Alex and if something happens to him, he wants me to know about it."

He put his head back and let out a deep sigh.

"Alex will be well off. I don't see the problem with it."

That sounded fine except the mafia aspect of it.

"What if it's blood money or laundered or illegal or whatever the hell else it might be? What if these businesses are set up as dummy corporations for some shady shit?"

"Stop it right now. Now you sound like you watch too much tv. Grant loves that girl. He's not going to put her in harm's way or bring her into some underworld. That's insane and you know it. I don't know what's going on with him, but maybe she's all he's got. Like you said, the daughter he never had."

I guess this is why I called my brother to have these conversations because, for some reason, he's the voice of reason. Go figure.

Chapter 19

ALEX

I walked into my office and found Shay and Darius working intently on some real estate projects. They looked worried when they saw me. I looked over at the desk to see a box on it.

I hesitantly said, "Hi guys."

They said hi back without smiling and their eyes followed mine over to the box and I walked over to see if maybe there was a severed head in it but, nope, just my awards and pictures.

"Alright, who did this?" I demanded then spun around as a loud voice commanded, "Shay can I see you for a minute?" Ryan was on a mission, stopping abruptly as he noticed me, looking like he'd seen a ghost.

"What's wrong with all of you?"

Ryan said, "Um, did you talk to Grant yet?"

I walked over to Ryan.

"Yes, Ryan, I quit while he fired me. I was just asking who packed up my stuff so I could thank them."

"Thank God." He pulled me into a hug then winced, stepping back abruptly and said, "I didn't hurt you, did I?"

"Ryan, I broke my ankle not my back. How are you going to run this place with a whimpy attitude like that? And why did you come in here talking to Shay like that?"

Shay laughed.

"Yeah, what was that about? What do you need to see me for?"

"Um, I'd rather not say in front of Alex." He whispered loudly covering half of his mouth to block me, as if I couldn't hear him standing right next to me.

"Oh, is it about Friday night?" Shay asked.

He didn't say anything, turning his head from me as he held up a finger in front of his lips.

"Ahh bars and beverages." I teased then laughed, shoving Ryan's arm. "It's fine, I know I won't be hanging out with you guys on the weekends anymore, but we can still get together, I hope, for lunch or dinner some-time, right?"

Shay said, "Duh, of course. It's not like I don't see you almost every day now at Roman's office."

"Cool. I thought you were in some kind of solitary confinement, and you couldn't talk about or be around alcohol anymore."

Come on. Everyone is so damn sensitive about this.

"Enough. I'm fine. It was more than alcohol I had to deal with, alright. One day at a time, but I'm doing great. By the way, did y'all get your invitation to my Christmas party at the farmhouse?"

"Sure did. Do I need to bring anything?" Ryan asked.

"Nope."

"Can I bring a date?" He winked with a smirk.

"Sure. Do you have one lined up yet?"

"Nope." He replied and I watched the wheels turning in his imaginary *little black book* of a brain.

Shay said, "Owen and I will be there."

Darius didn't answer right away so I asked him again, directly.

"Hey D. Did you get my invite?"

I rested my hand gently on his shoulder to get his attention. He looked up at me, with less enthusiasm than normal.

"Yeah. Grams got it. Not sure we're coming though."

"D, you can't say that to me without an explanation–you know that. Let's go for a walk."

He grabbed his coat, and I looped my arm through his as we walked outside by the creek.

"Tell me what's going on."

I reached over and took his hand in mine.

"It's nothing."

"Darius, it's not nothing. You know you can talk to me, right? I know Ella wouldn't want to miss this party or miss you boys being there and you know it, so tell me what's up?"

He blurted out, "I think Grams is sick."

My heart sank; it felt like the wind got knocked out of me. She didn't think he could figure it out, but I had a feeling he would. He was a smart young man. I instinctively squeezed his hand harder before I let it go.

"Why do you think that?" I calmly asked as I wrapped my arms around me to keep warm.

"Well, she's been going to the hospital a lot and the doctor and then crying when she doesn't think I'm watching."

"Has she told you anything, D?" He shook his head.

"Give me a second, stay right here. I'm going to make a quick phone call. I'll be right back?"

She picked up right away.

"Alex, what's going on, is Darius okay?"

"Hey Ella, why do you ask that?"

These two are thick as thieves that's for sure. She may not be his mother, but they have the same connection that my mother and I had.

"I don't know, I just got a weird feeling."

"Ella, you and Darius are on the same wavelength. He knows something's not right, and he knows you're hiding it from him. I'm here with him right now. He's worried. It's not going to make him less worried to keep this from him." I could hear her sniffling, and I added, "I'm going to walk over there and we're going to tell him together. Are you good with that?"

She managed to whisper out an *okay* and I walked back over to Darius.

"Let's go have a seat over on the picnic table. I have someone on the phone who has something she wants to tell you D."

We sat down and he looked so scared. I put Ella on speaker and said, "Big Mama, the floor is yours."

She told him everything she'd been going through and about the tests and that she was scheduled to hear the results of the second tests. He stared straight ahead, listening; never saying a word. When she was finished, he laid his head down on the table, placing his hands on the back of his head. He told her he loved her and would see her at home later. I put my hand on his back, and he turned to me shaking his head, reaching out to hold me.

We sat there and cried until the cold started to bite through our clothes.

"That's it we're blowing off the rest of the day. I'm taking you out to lunch and we're going to talk about this. I'll let Shay know you're done for the day."

He nodded and we hurried to my car, driving to Grant's restaurant where I knew we'd be able to get a table where we could talk in private.

I grabbed his hand across the table.

"Darius, I just found out a week ago. I called her when I was at the vet's office to talk to her about what a great job you're doing. She didn't want me to tell you, but I knew that wasn't a good idea when I saw you today." I paused a second to gauge his reaction, but his expression seemed blank. "She wanted to wait until after the doctor's appointment so she would know for sure. Do you want to go with us to that?"

He nodded but remained quiet. He was still processing; I could tell from the pinched brow. I was getting ready to say something else and his eyes got a wild look in them. Like that of a scared animal.

"What am I going to do without her Alex? I have two brothers that she took care of too. I don't know what I'm going to do."

My heart sank. He looked so innocent.

"First of all, there's a reason she told me and that was to help you and your brothers deal with this. Did you think I was going to let you do this on your own?"

He shook his head, looking down at the table.

"Why? Why are you always so nice to us? After how I treated you? I didn't deserve what you did for me."

Oh lord, it was like listening to myself degrade myself all over again. I'm not going to let him go down that same road.

"Darius, you look at me and you listen. I used to say the same thing and look what happened to me because of it? I almost ruined my life thinking like that. Of course you deserve this. By this I mean someone who treats you with kindness and respect. You're a good person. How could you not be, look who your grandmother is."

He put his head into his hands.

"She's the best and never let us do anything bad. She kept us out of trouble." He groaned as his hands muffled his response.

I nodded knowingly. She is the best, I agreed to myself.

"She's an amazing woman. I can't imagine how hard it was for her to have to raise her three grandsons after your father passed away. She's a strong woman and you're a strong man. No matter what happens you're going to be ok."

I felt like I've had this conversation so many times before recently, but it was always me who was getting the speech. I guess that's why I was given that speech so many times–just waiting for my turn to pay it forward.

I took Darius home and spent some time with him and Ella before the boys got home. I brought them takeout from the restaurant for dinner. We had a nice chat and Ella seemed like she had a cold, but nothing dire. The boys were excited about eating the "fancy" dinner, as they referred to it, then I gave everyone my signature hug, whether they liked it or not, letting them deal with the information their way.

About a mile from the house, the screen lit up with Matt's name.

"Hey Matt. Is this business or pleasure?"

I couldn't wait to get home. My foot was throbbing from being out on it all day.

"Hey Alex. It's business." He groaned and let out a sigh.

Hmmm. I don't think I like his tone. What business could there possibly be left? The judge already said both parties were absolved from any retribution after the fight, so what else could this be?

"What's up? Is he suing me for using performance-enhancing drugs?" I giggled. "Because I'm pretty sure alcohol is not performance enhancing."

I tried to lighten the mood. Maybe it's just unfinished paperwork or something, but he sounded weary, and paperwork doesn't bring that kind of weariness.

"Jack asked me to call you."

Jack was my main attorney because Matt couldn't get his hands dirty being a politician and all so why does he need to get in touch with me for Jack?

"It seems Tanner would like to see you. Says he'd like to apologize to you in person."

I let out a gasp as the air in the car thinned and I was having trouble breathing.

"Alex, did you hear me? Are you ok? Shit, are you in the car? Alex, are you driving?"

Am I driving? Am I in the car? What? What the fuck did he just say to me? This was supposed to be over and done with. I never want to see him again.

I gulped in just enough air to grit out through my teeth, "Fuck him" then hung up and immediately called Roman.

***

ROMAN

Spending the day with a puppy is not for the weak. That means, it's Alex's job from now on. Now I know why women are in charge of having the babies. I headed back up to the penthouse. Amelia still had Tao and was going to bring him up when she was done.

I changed my clothes, realizing I haven't heard from Alex since this morning except to say she was going to have lunch with Darius. I called her while I was headed out to the kitchen. She picked up after a couple of rings.

"Hey, can I call you on my way home?" She sounded a little down.

"Sure, where are you?"

"Ella's." She said with a sigh.

I told her I love you then let her visit. I'm guessing that was going to be a hard visit.

The doors to the elevator opened and in came Harrison, Amelia and Tao. Amelia was carrying the puppy while Harrison was carrying everything else.

He dropped all the puppy's bags by the door and stared at me as he said, "Dude, what the hell are you going to bring to work when you have a kid?"

Amelia looked over at him and said, "Hey!!! Language!!!"

I laughed as Harrison rolled his eyes while shaking his head at her.

"Where's Alex?" Harrison asked scanning the place.

"She's with Ella."

"Oh, when's she getting home? Was wondering if you guys wanted to go out to dinner with us tonight."

"Raincheck?"

Amelia walked over, handing me the puppy. I snuggled him in close, using his energy to calm my own nerves.

"Yeah, no problem. Talk to ya later."

I had a feeling Alex wasn't going to be in the mood to socialize when she got home from Ella's. I walked the puppy back to his crate, tucking him in for the night.

Out in the kitchen I poured a glass of wine and took Alex's vial of anti-anxiety out along with some tea so she wouldn't have to go looking for it when she got home. I left it on the counter next to a mug. She loved Greek food, so I ordered some from her favorite Greek restaurant. When my phone started ringing and her name was scrolling across it, I prepared for the worst before answering.

"Hey babe." She didn't say anything. I was worried so I asked, "You, ok?" Nothing, just silence. "Alex? I know you told me not to worry but you're scaring me. Is it Ella, Darius?"

Finally, I heard her take a big gulp of air and she yelled, "TANNER!"

Woah, Tanner, what? Shit, where is she?

Panic was setting in.

"What do you mean Tanner?" She sounded like she was hyperventilating.

Where the hell is she?

"Honey, are you driving? Where are you? I want you to pull over right now."

She finally said through gasps, "I'm... In... The... Garage."

I stayed on the line but got downstairs as quickly as I could. The puppy will be fine for a few minutes while I run downstairs and get her. I thought without looking back to see if the puppy was actually okay.

As soon as the doors opened, I saw her car. It was nearly sideways across three parking spaces. How long had she been driving in this condition? The door was locked so I knocked on the window. She screamed as she jumped out of her seat.

When she realized it was me, she opened the door, launching herself at me. I practically had to catch her. She was shaking so bad I could feel her to my bones.

"Come on, let's get upstairs and talk about this."

I got her comfortable on the couch and made her tea, placing it and the tincture on the coffee table in front of her. I didn't know how any of that worked, so I left her to do that part. Before I sat down my phone rang. The delivery guy was here. I told him to put the food in the elevator and I would do the rest. The food came up and I put it on the counter, hopefully giving her enough time to calm down.

She looked terrified as I sat next to her, rubbing her back up and down gently trying for some more relaxed vibes.

"Tell me what's going on, please?" I pleaded.

She looked at me like I just appeared out of nowhere.

"Was your day normal?" She asked in an eerie monotone voice.

Hmm what is this? Definitely not the vibe I'm looking for.

"Define normal? I had Tao with me, so it wasn't my normal."

She seemed to be in her own little world. I don't think she was even listening to me.

"I mean, I was just going to quit my job today and it kind of spiraled. One minute I'm getting fired, the next I'm telling someone their grandmother's dying, then I'm being summoned to talk to a monster."

I felt really hot suddenly as the heat rose to the top of my head. I know what monster she was talking about and hell no, that is not happening.

It was like I had no control, and I shouted, "No. Sorry. No. You are not going anywhere near that piece of shit."

I guess I'm the one who needs calming down now.

"I'm with you on this one." She agreed.

I felt crazed, jerking her into my body, trying to get a sense of peace. Her being safe at this moment should be enough, but I was having trouble with this information, too.

"Do you need me to do anything?"

I tried to bring the anxiety down and be strong for her, nuzzling my face in her hair, breathing in her calming scent.

"Lock up the liquor."

She actually laughed and it made me jolt away from her—my expression less than amused.

"That's not funny, Alex."

Was she serious?

"I know. I can't relax right now."

"Have you had some tea yet?" I asked, hoping she'd pick it over the alcohol.

"No, I haven't drunk any fucking tea, Roman. Do you think if I drink the tea, it's going to make what happened magically disappear?"

I got up and started pacing. I could feel the anger coming off of her and I needed to get away before it took hold of me as well.

"I'm sorry Alex..." I yelled back from the edge of the living room. "...I just don't know how to help. I don't think it's a magic potion. I wish it were because I would fucking drink it right now myself."

I stormed out of the room, knowing it could get worse if I didn't get some distance.

I made my way down the hall to the bedroom to check on the puppy. He was sound asleep and seemed so peaceful. I wonder if he would have the same effect on me that Alex does. I could use a little peace right about now. He was snoring softly as I lifted him from his crate and cradled him in my arms gently, so I didn't disturb his sleep. He was soft and warm, and I lifted him to my nose to smell him. His puppy shampoo was clean and fresh smelling, and I instantly felt better as I rubbed my thumb back and forth over the top of his head. I'm taking him out there to see if he'll work for her, too.

I was swaying slightly, from side to side, down the hall cradling Tao, staring down at him serenely looking at his face while humming.

"I see you found your magic potion." She said sweetly.

Her mood had changed drastically as she leaned up against the wall to take the pressure off her foot, waiting for me to make it further to her.

I smiled, the anger practically a distant memory.

"I did, and I was bringing him out here in hopes he might work for you as well."

Her eyes glistened with the threat of tears as one slowly slid down her cheek.

"Thank you for thinking of me with the tea. I added a few extra drops, and it did the trick. I think you and the puppy helped add a little extra something also..."

Handing her the puppy, I wrapped her in my arms before I could let her fully apologize. I can't imagine the weight of everything she's gone through, and I won't let her put all of this on herself.

"I'm sorry." There was a gentle shake of her shoulders before they relaxed, and I could feel the tension leave her body. "That was difficult news." I continued to stroke the back of her head as I held them both tightly to me.

"I know, but I shouldn't have reacted that way, especially to you."

Wow, the tea and the puppy might really be a magic potion.

Suddenly, I heard the screech of both of our phones at once on the counter and motioned us toward the kitchen to see.

"Is there a reason Matt and Jack are blowing up our phones right now?" She shrugged as she stared at the puppy. She was in her own little safe space, and I was good with that.

"I hung up on Matt." She said nonchalantly while gently bouncing the puppy leaning against the kitchen island. "I was driving at the time and wanted to concentrate on getting home."

I released them and ran over to grab my phone to call Matt and Jack, putting them on speaker. They both answered within a ring of each other.

"Roman, hey it's Matt." He sounded frantic.

Jack said, "I'm here too. Is Alex home? Is she ok?"

"I'm home. As for okay, I'll get back to you on that one."

"Alex, you don't have to talk to him in person or any other way at all." Jack insisted.

"I know that. I just wasn't ready to hear anything from or about him ever again, really."

"Alex, I'm sorry I didn't make sure you were somewhere safe before I blurted that out." Matt apologized. "That was bullshit, and I'm sorry."

I'd be worried as hell about giving her information like that while she's driving.

"Matt, it's fine. I'm fine now. Look, let me process this information and then get back to you."

"Get back to who about what?" I demanded harshly, slamming both hands on the counter.

"Jack, I'll call you tomorrow."

She ignored my outburst to end the call. She nudged my phone towards me.

"No. You can't go see him. If you're going to listen to me one time ever, let it be about this."

She nodded as she walked down the hall using the wall to hold herself up.

"Alex, I'm serious."

I poured a glass of bourbon and sat on the couch with the puppy, waiting for her to get out of the shower. We were definitely discussing this.

I heard her enter the kitchen, opening the bag of food that was still waiting on the counter. She plated it up for us with a smile on her face like none of this crazy shit just happened, or she's planning something sinister.

"What kind of tincture did you have in the shower?"

I turned and brought one leg up on the couch, sprawling my arm over the back to get a better look at her. I sipped my bourbon as I waited for her reply. She gave me a confused look with a scrunched up facial expression.

"That's an awful big smile you have on your face right now. I just assumed you had a vial somewhere called shit-eating grin."

She burst out laughing. Sinister motive then, I'm guessing.

"That would be so cool. I'm gonna work on that one."

That's one helluva one eighty she did in the shower. I squinted my eyes, trying to figure her out.

"So, is there a reason you're smiling? I mean, I'm not getting a happy vibe from it, if you know what I mean?"

She looked at me, rolling her eyes.

"Yeah babe, sorry, you aren't getting away with much around me. I'm pretty sure we've figured that out already, so let's just be honest with each other, please."

She nodded and stopped what she was doing. She wiped her hands off on a kitchen towel, laying it neatly folded on the counter.

"We should be honest, you're right. I'm just trying to figure out how to say this where you won't freak out. I'm being mindful."

She placed her hands flat on the counter and took a deep breath.

Okay, this was new and good, but I can already tell I'm not going to like it.

As she finished with the food and poured me a glass of wine, grabbing a bottle of water for herself, she said, "I really need to eat something first if that's alright?"

It was probably a good idea and I reluctantly agreed. I have no idea what she's been up to today since we haven't talked at all other than about Tanner. I put the puppy in his bed next to the couch and we ate in silence.

Damn, we were back to using food to control the atmosphere in the room.

"I'm just hungry. I haven't eaten since noon."

She looked like it too as she scarfed her food down. At least it wasn't just the silent treatment. I leaned over, kissing her cheek, and we finished dinner. I cleaned up the kitchen first because I knew how she hated leaving the kitchen dirty after meals.

"I know what he's doing, Roman. Matt told me he wants to apologize..." She began the conversation with no lead in.

"Like hell he does...." I interrupted. "...He's a piece of shit. There's no way he's planning to apologize."

She put her hand on my arm calmly.

"Relax, please let me finish."

She reined me back in and kept me from jumping out of my seat again.

"I already know where you stand on this. I know what he said he wants to do, and I know that's not true."

So why does she want to see him then? Just let him rot.

"I can't let him continue to think he got the best of me. He's going to get out in five years and then what? I'm on pins and needles again? I need to see him face to face in a safe space and let him know that it's over. He will never affect me again."

Can't she do that without going to see him?

"I'm going to do the right thing and forgive him. Set him free. Set myself free."

Chapter 20

ROMAN

I rolled over and groaned as she was reaching for the alarm and I took her phone out of her hand.

"No. Not 5:00 am. No, too early."

I sounded like a caveman. I rolled back over with the phone and scrolled to the alarm to change it to 6:30 am. She laughed, reaching over me, yanking the phone out of my hand.

"Look, I need the extra time in the morning." She insisted. "Early in the morning is quiet. You don't have to get up with me, but I need some quiet time to think." She explained matter-of-factly and I pulled her close with an exaggerated sigh.

"Okay, anything you want, beautiful. What time are you going to the gym this morning?" I mumbled.

"I'll probably head down there at six after I get changed, relaxed and have my pre-workout drink."

"I can probably get to the gym around that time too, I guess."

She laughed, wiggling out of my grip. I may or may not be going to the gym this morning after the night we had. I should go to work Tanner out of my head and think of a way to talk her out of going to see him.

"You can go whenever you want to. It doesn't have to be with me."

Good, I'm glad we agree on that, but I'm going to mess with her, anyway.

"Yes, yes, it does. I'm a sad, needy man now, who needs to be up your butt 24/7."

She gave me a seriously worried look. "Roman..." she said exasperatedly.

"You should really see your face right now. I'm just kidding, I promise." About stalking. "Go to the gym. I'll either be there while you're still there or see you when you get back. I love you. I'm going back to sleep."

I reached over and patted her butt, then rolled over and fell back to sleep.

It felt like my alarm went off minutes later. Now I'm even more tired than I was before. The door to the bathroom was closed and the light was on, which must mean she's back from the gym. I walked over to the bathroom door to see if she was getting in the shower. I think I'll surprise her and jump in with her. I grabbed the door handle, but before I opened it I heard heaving noises. Ugh. Sounds like she might be sick.

I knocked on the door instead and cautiously asked, "Hey babe, you okay?"

She didn't say anything at first, so I waited another second.

"Yeah, not feeling so hot." She groaned.

"Do you need anything?"

I definitely didn't want to go in there right now unless she needed me.

"No, I'll be out in a minute."

I stood next to the door, and she came out looking really green in the face.

"Alex, honey, are you sick? Did you eat something bad?"

She had the saddest look on her face while she shook her head no then weakly stated, "Roman, I don't feel so good. I feel dizzy..."

The words faded out and her eyes rolled back in her head. I knew that look. She was passing out.

Her body fell limp into my arms and I carried her to the bed, clutching her on my lap. I rubbed her face to get her to come to. She looked up at me in a daze.

"Hey there. What's going on, honey? Do I need to take you to the doctor?"

She looked at me with tears streaming down her face. I don't think being sick constitutes tears as I brushed them away, pushing her hair back from her face.

"I don't know what to do. I think the herbs are making me sick."

Oh, that could be a problem though.

"If that's what's happening I can't start this business. I don't want to make people sick."

She broke down sobbing and I pulled her to my chest, rocking her gently back and forth to try to calm her down but not jostle her. I didn't need her throwing up on me.

"Fine, I'm taking you to the hospital and we'll have them run some tests and see if the herbs are what's causing this. It may just be a virus."

"I've been feeling this coming on for days now. It gets worse when I drink the tea."

This is news to me. Why didn't she tell me this? She dropped her face to her hands. I held her as best I could, trying to reach for my phone. I didn't want to let her go. I also didn't want to upset her anymore if she was sick.

"Let me call the office and tell Amelia I won't be coming in today. You and me are taking the day off. I'll take the puppy down to Amelia before we leave. Let me get you some water. Do you want something to eat?"

The look on her face told me she didn't want any food, so I didn't need to worry about breakfast. I reluctantly let her go to call Amelia.

"Good morning Mr. King."

I shook my head, wondering when she was going to stop calling me that.

"Amelia, seriously, quit. Do you want to watch the puppy at work for me today?" She shrieked and I pulled the phone away from my ear.

"Yes, yes, yes!!!"

"Cool. Can you cover for me today? I have to take Alex to the doctor."

"What's wrong with Alex? What happened now?"

"I don't know. She thinks she's getting sick from the herb concoction she's been taking."

"Oh, no..." She gasped. "...are you serious? She's probably freaking out about that."

"I know. How are you feeling after taking it?" I asked to see if it was affecting her the same way since she had some the other night.

"I feel fine. I woke up feeling great after drinking it."

"She must just have a virus or something then."

"What's going on with her?"

"She was throwing up and then she passed out."

"Hmmm…okay let me know how it goes."

I thought I heard her snicker before I hung up. I grabbed the puppy out of his crate and got him ready for his day with his aunt Amelia.

"Do you still feel like you're going to be sick?" I asked her before we got in the car.

That's the last thing either of us needed was her puking in a confined space.

"Yes, but I don't think I'm actually going to throw up. I don't think there's anything left." She sounded weak and exhausted.

Lord, I hope she doesn't get sick again because then we'd both be sick. At least I haven't eaten anything yet.

We pulled up to the ER and I let her out, then parked the car. I grabbed her hand, walking in with her. We checked her in at the nurses' station and she ran to the restroom right after. She headed there at least three more times before she was called back. It felt like going to the ER was now our new love language instead of weird head games.

We finally got back to an exam room, and she told the doctor her concerns. The nurses took blood and hooked her up to all those damn machines again. One for her pulse, one for her blood pressure and one to check her heart. It was exhausting returning to those previous hospital memories. She laid back on the exam bed, and I encouraged her to close her eyes, but the beeping from all the machines and the noise from the doctors and nurses talking outside the room was making it hard for either of us to relax. I was staring at the wall rubbing her forehead gently, hoping that I was helping her.

She seemed to be fully relaxed but then came to when the doctor returned.

"Good news." He announced with a smile.

We both looked at each other like he was nuts. Whatever this is, is not good at all.

I quickly enquired about the tinctures. "Good news, meaning it's not the herbs?" mentally crossing my fingers as I sucked in a breath.

He confirmed, "Yes, the herbs that were in her system were so minimal and not dangerous. As much as she's been consuming, we did an allergy test—she's not allergic. There is no sign of a virus either, but we can do more testing for that too if you'd like. There's definitely another factor here." As our eyes met, I could feel the 'oh shit' vibe going back and forth between us. Then the doctor's eyes sparkled in Alex's direction and he said, "You're pregnant!"

Finally, I heard something other than the blood swishing in my ears and the incessant mind jerk about my five-year plan.

I looked up and said, "Did you say something?"

The doctor laughed.

"I'll give the two of you a minute."

As soon as he left the room, I took a few deep breaths before I looked up at her to see her reaction to this. She was laughing at me. Actually laughing.

"I guess this is kind of funny." I chuckled, but panic was still underneath the facade. "We came in here for you and now I think they're going to need to admit me."

I laid my head on her lap. All the oxygen felt like it was being sucked from the room.

"Did we mess this up, or are we happy?" I moaned into her lap.

She ran her fingers back and forth over my head. The movement was blissful, and I wanted to stay lost in it, but I really needed an answer right now. I rolled my head to the side, and she stopped, resting her hand on my cheek.

"I wasn't expecting that news, even though I guess I should have. I forgot all about birth control while I was at the retreat and didn't think about it again after I got back. Not until he said those words."

She blinked and a tear rolled down her cheek. I reached up, capturing it on my finger.

"I guess that explains my ridiculous forgetfulness recently."

I gazed at her to try and get a read on her expression. I didn't want her to be sad about this. It would break my heart if she thought having a baby with me was a bad decision since she's pregnant.

"But are you happy?" I asked, because I needed to know she was.

She smiled at me. That felt like a happy smile, but I haven't been able to read her in months. Not that I would tell her that.

"You know what I was thinking the other day?"

I can only imagine what this girl has been thinking.

"I was thinking how Tao was our first baby together and what would it be like if we had our own baby together."

She smiled again and another tear spilled over the edge and I let it fall.

"It scared me for only a second because I realized I was really in this for the long haul."

I let out the held breath through my nose.

"So, to answer your question...I'm happy! Scared but happy. Maybe a little excited, too."

A wide smile spread across her beautiful face.

Thank God she said happy.

I agreed, "Scared, yes. Scared as hell, but happy, happy as hell." I agreed.

She laughed and grabbed both sides of my face in her hands, pulling me to her—kissing me back to my senses.

"Good. Now they're going to take us for an ultrasound to see our little peanut." She informed me since I didn't hear a word the nurse just said to her.

***

ALEX

We were wheeled into another room, Roman holding my hand as we went and she sets us up next to a monitor. It was a computer screen with lights flickering, making those same repetitive beeping noises that drove me crazy, while another nurse came over and introduced herself.

"Hi, I'm Monica, the ultrasound tech. We're going to take a look at your baby if that's alright."

We smiled at each other excitedly and the noises didn't sound so bad anymore. Roman looked nervous and I gave his hand a reassuring squeeze. He smiled down at me and loosened his grip while rubbing his thumb over the back of my hand, sticking his free hand in his pocket.

"Yes." I answered for both of us, since Roman still looked like he might be in shock.

She pushed my shirt up to expose my belly, which didn't look any different than it did any other time, except I knew for sure it was empty of food.

The nurse said, "This is going to be a little cool." She put some gel substance on a wand, then pushed it into my stomach, rubbing it all over.

"Right there," she said and pointed to a little spot on the screen that looked kind of like a black hole with, well, a peanut in it.

"Is that the baby? It really does look like a peanut." Roman asked, and we laughed.

"That is your baby. I'm going to take some measurements and then I'll be able to tell you about how far along you are."

She was drawing lines and typing on the computer as Roman and I silently watched in awe.

When she was done, she confirmed, "You're about eight weeks. Everything looks normal."

"Will we be able to see the doctor again before we leave?" I asked.

"Yes, they'll bring you back to your room and the doctor will answer any questions or concerns you have before they release you."

The doctor gave me a prescription for some medicine for the nausea and told me to get some prenatal vitamins, find an ob/gyn then finally, good luck. A nurse came in, handing us an envelope with about ten ultrasound pictures and our release paperwork that I was going to thoroughly read over in the car on the way to getting that nausea medicine– because I'm freaking starving...I mean we're freaking starving.

Oh my god I'm having a baby!

We got to the car, closed the doors and just sat there, stunned. All of a sudden, we both let out the biggest breath and burst out laughing.

"Oh. My. God. I was not expecting that today at all."

"Ditto." He took another deep breath, running his hands through his hair.

He laid his forehead down on the steering wheel and turned his head towards me.

"Are you hungry or pukey?" He asked.

"I'm starving, but still feel a little pukey, so can we go get that medicine and the vitamins and try to eat something? I'd rather eat at home too, in case I have to, you know." I puffed out my cheeks and held my hand up to my mouth.

We picked up the meds, the vitamins, and some sandwiches to bring home.

Back in the penthouse, Roman said, "Hey, why don't you take the meds, have some tea, relax, and I'll run down and get the puppy. I forgot I haven't even called to check on him."

I nodded and did as he suggested.

After I took the medicine, I wandered around, not knowing who to call. In a perfect world, I would've called my mom. Should I even share the news yet? I grabbed a random hair tie off the kitchen counter and threw my hair up in a bun. This was starting to become sad and stressful, and I needed someone to share this with but, who? Wait, who am I kidding? I shook my head like an idiot.

"Hey Jerk. What's up" Maggie's intro was music to my ears.

It had been so long since the girls and I had a normal conversation.

"Hey Mags, Hey Abby." I greeted them nonchalantly.

I was pacing the floor, trying to figure out how to tell them and deciding if the medicine was working enough yet that I wasn't going to be sick again. I kicked off my flip flops, concentrating on the soft feel of the plush area rug between my toes.

Abby chimed in, "Hey Alex, what's going on?"

Blurting it out just wasn't my style, but I had no idea how to say it. I stopped pacing and put a hand on my tummy, then smiled.

"Had another trip to the ER. Roman and mine's new love language, I guess."

They both laughed.

Maggie asked sarcastically, "Who was the admittee this time?"

"Oh, you know, me, again."

Abby asked with more of a concerned tone, "Oh no, what did you break now?"

Maggie and I both laughed.

"Thankfully, nothing is broken. I thought I poisoned myself with the new tinctures."

"Oh gosh what happened?" Maggie was now more concerned.

"Lots of puking and dry heaving. I passed out..." The line went silent.

Finally, Abby responded, shock oozing out, "No freaking way..."

Maggie screamed, "You're pregnant!"

I put my hand–not holding the phone–over my ear as I pulled the phone away.

"Please stop screaming. That is not helpful, but yes, I'm pregnant, eight weeks. Looks like we're having a peanut." I exclaimed.

We made plans to continue the conversation for Saturday lunch, and I asked the girls who they used for a doctor, leaving me with a few names, before hanging up. I laid the phone on the counter just as Roman entered with the puppy.

"Hey babe. How's Tao? Did he have fun with Amelia?" He had a permanent smile on his face, looking at the puppy as he refrained from answering.

"What is that look for?" I asked.

"I had no idea how happy this was actually going to make me some day. I mean I knew I wanted children and I was going to be happy when it happened and then we got this puppy and I fell in love with him and he's like my baby, but this...this has truly put a whole other spin on what happiness is." He babbled on. "I'm so in love with someone who isn't even here yet. I couldn't stop myself...when Amelia asked me what I was so happy about after taking you to the hospital, it just came out. So, yes, they both know."

He slowly looked at me with a now worried smile on his face. I guess he thought I might be upset he told someone so soon.

I laughed, knowing exactly how he felt.

"That's ok, I just got off the phone with Abby and Maggie; so do they."

He looked relieved as he handed me the puppy, pulling us into an embrace that felt like he was just enveloping his new little family and, for once, the only feelings I got were love. Love that I never thought I would be good enough for.

We sat down to eat after the medicine kicked in. It felt so good to eat something and keep it down. Amelia called and asked if I was going to be up for shopping this week for the party.

"Um, yes. I'm pregnant, not sick or dying."

I swallowed the lump in my throat as I thought about Ella.

"I know, but you were feeling bad according to Roman and he doesn't want you overdoing it."

I wondered how overprotective he's going to be now.

"Can you do tomorrow?" I asked, not wanting to let this keep me from doing things.

"Of course. I'll leave work early and everything."

"Perfect. Just call me when you're finished and we'll head out."

I knew the day after tomorrow I'd be going to another doctor's appointment that I wasn't looking forward to. I let Roman know I was planning to announce the pregnancy to the rest of the friends and family at the Christmas party. That would be my end of the night announcement.

"Uh Oh!" He groaned and shook his head no.

***

ROMAN

When she said she was going to announce the news at the Christmas party, it just slipped out...

"Please don't tell me you already sent out an announcement."

I laughed but secretly wanted to tell everyone myself. This is the best thing that's ever happened to me and with the only person I could ever imagine doing it with.

"No, the only people who know so far are Amelia, Harrison, Abby, Maggie and I'm sure Matt and Jack, now."

"Then what was uh oh for?"

I took a deep breath because I didn't want to tell her, but I needed to make sure she knew now so she didn't overshadow the big proposal.

"Yes, our baby is exciting news..." I reached out and took her hands in mine, pulling them up to kiss the back of both of them. "...and it's the best news ever, but my mom and I are actually helping plan Harrison's proposal at the party."

Her eyes got super wide.

"Oh my God Roman, why didn't you tell me?"

She seemed a little offended as well as shocked.

"Well, I wanted it to be a surprise for you too and I wasn't sure how good you would be with keeping the secret since you're planning the party with Amelia, but I should know by now that you're pretty damn good with keeping secrets." Shit, I didn't mean to say that. It was a low blow and her face reflected it. I grabbed her, hurrying to apologize. "Sorry babe, that was shitty."

She shook her head like she was brushing it off.

"Nope, no worries, their secret is safe with me, plus look how scatter-brained I am right now. Most likely I'll forget about it, anyway." She said with a sigh, letting it roll off her shoulder, thankfully.

Speaking of the proposal, I needed to get with Harrison and mom so we can start planning that. I kissed her and headed to my office before I stuck my foot too far in my mouth.

"Mom, hi. Do you have time tomorrow for me and Harrison?"

"Sure, what's going on?"

She sounded excited, regardless of what it was.

"We need to plan something special at the Christmas party, and we need your help."

I wanted Harrison to be the one to tell her. I told her we were going to take her out to dinner to talk about it. I knew Alex and Amelia would be shopping all night and they'd want to take the puppy, and I figured this was the perfect opportunity.

I flopped on the couch next to Alex, who was snuggled up with the tiny furball. They were both wrapped in a blanket. I laid my head on her lap.

"Damn baby, we need a vacation." I announced almost like a joke, but I kind of meant it too.

She dragged her fingers gently through my hair, twirling the strands between her fingers. I guess I needed a haircut, too, if she could actually twirl my hair.

"Yes, we do."

Yes?

I rolled my head up to look at her, but she was fixated on the puppy.

"How about as soon as Tao is old enough to eat puppy food, we take a vacation. Someplace tropical?"

"Seriously, you really want to go somewhere?" I asked hopefully, because we absolutely needed a vacation.

"Yes. I have a feeling we're going to need a break after everything that's happened, happening and going to happen here very soon."

She was still combing her fingers through my hair. Damn this feels good. I might fall asleep. I wrapped my arms around her waist and snuggled in closer to her tummy, trying to listen and see if I could hear any sign there was a baby in there.

"Do you want to plan it ourselves or have my travel agent do it?" I asked.

She bent down and kissed my forehead.

"Please have your travel agent do it."

"Sounds good. Where do you think you wanna go, and when?"

"Caribbean in January? Is that a good time?"

She raised her eyebrows. Has she already been thinking about this?

"I'm pretty sure anytime is a good time to go to a tropical island in the Caribbean. I'll talk to Mark and see what he thinks. All-inclusive?"

As little as possible to do is what we need in our lives right now.

She mumbled out, "Mhm." *Perfect.*

Chapter 21

ALEX

Oh Lord, I can't sleep. For once no one set an alarm and I can't sleep. I tried not to roll too much with all this restlessness and wake him up. All this crap in my head is driving me nuts. I snuck out of bed and stood in the bathroom mirror, staring at my stomach, wondering when I was going to start showing. I couldn't help but rest my hands on this little person and let them know that their mommy and daddy love them so much already.

"We can't wait to meet you, but definitely take your time." I whispered, staring at myself in the mirror.

Geez, we were just getting used to the puppy's routine and he's not even old enough to eat puppy food yet. Gosh, am I going to be a good mother? Look how crazy my life was before this. I've barely had time to process everything that's happened and having to go to a rehab center to get my head straight.

Oh no, I'm going to be a terrible mother.

I took some deep breaths with my hands on the counter, looking back at my reflection in the mirror, and said, "Pull yourself together. This is a fresh start. Everything from now on is in your hands. You make it what you want." But that wasn't true and that wasn't what I learned at rehab.

Jesus had my life now. Not only mine but this baby's as well. It was something I was still getting used to. Letting go and letting God is not an easy task for someone who thinks they need control.

I grabbed the door handle, turning it quietly as I pushed open the door. The sight of a large shadow figure scared the hell out of me and I screamed. Roman threw his arms up defensively in front of his face.

"I'm sorry. I'm sorry, don't hit me." he laughed.

Laughter slowly faded into something heavier when he looked at me that way. The air shifted between us, familiar and electric, carrying the kind of connection that had always existed beneath everything else. The sight of him standing there pulled the breath from my lungs, and suddenly every thought that had occupied my mind moments before disappeared beneath the warmth of being wanted by someone who knew every fractured piece of me and stayed anyway.

His fingers brushed lightly against me as he moved closer, and the simple contact carried enough weight to make my pulse stumble. Weeks of healing, caution, and feeling fragile had created distance neither of us wanted, and standing here now felt like finding our way back to something we'd both missed more than we realized.

I held onto him tightly, grounding myself in familiarity. In safety. In him.

Emotion built slowly until it overwhelmed me completely, washing through me with enough force that it left me breathless and struggling to gather myself afterward. The intensity caught me off guard. Stronger somehow. Different.

I quietly logged that thought away for later. Maybe it meant nothing. Maybe it had everything to do with being pregnant. Right now, though, none of that felt nearly as important as the look in Roman's eyes. For weeks he'd treated me like I might break. Like healing made me delicate. Fragile. And while part of me understood why, another part of me desperately missed us. Missed normal. Missed feeling like we belonged to each other give it a test drive instead of going to a dealer and being annoyed by a salesperson, ya know?"

I looked at her, wondering if there was more to this proposal than I thought.

"Is there anything I should know?" I raised my eyebrows, blinking rapidly.

She laughed and said, "No, I've been thinking about getting an SUV for a while. Every time I go shopping, I have to borrow Harrison's truck, and I just don't look good in that."

I can't even imagine her in some souped-up pickup truck. The thought was amusing to say the least.

We had a late lunch at Giovanni's because she said she'd never been. I felt like I took advantage of Grant owning this place, but damn, the food was amazing and it was hard as hell to get into, even at lunchtime. Grant wasn't there, but apparently there was a note he left in case I came in about the food from the caterer. It had a list of the menu items and some changes they had to make because it was last minute. The chef came out and talked to us for a few minutes about the menu items.

"Hi Alex, good to see you again." I'd met Chef Anthony when I had come in previously.

"Hi Chef. It's great to see you too. This is Amelia." He went to say something but stopped and Amelia hesitated, then offered her hand to him.

"Hello, pleasure to meet you, Amelia." She smiled and they shook hands.

Something seemed familiar between the two of them.

"Same here Anthony. Nice to meet you as well."

That was a very odd introduction, but I brushed it off and we moved on to catering information. Anthony's wife, Beth, was the head chef for the catering company. They'd been with Grant since he opened both places. Amelia and I went over the list. It sounded amazing. I told Chef Anthony he was more than welcome to come to the party, too. He said he would probably come to help his wife break things down after the party, but that he would be working at the restaurant most of the night. Lunch was fantastic as always and the fact that I can keep it down because of the medicine makes it that much more amazing.

Amelia asked, "How are you feeling? Do you need to go home or anything?"

"I clearly don't know anything about being pregnant, but I'm pretty sure that eight weeks is not cause for needing a time out."

We both laughed, then headed out to our next stop. I wrapped my ankle though, in case the walking became too much again.

After we finished shopping, we went back to the penthouse. We left everything in the car since it was all going to the farmhouse.

Ok, maybe I was a little more tired than I thought I would be.

The doors to the elevator opened and my arms were hanging heavy at my sides. Even with the wrap around my ankle, I could tell it was swollen. All I wanted to do was lay down on that couch about twenty feet away from me. I wondered if I was going to have to crawl to get there until Amelia took the puppy and Roman appeared, throwing his big muscular arms around me, sweeping me off my feet. He brought me over to the couch and snuggled me into his body.

Party supplies, check. That part is officially accomplished, now for the big day tomorrow at the doctor with Ella.

***

ROMAN

Harrison and I looked like twins lately. His leg was bouncing all the way to our parents' house. I reached over and patted him on the shoulder, gripping him reassuringly.

"Hey man, you gonna be able to do this?" His head whipped in my direction.

"Huh, what? Do what?" I laughed. Damn, was he nervous.

"Um, what do you think? We're on our way to get mom so we can plan your proposal to Amelia." I think I can see sweat beading up on his forehead and his leg seemed to be bouncing even more.

"Sure, what makes you say that?" Now he was rubbing his jaw so hard I thought he was actually going to wear the skin off.

"Hmm, don't know, maybe the spastic leg and the profuse sweating?" He gave me a dirty look.

"Profuse sweating? Fuck you, that sounds gross. I'm not even sweating a little...am I?"

I smiled and shook my head.

"You know what? I'm proud of you. You love her and you're asking her to marry you. I think that once you get past the asking part, you'll feel great."

He almost stopped bouncing his leg until he realized, "But then there's the wedding. Dude, what am I doing? Can I really do this?" I laughed, back handing the side of his leg.

"Yes, you can do this. I'm positive. You're not doing it alone. You get to go through all of it with a pretty exceptional person. Amelia's great. You're a lucky guy and she'll be a lucky girl because she'll have me as a brother-in-law." He shoved my shoulder, but not enough to make the car swerve.

"What about you, man? I mean bombshell news. Holy shit, a baby?" I blew a big breath out of my mouth, nodding with what felt like a very strained expression on my face.

"This was not the way I had planned this. In fact, I'm pretty sure you're doing everything the way I was hoping to, and I'm doing everything the way I thought you'd end up." We both laughed as I pulled the car into our parent's driveway.

"Hi boys." Dad waved, from the sofa, as we walked in looking like he was happy he was going to have the entire house to himself for the day.

"Hey dad." We waved back.

"Okay, so what is it you need from me, boys?" Mom was sitting in the front seat, turned towards me and looking between the two of us.

"Well, I'm going to ask Amelia to marry me..." Mom screamed before Harrison could complete the sentence. "And can I finish?"

"Yes, sorry, oh my god, Harrison, this is so exciting." She reached in the back and grabbed his hand.

"I need your help coming up with a proposal. We want to do it at the Christmas party." I looked in the rearview mirror at Harrison's face, watching it turn ghost white at the thought of proposing or coming up with the perfect proposal, maybe.

She said, "I have no idea what the house looks like or the decorations or the yard. How am I supposed to help with the proposal?"

Good question.

"How about if you come this weekend to help us with the decorations? The girls love you and would love your help. We're only going to be the muscle, anyway."

"You'll need to ask them if they want me there to help. I don't want to assume they will."

Mom was the most thoughtful person I know and never wanted to step on toes or intrude if she thought she might be.

Harrison replied, "Mom, seriously? You know how they feel about you. I'll text Amelia right now."

HARRISON: *"Hey gorgeous, mom wants to help decorate this weekend."*

AMELIA: *"OMG are you serious? Of course...yes! We need all the help we can get. If she has some ideas, have her send them our way too. Alex says hi and yes."*

Harrison said, "There you have it. You're officially part of the decorating team."

After we agreed, she was going to help, we ate lunch and took her home. We also went inside and acknowledged dad for a minute.

"Hey dad. Sorry for the quick hello and goodbye earlier. We just needed to get some stuff done early."

"No worries, Roman. How'd it go?" He pointed to the bourbon as a silent offer, but we had to turn it down, since we needed to get back to the girls.

"It was good. So, mom is coming with us on Saturday to decorate the house. We figured we'd just have our family dinner out there then. Does that work for you?" Not like he had anything else to do since he retired except hang out with mom.

"Sounds like fun. I'd love to see the place before the party, anyway. From what I've heard, it's really beautiful." From what he's heard? Heard from who? That's interesting.

Chapter 22

ALEX

I managed to work some of the anxiety out at the gym, though Roman came with me since, according to him, he was "guarding two now," which somehow managed to make me feel both loved and mildly stressed at the same time.

That protective streak of his might become a problem when it came time to see Tanner. Matt or Jack would definitely come with me—possibly both. I had absolutely no idea what to expect from that visit, and maybe that was the hardest part. The uncertainty. The endless possibilities your brain created when answers refused to come. I needed a few minutes away from Roman's intense focus and constant watchfulness, so I slipped into the locker room and changed into my swimsuit before heading toward the pool.

The water moved softly around my feet while I sat at the edge twisting my hair into a tight knot on top of my head. The rhythmic sounds of movement around the fitness center blended into the background while I slipped in my earplugs—not only to keep water out, but to give my thoughts room to breathe without interruption. I glanced toward Roman without fully turning my head. He sat on the bench at the far end of the pool, looking entirely too comfortable keeping watch over me.

I turned back, concentrating on the water. Its temperature was cool without feeling cold. Warm enough to relax muscles but cool enough to remind you that you were completely submerged. Exactly how I liked it.

I took a deep breath and lowered myself completely beneath the surface, allowing my body a moment to adjust before beginning my laps. The world changed underwater. Everything quieter. Simpler. Cleaner somehow. As I came back up for air and pushed away from the wall, I noticed Roman still sitting exactly where I left him.

I shook my head. Hopefully he planned to work out at some point and not spend the entire morning supervising my existence.

My arms moved evenly through the water while my legs kicked lightly behind me, rhythm carrying me from one end of the pool to the other. Swimming had always felt meditative. The repetition cleared space in my head where chaos normally lived. I worked through every situation waiting for me—Tanner, the anxiety, the decisions piling up—moving through each thought lap by lap until answers slowly began finding their way forward.

By the time I finished and showered, I felt lighter. More certain.

As I walked down the hallway afterward, the smell of eggs and bacon drifted through the house, immediately finding every weakness I possessed. *Ugh.*

Food might actually be the death of me now. I wasn't entirely sure how eating for two was going to work out long term, but based on current evidence, I had concerns. I slid onto my usual stool at the kitchen island and watched Roman moving around the kitchen like he'd done it his entire life. I wasn't even sure he noticed me walk in until he casually asked whether I wanted tea. I sat there quietly watching him. Watching all of it. The small things. The thoughtful things. The things I never realized I could have. There were so many people who would never experience life like this, and some days I still wasn't entirely sure how to receive it without guilt finding its way in beside gratitude.

without fear standing in the middle of it. I could definitely get used to all the extra attention.

The shower had been wonderful. The entire morning, honestly. For weeks it felt like life revolved around healing schedules, limitations, caution, and waiting for things to feel normal again. Today felt different. Lighter somehow. Familiar in a way I hadn't realized I missed so much until it came back.

Even breakfast somehow felt different. Roman cooked in a way that made concentrating on anything productive nearly impossible, and between his distraction tactics and my own inability to focus, my carefully planned to-do list wasn't getting nearly the attention it deserved—not that I was complaining.

He kissed me goodbye before heading down to the office, leaving behind lingering warmth, a kitchen that still smelled like breakfast, and entirely too many reasons for my brain to refuse to cooperate this morning.

I grabbed my phone and called Amelia.

"Hey," I said when she answered. "What time do you think you'll be done at the office?"

"Roman informed me I could take the rest of the day off, so I guess I'm done now. Wanna meet me in the lobby?"

She sounded excited, which is great because I needed to do something normal and have someone who's excited to do that with me.

"Sure." I agreed, grabbing my purse and the puppy in his carrier and headed to meet Amelia in the lobby.

The elevator stopped on the 15th floor where Roman's office was, and Amelia was right there and she practically threw herself at me.

"Hey, be careful don't crush the puppy."

I guided her in the direction of my SUV because we definitely couldn't fit anything into her two-seat convertible.

"Do you mind if I drive?" She asked as I was heading towards the driver's side.

"No, not at all. Have you ever driven an SUV before?"

Not that I was worried if she was going to wreck it or anything because I knew she'd be careful since she drove a Mercedes and it was in mint condition. I was just worried that she'd never driven such a big car. They can be intimidating.

"Oh, yeah, I drive Harrison's truck all the time. I was just thinking about maybe getting an SUV and I really like the look of yours. Thought I'd

He leaned down and kissed my cheek before turning back toward breakfast. Warmth moved through me immediately. And somewhere beneath
the anxiety, uncertainty, healing, and all the complicated pieces life kept
handing us, something inside me finally understood a truth I'd spent far
too much of my life resisting.

I deserved happiness. I deserved love. No less than anyone else.

After kissing Roman and the puppy goodbye for the day, I called Jack
on the way to Ella's.

"Hey Jack. Talk to me about this Tanner B.S." I knew my snippy tone
wasn't really directed at him and he didn't deserve that, but it came out
that way, nonetheless.

"Good morning, Alex. I hear congratulations are in order."

Damn, he's good at putting up with me.

"Thank you and good morning." I brought my tone down a notch or
two. "Sorry, that dude puts me on edge."

"I completely understand. Not sure what his motivation is to do this.
I hear jail hasn't been pleasant for him. He might be trying to get in your
good graces to help him get early release, maybe."

Hmmm, I never thought of that, maybe because he's a monster and he
just isn't capable of doing something like that, even pretending. At least
that's the feeling I got from him during the fight.

I put my blinker on to turn right as I pulled up to the red light where I
turn to head to Ella's place.

"Jack, whatever it is, I need to see him. There's something I need to do
for me and it's important. I can't do it alone and Roman can't come. He's
going to fight me on this, but I need to have a clear head. With the baby,
it's already fuzzy, so I don't need him adding to it."

The light turned green and I turned; staying focused on the road and the
conversation at the same time, so I didn't lash out again.

"You're planning on telling him you're going, right?"

Jack was adamant that I not keep secrets. He was definitely one of the
good guys.

"Yes, but you and Matt are going to have to convince him to let me."

That was the plan I came up with while swimming this morning.

He laughed.

"How would you like us to do that? If it were Abby or Maggie, we
would feel the same way."

"How about this weekend? We're decorating for the Christmas party at the Farmhouse. Bring the kids out, we'll do lunch and dinner, spend the day just having a good time. There'll be plenty of people there to help, especially Roman's mom, who's also my therapist."

Maybe if they knew a doctor was there; a therapist, to be exact, that would help him say yes.

"Ok. let me talk to Matt and Abby and see if they're cool with it and I'll get back to you this afternoon."

"Thanks Jack."

At least he was going to try. That's all I could ask for. Plus, I didn't have a Plan B, so this had to work.

I pulled into Ella's driveway and the two younger boys, Dante and Isaac, were coming out the back door.

"Hi boys. You off to school?" They both nodded their heads and I gave them a quick hug. "Have a good day."

I'm sure they were getting used to my hugs by now. At first they thought I was some crazy lady for wanting to hug them–they gave in after the first couple of times. I love to give hugs, but I don't just give them to anyone. Ella's family was special to me. I loved them like my own and they were going to find out how much soon enough.

I yelled hello as I walked in the back door and spotted Ella cleaning up breakfast.

"It smells good in here."

I closed my eyes, inhaling pancakes and, I'm sure, sausage. Oh lord, I was actually starting to get hungry again. I'm in trouble if I'm this hungry so early in the pregnancy.

She looked over and said, "Good morning, Miss Alex. Just finishing up pancakes and sausage. We have a couple of pancakes left and a sausage if you're hungry."

"No thank you, Ella, I've already had plenty this morning."

Last thing I needed was to gain 100 pounds.

"How're you feeling today?" I asked, leaning against the wall with my hands behind my back, waiting for her to finish up what she was doing before giving her the hug I was saving specifically for her.

She said, "I'm doing fine, honey." Then she coughed and staggered slightly, and I instinctively jerked from the wall, reaching out to her.

Darius came running out to the kitchen. "Grams, you good?"

I pulled myself back to let him help his grandmother.

She responded, completely annoyed. "Darius, please stop doing that. I'm fine. Say hi to Miss Alex."

He hadn't even noticed I was standing there. He looked over in my direction.

"Sorry Alex. Hi."

I walked over and hugged him. His limp arms hugged me back and the look on his face was one of exhaustion.

"Good morning, Darius. Did you eat breakfast?"

He nodded, then took a deep breath, dragging his feet back out to the living room. I was hoping he was taking care of himself. I know this news has taken a toll on him and I didn't want it to take him over, too.

I whispered in Ella's ear, "Boys, just take things like this a little differently, don't they?"

She nodded her head. Seeing Darius like this has put into perspective why Ella wants me to watch after her boys. She doesn't think they'll be able to handle this if she doesn't make it.

"They sure do. I'll go get my things and we can go, I guess."

Before she turned, I reached out and gently took her hand in mine.

"Ella, I hugged everyone this morning. I'm not planning to leave anyone out."

I reached up around her shoulder and pulled her to me. We stayed like that for the longest time and when she pulled away, her eyes were sparkling.

She put her hands on my shoulders, looked down at my stomach and said, "Are you?.."

My mouth hit the floor.

"Ella, how the..." I was still stunned.

"I've always had a sixth sense of sorts." She admitted. "Guess I've got a strong connection with you."

"We just found out. It was a surprise that shouldn't have really been a surprise, but I lost a lot of time and apparently sense after everything happened."

I just babbled because, well, I was flabbergasted she guessed.

"Well, after all the bad news, it's finally nice to have some good news." She said, putting her hand on my cheek lovingly.

"Yes, it is. Let's go talk to the doctor and get you and Darius something for the Christmas party."

I'm hoping to get more good news from the doctor so we can have a celebration lunch and go shopping afterwards.

"You don't need to do that, Alex." She looked weary, like she already knew the answer.

"I know. I don't need to do a lot of things. It's something I want to do…"

I was trying to keep a positive attitude and hope it rubbed off.

"…You've been such a wonderful friend to me, and you know I think of you and your boys as family and I always will, Ella."

She grabbed me by the hand and yelled to Darius that we were leaving, and we hurried to the car to get this over with.

The doctor's office was nice and clean. Antiseptic, to be exact, maybe a little too antiseptic for my taste. It had no character or warmth to it. I reached over to one of the tables and ran a finger over it. Not a speck of dust anywhere. When we sat down, I reached down to put my purse on the floor so I could touch the floor without looking suspicious. I swiped the tips of my fingers on the floor and casually checked to see if there was any dirt. There was none. How were people supposed to come in here and feel hope in a place like this? It looked like something from a sci-fi movie where they did experiments.

Ugh, ok nice imagination.

Maybe I'll buy them some fake plants or flowers to brighten this place up. I mean, my God even the magazines are white with black writing, and they are all medical journals and learning about cancer. I'll just have some greenery delivered so they don't suspect it's me. Great, my brain is running in overdrive right now. I wonder if this is pregnancy brain too or if I'm just nervous and trying to take my mind off of what we might be hearing today.

Ella hadn't let go of mine or Darius's hand since we got here and then they called her name.

It took her a second and a couple of deep breaths before she nodded her head and said, "Okay, I'm ready."

We sat in the doctor's office for another ten minutes before he finally came in. I mean, didn't we wait in the waiting room long enough and now we're in the doctor's office and he makes us wait some more for potentially devastating news? If you're going to be that inconsiderate, you better have some good freaking news. I thought angrily as he sat down without looking at any of us before introducing himself while staring at the file on his desk.

I looked over at Darius and Ella and shrugged as I rolled my eyes.

"Good morning. I'm Dr. Patel, the oncologist." He finally said, with no inflection to his voice as he looked up, confusion plastered all over his face.

"Are you all related?"

Like that's important or something.

Ella answered, "Yes. This is my grandson and this is my daughter."

She had a powerful grip on my hand and hers was shaking.

"Alright then." He seemed to ignore the irritation he was causing. "Nice to meet you all..." Again, that didn't sound sincere. "...Mrs. Jackson I want to let you know that the news I'll be giving you today is from the results of the second set of tests that were taken at your last doctor's visit..." He was reading from the file, not making eye contact with any of us. "...Dr. Frederick had requested them as a precaution due to some irregular results from the preliminary blood work." My stomach was roiling. Not sure if it was from being hungry again or the baby or being in here. He was rifling through papers in the file now, probably trying to keep himself busy so he didn't have to engage in any real human interaction. I'm sure it's how he keeps his sanity when he has to deliver bad news or he just has no empathy, and he's a cruel, heartless bastard.

"You said, precaution. Does that mean they wanted to make sure it was nothing and that it was probably a glitch or something?"

He looked up for a quick second to see who was speaking and nodded at Ella before returning to staring at the file.

"Yes, that's what he wanted it for. However, after running a second set of tests, unfortunately, the results were not what we had hoped." He looked up at her with a blank, unfeeling expression that broke three hearts at once.

It's one thing to hear the information, it's another to process it. None of us shed a tear all the way back to the house or even spoke. I couldn't even think. Back at the house, Ella made some tea and we stared at each other, waiting for the boys to get home so we could tell them. I kept tapping my nails on the table and my stupid leg was bouncing.

Ella got up and said, "I'll make some lunch."

She heated some homemade chicken soup and buttered rolls. She got us each a bottle of water and slammed them down on the table.

"Ok, I can't do this." She said abruptly.

I practically jumped out of my seat.

"We need to talk about this. We have things to figure out now." Her hands were braced on the counter as if to hold herself up.

I nodded robotically. I didn't know what to do. I've never had to plan someone's death before or figure out what to do with their children. It puts my life in perspective now, knowing I have three godchildren. This is what I would be doing if something happened to their parents.

Ok, I need to be strong now and figure this out.

I took a deep breath, swallowing the lump in my throat.

"What do we need to figure out, Grams?" Darius stormed into the kitchen, growling. "How to make your cancer disappear?" He demanded.

She looked like she was about to get mad and yell at him, but she reined it in somehow. She was a strong woman and maybe that's where I'm feeling this abnormal strength right now.

"Darius, I understand you're upset. Hell, so am I but it is what it is now, and this is the hand we've been dealt. So we can fold or we can play it and I'm gonna play it."

I smiled, knowing that her strength was going to help us all get through this.

"Alex, I need to know you're going to help my boys when I'm gone."

I nodded, looking back and forth between the two of them.

Darius was mad when he said, "I've got the boys, Grams."

She looked at him deadpan.

"I was talking about all of you."

He crossed his arms over his chest.

"I don't need no babysitter."

His face was stony and I could feel the wall going up around him again, like the first time we met.

"Don't you talk to me like that, boy."

This was going to get heated, so I excused myself to go to the restroom, where I closed the toilet lid and sat down. I tried to relax and get some air. I splashed some water on my face, trying to pull myself together before returning to the kitchen, hoping they'd come to a truce.

We managed to talk calmly for a while, concluding we'd expedite the home renovations and get them moved ASAP.

"I'll talk to Roman, but I'm sure he'll agree this is something we can get done."

Ella took my hand and nodded, holding in all the tears. I knew what that felt like and I also knew they would come out as soon as I left, so I needed to hurry so she could process things as well.

"I'll make sure I'm available for the boys for whatever they need, Ella. Including Darius."

I was planning to remain upfront in the boy's lives until they could take care of themselves and make sure Darius was stable.

"Alex, I need you to be my power of attorney."

"Whatever you need, Ella. I have a couple of lawyer friends we can get your estate taken care of with. I will make sure everything goes in the boys' names and turned over when they are ready for that responsibility. Until then, I'll take care of things for them."

I had a lot of money put away for investing and I planned to invest in these boy's futures. I didn't want to bring that up right now, but I'll tell her when the time comes.

I pulled Darius to the side and said, "You know you can count on me, right?"

He nodded, but he was still so mad. His nostrils flared. This wasn't the best time to have a conversation when he couldn't really hear me.

"I'll let all of you talk about this without me here and you and I can talk next week?" I made him look me in the eye. "I'll have Amelia make us an appointment."

Keeping him thinking like a professional was my goal. He was my CEO, after all, and it will keep him focused.

He reluctantly softened his features after blinking twice.

"Okay, sounds good."

I hugged everyone and headed home.

I couldn't help but feel guilty that my life was so great while theirs was falling apart. At least I knew that there was always hope and that even in dark times if you look hard enough you can see that light especially if you have people who won't give up on you when things get tough.

***

ROMAN

As much as the news of the baby was fresh on my mind and the doctor's appointment with Ella was concerning me, I needed to get some work done today. I walked over to Amelia's desk and grinned while holding up all the bags. She nodded, reaching out to put them behind her desk. I took off the carrier, handing that to her as well.

"Do you mind if I put a little doggie bed behind my desk for him to sleep in?"

"He's not going to be coming here once he doesn't need a bottle anymore." I said as I walked to my office door.

"Ok, but for now?" She pleaded.

I nodded. "Sure, I guess that would be fine."

I hopefully wouldn't regret this decision.

She laughed and announced, "Good, cuz I already got one."

She pulled a little fuzzy blue puppy bed out from underneath her desk. I raised my eyebrow, shaking my head as I walked into my office. I turned back around before I closed the door.

"I'm going to need you to concentrate on work and not so much the puppy, though. Can you handle that?"

She was snuggling the puppy up by her face, not paying attention to me.

"No problem, right little Tao? We're going to let daddy get all his work done today." She said in that silly little voice again, while staring at the puppy.

Oh Lord, I need to have an adult day.

I finished all my morning meetings before Harrison barged in. The door swung open hard, but luckily he caught it before it slammed into the wall and he closed it behind him with less force.

"Hey Roman. You wanna go out for lunch today? I don't know how much more baby talk I can handle."

I was feeling his mood to a "T."

"You took the words right out of my mouth. I hope to God she hasn't been answering the phone like that."

We both laughed, even though it wouldn't really be funny if she had been. I stood up and walked quickly around the desk, throwing my phone in my jacket pocket.

"I've got the keys." Harrison said as I was about to grab my keys off the table next to the door where they usually land when I come in.

I nodded, ushering us out of the room.

"Do you want us to bring you anything for lunch?" I asked Amelia on our way to the elevator.

"Nope, I already have something being delivered. Tao and I are going to have lunch together."

Still in that damn baby voice.

"See you in an hour or three."

I looked at Harrison and he was shaking his head because she didn't hear a word I said.

We got in the elevator and looked at each other, then burst out laughing.

"How the hell did this happen?" Harrison asked, astonished. "We had a good thing going and now we're getting married, having kids and becoming all domestic and shit."

He leaned back heavily against the back of the elevator, putting his hand on his head.

"As fast as it all happened, I should be more freaked out than I am, but I've been expecting to be here by now. You know my five-year plan and all. I got the bug when we started hanging out with Matt and Jack's families. She was expecting to be here already too, so we're just kind of doing things backwards."

"Do you mind if we start hanging out with all of you? I think I need to see what this family life is like. I mean, I don't think we're going to be doing the club or bar life after we get married. We've already discussed it. She wants to settle down."

I gave him my shocked face. I mean, I am really blown away by this turn of events for both of us.

"Ok, but what about you? Are you ready to give up that life? Because if you're not, you need to tell her."

He looked sweaty and sick.

"I don't know. All I know is that I don't want to lose her. She's my person, ya know?"

I knew exactly how he felt.

"I do know. Look what I suffered through for Alex. She was not the ideal person for me. I would have never gone looking for someone who put herself through what Alex did, but she was the one and I knew it and I was going to sacrifice for her and I knew that too."

We got to the restaurant, and both had a strong drink of bourbon before lunch. We took an extra half hour to talk about our new situations before getting right back into work as soon as we returned to the office. It seemed like settling down was helping us both become closer and work more like a team than we had been before. I'm glad he wanted to hang out with the other families. He was so adamant about staying away from everyone and keeping his nightlife activities up; I was actually surprised when he mentioned he wanted to hang out.

I wondered how things were going with Alex? I know the doctor's visit was this morning and it's almost four now. Calling her making sure she's alright, makes sure I'm alright.

"Hi honey." She answered, sort of off, but not distraught. Sounded kind of melancholy which I'll take any day over distraught with her.

"Hey. How are you? How's Ella?"

She took a deep breath and hesitated before answering.

"I'm just saying goodbye to everyone, so I'll call you when I'm headed home. What's for dinner?"

I know that sounded like a normal response, but her tone of voice wasn't normal. She seemed calm so I'm not going to ask.

"I haven't thought about it yet. What if I make tacos?"

Keep the conversation neutral.

"Sounds good. I'm so hungry." Her tone was so monotonous—not like her at all.

I walked out of the office, grabbing the puppy and all his stuff as I went home. I fed him, gave him his sink bath, and laid him in his bed. He was getting a lot bigger and much more alert and mobile. He was still sleepy most of the time, which is what I needed to get shit done; like make dinner. In the middle of sauteing the veggies and chicken for the tacos, Alex's name was scrolling across the screen, so I hurried to answer it.

"Hey babe. You almost home?"

I lowered the heat on the veggies and put the phone on speaker, laying it on the counter. I grabbed a spoon and pushed the chicken around the pan, adding the taco seasoning and a measuring cup with water I had ready to go.

"Yeah. I'm about five minutes away. Can you make a chamomile tea for me and get out the calming tincture?"

I knew this wasn't going to be good news, but I'm happy she wasn't losing it while driving.

"Sure, it'll be ready when you get home."

I put the water in the microwave and grabbed a decaf chamomile tea and the calming tincture. Learning how to make her tea seemed like a good idea and I was getting a lot of practice lately.

She walked into the house and stood still with both arms heavy by her sides, tears streaming down her face. I turned off the stove and walked up to her as sedately as I could, embracing her. All I could say was "I'm sorry." I never let her go as I guided her to the sofa and helped her get comfortable. There was a lot of pain teetering in her eyes that needed to come out. I sensed it. Since the fight, I haven't sensed this kind of feeling from her. I had a feeling the news she was going to tell me was as bad as it could possibly get.

When she finally lifted her head, she said, "Cancer. Breast Cancer."

I shook my head.

"How advanced is it?"

She squeezed her eyes shut, taking a couple of breaths.

"Stage four and it's metastasized." She whimpered loudly, trying to hold in the genuine pain.

"So, what did they say the treatment would be, and what's the prognosis?"

She choked through each sob before finally catching her breath, letting out a deeply held sigh.

"Can I have my tea first, please?"

I reluctantly let her go, getting her tea. She took several sips and set it down on the table, looking at me with a swirling of green agony in her eyes.

"They said the usual, I guess, since he seemed to give us the information like he was telling us his damn grocery list, but something like three to six months. He said she could prolong her life with treatment." She gasped in some air. "Ella asked what the side effects of the treatment were and he told her all these really horrible things and she asked how long it would prolong her life, and he said there was no guarantee that it would, so she declined treatment..."

She let out a strangled noise. At that moment, my heart shattered along with hers.

"Honey, I know this is killing you, but I think Ella just wants to have the best quality of life she can with whatever time she has left and doesn't want to be sick from the treatment while doing it. How about we get her house ready ASAP, get her moved in and let her live the rest of her life knowing that her family will have the best life possible."

I rubbed my hand over her hair...over and over again trying to make the pain go away.

"Let's make sure that every day is her best day. How does that sound?"

I pulled her shaking body in close as she nodded her head in agreement and the tears were now falling from my eyes. I was never letting these people go.

Chapter 23

ALEX

G ym, shower, breakfast was finally our normal routine again.

    Now that the puppy was almost five weeks old, he'd be able to eat puppy food soon. He seemed to have doubled his size and weight in just the two weeks since we brought him home. I wondered how big he was going to get. I sat on the floor, playing tug of war with the little toy we got for him. His cute little growl made me giggle. Of course, I had to let him win.

"He's going to need a yard," I thought as I realized this dog would need room to run. I'm sure as hell not taking him in an elevator every time he has to go out to use the bathroom. The puppy licked my face as I laid down on the floor, exhausted by the thoughts overtaking me. I laughed because it tickled and I scooped him up, nuzzling my face in his tummy, managing to get us off the floor.

"Whatcha got goin' on in there?" Roman asked, startling me as he looped his arms around my ever-growing tummy.

"Oh, you know, Tao and I were just wondering which of us was going to risk taking him out for a potty break in the middle of winter?" I gave him a little wink and a nudge. "...You know, riding down twenty-four floors in an elevator and all?"

He laughed.

"Do you mean this winter or next winter?"

Like that matters.

"He's old enough now to use the potty."

"Well, we're going to have to take turns, I guess."

He looked at me seriously when he said it, but I laughed and used the pregnancy card.

In my best guilt trippy voice, I mused, "You'd make me do that pregnant and..." I quit while I was ahead, since I almost gave up that I was afraid of heights.

"Oh, okay, now you're a helpless pregnant lady. I gotcha." He distanced me from him by the shoulders like he just had an aha moment.

"Yes." I batted my lashes.

He drew me back to him tight, giving me a sweet kiss that made my head fuzzy when he slipped his tongue past my lips for a quick instant before he pulled away again, but I clung to him. "Alright." he said.

I mumbled through the brain fog from that kiss. "We can't keep him here. That's not fair. We need to look for a new place."

"What if I told you I was already thinking about that and I was planning to ask someone from Grant's office to house hunt for us after the party. I'll let you make the announcement first."

"Are you serious?" I screamed right in his face, and he let me go, backing up as he screwed up his face. "Can we look in Maggie and Abby's neighborhood? Do you care if I call them today and see if they know of anyone whose house is going on the market?"

I was hopping up and down on my toes excitedly.

"Sure, that sounds great and by the way, that's where I was going to suggest looking...." He winked. "...Just so you know, we're on the same page."

Agreeing doesn't happen very often for us. I kissed him one last time before he left for the office.

I called the girls on three way and this time Abby was the first one to answer.

"Hey preggo. How's the little mama to be?"

Maggie said, "Okay, how am I supposed to call you Jerk now?"

I laughed.

"Girls, I have fantastic news. I'm great, by the way. Roman and I are house hunting."

Abby asked, "House Hunting? Like a vacation home? You have the penthouse and the farmhouse. Where is this new house going?" Maggie was awkwardly silent.

"The penthouse is the penthouse. It will always be here because it's attached to the office, and he'd never sell it. The farmhouse is my Hallmark house just for the business and holiday parties. We need a home for our dog and our baby."

Maggie finally screamed, "Sharon Foster's house is for sale. She's such a pain in the you know what. The HOA was going to throw a good riddance party for her." Abby and I burst out laughing.

"When did it go on the market?" I quickly asked.

"It hasn't officially, yet, because it needs work."

"Well, she and I are actually friendly. Would you like me to talk to her for you? She's one street over from me," Abby suggestively mentioned.

I screamed, "Yes, hurry. Roman wants to wait till after the party to ask one of the Realtors in Grant's office to house hunt for us."

"Why the heck does he need to get a Realtor from Grant's office? You are a Realtor in Grant's office!!!"

Maggie threw it out there like I was an idiot.

"Oh, my God. Is this really my brain from now on? What the hell. Okay, Abby, go talk to Sharon and let me know if she has a Realtor that I can talk to or if she wants to skip a commission. She and I can just do the transaction between us. Can Jack do the legal shit?"

No one said anything.

"Abby?"

Maggie said, "I think she hung up."

"What...Okay, she's calling back in."

"Abby, where'd you go? Did you hear anything I said?"

"Yeah, I heard you say you were a Realtor! I just got off the phone with Sharon. She said she'd love to talk to you and wants to know if you can do the sale FSBO?"

"Perfect, that's the part of the conversation you must've missed."

We all laughed.

"I know you're friendly with Sharon, but would she let Jack be the attorney, or does she have her own?" I asked.

"Jack is her attorney." Abby confirmed.

Finding a house, check.

We talked about decorating the farmhouse tomorrow before we hung up. The information about Jack being her attorney was interesting, considering his actual title was divorce lawyer. He just did favors for me and he couldn't represent me during my divorce because they both worked in the same law office, which made my life more difficult than it needed to be at the time. Thankfully, Jack and Matt had some great friends at another office they set me up with to take care of my divorce.

ME: *"Hey babe, I found us a house." I texted as soon as I hung up with the girls.*

ROMAN: *"Where, what house? I've been scanning that area all morning and nothing is for sale in Abby and Maggie's neighborhood."*

As I was typing the next text, the phone rang with Roman's name scrolling across the screen.

"Hey." I said breathlessly.

"Hey babe. So, tell me, where is this house?"

I could tell he was trying to use his calm tone to get me to chill out. Taking a deep breath, I exhaled slowly before I responded.

"I called the girls and asked them if they knew anyone in their neighborhood that was selling, and they did. It's not on the market yet. Abby knew the lady. Jack's her attorney and she said she'd sell it FSBO." I gasped for air after spilling all that info in one breath.

"Damn baby, when you set your mind on something, you do it."

"Well, I would've had it done yesterday. You know Maggie had to remind me that I actually am one. You know...a realtor?"

"Yes, honey." He chuckled. "I knew that too, but I didn't want to add another thing to your already full dance card."

"I know, but..." I whined.

He cut in on me so I wouldn't go full-blown tantrum, I'm sure.

"What does this house look like and how much are they asking? I know we want to live in the neighborhood, but I'm not overpaying for a house just because they think we're desperate."

"I have no idea. Abby said the house was one street over from her. That's all I know right now. Maggie said the neighborhood is throwing the owners a good riddance party."

There was a loud sigh on his end.

"Oh lord, more drama."

"It apparently needs some work too, but in that neighborhood, it could just mean a better landscaper."

He chuckled.

"Okay, find out when we can go look at it and then we'll talk about it. I've gotta go to a meeting, so I'll call ya later. I love you."

"We love you too."

I rubbed my hand over my belly with a wide grin on my face. I still can't believe there's a little human in there.

I called Abby back and said, "Hey girl, can I get some information about the house? Roman wants to know some weird stuff like the address and the asking price." We both laughed hysterically. "Can I just come over? I only have phone calls to make today. I'm so bored. The puppy and I need something to do."

I scooped up the puppy with my free hand as I walked down the hall.

"Yes. Wait, puppy?"

I silently searched my memory bank, trying to figure out if I told them about the puppy. I guess not.

"Have I not told you about Tao?"

I was holding him up in front of me as his little legs were swimming in midair and it made me smile.

"Uh, no. When did this happen? I thought when you mentioned a dog a minute ago, you were speaking future plans."

"Two weeks ago. I found him in that neighborhood we're fixing up. He was the lone survivor. He was only three weeks old according to the vet. We're still bottle feeding him and carrying him everywhere."

"Jax is going to go crazy and then he's going to want me to get him a dog."

I laughed.

"How about Tao can be his dog too when we move into the neighborhood?..." Start that wishful thinking. "...He can't really play right now. He's only five weeks old, but he's so freaking cute."

I rubbed my finger back and forth gently over the soft fur on his head, cradling him to my chest. She asked the normal question I was always hesitant about answering.

"What kind of dog is it, do you know?"

I scrunched up my face, trying to think how to best answer this.

"We had a DNA test done to be certain, but the vet was pretty positive it's a Pitbull."

The line went silent and I patiently waited for her to process the information bouncing on my toes; holding Tao tight against me.

She finally said, "Are you sure you want that around a baby?"

I'm so tired of that response and rolled my eyes, releasing a strained breath.

"Not you too! Roman was the same way until the vet set him straight. He said he's going to take on the personality of his owners and how he's treated."

Leaving out the bit about natural instinct and all. She was quiet again.

"You're in trouble then, aren't you?"

"What do you mean?"

"I know what you can do."

That made me cringe.

"We're planning to get him trained, so it shouldn't be a problem."

***

I pulled up to Abby's house and was greeted by not only Abby but Maggie and all the kids as well.

Abby said, "Ok, first things first. We need to see this attack dog."

I unzipped the purse and everyone looked in, and that's all it took.

"Girls, this is bull." Maggie exclaimed out of the blue.

"What?" I asked, looking around wildly.

"You're going to make me look like an alchy at brunch now."

Her face fell, but something looked off about it too, like she was hiding her amusement.

"Get knocked up and join us!" I blurted out, like it was the easiest thing in the world to do.

"Too late." She squeaked.

Abby and I said in unison, "NO!" She shook her head rapidly.

"Matt didn't want me to say anything yet because it was harder for us to get pregnant this time and he didn't want anything to jinx it. I'm only seven weeks, but I had to tell you two."

I started crying mostly because I had all these crazy hormones but because this was what we had wanted to do, and now it's all happening, and I didn't want anything to take it away.

Abby called Sharon and we walked over to her house. It was an ostentatious, but gorgeous, two-story home with a basement. Light gray brick with five bedrooms and six bathrooms. A two-story foyer with a chandelier in the middle and curved stairs on both sides going up to the second level greeted you upon entry. The living room, family room, two offices, and a hearth room made up the lower level along with a giant chef's kitchen that boasted a walk-in pantry and a butler's pantry. There was a sunroom that went out to a huge second story deck all on the main level. The deck had stairs that went down to a covered patio with an outdoor kitchen that had a grill and a bar, perfect for entertaining. There was already a pool and hot tub along with plenty of fenced-in yard for Tao and kids to play. It also had a fully finished basement with a theater, bar and another bedroom and bathroom. An attached four-car garage connected to the mudroom leading into the kitchen was a plus as well—especially for Tao.

I leaned close and whispered to Maggie, "Now I know the work that needs to be done."

She nodded as we looked at all the different paint colors on the walls. It looked like the 90s threw up all over it. The wood floors were going to need to be refinished also, and the kitchen cabinets and counters would need replacing. It didn't look like it had been updated since its inception back in 1992. I took dozens of pictures and sent them all to Roman. He texted back.

ROMAN: *"How much?"*

I asked Sharon if she wanted me to do a comparative market analysis right there.

"Yes, that would be great." She said and handed me her laptop that was sitting on the kitchen counter.

We sat at her table as I worked up a pretty in-depth market analysis, printing it out for her. She said she needed to show her husband so they could talk about it. The result was the house was worth an estimated $1.5 million if it didn't need work.

I sent it to Roman.

ROMAN: *"What do you think? Is it worth that?"*

ME: *"Honestly, I wouldn't offer that because of the work that needs to go into it aesthetically, but it would be worth a lot more than that if it were fixed up. I'm sure it could use an inspection too, but it's the only house for sale in this neighborhood and I know they go fast, and don't you do construction or something?;) LOL."*

ROMAN: *"Wait there. I'm on my way."*

I turned to Sharon and asked, "Do you mind if my significant other comes out and takes a look?"

She replied, "No, when do you think he could come?"

I smiled sheepishly and said, "He's on his way."

Abby and Maggie were laughing.

Abby whispered loudly to Sharon as if I couldn't hear her. "You're going to want to take your own look, I promise."

Oh my God, Abby, you did not just say that.

I shook my head, putting my hand over my face.

Sharon said, "Okaaay...great, he's more than welcome to come."

Roman pulled up about twenty minutes later while we were all chatting and passing the puppy around. Maggie went out, walking him in—arm in arm.

Abby nudged Sharon and said, "Told you so."

She said, "Good Lord, who looks like that? Has he had work done?"

I whipped my head around.

"If either of you feeds that man's ego any more than it already is, I will be so mad." I said in a hushed tone.

They giggled as Abby shoved me towards Roman. I fell into his arms, and he smiled then kissed me. I turned and gave Abby a playful glare.

While we were walking around, he whispered in my ear, "Why is she staring at me like that?" Referring to Susan, who had not taken her eyes off of him since he walked in.

I rolled my eyes, as if he didn't know people have a tendency to stare at him.

"Because Abby told her you were hot and she believed it. She's probably wondering what the hell Abby was talking about."

He shoved my shoulder, slinging his arm possessively around me as if to let her know he was already taken.

After the tour, he asked me to come talk to him privately outside in the driveway. He was leaning against his car and pulled me over, resting his hands on my hips.

"It only needs some aesthetic work from what I can visually see. And yes, my crew can knock out pretty quick. Offer $1.5 with no commission due. I'll feel good knowing you're so close to your friends."

I smiled, laying a long lingering kiss on him, refraining from jumping up and down, though.

"I love you."

"I know." He winked.

I shoved him in the chest.

"Hey..."

He jerked me close.

"I love you too, babe. Now hurry up and get home. I need to spend some time with my baby. It's Friday night, I'm going to take off work early. Let's go on a date. I don't know how much more time we're going to be able to do that before our peanut comes."

"Ok, let me go talk to Sharon. I know she wants to talk to her husband first, but I'll give her the offer and see what she says."

I put my game face on when I got back inside, but that didn't last long when the kids were hanging all over me and the girls were talking baby talk to the puppy. Sharon was oohing and ahhing over Roman with Abby. It wasn't long before someone else coming into the house interrupted our little swaraj.

Awesome, her husband is home.

We won't have to wait for his input now.

Sharon said, "Hi, Rick." Her tone wasn't all that excited to see Rick, however.

He said, "What the hell is this, a party?"

Okay, sounds like a real creep.

She said, "This is Alex Kennedy. Alex, this is my husband, Rick."

He looked at me as if he knew me.

"Your name sounds familiar. Why is that?"

I've never seen this guy before in my life.

I politely mentioned, "I'm a Realtor with Johnson Realtors."

That was all I could think of. That he may have seen me in a local ad or something.

He replied, "Nope, that's not it. Anyway, nice to meet you but we're not hiring a realtor."

Nice to meet you didn't sound very nice. He turned away, throwing his keys and briefcase on the counter harshly.

"I'm not here to offer my services. I'm here to give you an offer on your house."

He spun around, looking me up and down in a way that made me want to delouse after.

Who is this creep? I thought with the feeling something seemed off about him.

"I didn't know our house was for sale." He sneered.

I looked at Sharon and now I know why everyone thinks Sharon's a bitch. She's married to a total jerk, and I didn't like the way he was eyeing me, but I'm good at this game.

"My fault, totally mistaken." I said, right to his face. "

Girls, let's go. Roman will be happy to know he wasted his time coming out here. I'll let him know his $1.2 million offer is no good because the house isn't for sale."

Sharon gasped. I looked at her and said, "Sharon, I'm so sorry we wasted your time. Thank you for your hospitality. You were so sweet."

Her mouth opened wide, looking at her husband like she was going to kill him. The argument that followed was loud but muffled by the walls of the house. We could hear it all the way out to the sidewalk but not the content.

As we were walking back to Abby's house, my phone pinged in my pocket. I pulled it out to see a text from Sharon.

SHARON: *"I'm so sorry and very embarrassed. I'll need to calm him down. I shouldn't tell you this, but we're getting divorced and have to sell the house soon, or file for bankruptcy. Once he gets over himself, I'm sure he'll take that offer."*

ME: *"Ugh. If it would help, we can write up an AS IS deal. No inspection necessary."*

SHARON: *"Give me 48 hours."*

ME: *"Sounds good, take care."*

I refrained from telling the girls what was going on. It didn't feel right telling her story.

I called Roman on the way home.

"That was interesting."

"So, what's the verdict?"

"The verdict is her husband came home. He's a real piece of work. Said he didn't know his house was for sale. I let him know I was sorry you wasted your time and that your $1.2 million offer was rescinded."

He was quiet and then laughed.

"I offered one point five."

"What? No! I'm such an idiot. What a forgetful brain I have."

He laughed.

"Good girl..." He praised. "...What did he have to say about that?"

"Nothing. We left. Sharon asked me to give her 48 hours. Mentioned they were getting divorced and needed the money or they were going to be filing bankruptcy."

I knew Roman wouldn't gossip about her predicament.

"An as is offer would make it quick, don't you think?"

"Agreed. Damn baby, you're turning me on." I felt a sense of victory for once.

"I'll see you in ten."

Chapter 24

ROMAN

"H ey man, I know I ask this an awful lot, just kinda hoping at some point you'll be available, but do you think you and Alex would like to go out to dinner with Amelia and me tonight?" I was in the middle of an email when Harrison asked, so I didn't even look up.

"Sure, where and when?" I knew we didn't have any actual plans tonight, so why not?

"Okay, fine, next.... wait, did you say yes?" He was ready for the usual rejection and responded aptly. I laughed, glancing up for a second.

"Hold that thought." I finished the email and hit send. "It's been crazy, but we finally have a night free, so where to?" I leaned back in my chair and held my arms out to the side, waiting for an answer. He looked confused.

"Shit, I'm used to you saying no, so I didn't actually have anything planned. Let me ask Amelia. She's good at plans on the fly." He practically ran out of the room. I called Alex.

"Hey babe. You almost home?"

"I'm pulling into the garage now."

"We're going on a double date with Amelia and Harrison. Is that cool?" She "eeeked." and it pierced my ears making me squint.

"Yes! We haven't been able to do that, and I know they've wanted to and so have I."

Alex was sitting on the floor playing with the puppy when I came in.

"I think he's old enough to be in his crate while we're gone, don't you think?" She looked up at me for confirmation. "...Nothing will happen to him in there. We can feed him before we leave and he'll sleep the whole time we're gone, right?"

Her eyes were wide, waiting for me to agree.

"Are you trying to convince me or you?"

A giggle slipped from her lips.

"Obviously, me!"

I sat with her on the floor, kissing her nose before stretching out on my side, propping myself up on my elbow. I scratched the puppy on the head as he tried to nip my fingers.

"The puppy will be fine." I tipped her chin towards me to look her in those beautiful green eyes. "You're going to be a great mom. This puppy is lucky you were the one to find him. Ella is lucky you were the one to run out of gas in front of her house. I'm so lucky you were the one who sold that property to my investors. Any other way and our lives would be very different. And not for the better."

She didn't have time to respond because Harrison and Amelia came in at that moment.

After Alex and I got ready, we talked to Harrison and Amelia in the kitchen to decide where we were going. We chose as nice restaurant downtown overlooking the River we could walk to. Harrison and Amelia looked as if they were having a silent argument with their eyes and it continued the entire ride down in the elevator.

Harrison finally said, "Ok. Sorry Alex, but even if you didn't have an issue with alcohol, you're pregnant and can't have it, anyway. Do you mind if we hit a nice bar for a cocktail before dinner?"

She looked at all of us, confused.

"Is that what all the whispering was about before we left? Are you serious? You idiots..." she said, irritated. "...If you want to have a drink, have a drink. Stop babying me. I have enough baby going on with Tao and the peanut now."

We got to the bar, which was not an overly crowded yuppie bar like Sebastians, thank God. It was a very nice upscale bar that I'm sure Harrison and Amelia frequented. It was bright, with lots of white painted wood and glass everywhere with colorful accents. There were low top tables with plush velvet chairs surrounding them. That's where we planted ourselves. Harrison and I ordered a bourbon, neat, and the girls got soda water with a splash of cranberry and lime. I was surprised Amelia ordered the same thing as Alex until she asked Alex for one of the tinctures. That's really cool that she's testing that out for her. Alex put a few drops in Amelia's drink and only one in her own.

"Why did you only put one drop in yours?" I inquired, remembering that I saw her put multiple drops in her tea at the house when I witnessed her first anxiety attack.

She said, "I haven't talked to a doctor yet about the interaction the herbs have on the baby. I don't want to risk it."

I wrapped my arm around her and hugged her, kissing the top of her head. She's so protective of our baby. It warms my very soul.

***

ALEX

We had a couple drinks at the bar before our dinner reservations. I noticed some guy staring at me and I didn't place him right away, but then it occurred to me it was Rick Foster, Sharon's husband. The way he was talking to that woman, I can only guess why they're getting divorced and why Sharon's been difficult lately. After he stopped gawking, I snapped a photo of him with his hand on the woman's rear and made sure to get a good pic of his face.

I wasn't paying attention to anyone at our table until Roman said, "Hey, did you hear me?"

I snapped out of it.

"Nope. What did you say?"

"Damn, I'm not very interesting, I guess." He chuckled.

I stared him right in the eyes and said, "We're getting that house whether Rick the Dick wants to sell or not."

"What the hell does that mean?"

I pointed to the guy groping the woman. His head turned and he squinted in Rick's direction.

"Who's that?" He asked.

"That's Sharon's soon to be ex, Rick. The one that said the house wasn't for sale."

"Yeah, so?" He sat back in his chair and casually crossed his ankle over his thigh, taking a sip of his bourbon after swishing it in a circle.

"Well, that's not Sharon, obviously."

I crossed my arms and wiggled my brows.

"Oh no. You didn't just send that pic to Sharon, did you?"

He sat up with a worried expression.

"Not yet."

He and Harrison started laughing, but I thought I heard Roman say the woman looked familiar.

Maybe I'm hearing things.

Harrison said, "I'd hate to get on your bad side."

"Look, this is divine intervention. I had nothing to do with this. He showed up here on his own, making bad decisions."

I got up to go to the restroom before we left. Amelia came with me and on the way out Rick was standing in the hall acting like he was on his phone.

"Alex, is it?"

He slipped his phone into his pocket, reaching his hand out to shake mine. I shrugged. I had my purse in one hand and my phone in the other so I pretended not to have a free hand.

"Yes. Rick Foster, right?" He nodded as he rubbed his hands together, irritated by the obvious snub.

"Mhm. So, I remember where I know you from now..." He smirked and his tone sounded unwelcome and creepy. "...You're the girl from the fight."

I felt a tightness in my chest as Amelia reached over, squeezing my wrist.

Roman and Harrison were on their way over—concern etched into their expressions.

Harrison asked, "Hey girls, what's the holdup? We're trying to get to dinner."

Roman put his arm around my shoulder and offered a snarky smile to the guy.

He smiled back and said, "I was just talking to Ms. Kennedy here about the offer on my house earlier today. $1.5 and you have a deal."

I looked up at Roman and gave him a knowing wink. I wanted to make sure Roman knew that's not what we were discussing.

"Well, Mr. Foster. It's not Alex you're negotiating with; it's me. For that complete and utter lack of disrespect, my offer is now $1.0 million. You can take it or leave it. We're leaving."

As we were walking away, the guy tried to get Roman's attention.

"Wait, wait, wait. We got off on the wrong foot. I had no idea she was negotiating for you. I thought she was buying this was her deal."

He was playing games...*But why?*

***

ROMAN

"Ya know what, Rick?..." I reigned in my temper. "...I think I would prefer to negotiate through your wife and her attorney."

He gave me a dirty look.

"I bet you would, but that's not happening. It's my fucking house and I say who buys it and how much."

I laughed, realizing I was starting to really piss this guy off and it was kind of fun.

"Yeah, I know how this works. You can bring your attorney to the table as well. So, you can either accept my $1.0 million offer, or not."

He smirked and there was something more behind those eyes than just trying to get a rise out of me. Rick was filled with bad juju.

"I'll think about it." He sneered. "Oh, and Roman, how did it feel watching Tanner manhandle your girlfriend like that?"

I let go of Alex and pushed her behind me as I turned around and got right in Rick's face.

That was not what I was expecting to hear from this dude. Who the hell was he? I can either play it cool or punch the guy in the face. I think I better just get Alex out of here.

"Hmmm, that's funny, if I recall correctly, Tanner not only got carted off to the hospital, unconscious, but he also got sentenced to five years in prison. So, I don't see how a cheap shot was any kind of manhandling, do you?"

I'm sure Alex could see my hand shaking, and she reached up and grabbed it.

"Please don't let him suck you into whatever game he's running." She pleaded.

I leaned down and whispered, "Not a chance, honey. I think a nice day in the attorney's office would be fun."

I glared at Rick.

"Well, it sure was fun to watch it over and over again. I recorded it."

He ran his tongue over his bottom lip while staring at Alex. But now Harrison was standing next to me. He must've pushed Alex out of this mess, thinking I was about to clock this guy.

"Interesting. What, do you work for Tanner or Marcus or something? Little errand boy?"

Harrison grabbed my arm.

"Man, he's not worth it."

I was starting to get angry now, but I wanted to know who this guy was.

"No, he's not and we've got dinner reservations."

He also seemed like one of those guys who needed his ego stroked, so if he thought we'd leave without knowing something about him that made him a big deal, it may not work for him.

He said, "I'm an accountant if you must know..." That's what I needed to know. "...A very successful one."

I laughed, knowing that filing for bankruptcy isn't the picture of success.

"Sure, well, you and your successful accounting have a nice night. By the way, my offer just went to $900K. You can now count that as a loss."

He can go to hell as far as I'm concerned. We can find another house.

He yelled, "Screw, You!" as we walked out of the restaurant.

I pulled Alex close to my side after we exited and said, "Hey babe. You ok?"

She laughed.

"I was just watching my man stick up for me. That was hot. I was getting turned on listening to you 'negotiate'." I kissed her before we walked in the restaurant.

"I'm not sure I'm hungry for dinner anymore." I whispered in her ear while getting a nice inhale of her hair. She wiggled her eyebrows at me and bit her bottom lip.

Harrison bellowed, "Either get a room or get in there, please. It's cold out here and I'm starving and you're making me nauseous."

I ignored him as we marched up to the hostess.

"King for four, please." Alex announced to the woman at the podium.

"Yes, Mrs. King, right this way." She turned abruptly around and eyed me. I was smiling from ear to ear, hearing her call Alex my wife.

"I like the sound of that," I whispered softly in her ear. Her cheeks lit up pink with the shyest of smiles escaping her lips.

Amelia and Alex got their soda water with cranberry and lime in a wine glass this time so she could get a feel for what her new non-wine was going to look like when it was released.

"I know bars don't want to serve non-alcoholic beverages, but if they were just as expensive in a restaurant, then why wouldn't they?..." She seemed to be having this conversation with herself. "...I shouldn't just limit the reach to people who shouldn't drink, don't you think?"

She snapped out of her little world and looked at us like we knew she was talking to us all along.

"I think it would be an excellent idea to sell it in places that serve alcohol..." Amelia and Harrison both nodded in agreement. "...Some people don't even like alcohol and some people are the DD. This way everyone can hang out together and no one feels left out. Especially when the bar tab comes."

We all laughed, but Alex had a sad look on her face.

"Honey, what's wrong?" I gently brushed her hair over her shoulder and laid my hand there.

"I just need to figure out how to make it available to everyone. There's a lot of people out there who won't be able to afford this on a regular basis."

This girl's heart was so big that sometimes I wish she cared a little less, so her heart didn't break so much.

Chapter 25

ALEX

Everyone helping with the Christmas party set up started to arrive at the farmhouse throughout the morning, and before long it shifted into organized chaos. Storage bins lined the walls while boxes of decorations covered countertops and half the dining table. Christmas music drifted softly through the speakers while conversations overlapped one another from different rooms. Someone was always asking where something belonged. Someone else was always moving whatever had just been placed five minutes earlier.

The guys handled most of the heavier work while the rest of us worked through details. Garland wrapped around stair rails. Decorations slowly found homes that somehow seemed obvious after twenty minutes of debate. Tables needed rearranged. Centerpieces needed assembled. More than once, I caught myself directing traffic like I was running some kind of small holiday construction site.

The farmhouse slowly started taking shape. Not finished. Not even close. But enough progress that we could finally picture what next week would look like. By lunchtime, we'd managed to get the place at least halfway done, which honestly felt like a miracle considering how much we still had stacked in boxes waiting for attention. Nobody planned food for lunch, so we ordered from the only place that delivered out this way.

When lunch arrived, everyone found places to sit wherever they could—kitchen stools, dining chairs, bar stools, even leaning against counters too tired to care anymore. For a little while decorating stopped, conversations took over, and the farmhouse filled with the kind of noise that somehow made a house feel more like home.

The kids were running and screaming through the house until we finally convinced them to head downstairs and watch a movie before someone broke something.

I pulled Abby and Maggie aside.

"Girls," I whispered dramatically. "I have a huge—you know—problem."

I fanned myself as if I were hot and sweaty trying to get them to catch my drift, so I didn't have to say it out loud.

Feeling overly amorous being pregnant felt like a medical condition.

Maggie immediately frowned.

"What kind of problem?"

Beside her, Abby pressed her lips together so hard I knew she was already figuring it out.

"I think she just told you, Maggie," Abby said.

I pressed my lips together, desperately trying not to laugh.

Maggie blinked. Looked at Abby then to me.

Still nothing.

"I don't get it—" Her eyes widened. "Ohhhh."

The three of us burst into laughter.

"Yep," Maggie said, shaking her head. "That's definitely a thing."

"How's Roman handling your problem?" Abby asked with a grin that immediately made me regret bringing this up.

"How do you think?" I muttered. "He thinks he's hilarious."

"Yeah, well..." Maggie snorted. "I was about to say something supportive, but honestly, I'm too entertained right now."

"Some friends you two are," I said.

"Oh no," Abby said. "We're excellent friends."

"Absolutely," Maggie added. "We're just enjoying your suffering a little."

"Traitors," I mumbled.

Everyone was passing the puppy around and enjoying themselves, and for the first time in a long time, life felt uncomplicated. Christmas music drifted softly through the farmhouse while conversations overlapped from different rooms, laughter carrying down the hallway as people moved from one task to another without much structure but somehow making it work.

The guys piled into Harrison's truck to go get the Christmas tree while Roman's parents unloaded bags of groceries and ingredients in the kitchen. Amelia stood beside them helping unpack everything, the sound of cabinet doors opening and dishes moving blending into the steady hum of holiday chaos filling the house.

Downstairs, the kids had completely taken over the basement. A movie played in the background while occasional laughter drifted up through the floor vents, reminding us they were having the kind of carefree fun kids always seem to create when left to themselves.

The puppy had officially reached his limit for social interaction and curled himself into a tight little ball in his bed, completely worn out from being passed around and loved on all afternoon.

The girls and I grabbed our tea and tincture and slipped outside to the porch swings. The cold December air brushed lightly against my cheeks while the gentle creak of the swings moved us back and forth beneath the soft glow of the outdoor lights. The farmhouse behind us buzzed with warmth and noise, but out here everything felt calmer.

I wrapped both hands around my cup and looked over at them.

"I need to talk to you guys about Tanner."

I paused before continuing to try and read the room so to speak.

"Abby, I'm going to ask for your opinion on this, but my mind is already made up and Maggie, I know what you're going to say already and I really didn't want to do this today, but it's one reason I invited everyone here."

The girls looked worried.

Before I said anything, Amelia came out and interrupted, "Hey girls, can I join?"

"Of course. You may have some insight for me about this as well."

It didn't occur to me we might be leaving Amelia out, or that she might not think she was welcome.

"Jack and Matt called me the other day to let me know Tanner would like to see me. Said he wanted to apologize..." There was a look of shock and terror on the girl's faces. I tried to pretend I didn't see it so I could continue. "...Jack thinks maybe being incarcerated is more than he can handle and wants me to put a good word in for him to get early release..." I had to hurry before one of the girls screamed at me. "...I, for one, think he's just trying to mess with me again."

I felt like Maggie was holding her breath as she slowly shook her head.

"Mags, I know this is tough on you..." I reached over to console her by putting a hand on her arm.

She blurted out before I could finish, "What does Roman think of this with you pregnant and all?"

"Before we found out about the baby, he was going to support my need to see him and tell him I forgave him so I could let him know he wasn't my problem anymore."

"And now?" She raised her voice.

"I don't know. We haven't talked about it again. I asked Jack and Matt to talk to him."

I tried to stay as calm as I could, knowing this really tested our friendship.

"Were you planning to go alone or with someone?" Abby's voice was calm, even though I could hear it shaking a little.

"I wanted to take Jack and Matt with me but have the conversation with Tanner alone. Or alone as it could be. I know they can hear from the other side of the mirror. I clearly would never do this by myself."

"How do you feel about going now with the baby? Are you worried about the stress?" Amelia's thoughtful question struck a nerve with me since all I've been lately is stressed and worried, regardless of Tanner.

"That's a good question. I know it's something I need to do and I feel like the sooner the better, so I can get on with my life."

The girls reluctantly agreed to support my decision, which should help with getting Roman on board. Less stress and worry were my priority for the baby.

***

ROMAN

Jack, Matt, Harrison and I took Harrison's truck to the nursery down the road, where we got all the plants to decorate the porch. We picked up a Christmas tree, mini pine trees for the porch, and Poinsettias for the inside. The whole back of the truck was full. On the ride back to the house, I hesitantly asked the guys if Alex's behavior was normal.

"I have a really weird question. Alex seems to have, how shall I say this, an increased appetite and I'm not talking about food. Is that normal?"

Harrison said, "Yeah, it's pretty annoying to be around, honestly."

Jack admitted, "It's a thing. Abby's the same way. The doctor said it has to do with an increase of blood flow to nurture the baby."

Matt said, "Yeah, Maggie's that way too right now."

All eyes were on Matt.

Jack boomed, "What?"

"Shoot, I didn't mean to let that slip. I'm the one who told Maggie not to say anything yet. It was just harder for us to get pregnant this time, and she's lost a couple really early."

"Well, congrats man. That's great news. Holy crap, the girls are all pregnant at the same time. We really need to get that house now, don't we?"

Things were starting to get really real now.

Harrison chimed in and said, "This better not be contagious. I'm barely ok with proposing to Amelia right now."

Jack turned with a shocked expression. "You're proposing to Amelia?"

"Yes, at the party next week. I'm freaking out."

Matt said, "Damn, that's awesome, Harrison. Congratulations. How does it feel to beat your big brother to the altar?" He put both hands on Harrison's shoulders from the back seat. Harrison laughed and then shoved my shoulder.

"It's pretty unreal, to be honest. This guy likes the white picket fence life and I never saw it coming for me, but when you find the one, you better do everything you can to keep her." I couldn't agree more. Harrison was definitely not beating me to the altar. I can't let her have that baby without us being married first.

"Roman, I guess you already know Sharon Foster is my client, right?" Jack informed me.

"Yeah. What kind of attorney are you for her? Real Estate?" I really had no idea what Jack specialized in. He took on that case for Alex, but that was because she's a family friend.

He smiled and said, "No, divorce." Okay, so he's a divorce attorney.

I wonder if he was Alex's attorney when she divorced Luke.

"Yeah, I met him at dinner last night." I sighed.

"Oh, yeah, what happened? Sharon said you told him you weren't interested in the house."

What a... He's not worth the thought.

"Actually, we're very interested in the house and very interested in making sure Sharon gets more than her fair share of the equity..." Two can play at this game. "...He has something to do with Tanner and he brought that up to Alex when he accosted her outside of the bathroom."

I'm sure he told her a lot of BS.

"What?..." Jack's hands were now on the back of my seat. "...What did he do?" He was on the edge of his seat.

"He just tried to 'negotiate'..." I held up air quotes. "...the sale with her and I got defensive and low balled the offer. He said he loved watching Tanner abuse Alex over and over because he recorded the fight. At that point, I really didn't give a shit about buying the house and basically told him to piss off."

"And you didn't lay his ass out?" Matt asked incredulously.

I sure wanted to.

"It was tempting, but Alex is my priority, and I just wanted to get her out of there." I mentioned honestly. "Alex has pictures of Rick with some woman, though, if you'd like them."

"What kind of pictures and how did she get them?"

I know I've seen her somewhere before.

"He had his hands all over some woman in the bar."

"Ok, well, at this point it may not matter, but if it's the woman Sharon accused him of sleeping with during their marriage, it may be a bargaining chip."

"Consider them yours. Also, I'm willing to offer $1.2 for the house, but only if Sharon gets a 75/25 split of the sale."

Jack agreed, with an "I'll see what I can do."

Jack stopped me on the way into the house. "Roman, there's one more thing I need to talk to you about before we go inside. Actually, Matt and I would both like to discuss it."

I didn't like how this sounded, and I had a feeling I knew what it was about.

I answered before they even asked. "The answer's no. She's pregnant. I don't want her anywhere near that mother..." I took a breath to compose myself. "...when she's not pregnant. I will not let my unborn child near him."

Jack put his hand on my shoulder and gave me an understanding nod. "Look, she's adamant. I'm glad she didn't try to hide it from you. That says a lot. I'd feel the same way if it was Abby. Matt and I will be right there with her." I took a deep breath and slowly exhaled.

"I'm going with her." I pushed my hair back and raked them down my face.

Matt shook his head. "Sorry, that's not going to be possible. They'll only let counsel go with her."

I doubt that's true. I'm sure Alex told them I couldn't go.

"Then no. Why the hell would I put her in that kind of danger?"

"She won't be in any danger..." Jack insisted. "...He'll be shackled to the table. He won't be able to get up or come anywhere near her, and we'll be able to control the whole thing."

So far no one has been able to control any of this situation.

"Sounds like he has all the control. What does he really want, anyway?"

How did this day turn into this? Alex must've invited them to talk me into letting her go.

Matt admitted, "We don't know. It seems like he's having trouble in jail and wants to see if he can make amends with Alex to help him get an early release, maybe."

"Give me a couple of days to think about this."

They agreed and we headed in.

After we finished dinner and decorating, everyone said good night. I snuggled Alex on the couch but never turned the Christmas music off. We turned off all the lights except the Christmas tree. She was leaning; her back to my chest and I was rubbing her stomach—deep in thought.

"Roman, did Matt and Jack talk to you?" She murmured.

***

ALEX

"Alex, I don't like this. This seems like a trap or something," Roman said with his head back and eyes closed. I know I've put him through a lot with this guy and now we're pregnant and I'm sure it's stressing him out, but I've got to do this.

"What kind of trap? For what? What could he possibly be trapping me into?"

"I don't freaking know, but you can't trust the guy." He threw his hands down onto his thighs in frustration.

Making tea seemed like the thing to do, so I pushed up from the couch and shuffled into the kitchen, dragging my now heavy legs with me. I knew there was more to this than some fake apology, but in reality, I wasn't even going there for him. I was going there for myself. Confronting him rather than ignoring his requests, to look him in the eyes and let him know he meant nothing to me, that my future would be beautiful, and that he could do nothing to stop it.

Lost in thought again, Roman walked up behind me, wrapping his arms around my waist, placing his hands protectively on my stomach as he did so often now that there was *"precious cargo"*, as he called it.

"Can I think about this at least? I feel like you're making decisions on your own again. I need to know we're in this together and we can make these decisions in a logical manner and not be so emotional all the time." He calmly breathed the words out into my ear and it was like a relaxing balm to the soul.

I took a deep breath and said, "I would like nothing more than for that to be the case here, but I'm afraid it's all emotion where this is concerned for me and probably for you." He looked stressed but he was doing his best not to lose it on me.

"I understand that and think you're right, but we can try to step back from it and look at it logically, don't you think?"

Logic, huh?

"Okay, what's the logic in this situation?" I turned around and he had me backed against the counter with both arms caging me in.

He laughed and buried his face in the crook of my neck, inhaling deeply.

"I have no idea..." He moaned. "...I personally think it's insane..." He picked his head up, placed his hands on my hips and relaxed as he peered into my eyes. "...But, I also think that it's going to eat at you until you do it..." I could feel him surrendering to the situation. "...It's also going to eat at me to let you go in there without me, but, 'logically', I know nothing is going to happen to you physically. However, mentally or emotionally is what I'm most worried about."

He had a point.

"You're right, if I don't go, it will bother me. To what extent, I don't know, but I don't want or need that kind of stress lingering over me, especially now with the baby..." I laid my head on his chest and rolled my forehead back and forth. "...I think the sooner the better to get this over with." He squeezed my hips tighter, feeling him tensing up again.

"Okay, when?" He responded, dripping with frustration. I snapped my head up in shock.

"Okay?" Surprised was an understatement.

He nodded, with pain written all over his face.

"How about this week whenever Matt and Jack can get it set up?" I asked hopefully.

"Do what you gotta do." Then he dropped his arms and walked out of the room, straight up the stairs.

Chapter 26

ALEX

In the morning, we had breakfast and cleaned up the house in mostly silence, other than a quick good morning greeting and peck on the cheek. We got the puppy all packed up and headed back to the penthouse to get ready for church. I felt like Roman was being really distant with me. Even my usual attempts to seduce him were being met with sudden deadlines.

"We have to hurry. We don't want to be late for church." Oh please, like that's really an issue.

In the car on the ride to church I said, "Roman, are you mad at me for the decision? I thought we agreed."

He groaned and said, "We did, but I've got a bad feeling about it and it's really messing with me."

"Let's not think about it, ok, let's just go to church and have a nice brunch with your family and go home. Maybe see if Tao wants to try to take a walk. I bought him some warm clothes, he should at least strut about in his new gear, don't ya think?" I insisted with a grin.

He faked a smile for me. "Sure. I mean, I'll try to relax about this, but I won't be able to until it's over." I was feeling a little overwhelmed myself.

"Then maybe we can get it scheduled for tomorrow."

But maybe tomorrow is too soon. I'm starting to feel sick.

We pulled up to the church and met everyone at the bottom of the steps and went in together. I had to get up a few times to go out in the lobby because the smell of the incense was making me nauseous. I forgot Roman's parents didn't know I was pregnant yet, so I was surprised at first when Lisette came out and asked if I wasn't feeling well— almost spilling the beans.

"The incense isn't sitting well with me today. Maybe too much fun last night." I offered as an excuse.

She hugged me and asked if I wanted her to stay out there with me. I told her I was fine. After she left, Roman came out.

"Mom sent me, said you looked a little green and I might need to take you home."

I think she was right. The anti-nausea medication wasn't helping even after we left the church.

We decided to just go home and call Matt and Jack to see if we could possibly get that set up tomorrow. I had a feeling the nausea was coming from this situation more so than being pregnant. I didn't want there to be any more secrets between us. I texted Jack and asked him to call me. The phone was ringing with Jack's name on the screen. I answered and he three way'd in Matt.

"Hi Jack. Roman's here too." They both greeted us back.

"Well, I've decided to go see him. I'd like to get that set up for tomorrow if that would work; the sooner the better."

I glanced at Roman who looked like he was in physical pain.

Matt asked, "Roman, I know you said you needed a couple days to think about this...is this going to be okay with you?" His face was in his hands.

"I don't know if I have a choice, really..." He mumbled harshly through his hands before slapping them firmly on the counter. "...It's kind of making me sick but to be honest it's making her sick too, not to do it...as soon as we can get this over with the better and then no more."

That's the plan anyway, *no more*.

***

ROMAN

After talking to Matt and Jack, I felt somewhat better. Not completely better, because I wasn't convinced anything short of canceling this entire ridiculous meeting would accomplish that, but better. They both assured me they'd be with her the entire time, and I believed them. They cared about Alex. Protected her. Looked at her the same way most people looked at family, and knowing she wouldn't be walking into that room alone eased some of the pressure sitting heavy in my chest.

Neither one of them was going to let anything happen to her.

Not if they could help it.

They got back to us later with confirmation and a time scheduled to see him tomorrow. Matt and Jack both got off work at six, which was when Alex agreed to meet them, completely rearranging her evening for what still felt like an utterly ridiculous conversation that never should have needed to happen in the first place.

Of course, being Alex, she planned to cram an entire day's worth of responsibilities into the hours leading up to it. She wanted to make all of her meetings at the office, finalize a few things involving the new wine business, and meet with Amelia to go over details for the gala.

Life kept moving.

Even when you wished it would slow down for five damn minutes.

We barely talked the rest of the night, but I did everything I could to help her relax. I made her a nice warm bubble bath, gave her a massage, cooked her dinner and put on a funny movie that we didn't end up watching and made love instead.

She was so preoccupied we didn't try to take the puppy for a walk like we had planned. In fact, the puppy just slept in his bed more than either of us even held him and I brought him downstairs and let him out for a few minutes.

I thought Alex had gone to bed, so I cleaned up a bit before Mary was scheduled to come in the morning and then went back to the bedroom to find her sitting on the floor crying.

Shit, I knew this was coming.

I calmly sat down on the floor beside her, wrapping my arms around her carefully. I stayed away from asking what was wrong because I already knew. There wasn't anything she needed to explain. She'd been through hell because of this guy, and now she was preparing to sit a few feet away from him and walk back into memories she'd fought hard to survive.

None of this felt fair.

Not for her.

Not after everything.

I still thought this was a bad idea. I probably always would. But I knew where her head was. I knew how she worked. Alex needed answers. Needed closure. Needed to look difficult things directly in the eye instead of spending years wondering what might have happened if she hadn't.

She looked up at me through tear-filled eyes. "Am I crazy to think this is going to bring some kind of closure? What if he doesn't give a shit and keeps coming after me when he gets out? What if I'm totally wasting my time here?" She sobbed as more tears stained her cheeks.

"You don't have to do it..." I pulled her to my chest, trying to comfort her or maybe comfort me. "...You can tell him to go fuck himself." She cried more.

"I know, so why am I doing this?" She really was a mess right now, and I wish I could do something to calm her down.

"I don't know, babe. Only you can answer that. Maybe you're just facing your fears. You said you weren't scared of him anymore. Show him you're not scared. That's all I can think for you to do." I held her tighter, then helped her into bed.

Chapter 27

ALEX

I needed something understated; I thought. Something that wouldn't draw unnecessary attention. I stood in my closet, willing the outfit to appear out of thin air. I finally chose an oversized gray cable-knit sweater, fitted white pants, knee high black leather boots and a black waist length wool coat. While Roman was getting ready, I yelled back towards him to let him know I was taking the puppy for a walk, as I covered him in one of his sweaters and carried him downstairs. He bumbled around, not really going anywhere. I couldn't even tell if he used the bathroom or not. Just as I was turning to bring him in, I caught sight of Amelia at the entrance to the parking garage waving.

"Hey Alex! I need to see my little buddy, Tao. You haven't brought him to play with me in so long."

"You saw him two days ago." I called out as I shook my head, waving back.

"Right, but not to spend a day at work with me. I have a bed and everything for him. Can he please stay with me today?" She was giddy, practically jumping up and down.

"Will it drive Roman crazy if you do?"

"Yes, most definitely."

Poor Roman.

"Okay, then it's settled. I'll bring him and his stuff when I come down." I looked down with a smile, thinking Roman was going to kill me.

Once I got in the office and handed Tao over to Amelia, Roman gave me a look that said I was in trouble, then motioned for me to come into his office.

As soon as I walked in, he said, "Don't give me that innocent face."

"What? I have no idea what you mean?" I rolled my lips, suppressing the laugh that was threatening to escape.

"Now I have to listen to baby talk all damn day." He looked less than enthused.

"She twisted my arm downstairs. I'm not ready for him to be crated all day either. He's too young." I gave him my best puppy dog face and fluttered my eyelashes.

"You don't have puppy dog eyes honey, they're bedroom eyes—I suggest you find another look." I backed up slowly towards the door, batting my my eyelashes.

"Promises promises." Then I winked and bolted out the door.

***

ROMAN

The phone rang, bringing me back to Earth. "Yeah Amelia, what's up?"

"Roman, there's a problem at the Burrow Township project."

"What kind of problem?" I sighed.

We need to keep this project on schedule. It's too big and we have too many investors involved.

"The foreman is on the line. I'm going to put him through."

"Hey Charlie, what's going on?" Charlie was my best foreman—always on time and always doing things right. He was in charge of almost all of my extensive projects.

"Hi Roman, sorry to be the bearer of bad news, but someone vandalized most of the buildings and destroyed a lot of the surrounding property." What the fuck!

"Do we have any idea who did this and why?"

"Not that I'm aware of. The police are down here now and are gonna want to talk to you."

"Ok, I'll be down there in thirty minutes." Shit, this isn't something I was planning for. I texted Alex.

ME: *"Hey honey, I have to go to the construction site for the Riverwalk."*

ALEX: *"Everything Ok?"*

ME: *"Not sure. The police are there. I'll be back in a while and let you know."*

ALEX: *"Ok, be careful."*

ME: *"Always."*

***

ALEX

I hurried down the hall to the first meeting of the day. It was an investor meeting for the non-wine biz. I needed to figure out a name for that already. The 'Non-Wine Biz' is not going to cut it. I know it's going to be an extension of the Kennedy-Jackson Foundation, but it's still going to need its own separate identity. I'll be needing a think tank for that one, I guess.

I walked in to find Grant and Mr. Santoro were already waiting inside talking. Harrison was coming down the hall as well. There were a few other investors already sitting down at the conference table. I said hello to everyone and we got started. We talked a little about the gala we were planning and let them know that the next meeting would be to go over more details about that and for them to have people in mind that we would need to invite. Amelia took notes for me.

Amelia and I went to lunch after to go over ideas for the Gala. She had some amazing ideas and really great connections that we made appointments to go talk to in a few weeks.

"Amelia, do you know why Roman had to go to the Riverwalk site? He said the cops were there." If anyone would know, she would.

Amelia shrugged and said, "The foreman on the project called and said there was a problem and they had to call the police. He didn't say what it was to me, though. I just put him through to Roman." I guess I'll find out later. I hope everything's alright.

Amelia and I ate lunch, then played with Tao before my next appointment, which was an update on the District five renovations and expediting the move-in date for Ella and Darius's house. I don't take much of a lead role on these because it really is Shay and Darius's baby now, but I have enjoyed hearing what's been going on with it. Usually Roman is here to make sure things are on time and the wheels and cogs are all working, but since he had to go to the construction site, I filled in.

Darius looked a little off his game this morning when I saw him across the table, but that's understandable with everything he's had to deal with since Ella's cancer diagnosis. I didn't do the hugging thing today to keep emotions at bay. I just sat quietly off to the side while they got things underway.

This foreman seemed to be getting off on the fact that Roman was absent from this meeting. When Darius started talking about pushing up the date to finish the renovations on the house, the foreman said it wasn't possible. One of the guys that worked for him said it shouldn't be a problem since it was the closest one to completion, but he got snarled at. I could tell Darius was getting irritated so I texted Harrison. I needed some insight into who this guy was. I personally didn't know him and I was getting a vibe that was more standoffish than helpful. I shot a quick text to Amelia, asking for a copy of the contract to be emailed to me. I didn't want to get Roman involved yet, since he was dealing with his own crap. He had mentioned to me that one of his foremen was kind of an asshole and they tended to butt heads. I wondered if this was the guy. I stayed calm and Harrison snuck in, sitting next to me in the corner.

"Tell me about this guy." I whispered.

"That's Donovan Lang. Roman's not a fan. The guy is a total egomaniac. Roman uses him because he does a good job, but he likes to do everything his way in his time and has such a shitty attitude." Okay, this must be the guy.

"Well, this project has a deadline regardless of his personal bullshit, and now the deadline has been moved up. I don't want to step on any toes here, but I know Darius isn't in a good headspace right now with Ella being sick, and I don't like this guy's attitude. I don't want D to get into it with him. What should I do?"

"Kick his ass." I snorted out a laugh.

Donovan said, "Excuse me, back in the corner. Is something funny?" I nudged Harrison with my elbow and took a deep breath.

"No, as a matter of fact, this isn't funny at all..." I sat forward in my chair and squinted. "...Why are you playing games with my CEO right now?" If looks could kill, I believe I'd be in trouble, but I was no stranger to getting shitty looks or giving them.

He looked at Darius, then back at me and said, "Your CEO? Who the hell are you?" Hmmm, I guess I didn't introduce myself when I came in because I was trying to stay out of the way.

"I'm sorry, it must've slipped my mind. I'm Alex Kennedy. Owner of this foundation." That's right, I said owner, asshole. I sat back, crossing my arms and legs.

He smirked and said, "I'm a general contractor for King Construction. I don't work for you." I chuckled and took a deep breath. The arrogance of this jerk is going to be his undoing. I am so versed on asshole antics I could write a fucking book.

"Mr. Lang, have you read the contract or were you more concerned with dollar signs?.." I looked directly at him and raised my eyebrows but didn't give him a second to answer before I continued. "...There is a deadline and there is also a potential to change certain deadlines as we see fit in case of an emergency. If you don't fulfill your part of the contract, our monetary obligation to you, goes away. Do you understand what that means?" I was deadly serious as I stared him down, waiting for his response.

He looked sharply at Harrison and shouted, "What the fuck is this bullshit?" He slammed his hands on the conference table and everyone jerked their heads at him. I on the other hand, didn't flinch.

Harrison said, "What are you looking at me for? Is she right?"

The guy didn't answer.

Harrison looked over at me and asked, "Do you have the contract?"

I softened my gaze as I nodded to Harrison.

"Right here on my laptop. I had Amelia email it to me a few minutes ago."

I put the contract up on the big screen and I scrolled down to the part I just mentioned to Donovan and tapped the screen with the mouse for him to read, then scrolled down to the bottom.

"Is this your signature?"

He continued with the dirty look, flaring his nostrils while his jaw ticked. It was not the sexy way Roman looked. It was more like a bull seeing a red cape.

"Is there going to be a problem getting this one house finished? That's all I'm asking for is this one house, Donovan, done by the end of next week." His guy looked at him and nodded. Clearly it wasn't a problem. The guy was just a jerk.

He shook his head and huffed, "Fine. I can get that one house finished by the end of next week."

He looked absolutely infuriated.

I threw a sweetener in and added, "If it gets done before the new deadline, that's great. If not, that's fine, too. Either way, I'll put a bonus in there for you and your guys. It is Christmas, after all."

I closed the laptop and sat back in the chair, relaxing with a deep breath while I waited for his response.

He gave me an arrogant smirk.

"Can I get that in writing?" He sneered as he crossed his arms over his chest. I wouldn't do business any other way with an asshat like him.

"Of course you can. I'll have the legal team write it up and send it over first thing tomorrow. I don't want you cutting corners to do it either. If you have to neglect other areas of this project to get this done, that's fine. This house is the most important."

How does Roman ever work with this guy?

***

ROMAN

"Charlie, what the hell happened here?"

I looked around at nothing but devastation.

"Roman, I don't know. Some punk kids maybe?"

I walked over to the officers and introduced myself.

The first officer said, "Hello Mr. King. Sorry about this mess. Do you have any idea who would do this?"

I shook my head while trying to come up with a reasonable assumption.

"Maybe disgruntled or displaced residents? I really don't know."

As far as the eye can see, the place was destroyed. My hands were balled up in fists at my side.

"They really trashed the place. We'll write up an incident report for your insurance."

I was in awe of the destruction. How many people did this take?

"Sure, that's fine."

I wandered around for a bit to see if there was any clue at all who would've done this. Charlie and I talked about a game plan and walked the entire property to assess the damage. Obviously, now there was going to be a delay, but hopefully I could get the cops to patrol more in here, so this didn't happen again.

We spent most of the day on the phone with the construction team and the investors, along with the insurance company and a lot of police officers and investigators.

My phone rang on my way back to the car. *I can't believe I've been here all day.* It's already 5:45.

"Hey Grant, what's up?"

"Hi Roman. I just heard some bad news about your Riverwalk project."

"Oh yeah, how'd you hear that?"

What does he know about this and why?

"Well, my guys overheard some people talking about a job they did. They were bragging about how thorough they were and even gave the address, so my guys went and checked it out." I shook my head, knowing this was not just some punk kids.

"Grant, do you know who did this?"

"I do. Looks like your friend Marcus isn't gone after all."

That's the last thing I needed, and the last thing Alex needed. I'm definitely not telling her.

"There's something else."

Of course there is. There always is with him.

"Do I want to hear this, Grant?" *W*

hy can't he just tell me everything and get it over with, so I don't have to be surprised all the damn time? I was already seething about the project. I didn't need this too.

"They overheard one of the guys say the job was to go after the Kennedy bitch's boyfriend."

"So, this isn't just about the King vendetta anymore, is it? Alex opened a real can of worms going after Tanner."

"I'm afraid so, but I still have her under close watch. And one more thing Roman...they know who I am and who the Santoros are."

Oh shit.

"How did that happen? She's going to talk to Tanner tonight. He said he wanted to apologize to her; they thought it was about trying to get early release. What if he's planning to tell her about you?"

"Can you stop her? This isn't how she needs to hear about this."

I didn't think she ever needed to hear about this.

"I don't think I can." I looked down to see a text from Alex saying she had to give the guard her phone.

"Maybe it's just what they thought. He's trying to manipulate her to get out early."

I somehow didn't think that was the case. I also didn't think he believed that either.

I got back to the penthouse where Harrison and Amelia were with the puppy.

Harrison said, "How did it go at the site? I heard it was destroyed."

"It was definitely that." I walked over to the bar and poured a drink.

"That bad, huh?" I wish it were only that bad. I downed one glass and poured another.

"Nope, worse." He came over and poured himself a drink, too.

"What's going on?" I looked at Amelia and back to Harrison.

"Does she know about Grant?" Harrison looked at Amelia, then nodded. I figured he would tell her.

"Okay. Tanner knows about Grant too. He called today to tell me that. Alex is there with Tanner right now. I have a feeling it's not an apology."

"So what if he does tell her..." Harrison said it like it was no big deal. "...She probably won't even believe him. And if she does believe him, so what? Grant isn't that person anymore." I nodded thinking, if it were only that simple where Alex was concerned.

"Do you remember how I reacted when I found out?"

"Uh, yep. Sure do."

"I barely knew the guy, and it bothered me. Alex gets so emotional and hurt when people hide stuff from her. How do you think she's going to take this news when she finds out we've all lied to her and kept this secret from her?"

"How would she know you knew? Grant's not going to tell her."

The laughter that slipped out was not the amused kind.

"Are you kidding me? She'll assume I knew. She's already accused me of knowing more about Grant than she does." I took another sip of bourbon, hoping it would help calm me down.

"Let's just pray he doesn't tell her then." Amelia made it sound so easy. *From your mouth to God's ear.*

Chapter 28

ALEX

J **ACK:** *"We'll pick you up in front of King Construction, we're pulling up in 2 minutes."*

ME: *"Ok, I'll be down in a minute."*

I climbed in the back of Jack's big white Tahoe.

Matt said, "You ready to get this over with?"

"Yes, it's been bugging me all weekend."

I practiced deep breathing techniques I learned at the retreat most of the day.

"Try not to let him upset you in there, okay? You need to think about the baby."

I nodded my head. Jack and Matt were like brothers to me and I knew they would keep me as safe and calm as they could.

"Yeah, I know. I had some tea before I came down— Anti-anxiety. I made a to go cup of calming tea for the ride back."

I patted my bag next to me to make sure I had everything.

"Does that stuff really work?" Jack sounded skeptical.

"So far so good but I haven't really tried it in this kind of situation yet. The closest I came was when you told me he wanted to talk to me. Poor Roman got the brunt of that."

I can't believe I yelled at him like that.

"What do you mean?" Jack asked sincerely.

"I thought about doing a shot of liquor to calm my nerves. It didn't go over well, even though I was half kidding. I yelled at him and he yelled back." They both nodded.

It was quiet for a second before I mentioned, "It turns out the tea does work and so does the puppy for calming both our nerves and we were able to talk about it rather than lose it on each other."

"I guess we should all look into getting some of your tea," Matt insisted.

We laughed, but my nerves were still on edge. My knees were shaking and I was wringing my hands as we were pulling up to the jail.

I hadn't heard from Roman after he told me about the site. He must've been doing damage control, so I texted him right before I went in.

ME: *"Hey babe. Hope everything's ok. I won't have my phone on me. We have to leave all electronics with the guard at the front door. I love you and I'll see you tonight."*

We walked in and I followed Matt and Jack as they stopped and shook hands with almost everyone in the place. I felt like I was in good hands. I sat down on a bench with Matt while Jack talked to the guard. An officer came over to me and was telling me what I could and couldn't do in the room. I wasn't allowed to touch him or provoke him.

I snorted and said, "I think just my presence is going to provoke him."

The officer said, "Would you like someone in the room with you?"

I thought about that for a minute, but I didn't think that would be necessary.

"Isn't he shackled to the floor and the table?" I was biting my lip nervously.

"Yes ma'am. He won't be able to touch you." I wish I could take one more swing at him while I was in there, but if he's shackled to the table, that wouldn't be as much fun. Plus, I had the baby to worry about now too.

"Then there's no need to have anyone in there. We both know you all can hear us, but I think not having someone in there will get this nonsense over with quicker."

He's not going to talk to anyone but me, I know that.

"Nonsense, ma'am? I thought he just wanted to apologize?" I'm sure this guy wasn't that clueless.

"He's a politician's brother, ya know. I doubt anything he's conveyed about this meeting is the truth."

The officer actually laughed.

"Well, if you don't feel safe in there for whatever reason, you just say the words, 'I'm ready' and we'll end it and get you out of there. Although I hear you can take care of yourself with this guy." He smiled and gave me a wink.

"Thank you, I appreciate that."

Thoughts of the fight from hell emerged in my head and left me with an uneasy feeling.

Another guard came out with Jack and said, "Miss Kennedy, are you ready?" As I'll ever be, I guess.

Through the grimy little square window in the door, I could only see the back of his head, a mop of brown hair. A frantic rhythm pounded in my chest; my heart was beating so hard I thought it might burst. I needed to calm down; the tension in my shoulders was unbearable. I wrapped my jacket around us, a thin defense against the world's cruelty, its soft fabric a familiar comfort against my skin.

Jack asked one more time. "Alex, are you sure you want to do this alone? I can go in there with you. Damn it, you don't have to do this at all. I'm starting to get a bad feeling about this."

I shook my head and took a few more deep breaths, thinking he might be right—this is a bad idea.

"It's okay, I'm ready."

Jack and I looked at each other uneasily, and he patted my shoulder to give me whatever encouragement he could.

The guard opened the door and Tanner didn't even turn around. The guard walked me over to the chair and pulled it out for me.

He looked at Tanner and growled, "You better watch it, you hear me?"

Tanner shot him daggers as he walked out of the room. As soon as the door closed, his whole demeanor changed. His face softened and he was smiling. If he wasn't such a piece of garbage, I would think he was a very good looking, attractive, possibly charming guy, but knowing what I know makes him evil and takes away from everything else he might be.

"Hello Tanner."

He smiled at me and damn, it was creepy. I felt like I was in a horror movie right now. I looked around the room with just my eyes to see if something was going to jump out at me.

"Hello Alex. I'm surprised you showed up."

I'm definitely second guessing that decision now. I took slow, deep breaths to get my heart rate back down.

"Me too..." Time to fake some serious control. "...They told me you wanted to apologize. I was a little surprised by that."

"Well, you know me, that's just the kinda guy I am."

No, you're an evil bastard, I thought and I wasn't getting any other vibe than that.

"Really? The apologetic kind, huh? That's hard to believe." Even his laugh was sinister.

"I do have a lot of things to apologize to you for. But first, why did you come here? Just to hear an apology? I doubt it. Did you miss me?.." *Is he trying to make me puke?* "...Were you thinking maybe there could be something between us? I mean, you had it bad for me, didn't you?"

Hmmm, I guess I did have a bit of an obsession with him, but clearly it didn't benefit him in a good way.

"Actually, you're right. I didn't come here to hear an apology. In fact, I don't care what you have to say..." It was time to end this and get the hell out of here. "...I'm here to let you know that I'm done with you. I've washed my hands of you. I forgave you and I'm letting it and you go."

I started to get up, and he burst out in maniacal laughter.

"Oh, darlin'..." That's weird. I don't think I've ever noticed he had an accent before. *Is it Italian?* No. I must be hearing things. "...I have a feeling that what I'm about to say you'll definitely care about..." I definitely don't hear an accent anymore. It must've been my imagination. "...It has to do with a few people you trust who've been lying to you. So much so that your entire career is just an enormous falsehood, among other things. You weren't successful; everything was handed to you on a silver platter..." He smiled and tugged on his wrist chains to put his elbows on the table. "...The only thing real about you is your pretty face. I'm wondering if you didn't use it to get to where you got in business—you know, screw your way to the top. You don't apparently have any other talent."

I could feel the heat rising through my body, but I needed to stay calm. I'm in control here and can leave whenever I want to, remember that.

But what is he talking about? Deep breaths, I told myself. I relaxed my face and forced a smile. I glanced over at the door where I could see the guard, nodding my head slightly to let him know I was okay.

"That didn't sound like much of an apology?" He didn't seem to like that response or reaction.

"I see you've been working on your anger management."

"Lucky for you I have." That wiped the smile off his face, but then it returned with malice.

"Okay, let's start with the apologies then..." He sat back, his posture relaxing. His eyes roaming over me with such judgement. "...I'd like to apologize for not getting to do more than grabbing your ass the first night I met you. I had a lot of dirty ideas in mind that I know someone like you would've enjoyed. Too bad we had an audience in the private room because I really wanted to..." He looked into the two-way mirror and winked. "Do more with a whore like you. I'd also like to apologize for not telling you sooner about your friends—Grant Johnson and The Santoros." Now I know I heard an accent. Especially when he said Santoro.

With that, the door cracked open and the officer looked at me, worried, offering me a thumbs up to check my comfort level. I nodded my head, letting him know I'm still okay, for now. I knew he'd go after me personally, but why is he bringing Grant and The Santoros into this? Who the hell is this guy?

the story began to take on a whole new twist, bringing my attention back to Tanner and something shifted. The air thinned. My chest felt heavy as the anxiety crept in.

What did I just hear? Mafia? Who's in the mafia? I don't know any hitmen.

"What in God's name are you talking about? Grant is not in the Mafia. He is not a hitman. Good lord what is wrong with you?" My face was frozen in shock.

He laughed and said, "His name is Andrea Di Giovanni..." He said that name with a perfect Italian accent. *What is going on here?* "...Personal 'Bodyguard' for the Santoro family of Italy. You can google them. Grant, however, you can't google because he's a ghost. They managed to hide him over the years because of all the people he's killed. I bet you think you're a really good Realtor too?" This was now just a game of screwing with me.

"I don't believe a word of this. You're insane. I thought you were just evil, but you are a whole other level of nuts." I feel like I should just get the hell out of here and I jumped out of my seat.

"I'm not done yet..." He demanded and slammed his hands on the table. I slowly sat back down. I had a morbid curiosity to hear this now. "...Grant had a family back in Italy. A wife and daughter. His daughter Emma looked just like you. They were murdered by one of the rival families. It would seem Grant escaped to the states. Apparently when he met you, he became attached because of how much you resembled his daughter..." This can't be true. This is messed up. "...and he handed you deal after deal letting you believe you had done it all on your own..." I always thought things were too easy for me. "...He probably did it to keep you from sleeping around so much. I'm sure it was hard to associate a slut like you with his daughter. He even broke up your marriage because he didn't like the guy, did you know that?"

I spit out through gritted teeth, "Luke was a cheating piece of shit."

It's getting really hot in here and I can't breathe.

"Doesn't matter Grant's the one that orchestrated the breakup, so you'd divorce him. Then he got you some big apartment deal that led you to King Construction, or should I say Roman King."

Leave Roman out of this you monster. I kept the thought to myself.

I was furious and yelled, "You're lying."

The evil smirk on his face got bigger.

"Am I? How do I know any of that? All you have to do is google the Santoros. They've never hidden who they are. Grant might not exist, but his family did. You can find them on google too."

Maybe I should be looking for you on Google instead.

I gained enough composure to ask, "Why would Grant have pushed me and Roman together?" He looked at me like he was searching for something.

"That is the only mystery here. I have no idea..." He was tapping his fingers on the table staring at me like maybe I knew something. "...I can't wait to find out though."

I could feel the room closing in on me. I needed to get out of there.

"Since all of this is bullshit, we're done here." I yelled "I'm ready!!!!"

The guard opened the door, and I practically ran out to where Jack and Matt were. My legs felt weak like they were about to give out.

Flustered and breathless I managed to huff out, "I need my phone, right now." As soon as we got our phones back, I started googling everything and there it all was in black and white just like he said. I couldn't catch my breath. I started shaking and getting lightheaded. I couldn't even hold my phone anymore and I dropped it and the whole face shattered. Matt and Jack went to help me.

"Leave me alone." My legs gave out and I collapsed to the floor. I heard yelling and then silence as everything went black.

***

"Ms. Kennedy, can you hear me?"

Oh my god it's so bright in here. Where the hell am I?

"My name is Dr. Reynolds. I'm a doctor here in the ER. How are you feeling? Are you in any pain?" I reached up to push the hands away from my eyes.

"No, what happened?"

"It seems you collapsed."

Oh yeah, now I remember.

"How's the baby? Is the baby okay?" He was holding my wrist and watching his watch.

"We're checking the baby as soon as the ultrasound tech gets here with the machine."

I rubbed my stomach with my free hand.

"Your heart rate and blood pressure are a little high."

Well, you go chat it up with a psychopath and see how you feel after.

"I'm not surprised." I admitted flippantly.

"Did something stressful happen?"

I nodded.

"Are you afraid for yourself or your baby?"

I know where this is going. He thinks this was a domestic thing.

"No, we're fine." I'm sure he's heard that one before, too.

"So I don't need to call a counselor or anything?"

"Um, could you actually call my psychologist for me? Dr. King?"

"Lisette King?" He seemed confused.

"Yes, please."

He gave me a worried look, like someone forgot to tell me something or I might have hit my head.

"She doesn't practice anymore, as far as I know." I almost laughed.

"Well, I'm a special patient. I'm carrying her grandchild."

He seemed relieved.

"Okay, I'll have a nurse call her, then."

"Baby, are you okay? What happened?"

Roman looked scared, tired and upset, but I don't care right now. He knows more about Grant than I do, and I know he knew about this.

"Don't baby me right now, you liar. Get out. Telling me I'm good at keeping secrets? I thought we promised no more secrets." I can't look at him right now.

"Excuse me, sir, you're going to have to leave."

Thank you, nurse whoever, for getting him out of here. I think the heart rate monitor just broke. I need to calm down.

"Alex, what can I do for you? Is there something I can get you?" A familiar voice. I could handle Amelia. She looked genuinely concerned. I didn't even notice she'd come in, but I'm really glad she had. I wasn't ok being alone right now.

"Yes, in my purse is the travel mug with my calming tea in it. I need it."

She nodded and grabbed the tea, handing it to me. I drank it as I squeezed her other hand. A few minutes later, I was feeling better, more relaxed. I took several deep breaths. It's a damn good thing I took that forty-five-day rehab vacation.

"Amelia, I need you to be honest with me right now, no matter what."

She kept hold on my hand as she braced herself for my next question.

"Did you know about Grant and the Santoros?" She nodded.

Okay, at least I'm getting some honesty.

"How long?"

Who else knew? I feel like such an idiot.

"Not long. Harrison told me a few weeks ago..." Jesus, Harrison knew too? "...He seemed to have had a lot on his mind and got pretty drunk. When I asked him what was going on he told me. Said it had been weighing on him..." I'll bet it was. "...I tried to get him to encourage Roman to tell you, but he wouldn't."

I shook my head and asked, "So, it's true then? Even after I googled it, I didn't want to believe it. Roman should've told me. Did you know about Grant's family?"

"No, what family? You mean the Santoros?"

She seemed a little quick to answer and nervous. But at this point, I'm skeptical of everyone.

"No. Apparently Grant had a family in Italy that was murdered by another mafia family. His daughter looked like me and that's why Grant felt he needed to be so protective or overprotective of me. Did you know I was being followed around by secret bodyguards 24/7?"

She nodded but didn't offer much else.

"I'm so sorry Alex. I don't know what to say. Roman wasn't doing this to hurt you. He was trying to protect you. According to Harrison, it was eating him up. Grant told him right before the court hearing."

I shouldn't be mad at her. She's just as innocent in all this as I am.

"Why did Grant tell Roman and not me?" I said more to myself than to her.

"I have no idea. Like I said, this all came to me from Harrison. I don't know what anyone really knows, ya know?"

"I'm sorry I brought you into this, Amelia. I shouldn't be asking you to tell me what they confided in you." I just wanted someone to be honest with me.

"It's fine. I told them if you ever asked me, I was going to tell you." I pulled her into a hug.

"Can I please text him and let him know that you and the baby are, ok?"

I nodded.

***

ROMAN

"She freaking threw me out. Called me a liar and said I was keeping secrets. I knew this was going to happen. Damn it, Grant."

With that Grant walks in and I managed to only roll my eyes instead of committing an act of violence.

"I'm so sorry, Roman. I never meant for this to happen. Is she okay?"

Frustration had definitely taken over.

"No Grant, clearly, she's not. I told you to tell her and you wouldn't. Now look what's happened. If anything happens to her or that baby, I hold you responsible."

His eyes went wide and he said, "Baby? Alex is pregnant?" I shook my head.

I didn't mean to tell him that.

"Yeah, Grant she is. We were going to tell everyone at the Christmas party. If that even happens now."

He ran his hands frantically through his hair then got his phone from his pocket and walked out of the building. *Oh great, now what's he doing, planning a hit?* That ought to make things better.

I looked at Amelia and said, "Can you go back there and try to check on her? I don't want her to be alone."

"I'll try." She said with tears in her eyes.

Amelia was gone for a while, so I'm betting she let her stay. Thank God. I sat next to Jack and looked at both of them.

"What happened in there?"

"It was a setup." Matt dropped his head into his hands.

"What do you mean, a setup?"

"Did you know about Grant and the Santoros?" He asked.

I nodded mindlessly.

"Grant asked me not to say anything. He told me when Tanner was released from jail before the hearing. He let me know that he was watching her."

"Watching her, how? Who was watching her?"

Who wasn't watching her?

"He told me it was ex-military snipers; hired as personal bodyguards only she didn't know."

"Are you sure they were just that?"

I had no idea who those guys were.

"No. Not a clue. Only what he told me, and I never met any of them."

"This guy knew a lot of personal stuff," Matt revealed. "...He not only knew who Grant was but that he had a family back in Italy that was murdered by a rival family and that's why Grant left Italy. Supposedly, his daughter looked a lot like Alex and that's the real reason he took Alex under his wing. He said he hand fed her all the deals that catapulted her business and made her the multi-millionaire she is. Said he's been pulling all the strings in her life for the past five years. He had a PI following Luke and he set up that deal for her with the investors on that apartment building apparently so she would meet you." This was all news to me.

"What the hell? What did I have to do with any of this?"

"He didn't know that. Alex, however, had a nervous breakdown in there thinking that you all are in on it and her whole life is somehow not her own and she doesn't trust anyone right now. Not even us."

"Hold on a second, Maggie's texting." Matt said.

MAGGIE: *"Matt, you and Jack get your asses home right now and watch these kids. We need to be with Alex."*

I nodded and the guys left.

"What the hell is going on, Roman?" Maggie came storming into the hospital.

"She won't let me see her. Amelia's been back there with her. Just see if they'll let you go back."

AMELIA: *"She and the baby are okay."*

Jesus, finally. Thank God.

ME: *"Thank you."*

AMELIA: *"She's upset."*

ME: *"I'm sure she is."*

So am I.

ME: *"Abby and Maggie are here."*

AMELIA: *"Ok, I'll let her know."*

Amelia came out right after Abby and Maggie went back there.

"What the hell have I done?" I said.

"I don't know, but you might as well go home because she's not going home with you tonight." Amelia informed me as panic set in.

"Where's she going?"

"She said she was going to stay with Maggie or Abby tonight." I nodded and felt a small sense of relief knowing she'd be with them.

ME: *"I'm going to leave. Can you just let me know that one of you has her, please?"*

ABBY: *"She's good. You can go home. She's coming home with me."*

ME: *"Thank you."*

MAGGIE: *"This is crazy, you know that, right?"*

ME: *"I do, yes. It wasn't my idea not to tell her. It's my fault for not telling her, though. I thought I was doing the right thing. Please tell her I love her."*

MAGGIE: *"I will."*

ABBY: *"We know. We'll tell her."*

***

ALEX

Maggie asked while pushing the hair back from my face, "Honey, are you okay?" I shook my head as the tears poured out.

"Okay, you're coming home with me tonight...." Abby wasn't taking no for an answer, and I wasn't going with Roman anywhere tonight. "...You don't need any more stress. We're going to eat Mac and Cheese and watch rated R movies."

We laughed, but it was short-lived when I wondered if my two best friends knew about this shit, too.

"Did you girls know?"

They looked at each other, baffled.

"Know what?" Abby questioned.

"About what Tanner was going to tell me in there today?"

Confusion bounced between them and I realized they were in the dark about this as well.

"I thought he was apologizing for something," Maggie insisted. "...We thought the stress of all of it was too much and that's why you were here. What the hell happened?"

"Ya know what? We don't need to know that right now..." Abby was in mommy mode, just like she used to do in college. "...Right now, I want to know how the baby is and how you are."

I could see the nurse wheeling the ultrasound machine down the hall.

"You're about to find out. There's the tech now."

I held both the girls' hands while we stared at the baby on the monitor. Our little peanut. After watching the baby and seeing that he or she was doing fine, I told the girls everything Tanner told me.

The doctor released me from the hospital, but the nurse said she wasn't able to get a hold of Dr. King. I'll call her as soon as I get a new phone, I thought.

Jax was already in bed when we got there and Jack hung out in the basement while Abby and I snuggled up on the couch in the living room with a fire blazing in the fireplace, mac and cheese and Hallmark Christmas movies instead of R-rated movies. It sort of resembled my life at the moment. Guy and girl fall in love; guy does something dumb to muck it up and they get back together after the whole thing is worked out.

How am I going to get this worked out?

Abby shoved my shoulder and said, "You know, I think Roman is a victim in this scenario."

"Why do you say that? He could've told me what was going on."

"Ok, let me play devil's advocate for a minute..." She sat back and put on her serious face. Living with an attorney, she must have some pretty good poker faces. "...Let's say he had told you. You told Grant you knew and now your relationship is ruined with Grant and Roman blames himself."

"He'd get over it."

She laughed while saying, "Okay, what if I said that to you? This is no big deal. You'll get over it?"

I rolled my eyes.

"Any other scenarios?" I huffed.

"Yeah, it's not good. What if Roman told you after Grant told him not to and he puts out a hit on Roman?" Both our eyes popped and then we burst out laughing so hard I almost threw my mac and cheese on the floor.

"Give me your phone." I pleaded through the hysterics.

"What do you need my phone for?" I pulled my phone out of my purse and showed her today's casualty. She nodded and handed it over.

***

ROMAN

ALEX: *"Hi".*

ME: *"Hi Abby."*

ALEX: *"It's Alex"*

ME: *"Hey baby, how are you?"*

ALEX: *"Been better."*

ME: *"I'm so sorry. I wanted to tell you. I swear to God I did."*

ALEX: *"Obviously, we need to talk, but tonight's not the night. I need a new phone. Mine shattered at the police station when I dropped it."*

ME: *"Ok, no problem. Do you want me to get you one? Do you want me to pick you up from Abby's tomorrow and we can go together to get you a new one?"*

ALEX: *"Yeah, you can pick me up at noon if that's ok."*

ME: *"I'll see you at noon. I love you. Good night baby, get some rest, please. I'm so sorry."*

ALEX: *"Good night. I love you too."*

At least she's talking to me and she's okay. Damn, I'm lucky she has good friends. Well, I don't know how lucky I am with Grant as her friend.

ME: *"Grant, Alex and the baby are fine. She's staying at Abby's house tonight."*

I don't need him going all mafia right now.

GRANT: *"Thanks for letting me know."*

ME: *"I know you probably want to explain things to her but if you could wait until she reaches out to you, that would be great."*

GRANT: *"Sounds good."*

This didn't seem right. He's usually got a lot more to say than that. I'll just call him. He sent it straight to voicemail. I'm sure he's hurting pretty good right now too.

Chapter 29

ROMAN

I headed to the gym in the morning and took Tao out for a walk. Now I know what Alex was talking about when she said she couldn't tell if he actually went to the bathroom or not. He waddles then stops then waddles some more then stops and that just goes on and on until he's literally made it two feet. He's so damn cute though. I took him back up to the penthouse, put him in his crate and got ready for work.

It was a somber feeling in the office today. Amelia was not her bubbly self.

"Good morning."

"Good morning. Have you talked to Alex?"

She sounded sincere.

"Yeah, she texted me last night from Abby's phone. She's fine."

Amelia exhaled loudly, relieved, I'm sure. She did look a little nervous though.

"Hey, are you alright?" I asked, just to make sure there wasn't something else I needed to know.

She nodded and said, "I hate seeing her go through all this craziness. It never stops, especially with the baby an all."

"Yeah, she's a magnet for this crap."

We both chuckled uncomfortably.

"Are you glad you don't have to lie to her anymore?"

Her eyes pointed down like she wanted to know for more than just the obvious reasons. I was getting the feeling there actually might be something Amelia would like to get off her chest, but that may have to wait for another time. I can't try to figure out both of these women. I'll let Harrison handle Amelia.

"I do feel a sense of relief, but I also know that it's hard to gain trust back once you lose it."

She nodded, worry etched all over her face as I headed into my office.

Harrison came in and sat down in the chair across from my desk. Work had to be my focus, so I'm hoping, he can help me do that.

"So, what's this email I got yesterday about Ella's house from Donovan? Oh, Alex is good, by the way. I'm picking her up at noon from Abby's."

"That's good news. I was going to ask you how she was." He admitted. "I don't know, what does the email say?"

"Something about having this house finished in two weeks is bullshit and the person running it is a total bitch. Is he talking about Shay or Alex?"

Harrison laughed.

"Oh yeah, I almost forgot about that meeting. He was definitely referring to Alex. That was the meeting to talk to expediting the move in date for Ella. Donovan is the foreman on that project. He was basically telling Darius that it wasn't going to happen and that shit gets done when he gets it done—yada yada. Alex set him straight." Oh No. Did they get into a fight in there or something? "...She told him his contract says do it or we find someone else. Even offered bonuses if they complete it on time. The amended contract was emailed to him this morning. So I'm, really, not sure what his problem is other than he didn't enjoy being put in his place by a woman."

"Damn, sorry I missed that meeting." I smiled as I sat back, wishing I had seen Alex in action.

"Yeah, but that guy would've never gone off the rails if you were there. This was way more fun."

That's my girl. Not sure how anyone could think she wasn't a successful businesswoman. So what if Grant helped her get her foot in the door?

After the morning meetings, I headed over to Abby's to pick up Alex. Abby answered the door and gave me a hug.

"She's in the bathroom." She pointed to the door in the hallway behind her.

"How are you? Did you two have some nice bonding time?" I asked sincerely.

"We did. I hope I helped."

"You must've since I'm here to pick her up." She smiled as I glanced at Alex, grabbing her purse off the hall table and walking straight into my arms. I mouthed "thank you" to Abby and guided Alex to the car.

Before I opened the door, I grabbed her face with both hands and kissed her, enveloping her, pulling her tight to my chest to whisper in her ear, "I'm so sorry. I will never keep anything from you again, I promise. I love you so much. I don't want to lose you again."

Low whimpers vibrated my chest as she nodded softly. I got her in the car, stopped at the store to get her a new phone and back to the penthouse.

"Have you eaten?"

I was so concerned about her mental, emotional, and physical health now.

"I had breakfast, but not much."

"Ok, I'm going to run across the street and get you some food. I don't think we have anything that doesn't need to be cooked here." I was hurrying and she grabbed my arm.

"You don't have to do that. I can make something here. I'm fine, Roman, I'm just processing information."

"What do you need me to do for you?" I asked as I pulled her close and planted a soft kiss on her forehead.

"Not whatever this is..." she exclaimed while flailing her arms around as she pushed me away from her.   "...I need you to go back to work because you have a company to run and I'm going to take a shower and put on some sweats, fuzzy slippers and a mud mask, then play with the puppy."

I smiled and said, "Okay, that sounds good. Can I cook you dinner tonight?" She nodded.

I kissed her and headed back to the office.

I picked up the phone and called Donovan to find out what his actual problem was with getting the Jackson house finished.

"This is Donovan." Nasty tone, check.

"It's Roman. I have a question about your email."

He said condescendingly, "Yeah, what is it?" I'm going to freaking fire this guy.

"I'd like you to explain to me please why you would call the owner of the Foundation a bitch."

No need to be nice about it, I guess.

"I was told I'd be dealing with you and Darius, the CEO, not some hoity toity bitch telling me how to do my job." If he were in front of me right now, I believe I would've punched him right in the face and asked forgiveness later or never.

"Donovan, first of all, we don't refer to our clients that way, ever. They pay our bills. Second, I heard she offered your team bonuses. Is that correct?"

He huffed out a breath and said, "Yeah, throwing her fucking money around to let us all know who's in charge is really noble."

"Well, I think I've had enough of this bullshit. If you ever talk to Alex, Ms Kennedy, that way again, I will not only fire you, but you'll have a lot of trouble finding a job in this city ever again. She was more than fair to you, asking you to finish one fucking house and offering your entire team a bonus, which I'm sure they're ecstatic about." His tone definitely deflated after that.

"Fine. I'll get the house finished. Have a good day Roman." I bit my tongue and hung up the phone. This will definitely be the last project I work on with that guy. Harrison was right; he does seem to have a problem with women in authority. I can't have anyone like that around Alex. She exudes a lot of authority, even if she isn't trying to.

***

ALEX

ME: *"Grant, we need to talk."*

ABBY: *"Hey girl. Everything good?"*
ME: *"Yeah, we stopped and got a new phone, so all's right with the world again."*
ABBY: *"LOL, ok good.*
MAGGIE: *"Alex, you home?"*
ME: *"Yep, safe and sound."*
MAGGIE: *"That's what I like to hear."*

Maybe I should send out a group text to everyone I know and say, *"I'M FINE!!!!!"* I swear my life is a never ending drama. I need a vacation for real.

That's it. I'm talking to Roman's travel agent guy and getting that trip booked.

ME: *"Hey babe, can you send me your travel agents' contact info please so I can get us the hell outta here?!"*
ROMAN: *"I'll get it to you in one second..."*
ROMAN: *"Done! I sent it to your email. Where are we going?"*
ME: *"Don't know yet."*
ROMAN: *"Ok I can't wait to hear about it. See you later."*

I spent two hours on the phone with Mark, the travel agent, customizing our fourteen-day private resort trip to Anguilla for the middle of January. For two solid hours, my brain focused on something other than court cases, difficult conversations, business meetings, healing, and all the chaos life seemed determined to throw at us lately. It felt nice. Normal, even. I tried to pay for the trip, but Mark informed me Roman had already arranged payment for whoever handled the booking. Apparently, the man had a plan. Of course he did. Most of the trip had already been mapped out, which honestly shouldn't have surprised me. Roman planned things thoroughly. Occasionally annoyingly so.

Mark did mention there was one day the resort would be closed for a private event, but otherwise we'd have full access to everything. Strange. Who closed an entire resort for a day? I shrugged it off. We'd go explore the island or find something else to do. Not exactly a hardship. I leaned back in my chair after we finished finalizing details and stared out the window for a moment. I hoped Roman didn't mind me taking over the planning. More than anything, though, I needed the distraction. Needed something exciting. Something normal. Because lately life felt so surreal I was beginning to wonder if someone accidentally handed me the script to somebody else's story.

ME: *"Hey Jack. Thanks for letting me crash last night. Sorry for all the drama. Just wanted to inquire if there was anything new as far as the Foster house goes?"*

JACK: *"No worries, you're always welcome, you know that. Can you send me those pictures of Rick and that woman and then write up an FSBO offer to purchase on the house? Roman offered $1.2, is that still on the table?"*

ME: *"Yes, that's still the offer and I'll get that taken care of by the end of the day. Would you like me to email or text those pics to you?"*

JACK: *"Text is fine."*

I texted him the pics I took at the bar, then sent a text to Shay.

ME: *"Hey honey. Sorry about that guy yesterday. Hope he didn't ruffle anyone's feathers."*

SHAY: *"No big deal. You take care of it."*

I was just trying to get things done without causing a fight. Hopefully, it worked.

ME: *"Can you do me a favor? Will you write up an FSBO offer to purchase for me and Roman, please?"*

SHAY: *"Yeah, are you buying something?"*

ME: *"I hope so."*

SHAY: *"Didn't you just buy a house?"*

I laughed, but houses are a good investment regardless, and it was my intention to start investing. This just wasn't exactly what I had in mind.

ME: *"I did, yes. I'll send the info to your email."*

SHAY: *"Ok, sounds good."*

ME: *"Is Grant in the office today?"*

SHAY: *"He came in early and then left. He didn't even talk to anyone. Do you know if everything's ok?"*

ME: *"I'm sure it's fine."*

A response from my earlier text to Grant finally came.

GRANT: *"You're right. We do. Can you meet me for dinner tonight at Giovanni's?"*

ME: *"Yes, if Roman can come."*

GRANT: *"I think that would be for the best."*

ME: *"Will 7 work?"*

GRANT: *"Perfect. See you then."*

Now to disrupt Roman's day, and his plans for cooking me dinner tonight.

ME: *"Hey babe. Hope you're having a good day."*

ROMAN: *"I am now. How are you?"*

ME: *"I'm good. I made us dinner reservations tonight at 7."*

ROMAN: *"You did, huh? Where might we be going? Is it a special occasion? I thought I was cooking for you tonight?"*

Just going to rip the bandage off.

ME: *"Giovanni's."*

ROMAN: *"Hmmm...I guess we're not having dinner alone then, are we?"*

ME: *"Nope."*

ROMAN: *"Okey Dokey."*

***

ROMAN

The door opened and Amelia and Harrison walked in.

"Hey, we're going to cut out of here early. We're going to do some Christmas shopping for the party." Harrison said.

Lost in thought, I responded without effort, "Cool, have a good time."

"Everything okay?" Amelia asked.

"Is it ever?" I smiled and glanced up quickly before finishing up the last bit of what I was doing.

Harrison asked with a sigh, "What's wrong now?"

That sounds like a recurring question.

"You were right about Donovan having an issue with women in charge, and Alex and I are having dinner with Grant tonight."

They both stared at me, worry etched on their faces, and I smiled back, not knowing what tonight might reveal.

"You two have a pleasant evening. I'll see you tomorrow." They said bye and left without saying another word.

I couldn't really wrap my head around this whole conversation we might be having tonight. I mean, what was he going to say to her? What was she going to say to him? I'm at a total loss how I'm any part of this.

The doors to the penthouse opened and Alex was sitting on the floor in a fluffy robe, slippers and some green stuff on her face. I'm guessing it's the mud mask she was talking about earlier, just like she said she'd be. She was playing tug of war with the puppy and a little chew toy. I chuckled at the sight.

"I need calm to be my superpower right now..." She looked up at me wide eyed. "...I'm more nervous about talking to Grant than I was Tanner. Is that weird?"

I know exactly how she felt.

"Do you remember when I told you I was all messed up in the head when you finally moved in with me? You thought there was something wrong with me?"

"I do. Thought you were sick."

"I was sick alright. That was the day Grant told me most of what you heard in there from Tanner."

"Most of?" She had a skeptical look on her face.

"I didn't know anything about his family or feeding you deals or anything that had to do with me..." I said, shaking my head. "...I'm really confused about that and hope that can be clarified this evening."

She took a deep breath and said, "I can't have this conversation with this..." She pointed to her face. "all over my face."

We burst out laughing and I sat on the floor with her, pulling her into my chest, laying my cheek on top of her head in our familiar way.

***

"Are you ready?" I asked cautiously, as we pulled up to the restaurant.

"I'm not sure I'm ever going to be ready to hear any of this. All this time I've thought I was just the biggest fraud, and I was right. I'd actually told myself it wasn't true, and I was starting to believe my own bull; that I did this all myself." I turned her face to look at me and I kissed her.

"Look, I don't care what Grant says he did for you. I don't care what anyone says they did for you. You are not a fraud..." I kept my hands on her face so she had to look in my eyes the entire time, so she'd know I was telling the truth. "...I heard what you did for Darius in that meeting yesterday. No one did that but you. Do you think I got to where I am on my own? My dad walked my ass all the way to the top. In fact, he handed me this company while it was already successful. Does that make me a fraud?"

She sniffed and said, "I hear what you're saying, but I feel like a puppet now. I don't know how to unfeel it."

"Okay, let's just go in there and hear what he has to say for himself and then go home and have a nice, quiet evening." She nodded and I took her hand, leading her into the restaurant.

The very attentive woman who worked the hostess station, most days I came in here, wasn't there today. I don't know why that seems strange to me, but it does. I feel like I've seen her somewhere else recently. We were escorted by one of the male servers and I glanced back to see if she'd reappear and I could get a look at her again to jog my memory. He led us to the private room off the kitchen where Grant and I met for lunch for the first time. When the door opened, the air was sucked right out of my lungs with a gasp, and I'm pretty sure by the look on Alex's face, she felt exactly the same.

Chapter 30

ALEX

I figured we were going to be sitting in some secluded area of the dining room, but I'd never seen this room before. I glanced over at Roman to see if he knew anything about it. The forced smile on his face immediately told me he did.

My stomach tightened.

As the door opened, my mouth fell open slightly and butterflies erupted uncomfortably in my stomach.

What were the Santoros doing here?

Mr. King Sr. too?

Roman's grip tightened around my hand, and suddenly I felt every step we took walking into that room. One by one, everyone slowly stood from their chairs.

Grant reached me first.

He stood and pulled me into a hug, but something felt different. Off. Familiar somehow while also feeling strangely unfamiliar at the same time, like hugging someone I knew while suddenly realizing I didn't know them at all.

The Santoros hugged me next, warm and kind like always, but this time tension pulled tightly through my shoulders knowing what I knew now.

Roman moved through greetings beside me, shaking hands while I quietly watched him. His attention stayed fixed on his father longer than normal. Too long.

Lisette wasn't here and that realization hit harder than I expected because I still hadn't talked to her.

Across the table, Fitz offered me a small smile and lifted his hand in a quiet wave but didn't come around to hug me or shake my hand like everyone else had. I think he knew. Knew I was uncomfortable. Knew I was confused. And somehow—That made it feel worse.

After the initial greetings and drinks were ordered, I couldn't take any more of the awkward silences and meaningless chitchat, like this wasn't weird.

I blurted out, "Okay, so who wants to start?" I glanced around the table to see if anyone wanted to get the ball rolling. When no one volunteered, I chose. The Santoros seemed to be the only ones with nothing to hide, so when no one said anything, I looked straight to Mr. Santoro and asked politely, "Alessandro, I think I'd like to start with you, If that's okay?"

He smiled and responded, "Alexandra, I would be more than happy to address any questions you may have, my dear." Roman nudged my leg, shooting me a worried look. I rested my hand on his knee, understanding immediately what his concerns might be, but we needed to get to the point.

"First, I'd like to think that I'm among friends and anything that I may say or ask isn't going to have any negative repercussions. I've had a lot of unwanted surprises recently, but I've invited all of you into my life because you mean a lot to us and I think we deserve to know what's going on, don't you think?"

That was the nice way of saying, *"You're not going to put a hit out on me now, are you?"*

I waited for everyone's agreement before I continued, "Mr. Santoro, could you please give me a little background on your family." He looked very relaxed and calm, like he explained this all the time—no big deal.

"My family goes back many years in Italy. We started as farmers and shepherds and grew. I was raised in 'the life' as you all refer to it here in America, but I didn't really want that for my own family. Lucia and I built wineries all over Europe and Australia. We stayed away from the unsavory parts of the family business. Even though we weren't part of those businesses, we were still part of the family and needed protecting. Grant or Andrea, as he was known back then, was the head of security for our family. Not just my family, but the entire Santoro family. It's not a life for the faint of heart." He looked towards Grant and said, "Grant, would you like to tell your story?" He shook his head and I'm pretty sure I saw a tear fall. Alessandro continued, "Grant found the love of his life during that time and he got married and had a beautiful daughter, Emma. He was very protective of them and very loyal to our family. We had talked about him getting out and taking his family with him. When Emma was around ten years old, she met a boy around twelve who was on vacation with his family at one of our wineries. It was the cutest puppy love I think we've ever seen." He looked lovingly at his wife. " I'm not sure the boy thought as much about Emma as she did about him, but nonetheless, the parents talked and got to know each other and vowed to keep the kids in contact. They even made a pact that one day their children would marry; kind of a family merger that would help both families achieve their goals. One to not have to work outside of his city for business to be closer to home for his family and the other to get his family out of Italy and this business..." My mouth felt like it was gaping open as I hung on every word of this story. "...That all came crashing down when Grant's wife and daughter were tragically murdered. That ended the pact and the family merger, but I still wanted to get Grant out of Italy and away from this life where he could move on from the memories. We kept in touch with the other family as well..." He turned to Roman's dad and nodded. "...I sent him to the states to find some winery locations and he finally settled in Cincinnati where the Kings lived, and you, Alex."

"What do I have to do with any of that?" I looked at Grant, who was looking down and I inquired, "Grant, do I look like Emma?"

He pulled a picture out of his pocket and handed it to me. I looked at the picture of a girl about fifteen.

"Oh my god..." I handed it to Roman, and his face went pale.

"Dad, I'm going to need you to start talking." I looked at Roman and things were starting to click.

***

ROMAN

I was just a kid. My stomach launched into my throat.

I remember our trips to Italy. I remember Emma, but I never had any feelings for her. If I'm hearing this story straight, my parents were arranging a marriage between me and Emma. This can't be real. Dad said he only built them a real estate office and a restaurant. Most likely the restaurant we were sitting in right now. I looked at my dad the whole time Alessandro was telling the story. He only looked back at me once. After Alessandro was finished with his story, I let my dad know it was his turn and I was not asking.

He took a big sip of his bourbon and said, "I'm sorry, son. I never thought I'd need to explain this. After Emma died, there was nothing more to talk about, or so I thought." I felt like the world had just disappeared and it was just me and my dad right now. I looked up to him. He taught me everything he knew about business. He was so successful and even though most of the time I was kind of scared of him the way he ran his business, I couldn't believe I was sitting here listening to someone tell me my father was making deals with the mafia and promising his child in marriage as a favor or business transaction of sorts.

"Was mom in on this?"

I was furious.

"No. She thought we were crazy because you kids were so young. She didn't know about any of the business deals that kept me from taking the business out of the state."

"What kind of business deals?"

"Nothing for you to worry about..." He said with a stone-faced expression. "...and there's nothing tied to King Construction—those businesses no longer exist." I thought I was going to be sick.

"Dad, what the hell have you done?"

"Look Roman, it was the only way I could give you and your brother the life you have now and be there to help your mother. She had some pretty serious mental illness issues and I needed to be there to help with you boys and her." He looked like he was in actual pain telling this story. As much as I wanted to hear what was wrong with mom, I didn't want him airing her dirty laundry out here, in front of all these people.

"And...?"

There has to be more to this. I turned to Grant to take the spotlight off my father. It was his turn to spill.

Grant finally started talking, but his voice was hoarse and broken. All eyes were on him.

"Six years ago, a very naïve, beautiful young lady walked into my real estate office with her brand-new Realtors license. My heart stopped. I felt like I'd seen a ghost. I'd never believed in reincarnation or even the afterlife until that moment and I felt like I was getting a second chance." He looked adoringly at Alex, and she faked a smile. She looked more scared than anything at the moment.

He continued, "I guess that sounds pretty messed up, but it's the reason I didn't let you into my life. I knew if you came to my house or knew too much, you would think that I had somehow orchestrated all of this. For me, it was fate. I didn't pick Cincinnati because I knew you were here. I picked it because the King's were here. I didn't find you; you found me."

Tears were streaming down Alex's face.

"So, I'm only in the position I'm in right now because you think I'm your deceased daughter?" She said.

"I never thought you were actually my daughter, but yes, in some weird way, I suppose I did. You are so much more than that, Alex. I know you're not my daughter, even though I have thought of you like a daughter since the moment I met you. Yes, I helped you rid yourself of Luke. Did you really want to be stuck in a horrible marriage to him? I doubt that, but I'm sorry for not minding my own business and letting you make that decision for yourself."

He sounded like a father talking to his daughter.

"All of that is weird and kind of creepy, to be honest, but why did Tanner say you all put Roman and I together?" She asked.

Did they still have the pact? I wondered.

I asked cautiously, "Grant, did you and my dad start up that deal again when you found Alex?" Neither of them said a word and I knew right then it was true.

"*How?* Someone start talking." I demanded.

Dad tried to be stern. "First of all, you need to calm down..." *Calm down?* "Grant called me after he hired Alex. Mentioned she was married, but he found some things out and would take care of that. You were engaged to Caitlin at the time, so neither of us could really do anything until Amelia got your mother involved in your breakup with Caitlin."

"I thought mom didn't know about any of this?"

"Like I said, she thought it was a joke until I told her about Alex. That's when she got really protective of you boys and wanted all women away from you. She thought that this was somehow going to bring you trouble. She had no idea who she could trust at that point, and she wasn't particularly fond of me for putting her and our family in this position. That was part of the reason she spent those forty-five days in Bali the first time and quit her practice. When you asked her to start seeing Alex professionally, she thought it would be the best way to keep an eye on the situation this time."

He seemed rather distraught talking about what happened to mom and he took a large sip of his bourbon before adding, "Alex did not fall for your charms like Emma did. Looking back, though, you weren't really that interested in Emma," He looked to me before turning to Alex. "But he sure does love you Alex..." He cleared his throat. "Yes, we pushed you two together for our own selfish reasons, but in the end, it was fate that got you to this moment."

I threw the rest of my bourbon down my throat, then grabbed Alex's hand and left.

***

ALEX

Roman was dragging us to the door, and I pulled my hand away abruptly.

"Stop. We can't just leave. I know you're upset, and God knows, so am I but we need to go back in there and find out what their freaking deal is about. I don't want to be a part of some illegal mafia, who knows what." He was rubbing his face in his hands.

"I need to go throw some water on my face or something before I go back in there. What the fuck?"

"Well, I'm going back in."

He looked freaked out.

"I don't want you in there with them on your own."

I laughed and acknowledged, "Roman, I'm pretty sure it's the scariest place but also the safest place in this entire city right now—for us at least." He rolled his eyes and I headed back while he stormed off to the restrooms.

Lucia, came over to me when I walked in and wrapped her arms around me to whisper in my ear, "I know this must be such a shock for you, but we promise that no one has ever wanted anything but the best for you my dear." I nodded, hugging her back, getting nothing but honest, caring vibes from her.

"I really do believe that. This is rather fantastical and a bit much to have to digest all at once, but I know what loss can do to a person, don't I?" Thinking about what Grant must've endured when he lost his family.

Roman settles back in his chair with another drink in his hand.

I leaned over to him and suggested, "I'll drive home tonight. Can you give me your keys, please?" He handed me his keys, and I put them in my coat pocket.

We decided to eat something before we got into any more discussions. Despite all this information, I needed to think of the baby.

Dinner was incredible, as always, at Giovanni's, and we managed to have less serious conversations before I interrupted the flow.

"I need to clear one more thing out of the air before we leave tonight. Alessandro, Lucia, you both have been very wonderful to Roman and me and going into business with you for my new business is a dream come true, and we are so grateful..." I wanted them to know I was truly thankful for all they've done before I knew any of this. "... Grant, I know you are a major investor in my foundation, and I'd like to thank you as well. Mr. King, Fitz, I love Roman and your family regardless of how we got here. I need to know that for the sake of any future children that there is nothing else going on. No pacts, no deals, no shady transactions...I can't have my children brought up in that kind of black cloud."

Alessandro was the first to speak. "Alexandra, my dear. You are a breath of fresh air in all our lives, and we are just as grateful for you as you are for us. We will never jeopardize you or your family."

I nodded, tears pricking my eyes. Being pregnant wasn't helping to contain the emotion this ordeal was causing.

Grant said, "No, Alex, nothing we've done is illegal and I've never done anything for you that was illegal."

I smiled as Roman looked at his father and Fitz said, "Alex, thank you for loving our son and our family as your own. I'm sorry if any of this hurt you. Neither of you deserved it and I truly thank God that you both found each other, regardless of how you got here."

After dinner, we said our goodbyes and went home. Roman went straight to the liquor cabinet and poured a bourbon. It was still early when I saw a message from Amelia.

AMELIA: *"Just checking in. Roman said you were having dinner at Giovanni's tonight."*

ME: *"We did, yes."*

AMELIA: *"Everything ok?"*

ME: *"I think I'll leave that for Roman to decide."*

AMELIA: *"HMMMM...I don't know how to take that."*

ME: *"Weird question...Did someone ask you to talk to Lisette about breaking up Roman and Caitlin, or did you do that on your own?"*

AMELIA: *"That is a weird question. The day I did it Mr. King Sr. was in the office and told me the best way to do it would be to go through the misses."*

ME: *"Good to know. Ok, I'll talk to you later. Good night."*

AMELIA: *"Good night."*

I let Roman process everything he heard, and I took the dog out for a walk. My phone was buzzing in my pocket, and I pulled it out to see Roman was calling.

"Hey what's up? I'm just downstairs with Tao."

"Please don't leave the house by yourself without telling me." His words were slurred, and I knew he wasn't taking the information well and probably distorting everything he heard with all the alcohol.

"I'll be up in a minute as soon as the puppy is finished." Five minutes later he's outside, grabbing me around my waist after I picked up the puppy, hurrying to usher us into the elevator.

"Roman, what the hell is wrong with you?"

He's losing it.

"We have no idea who they've pissed off."

"What do you mean?"

"I didn't get to tell you about the construction site."

"What are you talking about?"

"It was trashed. Burrow Township was destroyed, and we have to start all over from scratch."

"What the hell happened?"

This was news.

"Marcus Ellington happened. Grant told me his goons overheard the people who did it say they were coming after the Kennedy bitch's boyfriend." I was in shock. That happened the same day Tanner told me about Grant.

"Do you think we're in danger now?"

He nodded frantically. "Why else would Grant have people watching us all the time?"

"Who are these people watching us? I'm going to need to know who they are and where they are at all times."

"You're going to have to talk to Grant about that because I have no idea."

I'll, definitely be doing that in the morning.

Chapter 31

ALEX

Roman pulled the covers up over his head the second the alarm went off, burying himself deeper into the warmth of the blankets with a low groan that told me everything I needed to know.

Someone wasn't feeling the gym this morning. I, however, was. For once, my body felt restless in a productive way instead of an anxious one, and after everything lately, I wasn't about to waste that.

By the time I made my way back upstairs, that familiar post-workout feeling had settled in—the pleasant heaviness in my muscles, my heart no longer racing, and the quiet satisfaction that came from clearing my head before the day had a chance to take hold of it.

The penthouse was still peaceful when I stepped back inside. No movement. No voices. Nothing except the soft hum of the heat coming on. Roman was apparently still fully committed to avoiding responsibility beneath a mountain of blankets. I smiled to myself. Since everything was still quiet, I decided to see if Grant was up. I sent a quick text first.

ME: *"Good morning. I was wondering if you could talk?"*

GRANT: *"Yes."*

I pushed send and he answered on the first ring.

"Good morning, Alex."

"Good morning. I feel so awkward now. This isn't my favorite way to feel, Grant." I wanted him to know how unnerved I really was.

"I'm sure it's not. I wish I could've told you about this in a different way, but that's the way it goes sometimes." I nodded, thinking about everything that we talked about last night and I almost forgot why I was calling.

I cleared my throat and said, "I'm calling because I don't feel comfortable with people following me around that I can't see. It's making me feel paranoid and stressed. Can I at least meet them and know where they are?"

He was silent momentarily before responding. "I'd rather not bring attention to them for both your sake and theirs."

"Why?"

"If no one knows who they are and where they are, they stay safe. Some of them have families, too." I nodded, thinking that was at least understandable, since his family was murdered for the same reason.

"Grant, why do I need protection like this?"

"Marcus and Tanner are bad people, Alex. Their father was a bad person. They were working with corrupt police and other corrupt politicians, —no one stood in their way. You were the first person to stand up to any of them. You ruined Marcus's career in politics and business, regardless of its legality. That judge turned your information over to the authorities and had it investigated. Marcus would be in jail next to his brother right now if they could find him."

I gasped, thinking of what my actions had really created.

"Do you think they'd try to hurt me or Roman?" He was quick to respond.

"Alex, they already have. That's why I'm keeping such a close eye on you."

I can't help but wonder if there's more he's not telling me about these people.

"What do Tanner and Marcus have to do with any of the stuff you told us last night?"

He hesitated before saying, "Nothing. That is a separate situation." *I'm having a hard time believing anything he says now.*

"Well then, how did they find out about it?"

He sighed. "Come to find out that our front of the house manager was somehow involved with Marcus and relaying information back to him."

"I guess that's what Roman meant when he said she seemed extra attentive. She wasn't just checking out his goods." Grant laughed and for once I felt that fatherly bond we had come back.

"I hope you can forgive me and know that I wasn't doing anything to hurt you..." He sounded sad and sincere. "...I care deeply for you and not just because you look like Emma, but because I've grown to love you like a daughter, regardless of that."

Getting choked up was a daily occurrence these days, with the pregnancy.

"I know, Grant. I feel the same way and look forward to seeing you at the Christmas party." I suspected there was more—but what more could there really be?

***

ROMAN

Ugh! Big ass headache. It wasn't my imagination last night, after all. *Damn, my head hurts.*

I rolled over to find the bed empty, and panic hit instantly.

My eyes moved across the room while my brain ran through possibilities I knew were irrational but couldn't stop anyway. Then I noticed the bottle of water sitting on the nightstand beside a few green gel tabs Alex must have left there for me.

Of course she did, I thought as I tried to smile.

I tossed them into my mouth and chased them down with half the bottle of water before pushing myself upright. A pounding headache sat behind my eyes while exhaustion still clung heavily to me as I made my way toward the bedroom door.

Then I heard it. Alex's voice. Faint and somewhere down the hall. Relief moved through me immediately because at least I knew she was in the house. Good. I need to take a shower.

The heat from the water slowly worked tension out of my back, my neck, and the pounding pressure sitting behind my eyes. Steam thickened the glass around me while hot water rolled down my shoulders and disappeared beneath feet planted firmly against dark tile. The shower usually helped clear my head. Usually.

Not today. Thoughts I'd been trying to avoid kept forcing their way back in one by one, circling until they became impossible to ignore. I found myself wondering why I hadn't heard from Mom yet. After everything that had been said the night before, after everything we'd uncovered, I questioned whether she knew more than she let on. When she saw them at the courthouse, I genuinely thought she didn't know who they were. The confusion on her face seemed real. But now? Now I wasn't so sure. Maybe seeing them there caught her off guard. Maybe she forgot. Or maybe she knew more than I realized. that possibility sat heavier than I wanted it to.

Water streamed over my face as I leaned one hand against the tile wall, closing my eyes while pieces continued falling together whether I wanted them to or not. The courthouse felt like a lifetime ago now. If I was twelve when all of this happened, that meant we were talking about nineteen years ago.

Nineteen years. Grant said he immigrated to the United States fifteen years ago. My chest tightened. I dragged a hand across the back of my neck. Was that one of the last pictures he had of his daughter? The one he showed Alex. Damn.

What they did was wrong. Completely messed up. There wasn't any version of this story where it wasn't. But standing here beneath water hot enough to sting my skin, forcing myself to think about it from every angle, I couldn't ignore the other side either. He lost his wife. His daughter. I forced myself to sit in that reality for half a second and immediately regretted it. I didn't know what I'd do if I lost Alex. Or our baby. Much less both. The thought hit so hard it stole the air from my lungs.

Steam wrapped around me while water continued beating steadily against my shoulders, but suddenly none of the heat reached far enough...Harrison. The realization hit hard enough to make me straighten. Did they do the same thing to him? I'd confided in him more times than I could count. Business. Family. Alex. Life. Things I didn't tell anyone else. How the hell was I supposed to have this conversation? I dragged both hands down my face and stared at the tile wall through drifting steam...Just tell him. Because regardless of how uncomfortable it felt, he deserved the truth. Even if this landed harder on me than it ever would on him.

Once we got in the office and resumed business as usual, Harrison came in at lunch.

"Do you want to go out for lunch today or get delivery?"

"Best we get delivery today. How much time do you have for lunch?"

"How much time do I need?" I called out to Amelia to have her order us some sandwiches from across the street.

"You know how I like to tell you things that I can't handle on my own, right?" He laughed, but I could tell it was to cover up something else.

I said, "It's ok, Amelia told Alex that some of that information was a little heavy for you."

He dropped his head and said, "It was kind of funny when you were telling me, but when I got home and thought about what you were saying, it freaked me out."

"I know how you feel. You should've told me that the information I was giving you was too much, though."

"Look Roman, I know I'm just your little brother, but I'm your brother and what happens to you happens to me." I shook my head and put my hands on my face.

"God, I hope not." I said under my breath.

He chuckled and said, "What was that?"

"I have more shit to tell you." I laughed through that one.

His face went blank as he asked, "How the fuck can there be anymore?"

"Oh, you have no idea how much more there really is."

While Amelia and Alex had gone up to the penthouse for lunch, I proceeded to tell Harrison everything that was said last night at dinner. I thought he was going to be sick.

"You don't have to keep any secrets this time. The cat's out of the bag. I just thought you should know."

"Wait, I know I said whatever happens to you happens to me, but do you think they really did this to me, too?"

I shook my head and said, "Thankfully, Grant didn't have any more children." We both laughed but it wasn't really a ha ha kind of laugh. More like relief.

Chapter 32

ALEX

IT was the morning of the Christmas party. We changed into clothes we could mess up while helping get things ready and packed an overnight bag with clothes to change into. We ate a quick breakfast, drank coffee and left for the farmhouse. Amelia and Harrison were meeting us there early to help set up before the caterers arrived. We pulled in at almost the same time and brought everything into the house. I took Amelia up to show her where they'd be sleeping tonight.

When we got upstairs and into the room, Amelia said, "Harrison told me about your dinner."

"The food was good." I said, trying and failing not to find the humor in it now.

"Holy wow." She looked genuinely surprised.

"I know…" I deeply sighed. "…I'm still trying to figure out if it's real or just my imagination. I mean, come on, really? Does that kind of behavior really exist?"

She shook her head and said, "I guess it does."

"I can understand why Lisette would be so protective of her boys." She said under her breath. "Although Caitlin was horrible and needed to go regardless of this little deal they had."

Roman never talked about Caitlin, but apparently no one was a fan.

The caterers got there right at noon and started setting up. The place was decorated to perfection. My mother would've absolutely loved it. There were lights all over the house and all over the yard. The trees had big orbs hanging in them and candy cane lights lining the driveway. There were wreaths and candles in every window. The inside was covered in garland and ornaments. We had stockings on the fireplace filled for the kids. Under the tree were all the presents. Baby announcements in a box by the door that we would hand out at the end of the night. Once I was satisfied we had everything ready, I headed upstairs to shower and change.

I found myself standing in the middle of the room, staring into space. I felt mentally and emotionally exhausted. I heard the door shut and the click of the lock. Roman wrapped his arms around my waist, pulling me in close as he kissed my neck. I turned around in his arms and threaded my hands through his hair, pulling his mouth forcefully to mine. I just needed to feel him and know that he was mine because we wanted each other and not because we were forced on to each other. There was no denying I wanted this man. I loved everything about him.

Everything about the way he was touching me and kissing me let me know that he was desperate to know the same thing. As our clothes hit the floor, he picked me up and carried me to the bed, gently laying me down as he hovered over me. He looked into my eyes with a level of intensity I've never seen from him before.

"I love YOU." He emphasized the you. "…I love you because I do, not because of anyone or anything."

I smiled, knowing that we definitely still had that strong connection to each other. We were together because we were meant to be together. "I love you too, forever."

***

ROMAN

We laid in the bed for a little while talking about the baby before we got up to take a shower and get changed for the party. I got ready first and told her I would meet her downstairs in case any of the guests came early.

I had on a festive red and green plaid shirt with dark blue jeans that Alex had picked out for me and brown dress shoes. When I got downstairs, I started laughing at the sight before me. Harrison was wearing the exact same thing. We looked ridiculous.

I said, "Let me guess, Amelia picked out your outfit?" He nodded and we went and poured ourselves an eggnog with extra bourbon.

About fifteen minutes later, the girls came giggling down the stairs. They were wearing the same outfit as well, only one was green and one was red.

Harrison called up the stairs. "Real cute girls."

"We are, aren't we!" Amelia agreed, flipping her hair. It was definitely more of a statement than a question.

They laughed and Alex exclaimed, "Oh, come on, have a little Christmas spirit! God knows we need it."

She was definitely right about that. Anything to forget the last week.

"I'm going to need another drink if I have to look at you all night and not be able to touch you wearing that dress." She had on a tight long sleeve red sequin dress that came mid thigh and high on the neck with high heels. Amelia's was the same in green. They both looked absolutely stunning.

Alex informed us, "I brought some fuzzy boots down to change into because these heels are not going to make it the entire night."

I saw her foot wobble a little in the heels at the top of the step. She put the boots in the hall closet after she made it down safely. She gave me a knowing smile that we both saw that little wobble.

The first car of the day has arrived; let the party commence.

There was a lot of handshaking, small talk, drinking, and grazing. I don't think I got a chance to really hang out with Alex once the people started showing up. There were friends, family and maybe neighbors that came to check things out; I'm not too sure anymore who all these people are. I thought there were only fifty people coming. This seems more like 100.

"Hey Roman, good to see you." Alex's brother Edward made it with his wife Bianca.

Alex's brother Patrick and his girlfriend Rose and Mr. Kennedy, too. Alex's dad spent most of his time talking to my parents and Grant. Grant showed up with the entire Santoro family; all four of the kids came. It looked like the entire staff of Johnson Realty had shown up as well. Ella and all three of her grandson's were with her. It was a great turnout and the food was amazing.

Alex had taken Tao up to our room and put him to bed so he didn't get overstimulated. She let the kids play with him for a while before she did, but then she told them it was his bedtime. I think she was afraid she wouldn't be able to keep an eye on him with all the people here and didn't want him to get lost or stepped on if someone put him down. I loved watching her be motherly. It solidified my thoughts of wanting a house full of kids.

I joined Alex out on the front porch. She was out there with Maggie, Abby, Amelia, and the guys.

"Hey buddy, great party." Matt waved his bottle of beer at me.

"Uh, thanks, but all the credit goes to Alex and Amelia." They bowed, accepting all that credit.

Jack interrupted in a more serious tone. "I almost forgot. I thought you'd both like to know that after a quick conversation with someone's lawyer, the $1.2 million offer you sent over the other day was accepted. I was in court most of the day yesterday and hadn't had the chance to tell you yet."

Alex blurted out, "Are you serious? We got the house?" Jack nodded, and the girls started screaming. Everyone came running outside, wondering what the heck was going on.

I shook Jack's hand, then Matt's and said, "Howdy neighbors" then I walked over and grabbed Alex, planting my mouth right on hers.

***

ALEX

Oh. My. God. I'm going to be living in my best friends' neighborhood and we're all pregnant together. Holy smokes, it's a real Christmas miracle. After hugging and kissing Roman, I was just overcome with emotion. Abby and Maggie, both saw it on my face, and they grabbed me into a hug and the three of us cried tears of joy that our pact to raise our children as a trio of best friends was going to happen after all. I could only assume that my mother was looking down on me, smiling. I just knew she had a hand in this, even if everyone else said they did.

As the night went on, Harrison was getting sweaty and nervous. I hope he didn't drink too much. I think Roman was monitoring him, just in case.

I asked Amelia, "Where did the guys go?"

I was not privy to what the plans were for fear I might let it slip.

She looked around and shrugged. "I have no idea. Maybe they went to help clean up the Santa station." I looked in and noticed Santa's chair was still there, but everything was gone.

Oh no. I hope he's not flaking out on her.

"Alex, could you come help me for a minute?" Lisette, called from the kitchen. I hadn't had a chance to talk to her tonight for any real length of time, and I wasn't able to get through to her this whole week after all that happened. When I heard how all this stuff affected her, I wasn't going to bring any of it up to her tonight; that's for sure.

I got in the house, stopping at the closet to change my shoes to the fuzzy boots I had deposited in their earlier.

"Hi, what do you need me to do?" I sounded out of breath.

"First, I need to give you a hug." She gave me a big, warm hug and kissed my cheek. She continued, "You look beautiful tonight. Second, I need you to arrange to have all the adult girls sit on Santa's lap and make sure Amelia is last." I smiled and nodded, realizing it was time for the big proposal.

I went around and gathered all the ladies.

"Girls, it's time we tell Santa what we want for Christmas. We need to line up shortest to tallest. Sorry, Amelia, that puts you last. I hope Santa has something left for you."

She laughed and we lined up shortest to tallest.

Finally, Santa made it to his chair. He had a freaking hot elf next to him, too. I tried my best not to laugh at Harrison dressed as Santa and Roman as Buddy the Elf. But how freaking cute.

All the ladies got a quick turn on Harrison's lap, and he whispered in my ear on my very quick turn, "Did you have to find every damn woman in this place?"

I laughed and said, "It needed to be believable." I nudged his stomach with my elbow. He grunted.

Roman handed out candy canes until it was Amelia's turn and she sat on Harrison's lap and he did his best, "Ho, Ho, Ho. What can I get you for Christmas this year, my dear?"

She was giggling as she announced, "World peace."

Santa let out a big Santa laugh and said, "I have just the thing." He helped her up and turned around as I distracted Amelia at Roman's insistence.

Harrison took a box off the Christmas tree and got down on one knee behind her, flipping off his hat and beard, then cleared his throat.

"I can't offer you World Peace..." When she turned around, he had the box open and a beautiful princess cut solitaire diamond sparkling at her. "...But I can offer you peace in our world. Amelia, will you do me the honor of being my wife from this Christmas and every Christmas till forever?"

Her hands flew up to her face and she barely got out the words, "Yes, Santa, yes I'll marry you!!!"

The cheering drowned out the music that was playing through the speakers in the house. That was the perfect ending to the night. I'm so glad Roman told me about it, so I didn't spoil it with news of the baby.

People started leaving and congratulating the newly engaged couple and I handed everyone a card with baby King's announcement and a cute Christmas ornament. The "OH MY GOD!!!" screams and car horns were the perfect ending to the night.

After most everyone left, the only people to stay were Grant and Roman's parents. We sat in the living room with the Christmas tree and the fireplace roaring. I looked at Amelia's ring, feeling so much happiness and joy for her. Harrison did a great job keeping it together. Roman had his arm wrapped around me and Mr. and Mrs. King were cuddled up on one end of one couch with Grant on the other. Roman, me, Harrison and Amelia were on the other couch. The silence was deafening even with the Christmas music playing.

Finally, Harrison blurted out, "I have to know if you all did this to me, too?" There was a short awkward silence.

Fitz said with a little bit of a shakiness to his voice, "No, Harrison." Lisette got up and went out to the kitchen and Roman started to get up to follow her and I put my hand on his arm.

I whispered, "Let me, please." He nodded, and I followed Lisette.

The kitchen was far enough away from the living room so we could talk without being overheard. I gave her a hug and asked if she got her card yet. She said she hadn't.

"Even though everyone got the same gift, it's more special to some of us. I'll go get yours." I came back and handed her the card with the star ornament attached.

She held it up and said, "It's beautiful." It was a Swarovski Crystal star.

"That's not the gift." She opened the card and took a deep breath. The outside of the card read, "And unto us a child is born" there was a picture of the manger with the star of David over it. She smiled and opened it up as tears rolled down her cheeks when she saw the ultrasound picture. She turned to me, wrapping me in her arms.

"Oh my god, I'm so happy for you and Roman..." She was now full on crying. I hope these were tears of joy. "...I'm so sorry for everything you went through and everything that's happened. I'm so sorry I couldn't be there for you when they decided to tell you that awful news."

This wasn't supposed to happen. Those are not tears of joy. This was supposed to be cheerful news. I waved to Roman to come over.

He hurried over and said, "Mom, are you okay?" She shook her head, forcing out a smile.

"I'm better than okay, Roman. My boys are with wonderful women and I'm going to be a grandma. How could I be anything other than happy?" He pulled his mom into his arms and gave me a look like he didn't believe what she just said. He grabbed a tea bag off the counter and looked at me.

Good idea babe, I'll make her some tea and some calming tincture.

After I made the tea, I walked back out to the living room as Roman guided his mom over to the dining room table.

***

ROMAN

I stood there, letting mom cry while Alex made her tea, then I took her to talk in private.

I hope this freaking tea really is magic.

She drank her tea and said, "This has an interesting taste to it, doesn't it?"

"Yeah, Alex added the calming tincture to your tea. She said it has a strong taste, but not always good. That's why she wants to drown out the taste with other flavors like that of wine without the alcohol."

"That's incredible." Her entire face relaxed and lit up.

"Yeah, it's really cool." I'm glad she was excited for her.

"No, I mean, I can feel the calm come over me."

I guess this stuff could really be a magic potion.

I genuinely asked, "Mom, are you really okay?" It looked like she felt better now.

"Roman, I'm going to be fine. I'll have a wedding to help plan and a grandbaby to spoil." I smiled, hoping she wasn't blowing smoke up my ass, but it seemed like she really was okay at the moment.

"You'd tell me if you weren't, right? I heard some things in there from dad I wasn't aware of."

Now she looked pissed. *Oops, maybe I shouldn't have brought that up.*

"I'm sorry you had to hear about any of that. It's almost laughable that I'm the one diagnosed with a mental illness, and that's the kind of shit they've pulled." Damn, I don't think I've ever heard my mom talk like this before.

Cautiously, I asked, "What exactly were you diagnosed with?"

"I have depression on top of all the empathy I have. It happened after you were born. It was called postpartum depression. I couldn't take care of you and wouldn't let anyone else take care of you either. Your dad tried his best to stay home with me and help, but he had to go to work and I wouldn't let him hire anyone to help. Once it subsided, I was better, but then I got pregnant with Harrison and the same thing happened. That's why we only had the two of you. I figured it was gone after that, but during my years as a psychologist I was just absorbing all the negativity, and it was causing severe depression." She started crying again. I had never heard this story before. I had no idea. I can only imagine how hard it was for her to listen to all those problems and try to raise two boys who had their own problems.

"It was probably for the best that you stopped after two. We weren't the easiest, from what I remember. I'm sorry, mom, I never knew." She shook it off like it was in the past.

"Well, let's not rehash those times. Let's get back to everyone and then we'll say goodnight." I didn't bother to bring up anymore about the conversation from the other night. I'm sure that was weighing on her as well.

I walked mom back out to the living room and my dad took her and Grant home after saying goodnight to everyone. Now it was just the four of us and the puppy who was snuggled up in Alex's arms.

***

ALEX

When I sat back down, everyone was sitting in a frosty silence. I decided to chip the ice.

"So, Fitz, I'm pretty sure you're the only one who hasn't heard yet, but Roman and I are having a baby." His eyes went wide.

"Alex, that's the best Christmas present you could've ever given us." I'm so glad that was his reaction. Just hoping he's not going to try to plan this little one's future.

"Let's just enjoy the rest of the night and look forward to more happy times, with no more surprises, unless they're good ones."

Everyone agreed as Roman, and his mom came back over to join the group.

When everyone left, the four of us let out a big group sigh and burst into laughter.

Amelia said, "At least they had good taste setting you up with Alex, Roman."

He smiled and said, "They sure did. Boy, did she get lucky." I smacked his arm.

"Hey now. I think you got the better end of the deal." The more we joked about it, the quieter Harrison got.

He left the couch for the kitchen and poured himself another healthy sized bourbon.

"Let me talk to him for a minute. He was there for me during a pretty dark time. I'd like to repay the favor." Roman and Amelia smiled and nodded as I went out to the kitchen, putting my arm around my future baby uncle.

He turned and hugged me, whispering in my ear, "I used to think you were the most fucked up person I'd ever met until this." I laughed, thinking how right he was.

"Harrison, I didn't know this was affecting you the way it has. Might be because we've been extremely self-absorbed."

"Well, you're pretty much at the center of everything, whether you want to be or not." I looked up at the ceiling and exhaled.

"I don't wish it upon anyone." He looked like I felt—exhausted.

"I'm sure you don't. Try to keep it away from me and Amelia." We chuckled and I hugged him before we sat back down.

Amelia looked a little uneasy now, however.

Harrison gave his brother a little brotherly poke. "You know Roman, I really thought you'd be married before me."

Roman rolled his eyes and said, "I would've been if Amelia hadn't ruined it."

Amelia laughed and said, "You mean you'd already have one divorce if it weren't for me."

I laughed and said, "Thank God for Amelia then, because divorce isn't something that is easily forgotten."

Roman wrapped his arm around me, kissing the top of my head. Marriage scared me now because divorce scared me so much more.

***

ROMAN

I looked over at Amelia and said, "Has it always been this complicated working for me, or is this new?"

She laughed softly before shaking her head. "Harrison is pretty dramatic even when there's not something going on, to be honest. But..." She paused for a second. "I've seen a new side to him through all this craziness. I feel like he's matured through it instead of letting it overwhelm him."

I scrunched my brows, not entirely sure how to take that.

"Is that why you agreed to marry him?" I asked. "Do you think you would've said yes before?"

"I don't think he would've asked before." A small smile crossed her face. "He knew he wasn't ready before..." Her voice lowered slightly as she added, "...He had that going for him, at least."

That felt like an understatement. I studied her for a second. Maybe longer than I should have.

"I may be a little paranoid," I admitted, "but is there something going on with you I should know about? I'm getting a weird vibe from you whenever you're around Grant."

Something shifted in her expression. Nervousness. Or maybe I imagined it. At this point, after everything that had happened lately, I wasn't entirely sure I trusted my instincts the way I used to.

"I don't think so," she said carefully. "You've heard a lot of stories lately. I can't even imagine how I'd feel if I were in your position."

The answer felt polished. Maybe rehearsed. Or maybe I'd officially crossed into overthinking territory.

Honestly, who was I to decide what felt real anymore?

I simply nodded and shifted my attention toward Alex and Harrison as they made their way back over.

Later that night, after we finally climbed into bed, I wrapped my arms around Alex while we talked quietly about nothing important. Small things. Ordinary things. The kind of conversations that somehow mattered most.

I thought about bringing up Amelia. Then decided against it as the house fell silent around us while sleep slowly pulled us under.

Chapter 33

ALEX

We spent the morning making love before meeting Amelia and Harrison downstairs for breakfast. When we made our way into the kitchen, there was food everywhere. Plates covered the counters. The smell of bacon and coffee filled the space while sunlight poured through the windows, giving everything that warm Sunday morning feeling that made you want to slow down and stay awhile.

Amelia smiled when she saw us. "This is what we do on Sundays when we don't do brunch at the King house. Brunch is my favorite."

"I'm beginning to see why," I said.

I fixed myself a plate with waffles, eggs, and bacon along with a Virgin Mary while everyone settled around the kitchen talking about nothing important and somehow everything important at the same time.

After breakfast, we took Tao for a walk around the property before packing up to head home. The cool air carried that quiet stillness that comes with late fall edging toward winter. Tao seemed like he was finally getting used to walks. He'd trot along confidently for a while, then suddenly decide life was too difficult and want to be carried, only to change his mind again a few minutes later.

As we walked, my brain kept building lists.

Santoros.

Call Melati.

Get the contact information for her friends in Ohio.

Meet about the property.

Figure out the herbs.

Figure out staffing.

Figure out timelines.

The list kept growing. It felt exciting. Overwhelming yet necessary.

By the time we got back to the house, I already knew the first thing I needed to do when we got home was sit down and organize everything before my brain lost track of half of it.

We cleaned up, locked the house, and headed home. The ride back felt quieter than normal. As soon as Roman pulled into the garage, he looked over at me.

"Alex, is everything okay? You were really quiet on the ride home."

I let out a long breath.

"I'm good. Just thinking about everything I need to get started on and trying not to forget anything. I'm so forgetful lately and I have so much to get done."

He laughed softly.

"Understandable. But don't forget you have a ton of help. Feel free to delegate."

"I know." I smiled. "But you know me. I like to know everything that's going on."

"Unfortunately," he muttered.

"Hey."

"I'm kidding."

Mostly.

Once we got upstairs and unpacked, we took Tao down to the river. The crisp air brushed against my cheeks while he wandered beside us, growing more confident with every walk. He still wanted to be carried after a little while, but then he'd decide he was perfectly capable again, and the cycle would repeat.

We stopped at the swings with Tao in our laps. The river moved quietly beyond us. Wind stirred lightly through the trees. For a minute everything felt normal. Then panic found me anyway.

I looked over at Roman.

"You know we just did something normal." My voice felt smaller than I intended. "We went for a walk and now I'm panicking."

"Why?" he asked.

"Because there are lunatics out there trying to hurt us and God only knows what—or who—is watching us. I don't feel like my life is my own anymore."

"Yeah," he said quietly. "It is kind of surreal to think about." His hand moved over mine. "I'm guessing if we're being watched, we're safe though, right? I just hate thinking someone out there is risking their own life for us."

"I know." I stared toward the river. "I feel the same way. I think I'm more upset there's a need for it at all. Why would anyone want to hurt either of us? What was all this even about? Power? Revenge? If that's really it..." I shook my head. "That's a sad way to live."

He pulled me closer.

"You're right," he said quietly. "Someone like that could never be happy. No amount of money. No amount of power. It would never be enough."

As if the universe heard him and decided we'd had enough peace for one afternoon—

My phone rang.

Grant.

His name illuminated the screen.

***

ROMAN

"Hi Grant. Is this a private call? We're out on a walk. Can I put you on speaker?" He agreed and she put him on speaker.

"Hi Grant." I said to make sure he knew she was safe and I was with her.

He said, "Hi you two. Sorry to bother you on your walk, but I feel like you should know this information." Matt was calling on my phone and Jack was calling on Alex's phone too.

"Grant, Matt's calling me so I'm going to answer this." He said ok and I walked a few feet away holding the puppy in one hand, answering the phone in the other. I glanced back at Alex to make sure I had her in my sights and didn't get too far.

"Hey Matt, what's up?"

"It's not good. Tanner hung himself in jail this morning." I swallowed hard, whipping my head around to get a glimpse of Alex to make sure she was alright.

"Matt, was it a suicide?" I kept my gaze on Alex for any reactions she might have.

"It definitely looks that way." I couldn't bring myself to believe that it was a coincidence that Grant was the first to pass along this news.

"Let me call you back. I need to get over to Alex and see what she's heard." We hung up and I hurried back over to Alex, whose eyes were glazed over and she had tears streaming down her face. Her phone was now hanging down beside her in her hand.

I cautiously asked, "Alex, what did Grant tell you?"

"That Tanner killed himself." She said through tears. Ok, so he's saying it was suicide. I'm not going to let her mind wander to where mine is.

"Roman..." She looked at me with big, worried eyes. "...Do you think Grant did this?" Shit, too late.

"No babe, I don't. I talked to Matt and even he said the guards, and everyone think it was suicide. He had mentioned that Tanner wasn't doing too good in there." She fell into my arms and I held her and the puppy tight.

"Ok, come on, we need to get you home." She nodded, and we walked back to the penthouse.

She went straight to the kitchen and started making some tea.

Her phone was ringing and she looked through me and said, "It's Maggie and Abby. I'm going to take this back in the bedroom, then I'm going to soak in the tub."

"Do you want me to get it ready for you?" She shook her head no, gave me a weak smile, and dragged her feet back to the bedroom.

I sent a text to Harrison to let him know what was going on.

ME: *"Dude, you're never going to believe what happened."*

HARRISON: *"Oh, you mean like Tanner killing himself in jail?"*
ME: *"WTF!"*
HARRISON: *"It's all over the news. Is Alex ok?"* I hit the call button and Harrison picked right up.

"Good lord, what next? I guess I shouldn't say that if I don't really want there to be a something next, if this is what we keep getting." Harrison started laughing.

"Hey, you don't think..." I cut him off.

"No, I don't and I don't want anyone else thinking it either, okay?" I know exactly what he was suggesting.

"Okay, Okay. I take it that's already crossed your mind?"

"Hell yeah it has. Wouldn't you after the bullshit we found out?" I sounded maddened.

"That was the first thought in my head and even if they rule it a suicide, I'm not too sure I believe it. That guy was pretty narcissistic, and those kinds of people don't just kill themselves. He probably thought he would somehow get out." I had to agree with his logic but I was still going with the fact that everyone has told me it was a suicide and that is all I care to believe, for Alex's sake; and mine.

I grabbed a beer and turned on the TV to quiet my mind, but the news was on and the first thing on the screen was news of Tanner's demise. I didn't even hear Alex come into the living room until I heard her start crying. I sat my beer down and walked over, engulfing her in my arms as I guided her to sit on the couch with me. I changed the channel, holding her tight.

She sobbed. "Why am I crying?"

"Because you're not a monster and even though he was, you still care about what happened to him. He could've made better choices in life. To think that the choices he made in his were his only options; now that truly is sad." I asked her if she wanted more tea, but it seemed even the tea wouldn't be enough for this. I ended up turning off the TV and playing Christmas music instead.

***

ALEX
I walked like a zombie to the bedroom as I dialed the girls.

Maggie answered first, "Hey honey, you okay?" I stayed silent for a good minute.

Abby said, "Alex, girl, talk to us."

"I don't know what I am. I'm so many things right now, you know? I'm pregnant. I'm in the middle of a million projects. I'm Roman's girlfriend because of a pact by the mafia. I'm being watched by who knows who. I'm the girl who put Tanner Ellington in jail, and now he's dead. What does that make me now?" I was staring at the wall, waiting for some weird story of my life to pop up on it like a movie reel.

Maggie said, "First of all, what he did to himself in jail is not your fault. In fact, every damn thing he did was his fault, not yours. It had nothing to do with you. And what did you just say about you and Roman?" I started crying.

Abby said, "Honey, do you need us to come over? Is Roman there?"

I caught my breath and sniffled. "I'm just going to take a bath and try to relax. Roman is out in the living room. How did all of this happen? Why are people so damn crazy? Why was I so crazy? I'll call you later." The girls assured me I wasn't crazy before we hung up, but I wasn't really looking for reassurance.

They sent a text in the group chat to let me know we were officially having a girls' day after Christmas to help get my mind off everything that had happened lately. Maggie was also planning a New Year's Eve party at her house, which honestly felt impossible to think about right now. New Year's Eve. New beginnings. Fresh starts. My life felt like it had hit fast forward and pause at the exact same time.

I soaked in the tub with a cup of tea resting nearby while warmth wrapped around muscles I hadn't realized were still carrying tension. Steam drifted softly through the bathroom while the quiet gave my thoughts too much room to wander. For a few moments, calm finally found me.

Or at least I thought it did.

Wrapped in my robe afterward, hair still damp and skin warm from the bath, I made my way toward the living room.

Then I saw it. Tanner. Everywhere. The television glowed across the room while headlines and footage immediately pulled the air from my lungs. Tears hit before I even realized they were coming, and once they started, the sobs followed right behind them.

"Seriously?" I whispered to myself.

Was this hormones? Exhaustion? Stress? Or was I just going to spend the rest of my life crying over everything now?

Christmas music drifted softly through the penthouse—the playlist Roman turned on earlier filling the quiet—but my brain wouldn't stay there. It kept circling back to Tanner again.

How was it possible that someone could take up so much space in your head even after they were gone?

What did this mean now? For us. For our life. For our safety.

Did we even still need protection?

Were these bodyguards—security—whatever we were calling them now—still necessary? Was the threat gone? Or had this created another ripple I couldn't see yet?

My fingers tightened around the edge of my robe. I thought baths were supposed to calm people down. Apparently, mine had expired early.

I looked toward the kitchen. Yeah. I was definitely going to need more tea.

Chapter 34

ROMAN

The alarm went off along with both of our phones blowing up.

Now what?

Dad's calling me, I realized. I looked at the clock…5am…I better get this.

I couldn't see who was calling Alex, but she answered and went into the bathroom. I was looking at my phone trying to figure out why I couldn't shut off my phone alarm when I realized it was actually the alarm for the building blaring.

"Dad, what's going on?" I rubbed my eyes because I was barely awake and felt exhausted.

"Son, are you and Alex at the penthouse?" He asked, sounding more worried than I've ever heard him.

"Yeah, why?" I didn't mention I thought the alarm was going off though.

"Stay there. We need to talk." I really hate hearing those words now.

"What the hell is going on?"

"Just stay in the house and don't let anyone on that elevator if they don't have a code. Text Harrison and Amelia and tell them to stay away from the building."

"Dad, you're freaking me out."

"I know and I'm sorry but just stay put. I'll be there soon. The police should be downstairs talking with your security."

Anxiety was replaced by fear when Alex came out of the bathroom, her mouth hanging open, looking absolutely terrified. I crossed the room to her and took her in my arms.

"Baby, who was that on the phone?"

"Grant." She looked like she was in shock.

"What did he say?" I asked a little bit louder than I meant to because of the building alarms, but he didn't respond.

I grabbed her by the shoulders and asked more assertively, "Baby, what did he say?"

That noise is driving me crazy.

I opened an app on my phone and stabbed at the button to shut off the alarm.

She looked into my eyes, and I saw horror swirling, "Someone tried to kill us."

My chest tightened and my throat practically closed with the size of the lump that formed.

"Did he say how?" My voice was shaking and hoarse no matter how hard I tried to control it.

Before she had a chance to respond, I dialed Grant.

"Roman?" Grant sounded scared for once.

"Tell me right now, what the hell is going on?" I growled and moved away from Alex but didn't let go of her hand.

"They set bombs in the garage and in the lobby; security handled it."

I sat down on the edge of the bed, pulling Alex on to my lap as she clutched me tightly around the neck. I possessively clung to her before putting the phone back to my ear.

"Grant, are you on your way here with my dad?"

"Yes. We should be there in a few minutes. We're going to bring some of the guys up for you to meet. They're going to be your personal bodyguards until they can find Marcus." I hung up the phone without saying another word, dropping it on the floor. I buried my face in her chest in an attempt to quell this overwhelming sensation I had no control over protecting my family.

She was rubbing my head and asked calmly, "Roman, what did he say?"

I just moaned because I didn't want to tell her any of this and put this kind of stress on her and the baby.

"Grant and my dad are on their way here. They're going to introduce us to our new bodyguards." She either took it surprisingly well or this was the calm before the storm.

"At least we'll be able to see them now and won't have to wonder where they are and if they're going to be there when we need them."

That was a surprising revelation that she wanted them to protect us, but she sounded extra pissed now.

We had some tea in the kitchen while we waited for them. I thought I should test out the tinctures at this point.

Damn, they really have a profound effect on stress, which is pretty amazing.

The elevator doors opened and six people got out, including Grant and my dad. My anxiety soared as I watched them walk in. Four strangers, completely obscured by black clothing and baseball caps, stood before us. Their swat gear, body armor, and large caliber firearms, made them look ready for anything. Alex and I were introduced to the men who were now our full-time security until this bullshit was over. We were informed that the police would arrive soon after they finished processing the crime scene.

Alex was watching everyone like a hawk until she finally said, "Ok, so who are they? Who do you have in custody?"

One of the guards said, "They were just some local thugs. There is a kid from the Burrow Township community in custody. Said he knows you." He was looking at Alex.

"The only kids I know from there are Ella's kids. Is his last name Jackson?" The guy shrugged his shoulders.

"Not sure ma'am." He continued, "He made a strange comment about having pulled a knife on you once? Are you familiar with that?"

She took a deep breath and said, "Yes. I know the kid. Sadly, I had a feeling he wasn't one of the fixable ones." My heart sank as her face fell. I remembered that day well.

He nodded and said, "Yeah, unfortunately we see that a lot. I'm sorry. How did you get out of the knife conflict?"

"I had help." She almost seemed upset she had to admit that.

The elevator door opened again and in walks the police officers. Officer Lewis, from the case with Tanner, was with them and she came over and shook our hands.

She said, "I thought you might be more comfortable with me being here, Alex."

Alex nodded and said, "Thank you. Can you tell me anything about what happened?" I asked her if she was going to be alright without me for a minute and I left her alone to talk to officer Lewis.

I made my way over to talk to my dad, Grant, and the other officers. They introduced themselves and shook my hand, asking if we were aware of anything that had gone on downstairs.

I said, "No, we didn't know anything until the phone calls this morning. What time did all of this happen?"

One of the security guards said, "We saw unusual activity around three am. There are normally just two of us watching, but we noticed more movement than normal, so we called for backup. We all have bomb training, but there were about six guys with bags all dressed in black with their faces covered. They seemed familiar with your camera locations and the structure of the building because of the location of the bombs. My guess is they'd been in here before and had some kind of knowledge of building demolition. We neutralized the threat immediately and found all the bombs and diffused them. The kid was hiding behind a car crying, so we zip tied him and waited for police."

"You called the police after killing five guys?" My eyes were wide with surprise. I mean, at this point, anything's on the table, right?

"Roman, it's what we do. We aren't mercenaries, thugs or assassins."

I looked over at the police officers and one of them confirmed. "Yes, they're registered with the department and have the authority to neutralize a threat with force if necessary. Clearly, this situation was a necessity. Obviously, they have a clear picture of the lines they may cross or that kid would be dead." I had to admit that I may have been wrong about who these guys were.

***

ALEX

"Detective, I didn't think I'd ever see you again and I was ok with that."
She laughed. My eyes scanned back and forth between her and Roman
across the room.

"I know, same here. How are you after the fight and your vacation?"
She winked and patted my shoulder.

"Oh yeah, my vacation..." I rolled my eyes and smiled, thinking about
it. "...It was therapeutic, to say the least. I'm doing really well and we're
having a baby." I put my hand protectively on my stomach. Thought I
could throw in a little good news for once. She congratulated me.

"So, let me tell you what I know so far."

I interrupted and asked, "Did they bring you for my benefit?" I felt like
everyone was always cautious about my reactions.

She smiled and said, "Actually, I offered to come, since it seemed related
to Tanner. I think most of the guys are pretty intimidated by you and
aren't sure if you have a thing against men, or just that one in particular."
I took a breath and nodded, wondering how intimidating I am these days
with all these anxiety attacks.

"And you're not?" I asked jokingly.

"I admire you for what you did. No need to be intimidated." She gave
me another quick wink. I'm sure there was some girl power solidarity
behind it.

I nodded with a smile and stated, "It isn't my goal to intimidate people;
only Tanner and there's no more reason for that, is there? He took the
coward's way out."

"He sure did. We think this was his brother's way of getting revenge.
We don't know how many more people he may have working with him,
but we like that you have guards on you now."

"We've had them for a while, it would seem."

"I heard that around the precinct. Never thought we had those kinds
of people here in our city. It seems you can hide a lot in the shadows." I
wonder what people she was really referring to. Did she know?

"Yeah, I'm starting to see that. Well, detective, I appreciate you coming
today and talking to me. I guess I'll be working from home today if you
need to get a hold of me." She handed me her card again and said to call if
I ever needed anything.

I walked her to the elevator and she and the rest of the officers left. Roman was still talking to Grant, his father, and our extra security when I turned around.

I looked between all of them, trying not to let this all affect me before I asked with as much stoicism as I could muster, "Would anyone like to stay for breakfast?" When everyone said no my hands shook and the anxiety tried to creep in but instead was being replaced by anger and frustration.

"Well, too freaking bad..." I yelled. "...I'm going to cook some damn breakfast, and everyone is going to stay and eat damn it." Roman came over to me, putting his hand on my shoulder, and I snapped at him.

"Don't!" He pulled his hand away, lifting them before taking a step back. I don't need to be placated right now. I took a couple of serious inhales and exhales to find my center.

"Ok, what do you need me to help you do?" He asked slowly and cautiously. I took another deep cleansing breath to relax and try to get control again.

"Can you make coffee, please?" I hadn't meant to sound like such a bitch, but someone was trying to kill us and strangers were putting their life on the line for me.

I'm not okay right now. Focusing on something I can control will help. He nodded and got the coffee started.

Grant came over and said, "Honey, you really don't have to do this." I put my hands over my face and shook my head.

"Yes. Yes, I do. These four men right here saved our lives. The least I can do is feed them. I don't want them hiding outside anymore. I don't know how all this works." I threw my hand in the air and flung them out straight toward the four strangers.

I turned my attention to our new security and asked, "Do you all have families?" Two of them nodded yes. "Ok, and how does your family feel about this job? Do they know what you do?"

"Yes, ma'am." One of the guards said.

The other said, "It's not their favorite of our jobs, but it pays the bills."

"Well, after breakfast we need to have a conversation because I'm starting a family very soon and there is no way in hell that I would want Roman putting his life on the line every day to guard some stranger." They needed to know who they're protecting.

They looked around confused, nodding at each other and Grant for affirmation. "Ok, sure. Yes, ma'am." Grant had a goofy smile on his face and nodded back at the guys.

I turned to Grant. "I need you to set the table, please." I pointed at the cabinet, then to the table in the other room. He shook his head and grabbed the plates and silverware, taking them straight to the dining room.

Fitz looked at me, smiled and asked politely, "Alex, what would you like me to do for you, sweetheart?" I wasn't really used to hearing him be fatherly like Grant, so it took me back a little and kept me calm.

"Go help Roman with the coffee and beverages, please." He nodded and headed over to Roman.

One of the guys came over, tapping me on the shoulder. "Ms. Kennedy..." I turned slowly at the unfamiliar voice. "...have you ever been in the military?"

"Nope, I'm just bossy sometimes with a huge chip on my shoulder." Thinking to myself that right now, that seems like an understatement.

He laughed.

"What's your name?" I asked with a forced smile on my face.

"Scott, ma'am." Okay, there we go, names with faces.

"Well, my name is Alex. Not Ms. Kennedy and not ma'am. Just Alex."

He asked if there was anything he could do to help.

"No, the four of you have done enough this morning. I want you all to relax and eat breakfast in peace. Is that clear?"

He nodded with a smile and went back to his spot at the table with the other men.

Roman and I ate breakfast at the kitchen island with Grant and his father.

"We need to talk about how this is going to work. It's cold outside and they have families and it's Christmas in a few days. I'm not comfortable with this."

Grant looked over at the four men and back to me. "What do you suggest?"

"Well, I think the guys who are single could stay here and the other ones should be at home with their families, and they can work the day shift, while the others stay the night here if that works for them."

Roman said, "We actually have another apartment in the building. It's a two bedroom and the guys can stay there. We can set up surveillance in that apartment as well." I looked at him bewildered by the fact I didn't know that.

"Why is there another apartment here?" I honestly thought there was just the penthouse, because he didn't want to feel claustrophobic.

"Nothing crazy." I'm not sure I was thinking anything at this point, but there must be something on my face that suggests something else.

"Then what do you need another one for?" I wonder if it was for a potential girlfriend at some point.

"It was going to be for Harrison, but he didn't want to live here with me."

That makes sense. Both reasons, actually.

"Well, can you blame him? Look at the pickle we're in." All eyebrows raised and heads nodded.

"Good. At least now that's taken care of. Grant, are these all the guys you have working for us?" I thought I remembered him saying some of them were here. Could there be more?

He nodded and said, "Yes, these are all your guards, but we've been recruiting more for everyone else."

Everyone else?

"Not to make light of what just happened, but do you really think we're going to need more than this?"

Grant said, "Right now we're recruiting because we're worried about everyone who was involved with the case." I gasped. Oh my god, not Abby and Maggie.

"You mean like my attorneys and their families?" Roman grabbed my hand, as anxious to hear the answer as I was.

Grant said, "Yes, there have already been threats."

I jumped up off the stool and said, "Roman, the rest of this insanity is up to you. Get those guys situated. I need to call the girls."

I grabbed my phone and ran down the hall towards our bedroom.

Chapter 35

ROMAN

"When will you guys be moving into your house?" Dad looked toward Alex as she ran down the hall.

"Not sure. We have to close on it and start the reno and who knows with all the crap we have going on."

He laughed and said, "I bet if you put Alex in charge of the renovations, it'll get done a lot faster."

She could definitely get a room moving.

"Yeah, she's just freaking out right now."

"That's what you call freaking out? It looks like control to me."

"It sure does, but it's the wall she throws up when she feels threatened."

"I guess that makes sense, but what's behind the wall? Is that something we should be worried about?"

Good question. The last time she showed us what was behind the wall, she ended up across the world in rehab.

"I don't know. I hope not for the baby's sake."

After dad and Grant left, Alex and I sat down with the four security guards. Two of the guys were in their late twenties and the other two were in their late thirties—early forties. The older guys had wives and kids; they were all ex-marines. There was Scott, Randy, Franco and Boss, who swears that's his real name—*who am I to argue.* Scott and Randy were the younger ones that would be moving into the apartment that was just downstairs next to the gym. Franco and Boss would be with us during the day, whether it be in the penthouse while we work or in the office.

I called Harrison to let him know that he and Amelia were not to come to the office today. I sent out an office memo letting everyone know the office would be closed for the day but resume as usual tomorrow, tentatively. I had Scott and Randy go home and pack whatever they needed and rode the elevator down with them to show them the apartment and give them each a key to the building and a passcode to the elevator. I gave all of them a different passcode, so if they gave it away, I would know who did it.

We got in the elevator with Franco and Boss to take the puppy outside. Alex slumped against me, letting out a weary sigh as her eyes glistened with tears. I smiled weakly, knowing there was nothing I could do to alleviate her troubles.

When we got outside, I pulled Boss aside while Franco stayed close to Alex as she wandered to the grass with the puppy.

"I just want to give you a heads up about Alex." He started laughing and it caught me off guard.

"I watched the video. It was part of our get to know who you're protecting training." I think that would've probably scared the shit out of me, but I laughed with him instead.

"Yeah, well, she hates this more than she's letting on, so if she takes it out on you and I'm sure she will, she's just frustrated."

"That's normal and we won't take it personally...." He nodded. "...We have wives. I think Alex has gone through enough and with a baby on the way, you have our complete loyalty and trust. We'll do whatever it takes to keep you both safe." I shook his hand, patting him on the back.

Boss was a good name for him. He reminded me of Bruce. He was like a brick wall. I had no doubt he could take care of business.

"Roman, what the hell is going on?" Harrison sounded frantic and out of breath when he answered the phone.

"Harrison, are you and Amelia, okay? Safe?"

"Yeah, we're fine, but the police are here checking the place out. They said they're not allowed to leave until our security shows up. Why do we need security?"

"This is really gonna suck, buddy." Harrison likes his life quiet and he's going to be pissed.

"What are we talking about?"

"The kind that will be in your business, I'm afraid. Looks like Tanner's little stunt has really made his brother, Marcus, mad, and he's coming after us all now."

"What do you mean, coming after us? What the hell happened? Did he come after you?" Damn, if the last bit of information I gave him wasn't bad enough, now I had to tell him this.

"He did. He tried to blow up the building last night." There was silence on the phone, then the line went dead. I called back and it went straight to voicemail.

"Roman, are you and Alex, okay?" Amelia picked up on the first ring.

"Yes, thankfully, we're fine. Is Harrison alright?"

"He turned off his phone and threw it across the room. What happened?" She replied.

"Marcus sent some unlucky folks to blow up the building."

"How unlucky?" She whispered harshly.

"As unlucky as it gets." It was quiet for a minute, but before I could ask if she was still there, she responded.

"Good. I'm sick of being nice about this. You and your family did nothing to deserve any of this and if that's the way they want to play, then they deserve everything that's coming to them." She whispered harshly. I'm not sure I was ever expecting that from her.

"Amelia, is there anything I should know about you that I don't?"

"Nope, not at all. I'm just a normal Italian, Irish gal." She laughed as she said it, but why did I feel like that was code for something? Like I'm supposed to know what a normal Italian, Irish gal is.

"Do you own a gun, by any chance?" I know Harrison didn't, but something told me she did.

"Yeah, why?"

"No reason. Do you know how to use it?" Yep, I was right.

"I hope so or I don't belong owning one." Smart girl.

"Good answer. Does Harrison know you have a gun?"

"Yeah. I've owned it for years. I'm a woman and I lived alone." Nothing odd about that, I suppose.

"Ok, that makes sense. It's good that someone can protect the house." She giggled.

"So where is Harrison right now?"

"He's sitting on the sofa with his head in his hands."

I can relate to that all too well.

"Do me a favor and have him call me later."

"Ok, will do boss." She sounded almost happy. Where the hell do we go from here and why am I so paranoid about everyone now?

How am I supposed to work like nothing happened? I went through all my emails and followed up on calls. Alex was in her office, seemingly focused on work every time I walked past to check on her—and I did that several times.

Franco and Boss were patrolling the building while Scott and Randy checked all the cameras and made sure there were monitors for all the cameras in their apartment. Our normal security team for the building was updated on what happened and given new assignments to watch their monitors and focus on all entrances and exits to the building. Two of the guards quit, saying this wasn't something they signed up for and I couldn't blame them. I hired security to make sure people weren't breaking in or camping out in the garage or lobby; not to protect us from people trying to blow the place up. This was definitely not in their job description. Luckily, so far, all of it was being kept out of the news. We didn't need that circus either.

"Hey baby, do you want me to make you something to eat?" I was standing in the doorway to her office, watching her, contemplating how the hell things got to this point.

She snapped out of her daze and said, "What were you thinking?"

"We have some leftover sandwiches from the party. Would you like one? I think there's some tortellini soup in there too. How about half a sandwich and soup?" Most everything was going to be leftovers since I also told Mary she could have a couple of weeks' paid vacation.

She nodded without turning her gaze from her computer and said, "That sounds perfect. Would you like me to make you some tea?" She said casually and smiled but it didn't reach her eyes.

Uh Oh, she's doing that normal thing again.

"Sounds good." Her tea might be a good idea.

"So, what all have you gotten done today?" I asked as we walked out to the kitchen.

"Well, Amelia and I picked a date for the Gala—the end of March. We got the invite list narrowed down and the caterer and music. I think that's a good start to the day." I was definitely impressed with her ability to focus during all this craziness.

"Anything else?"

"I spoke to Alessandro about going over the plans for the renovations to his property for the non-wine biz that I need to name, and he said Lucia would be the perfect person to help me name the business and design the label. He said he'd prefer to get together after the new year." She took a breath and continued. "I talked to Maggie about her New Year's party. I don't think it's the best idea with everything that's going on, so we're going to revisit that in a couple of days right after Christmas. I also don't think we should go to the farmhouse for Christmas this year; It's too remote and I don't want anyone away from their family." That was a lot of information, and her eyes were glazed over, staring off into the distance. She shook the look off her face, then handed me the tea as I finished getting our food set up on the island.

"You might be right about not having a party or spending Christmas at the farmhouse, and that is a tragedy. Do you want to decorate the penthouse, and maybe we can have a small party here?"

She looked so sad as she nodded her head.

"I want to see my family for Christmas, but I don't want to put them in any danger; I don't want them to know about any of this. What should I do?" A single tear slid down her cheek as she looked to me for the answer.

"First of all, Edward does security for a living and second, you need to be honest with your family so they don't think something's wrong and come looking for you and something happens to them. I'm sure Grant has already put a detail on them, but..."

She casually interrupted, "I should call Edward at least and let him do the informing, shouldn't I?" I nodded my agreement as I reached over and wiped the tear from her face.

***

ALEX

I placed the phone on the desk, putting it on speaker, lowering my head as I gasped for air, trying not to hyperventilate when I called the girls.

"Jesus Alex, are you okay?" Maggie was definitely wound up. Of course, they already knew. Everyone seems to know everything before I do, especially when it's about me.

"Mags, I'm fine in the sense I'm not hurt and I'm trying to stay calm for the baby, but this is not helping. This is insane. How are all of you?" I dragged my head to an upright position, feeling a bit dizzy from the events of the morning while trying to safely grow a baby.

"I don't know if I'm okay yet. How did this happen? Jack's getting death threats and there were police on our doorstep bright and early this morning. Jax loved it, but Jack and I, not so much." Abby said, just shy of hysterical.

"Well, thank God they're there." I would die if anything happened to any of the people I loved because of me.

"One of the officers told Jack that we would be assigned a body-guard." Abby said.

"Good." I said with a sigh of relief.

Then Maggie yells, "Hey Alex, you have some explaining to do."

I exhaled and loudly replied, "What do you need me to explain, Maggie? That your life has been upended because you're my friend?"

She yelled, "No, jerk. What the hell were you talking about? You and Roman were set up by the mafia?" I actually laughed, thinking this story was now the lessor of the insane.

"Oh, that? So, you're not as concerned with a lunatic coming after you as you are something about me and Roman being arranged?"

She laughed and said, "Right now? Not worried about lunatics. This shit happens to Matt all the time, unfortunately, mostly empty threats. Now start talking." I laughed because only Maggie would brush something like this off as an everyday occurrence.

I retold the conversation I'd heard, straight from the horses mouth.

They both gasped and said in unison, "Are you fucking kidding me?"

I wish.

"Nope. They assured us they only made sure we met. But they basically encouraged it." I figured from the long pause; they thought the story was as nuts as I did.

"Oh my god..." Abby exhaled loudly. "...Besides it being completely insane, it's almost sweet how they did this for you both. I mean, you have to admit you're really freaking cute together and so in love and you've gone through hell and he's still around. That says a lot and it has nothing to do with an arrangement." I knew she was right, but I was still having my doubts about us being together if this hadn't happened.

"I don't know if I can survive much more of your life, Alex." Maggie's voice sounded strained and exhausted.

I needed my friends to get through this; especially now.

"I don't blame you, Mags. This is a lot to swallow, and I have a baby on the way that I have to raise in this very traumatic environment. I'm really going to need my village to help me do that though—and we're going to be neighbors, don't forget." Maggie started screaming.

"Oh my god that's right! How did I forget about that? When are you moving in?" Maggie screamed.

I pulled the phone away from my ear.

"We haven't closed on it yet and we'll need the current owners to move out before starting renovations."

She laughed and announced, "I'll go kick those assholes out right now if you need me too." I knew she meant it too.

We laughed and Maggie confirmed, "Yes, by the way, I definitely want to be part of your village. Screw all those monsters, bring 'em on."

"Speak for yourself..." Abby interjected. "...Do not bring any of them, please. I'll totally be a part of your village, but not to the rest of that."

As happy as I was that everyone was safe for the time being, I started to feel like a prisoner again. What about my family and Christmas? Roman thought I should talk to my family and honestly, I did too—I just didn't know what to say. We talked about having Christmas here in the penthouse and I thought that was a great idea because this seemed to be the most secure place of all of them, and we had the most security.

The thought of this place looking like a Die-Hard movie on Christmas, sent me into a fit of laughter. If I didn't laugh—what else was there to do except cry.

I decided to bite the bullet and call my brother. He answered and said, "Hey there. How are you?"

I thought he was much too chipper.

"I'm good. How are you?" Something wasn't right with this conversation, and I shifted nervously in my seat.

"I didn't get a chance to congratulate you on the new addition coming." He said politely. I forgot all about the announcement, damn my head is really in the clouds.

"Awe thanks. Yeah, we found out Amelia and Harrison were going to get engaged as a surprise, so we decided to give them the night." No, brother sister poking going on, something's up.

"It was a great proposal. He did a good job." He paused and the silence was deafening. "...So, Alex, clearly, I know about Tanner, so why don't you tell me how you're really doing?" I'm sure he's got more to say than that.

"Ok, I guess I should just shoot straight then, right? Things are bad. Marcus didn't take the news of his brother well and he tried to kill Roman and me last night."

Before I could elaborate, he yelled into the phone, "Why am I just hearing about this from you right now?!" I took a deep breath, so I didn't yell back. I know he was angry and upset with me for not going to him immediately, but I can't afford to get worked up right now.

"Because we didn't know until this morning and we've had security with us since before Tanner got out of jail the first time and I'm not trying to freak everyone out..." I took another breath to calm down. "...I had no idea how bad this was. We have fulltime security, so we're fine. The major reason for my call is to let you know that you're not safe and neither is the rest of the family."

"Does dad know? Does Patrick know?" At least he sounded calmer, but off somehow—rehearsed.

"No, I figured you should be the first one I call."

"Ok, why didn't you call me sooner? You do know I run a security company, right?"

I nodded and said, "I Know that, yes, and I also know that none of you are without protection right now. Grant put some detail on the family."

"Grant? Why Grant?" He sounded highly annoyed with me.

"He owns a lot of businesses and apparently one of them is a security business, so he took it upon himself to take care of that." I could hear him grumbling to himself and I rubbed my forehead incessantly, hoping this was enough information for him.

"Ok, well can you give me Grant's number or give him mine and I can at least help out too?"

"That would be great, actually. He's trying to recruit more security, anyway. I'll text it to you."

"What about Christmas? Are you still planning on having it at the farmhouse?" I shook my head with my hand still on my forehead.

"No, we're going to have it at the penthouse now because this place is like Fort Knox."

"Wasn't that the second Die Hard movie and didn't they manage to break in?"

I laughed.

"Oh my god I was just thinking that this place was going to look like Nakatomi Tower on Christmas with all the security and guns."

We both laughed. At least we can find some humor in a movie reference, I guess.

"Ok, just tell us what you want us to bring, and we'll be there." That was a weight lifted I didn't know needed lifting.

"Thanks, and I love you. Can you tell dad and Patrick please? I'm sure they'll come for Christmas, right?"

He said, "Yeah, sure, I'll tell them and they're coming. Love you too, Alex, and we're really excited about our new niece or nephew." I sent Grant's contact information via text to Edward right after we hung up.

I sent out email invitations for Christmas and realized that we didn't have a tree or decorations or anything in here; no stockings, nothing. I put my head on the desk, feeling defeated.

The knock at the door was followed by Roman's voice. "Hey babe, I got your invite to our Christmas party, so I made a few phone calls." I looked up, totally exhausted.

"Yeah?" I had nothing else to offer at this point.

He smiled and said, "I have all the Christmas stuff in a storage unit. I called the team I use and they're going to bring it all tonight and get this place decorated. Do you have all the gifts you need for everyone here?"

How did I get so lucky, and he can read my mind now too. I managed to pick my head up enough to smile back.

"You're the best. That would be amazing, babe, and yes, I've got all the gifts I need, but I would like to do something nice for our four security guards and their families."

"You let me know what you want to do for them, and I'll make that happen. I also decided to close the office from Christmas Eve until January second. We don't need to be open for anything, and that gives the security team time to make sure this place is fully secure."

I called Amelia and had her help me make a grocery list. She said she would come over and assist me in putting a menu together for Christmas. The dining room can hold twelve comfortably and it was just going to be my family, Roman's family and Ella's family. I tapped my pen to chin as I looked around trying to jot down the growing list.

My phone rang; Ella's name illuminating my phone, bringing me out of my thoughts. There were a lot of people affected by my crazy life and she and her family included.

"Ella, hi, how are you Big Mama?"

She coughed and said, "Miss Alex, I am so happy you and that fine young man are having a baby together. I'm also grateful for all you've done for my grandchildren and thank you for the Christmas invite. We will all be there." She paused for a coughing fit before continuing. "Now tell me what the hell these police are doing at my house, telling me they're here to protect me and my grandsons. They wouldn't tell me what's going on, but they assured me that it had nothing to do with any of the boys, so I'm assuming it has everything to do with you."

I changed the subject because I knew she had moved into the new house.

"Ella, first things first. How do you like your new house? I was able to get a moving team last minute, thankfully, because I wasn't going to be able to help you move in my condition."

She laughed, then coughed again before saying, "Oh, that's a bunch of crap you couldn't help in your condition... What condition might that be, because being pregnant isn't stopping you from doing anything, I'm sure of that and the house is wonderful. Thank you."

I laughed and said, "Oh Big Mama, I'm so glad to hear that."

"Ok, so tell me what's going on then." She asked again.

"Tanner committed suicide in jail, and his brother didn't like that. The police are worried that anyone close to me is at risk."

I assume she had me on speaker because I heard Darius say, "I can take care of this family. We don't need no cops hanging around." He was not a cop fan and I couldn't blame him for that. The way the previous ones treated him, and his family was a disgrace, but they were no longer on the job.

"Darius, I get how you feel. You know that, right?"

"Yes, ma'am I do, and I can't believe you ok with havin um here after what they did to you." He's a very protective young man, that's for sure.

"I'm betting this isn't the same group. Those other ones got arrested."

He was quiet for a minute before asking, "So, you think we should trust em then?"

"I'm going to talk to someone I know about getting you guys a body-guard until Marcus is found. I want to make sure whoever's looking after you is someone getting paid specifically to look after you." I don't know if that meant I didn't really trust them or not.

Darius said, "Alex, there's four of us and we don't always do things together."

I know, I think as my hands start to sweat just thinking about all the chaos this has created.

"Let me figure that out. Can you talk to the boys and let them know what's going on? If I have to bring you here to stay with me to keep you safe, I will."

Ella chimed in and said, "Now, you know we ain't gonna do that, don't you, sweetie?"

I smiled and replied, "Yes, of course I know that, but I want you to know that the invitation is open." They both said they would see me on Christmas, and we hung up.

I finally finished in the office for the day and walked out into the living room to see Boss with Tao on the sofa. For someone I know is tough as nails and has at least one kill under his belt, it was the sweetest thing in the world seeing him with that puppy. He caught a glimpse of me and tried to play it off.

"Sorry ma'am, Mr. King asked me to watch the puppy for a minute while he went to get his sweater and leash." I laughed, knowing how ridiculous that sounded, even to me. I'm sure Roman made a face when he told him that.

"Mr. King? He would hate that. Call him Roman, please. And I'm Alex, ok?" I hate formal names. It's just not who I am or ever will be.

He said, "Ok." then quickly put the puppy down.

"You can hold him if you want. He's the sweetest little boy, isn't he?" He nodded, picking him back up with a special kind of care.

"What kind of dog is he, if you don't mind me asking? He looks like a Pitbull."

I smiled and agreed with a nod. "You know your dogs. He is a Pitbull. I think after all this, I'm going to get him trained to protect this family." I laughed to myself, picturing this dog guarding this whole family like a superhero.

He smiled back, nodding his head knowingly.

"Alex, I own a company that trains Pitbulls." Is this some kind of divine intervention? I mean, first Bruce trained me to fight and now Boss is here to train my dog on how to fight. So weird.

"Are you serious?"

He waved his hand for me to come closer. "Let me show you my website."

I walked over and sat down next to him on the sofa. He opened his website and began to play the videos. Those dogs looked like vicious killers when they were commanded to. Then he showed me videos of the same dogs in the house playing with the kids, rolling around on the floor—sharing food. I was completely blown away.

"Boss, when do you have time to do that?"

"Well, I just run the business these days. My sons and some trusted employees train the dogs now. My wife and daughter are kind of the softies where the dogs are concerned but they also know their commands if they need them. I would be more than happy to train Tao."

"Do you trust them with babies after that kind of training?" He showed me some more videos with the dogs and babies.

"These dogs were used as nanny dogs back in the day to guard the kids. They've been used to herd and, of course, we know they were trained to fight." He sounded so adamant that the baby would be safe around Tao.

"I think I may have been half kidding when I said I was going to get him to guard our family until I saw that..." I was mesmerized by the videos. Especially the ones in slow motion. "...How old does he need to be to start his training?" He told me at least twelve weeks, so we still had time, but that he was looking forward to it if we'd let him.

***

ROMAN

"Roman, look at this." She showed me a video of a Pitbull attacking some guy in a big suit. Not really sure why she wanted me to see that other than to question my decision to bring Tao home.

"Ok, what am I looking at?"

She just blurted out, "Boss trains Pitbulls."

I looked at Boss and said, "Oh yeah? Do I want my dog to be vicious like that? I thought we were trying to break that stigma." That scared the shit out of me.

Boss calmly educated me. "Pitbulls are wonderful, loving, and very loyal dogs. They are also very easy to train and really smart. It's definitely best if both of you agree on training because you'll both need to understand the commands..." I looked at Alex, who was smiling from ear to ear on the edge of her seat. "...I know I feel much better about my family being home alone when I'm not there with all of our dogs than I would without them being there. I've never been worried about one of the dogs becoming aggressive with anyone in the family." I nodded my head and handed Alex the sweater to put on the puppy.

"That's definitely something I'll need to think about and discuss with Alex." I don't know if I can handle that kind of training. Maybe obedience training, but not that.

She smiled and said, "Yeah, I definitely want to discuss it with you." First her training to fight and now the dog? I don't know if this is such a good idea. I think she's just amp'd up about Marcus's attack.

The four of us took the puppy on a walk down to the river. I asked the guys to look as much like regular people as possible. I hated the thought of looking like some asshole with a bodyguard, even though that's exactly what I was.

We made our way to the coffee shop, and Alex got our table by the window. She and Boss took a seat, deep in conversation about Tao, while Franco and I got the coffees and muffins. Franco wasn't much of a talker, but Alex and Boss bonded over Tao. I was just happy to be out of the house and not looking over my shoulder. I'll leave that to the guys.

Back at the penthouse, we got the place ready for Paul's team with the decorations. As soon as they got there, we helped unload the decorations from the crates while Alex cooked dinner for everyone. When we finished, the place looked like Christmas threw up all over.

"Hey babe, it's finished. You wanna look around, first, before we eat?" She spun around, nodding enthusiastically as I took her hand, leading her into the dining room first. It was all red and gold decorations, with pinecones and candles embedded in each one. Next, we walked down the hallway, where sparkly snowflakes hung from the ceiling. The living room had thick garland with red and gold decorations strewn everywhere in a perfectly designed pattern. Plain gold stockings hung with no names on the fireplace, with thick green garland covered in pinecones and red ornaments situated across the mantle. The Christmas tree was a ten-foot artificial spruce pine with white lights and red and gold ornaments, gold garland, and a big gold star on top.

Paul and his wife decorated the balcony with a boatload of white lights and a couple small pine trees with white lights. They had to be weighted down pretty good since we are on the 24th floor and it can get windy, but the railing is concrete, so it does block a lot of it; plus, it's covered.

The smile on her face meant everything to me until we came in from the balcony and the tears started to flow. I pulled her into my chest, looking at Paul and his wife, who thought something was wrong. I shook my head slightly at them and mouthed, "She's pregnant."

They both smiled and mouthed, "Congratulations" back at me, and I almost started laughing.

I leaned down and whispered in Alex's ear, "Honey, is everything ok? Do you like it?"

She looked up, smiling from ear to ear as she whimpered, "Yes, it's amazing. I'm just so overwhelmed..." She sniffled. "...I thought it wasn't going to be Christmassy enough. My mom would've come over with a ton of decorations and put me in my place." She laughed as she wiped the tears. I realized she just missed her mom. I can't imagine how hard all of this is for her.

After dinner, everyone left, including Boss and Franco. We got things cleaned up, then sat on the couch, listening to Christmas music. Scott and Randy came up to check and make sure we were secure before they went to check the building and the garage. They texted all their security checks to me because I didn't want Alex getting anxious. She was sitting next to me with a cup of tea, and I had a bourbon.

She said out of nowhere in particular, "Ya know something? I don't miss it."

"Miss what?" The fire in the fireplace was so peaceful, even though it was just a gas one. The light was glowing off of Alex's face and I was mesmerized by how beautiful she looked as the flames danced in her eyes.

"Alcohol. I don't miss it a bit." Oh shit, she was being deep. That's good to know.

"Well, I guess that's a good thing, right?" She did look more relaxed now. I forgot I poured a drink. I'm just so used to having a drink whenever and not worrying about it bothering anyone.

"So this bourbon doesn't bother you, does it?" I moved it to the hand farthest away from her and set it on the end table.

She shook her head and said, "No. In fact, it kind of smells bad to me now. I used to like the smell of it." Does that mean I have to stop drinking it? Please say no.

"I don't have to drink it if you don't like it."

"You can drink it if you want. It doesn't bother me like that. I just have no desire to drink it myself." Definitely good to know and thank goodness.

"You know you can tell me if you don't like something I'm doing, right?" I wanted her to feel comfortable coming to me with anything.

She laughed and said, "Have I ever had a problem with that?" The answer to that is definitely no and I already knew that.

"I think we can agree that you say whatever is on your mind." I gently reached for her face as I kissed her passionately. She wrapped her hands around the back of my neck and up the back of my head, holding me firmly to her mouth. This felt like the first time in a long time I felt safe and secure with her.

Chapter 36

ROMAN

The next couple of days, we worked from home again. We also prepped dinner for Christmas and wrapped presents, placing them strategically under the tree, so we knew where each person's presents were. Christmas Eve came quickly, and we sent Boss and Franco home with dinner for their family as a thank you for all they had done. Scott and Randy said they weren't planning to go home for Christmas anyway, so they had no problem staying with us all day. In the morning the four of us walked Tao down to the river, then to the coffee shop as per our usual routine. Tao seems to have made everyone fall in love with him. Now every time we go to the coffee shop, they have a pup cup waiting for him.

This is the week we started him on wet food; no more bottle feeding. I felt kind of sad about that, but with a baby on the way, I guess we'll be right back into it soon enough. He was now almost fifteen pounds, at only seven full weeks old. He was already growing out of his Christmas sweaters, which I was very thankful for.

Amelia and Harrison decided to stay with us for Christmas Eve and spend the night so Amelia could help get everything ready for the party and not feel rushed. I wanted to keep Amelia close and see if there was something she would let slip about what she might know about everything that's going on. She swears she doesn't know anything, but the more shit that happens, the more I feel like everyone is hiding something.

Scott and Randy went on a sweep of the building while we waited for Harrison and Amelia to arrive. They had their own bodyguards with them. I didn't know how this was going to work if everyone had bodyguards. I guess we could just set them all up in the lobby with their own Christmas party or something. Hell, this whole thing was starting to get out of hand and all I wanted to do was have a small family Christmas dinner. Ok, now I know that overwhelming feeling that Alex always had when she was over thinking things.

"Hey babe, what's on your mind?" Unlike her, I can't hide the looks on my face. I snapped to attention.

"Just wondering where we're going to fit everyone if everyone has a bodyguard." I put my hands on my head, taking a deep breath and blowing out my cheeks as I exhaled.

"That's awesome." She threw her hands on her hips and looked around wildly. "I never thought of that. Where are we going to put them?" The puppy was running around chasing after his toys and Alex just flopped on the couch laughing.

Harrison and Amelia come out of the elevator as Harrison yells, "Merry Christmas Eve! What's so funny?"

"All these extra people, apparently." I said, as Amelia sat with Alex on the couch.

"Yeah, we told our guys to just hang out in the lobby. I feel bad, but we don't need fifteen bodyguards up here. In fact, it would be best if they were outside the building casing the perimeter and in the lobby so no one can get in." Amelia casually gave instructions like she had some kind of knowledge on the subject as opposed to just being my assistant. I shot another puzzled look her way.

"Oh, so now you know what they should be doing? Do you have some kind of bodyguard training?" I snapped, then immediately felt bad, but not really.

She laughed, and Harrison smacked me on the back. "Dude, what's your problem? That sounded kinda shitty." *Well, that sounded kind of militaristic,* I thought.

"No, I was just thinking rationally; using a little common sense." Amelia interjected. Again, I wasn't buying it for some reason, but it was Christmas, and I didn't want to get into a fight with anyone causing any more stress for Alex.

Alex agreed. "I was thinking the same thing. If we know how many of them are actually coming, then we can make them food. I hate that they'll be spending Christmas doing this."

I put my hands through my hair and said, "I'll call Grant and see who he's got protecting who, so we have a count."

Ten total extra people, so not too many, is the count I got from Grant. As I was coming out of my office, Harrison was at the door, asking if we could talk for a minute in my office. He followed me back in, closing the door behind us.

"What's up?"

"What was that all about that you said to Amelia out there?" He growled. Whoa, not what I was expecting. My defenses went up and I shoved my hands in my pockets, balled up in fists to regain some control.

"What? About bodyguard training?" He looked pissed as he walked closer towards me.

"Yeah, that. It didn't sound like you were just messing with her, either. What's going on?"

I'm tired of tiptoeing around everyone so I don't hurt feelings, that's what's going on.

"I don't know Harrison." I stood up tall, toe to toe with him, taking my hands out of my pockets before stretching my fingers to let him know he needed to back off out of my space. "I've been getting a weird vibe from her ever since this shit with Grant came out and now, I'm paranoid, maybe, that she's involved somehow."

He didn't back off as he stood nose to nose with me and said, "Leave her the fuck out of this. She isn't a part of this bullshit, and I don't want you making snarky comments at her trying to start a fight because your girlfriend and you, for that matter..." He began to poke me in the chest but thought better of it, pulling his hand away and resting it back down at his side. "...are at the center of this crap. Enough is enough and I won't have you upsetting her." My little brother getting protective of a girl is very new to me. I felt it was my duty as a big brother to back off and not escalate this.

"Harrison, I'm sorry. I'll try not to upset Amelia, or you, for that matter. It's Christmas and you're right, enough is enough." Both of our tense stances softened, and he slapped me on the back as he went back out to the living room.

Buddy, *I will say whatever you want to hear right now to keep the* peace, *but if I find out Amelia is a part of this too, I will have major issues and peace is the last thing I'll be thinking about.*

***

ALEX

I watched Roman trudge to his office to call Grant while Harrison probed for information in a tone, I'm unfamiliar with from him. "Alex, what's up with Roman? Why did he lash out at Amelia like that?"

"I don't know. Do you think he was kidding?" I know he felt something weird going on with Amelia and, frankly, so did I.

"It didn't sound like it." He looked on edge too.

I can't wait for all of this to be over so we can get back to our plain old vanilla lives.

Amelia spoke up, "Oh please, he's said way worse things to me than that at the office." For some reason it sounded like she was covering for Roman.

"Well, I can't attest for Roman, but I know we've been through a lot lately and it's easy to get triggered right now."

Harrison nodded his head, storming over in the direction of Roman's office.

"Amelia, is everything okay?"

Her smile looked forced, but Harrison just made it a bit awkward, so I'll give her that.

"Sure, I mean all that's going on has become the norm, right?"

I started laughing and she followed my lead. I think she was feeling me out. I think Roman might be right. I think something's up with Amelia.

"Well, I'm definitely glad I have a friend like you in my life. You always seem so calm and in control. I'm pretty jealous of that, actually." I hate that I'm trying to figure this out rather than just being her friend. Everything is weird right now and it's making me do weird things.

She laughed, sort of, and said, "You'd be surprised at how you act when you have to."

That sounded cryptic, but I let it go.

"Don't I know it. I've tried my hand at acting—I think I might actually be an open book. I pretty much wear my heart on my sleeve. I'm terrible at hiding things." I said.

"Same. Boring as hell."

I smiled, but there was nothing boring about Miss Amelia Wright. With that thought, the guys came back out smiling. I guess Roman is also a good actor because I knew what he said to Amelia wasn't a joke; he was trying to figure out what she was hiding.

After Amelia and Harrison put all their things in the spare bedroom upstairs and their presents under the Christmas tree, we had dinner and watched a movie.

Roman whispered in my ear, "Did you talk to Amelia tonight?"

I whispered back, "I did."

"And...?"

"And nothing. I get what you're saying, and I feel something is off too, but she's not going to spill it, and if you keep prying, you're going to upset Harrison."

"Ok, I'll let it go for Christmas, but I'm going to find out what she's hiding."

"I thought you trusted her. Why don't you just trust her enough to let whatever it is go. If she's involved with Grant, she's on our side, anyway."

He wrapped his arms around me and pulled me onto his lap, nuzzling his face into the crook of my neck.

"I just want my normal boring life back." He muttered.

I giggled a little and said, "Then you're going to lose me and our beautiful baby."

"Hey, don't say that."

"Well, I'm the reason your life isn't boring anymore and I'm the one carrying the baby. Package deal, I'm afraid." I leaned in, kissing his cheek.

"Ummm, no, that's not true at all. In fact, I'm the reason your life isn't boring. My father is the reason my life isn't boring anymore."

I combed my fingers through his hair, pushing the hair off his forehead to place a soft, calming kiss there, too.

"As much as I hate how we got here, I'm still glad we got here and I'll do whatever I have to—to keep us." I moved my lips to his, humming my appreciation for their full, soft texture.

He mumbled out, "Me too."

"Good, then let whatever this is with Amelia go." I held his face, looking deep in his eyes to get a read on him.

He took a deep breath and said, "Fine."

Not a chance in hell he was going to let this go. I could see the determination swirling behind his pupils.

In the middle of the night, I woke up thirsty and realized I hadn't brought any water with me to bed like I had been lately. I decided sneak to the kitchen to get some water. As I was getting closer to the end of the hall, I could see a faint light in the direction of the kitchen. I cautiously looked around the corner first, spotting Amelia sitting at the island texting on her phone.

"Hey." I said, quietly, from a distance so she didn't think I was spying on her.

She looked tired but remained friendly as she acknowledged me with a faint smile.

"You couldn't sleep either, huh?"

She shook her head. I was testing the waters to see if she wanted to talk. I went to the fridge and grabbed a bottle of water, offering her one too. She shook her head no, but didn't say a word. Now she looked more sad than tired. I felt for her. I knew this feeling emanating from her. One, you had to bear the weight of everything, all on your own. I wonder what she was carrying–and did anyone know?

I sat next to her and put my arm around her shoulder, hoping she would understand that I was here as a friend.

"I know we haven't known each other for that long, but if you need someone to talk to, I'm here for you." I was being sincere. This had nothing to do with trying to get information.

"I appreciate that..." she acknowledged and seemed to relax. "... I've actually never had that before." This was news.

"Oh no? You don't have any girlfriends you confide in?"

She shook her head again and admitted, "I moved around a lot as a kid and got used to being a loner."

I always thought Amelia was one of those people who was uber popular, loved by all.

"That must've been hard. Was your dad in the military or something?" I realized I didn't know anything about Amelia, really. I wonder if Roman did.

She tilted her head and shrugged. "I wish. I was raised by family friends, actually."

Um, was asking what happened to her parents pushing the limit with her? I wondered.

I asked with hesitation, "What happened to your parents, if you don't mind me asking?"

She took a deep breath and said, "They died in an accident when I was ten."

Oh no, maybe the holidays are hard on her too.

"Amelia, I'm so sorry. I had no idea." She twitched her shoulders, but I could tell she was affected.

"Well, it was a long time ago. I don't think too much about it anymore except around the holidays, I guess."

I rubbed her arm, trying to comfort her the best I could while suppressing my own grief.

"Well, you know we all think of you as family and even if we aren't your blood, we come in handy when you need a shoulder to cry on, an ear to listen or someone to help you bury the body." We both started laughing and I couldn't stop when I tried to bring that one back.

"I meant that figuratively speaking, of course." She pulled me into a hug.

"Thank you so much, Alex. I needed to hear that. I've always felt very close to you and hope that we'll be sisters one day."

"I agree. I always knew we were going to be friends and I hope sisters one day too. Sounds like a great Christmas present to me." I ended up making us some tea before going back to bed.

Roman rolled over and asked, "What were you and Amelia talking about out there?" His deep sleepy voice was sexy, but putting me to sleep.

"Oh, so you were awake?.." I murmured through the sleepy haze. "...How did you know I was talking to Amelia?" Trying to figure out if he actually heard the conversation or not.

"I rolled over to wrap myself around you, only to find an empty bed..." He put his hand on my hip and slinked it around my back, pulling me close. "...That made me anxious. I noticed the door was open and I could hear talking from the kitchen. Since both voices were pretty feminine, I'm assuming it was Amelia you were talking to. There aren't any other women here, are there?" He yawned and I snuggled into the crook of his arm, laying my head on his chest.

"Oh, so you only heard voices and didn't come and eavesdrop?" He smelled so good, but I wasn't going to be able to finish this conversation. On top of his voice, making me sleepy, the tea was doing its job as well.

"No. I told you I was going to let it go with Amelia. If, however, there's something you want to tell me about her, I won't stop you." He kissed my head, wrapping his arms firmly in place.

I giggled. "Nope, there's nothing..." At least nothing that I could remember at the moment. "...There's just been a lot going on lately and neither of us could sleep, so I made us some tea. She's hoping we're going to be sisters, because she's never had a sister or even a girlfriend." I could almost feel the guilt oozing out of him now.

"Are you serious? She has no friends?" He perked up, but I needed him to go back to sleep.

I nodded. "She does now, so let's keep it that way, okay?"

He apologized, hugging me tight.

"Let's go to sleep and get a good workout in the morning before everyone gets here. I'm pretty sure they're coming around noon."

He kissed my lips, moving eagerly down to my neck. "I'm ready to start that workout early." His tone was low and hungry; not sleepy at all anymore. Oh, my god I'm never going to get any sleep.

Chapter 37

ROMAN

H mmm, I don't think I'll ever get enough of waking up with her in my arms. I reached over, turning off the alarm. The smile on her face was enough of a Christmas present for me after all the crap we've been through lately.

"Good morning. Merry Christmas." She practically sang it.

"Merry Christmas and good morning to you." I said as I nuzzled my face into her tummy and muttered, "Merry Christmas to you too, little one."

We got up to head to the gym before Tao got up and needed to go outside. While Alex went to change, I threw on some shorts, a t-shirt and grabbed some socks and shoes to put on in the kitchen while I made a pre-workout drink. Alex wasn't drinking those these days because of the baby, but I didn't know which tincture she was going to use for her tea, so I made her some tea and let her sort out the rest.

"Oh shoot, you scared me." I said as I rounded the corner to the kitchen. Amelia was startled but then laughed.

"Sorry, I'm an early bird." She confessed.

Time to extend the olive branch. Hearing that she didn't have any friends was kind of disheartening, and I didn't want her to feel like an outcast.

"Do you want to go to the gym with us? Oh yeah, and Merry Christmas. I also wanted to say I'm sorry for yesterday. I didn't mean to be such a jerk."

"No worries. You guys are going to the gym this morning..." She sat at the kitchen island staring at her hands. "That's right, Merry Christmas." She repeated, looking rather forlorn.

"Yep, we're going to hurry before Tao wakes up." I said as I was shaking my pre workout drink and heating the water for Alex's tea.

"You don't mind if I go with you?"

"Not at all. Would you like some tea or one of these?" I asked, holding up the shaker with my drink in it.

"Yeah, I think Alex told me about an energizing tincture she made. Could I maybe try that one?"

With that, Alex bounces out into the kitchen and says with a skip in her step, "Oh, the energizing tincture is awesome. I took it by accident one day and cleaned the entire house, then had an awesome workout. It was amazing."

It doesn't sound like Alex really needs it, though.

"Cool, I'll try the tea then." She said.

I asked if Harrison was coming to the gym, and she said he just wanted to sleep in this morning.

Alex and Amelia worked out together. I watched them as I ran on the treadmill. They seemed to get along really well and looked like they were genuinely having a great time. If Amelia did have a connection to Grant and that life, she was definitely one of the ones on our side and I should be grateful, like Alex suggested.

Right before we left the gym, I got a text from Scott asking if they could use the gym. When I opened the gym door, the guys were right there. "Good morning..."

Alex and Amelia interrupted by shouting, "Merry Christmas" at the same time in a sing-songy voice as they giggled their way into the elevator.

I think that tea has something else in it too. I raised my eyebrows, shaking my head as I watched them.

"Yeah, Merry Christmas and you all are free to use the gym whenever you want. Just use the same code as the elevator that I gave you."

"Thanks. Merry Christmas to all of you, too. We'll alternate using the gym, so someone is always keeping an eye on things. Thanks again."

I had a lot of trouble with this setup and hoped that it would end sooner than later so we could all have a life again.

The guards in the downstairs apartment had a fully stocked kitchen, so they were good for breakfast and lunch. All the guards would be out and about downstairs when everyone arrived. Amelia and Alex were going to make ten extra dinners for them, and we'd deliver it to them in the lobby. They had set up a whole Christmas dining area for them in the green space. As soon as everyone arrived, we were locking the place up tight, including the parking garage. Then all they would have to do is watch the monitors. This seemed like a lot to go through for a small get together, but safety first and foremost.

Scott took Tao out for his morning walk while we got ready for the party. The girls were dressed in yoga pants and t-shirts while food prepping before they pranced down the hall to change. Harrison and I had one job and that was to set up the bar.

"Alex and Amelia are in really good spirits. They seem really close, don't you think?" Harrison said and he seemed happy about that.

"Yeah, Alex really likes her and wants her to feel like part of the family."

He smiled, smacking me on the back with a little more force than necessary.

"I knew I liked her. You, I have a problem with, but Alex is cool."

She is definitely that, and so much more.

"Yeah, I guess they're both pretty cool. I mean, I wouldn't know what to do without Amelia at the office. She keeps me organized and on track."

Harrison nudged me. "Ya know, I'm not going to stop her if she ever wants to quit working for you."

"Oh, I'm sure you're not. I'm not looking forward to that day. I hope there's someone out there half as competent as she is when that day comes."

"But if they're smart, they'll stay the hell away from you." He chided.

***

ALEX

We got up to the gym and Amelia asked if she could do my workout with me. I told her sure but that I toned it down because of the baby and couldn't enjoy the hot tub or the sauna right now, and she seemed fine with that. We lifted weights, did some yoga and swam laps in the pool. She looked an awful lot like she had a workout routine of her own already, though. The girl's physique was perfectly cut and toned.

"So, what do you do to stay in such good shape? You look incredible." I asked, remembering the day she told me she bruised easily so she wouldn't be taking kickboxing classes with us.

"I've always had a gym wherever I've lived, and Harrison's house had one when I moved in. I make working out a priority along with healthy eating and drinking." Maybe I should ask her what her workout regime is?

"I wish we had been friends sooner and maybe I wouldn't need all this tea." She seemed like she had a good head on her shoulders. She may have been a better influence on me than the work crew. I shouldn't put the blame anywhere but myself, though. The choices we make are, inevitably, our own and we are the ones who pay the consequences.

"But if you think about it, you actually took one for the team in a sense because if it wasn't for you and what you went through you would've never found out about these herbs and come up with this incredible alternative to drinking."

I looked up to the ceiling and said, "I never thought of it that way. To all the alcoholics out there...you're welcome."

***

ME: *"Did you take the puppy out for a walk?"*

ROMAN: *"No, Scott did so we could get ready."*

ME: *"Ok, great. Thanks for taking care of that. I'm kind of spacy right now. I don't think we should have more than one kid."*

ROMAN: *"LOL! Ok, we'll talk about that later."*

ME: *"I love you."* Talk about what later?

With that, the door opens and Roman pulls me in for a kiss and says, "I love you too, baby, and we're having at least six kids." Then he kisses me again and leaves before I can respond. I hope he was kidding.

I put on a soft baggie off-white sweater with matching wide leg pants. I completed the ensemble with UGG slippers, also in off white. Today, comfort was key. My belly was already noticeably larger than I expected, and frankly, I was still learning the ropes of pregnancy. My hair was down in big beachy waves and minimal makeup with the famous red lipstick I know Roman has come to love. Good thing we can only get pregnant one at a time, or I'm sure he would try to knock me up with all six of them today. There is a look in his eyes when he sees this red lipstick that's so primal. Sexy caveman. He can probably talk me into having six kids.

As I came out of the bedroom, Amelia was on her way out as well. We laughed when we saw we were both wearing almost the same thing. She was in an off white sweater with matching pants as well, except hers was form fitting and mine was flowy and she had on heels. She wore her beautiful blond hair down with no makeup. The girl didn't actually need a drop. She was naturally gorgeous with her flawless ivory skin tone.

The party started promptly, with everyone arriving on time and a brief discussion of recent events. I explained a few things to my dad, and he seemed to accept them as well as could be expected. The joyous occasion was filled with double the celebration as Patrick and Rose announced their engagement, the happy news immediately followed by Edward and Bianca's announcement of their pregnancy. I was overjoyed at the prospect of our baby having a cousin so close in age—it felt like a wonderful gift.

When Ella's grandsons opened their stockings, they started crying and handed the envelopes to Ella. This was the big gift of the day. She looked over at me and I saw tears falling. I didn't want to cry right now, but the tears were filling up in my eyes too, and I did my best to hold them back with a smile. Roman grabbed my hand as we walked over together.

"I know I asked you to take care of my boys, but this is too much, Alex." Ella said through soft sobs.

Roman squeezed my hand and we looked at each other and smiled knowingly. Ella was the sweetest person I knew and having a cancer diagnosis was breaking all our hearts. Nothing was too much as far as I was concerned.

"Ella…" I reached out and took her hand in mine, still hanging on to Roman for support. "…Roman and I agreed we were going to do this. It's not too much..." I looked at Roman, who was smiling at me so lovingly, squeezing my hand in return. "...It's everything I've ever wanted to do with this money. You're like family to me now. You and these boys are not getting rid of me."

Roman and I put $500,000 into a trust for each of the boys to pay for school and to help support them after she's gone. They can't touch the money until they're either graduated from college or turn twenty-five years of age, whichever comes first, and we put Bradley (my money manager) in charge as executor until that day comes. Darius drags himself over and falls into my arms, mumbling a thank you through unshed tears.

He lifted his head. His eyes were red from trying to hold back the emotion. "I don't know how I'm ever going to pay you back for everything you've done for us."

Pay me back?

Clasping his face, I looked intently into his eyes to convey the gravity of my words. "I just want you to live a good life, Darius. That's the only payback I'll ever need. If you can accept that you deserve to have a good life and you go after it, I will never need anything else from you." I pulled him in for another hug as he let the tears finally fall.

Roman hugged him, patting his back. "Merry Christmas Darius."

We made the rounds of the rest of the family, then enjoyed an amazing Christmas dinner before everyone went home.

I called Maggie and Abby on three way, to wish them a Merry Christmas. I knew that they'd be running around seeing family all day. So I didn't even know if they'd answer.

After a quick chat with the girls, I collapsed on the couch. Roman sat down and I laid my head on his lap.

I let out a deep sigh. "Someone needs to find Marcus and put a stop to this. No one had a normal Christmas this year. Everyone was on edge, and we had ten bodyguards in the building. This is insane." And exhausting, I thought as I groaned.

"You're absolutely right..." *Seriously, he's agreeing with me? That's a first.* "...I don't know what to do. How are we supposed to raise a family with this kind of craziness?"

"We need to draw him out somehow."

He practically threw me up to a sitting position and grabbed my shoulders.

"What? Are you f'ing crazy? You are not drawing anyone out—do you hear me?"

Not me. Good lord, no.

"Sorry, that must've come out wrong..." His shoulders relaxed as he wrapped his arms around me, pulling me aggressively back to his chest. He laid his forehead against my shoulder as his grip tightened around my stomach. "...I didn't mean me personally. I meant whoever's looking for him..." He nodded his head silently. "...I mean, is he hiding that good, or are we just being reactive? Again, by we, I mean whoever, is trying to find him." He seemed relieved as he took a couple of deep breaths and slouched back into the couch.

"Please don't mess with me like that. I'm tired and overprotective."

Just a little.

"I know. I'm going to call Grant tomorrow and see what's going on. I'm not sure he'll talk to me anymore about this, though. I think he's more amenable to telling you things now that we all know who he is."

Roman's eyes closed and he let out a breath that felt more like anxiety than relief. "There's something I think I should tell you." My eyes went wide as I slowly turned my head to look back at him.

***

ROMAN

"Oh yeah, what's that?" She said slowly, sitting up straighter to pay attention as she inched slightly away from me.

"I don't want you to think I was keeping it a secret from you. I just wanted to find the right time to tell you."

"Mhm." she said, scrunching her brows as she wiggled in her seat and peered into my eyes.

"Given the plethora of information already revealed, this isn't as significant as it might seem." I was hoping it would soften the blow.

"Just don't tell me I'm adopted or something and my parents didn't want me to know." She relaxed back on the sofa.

I smiled, angling myself into the corner so I could look at her.

"Cool, cuz that's not what it is, but weirdly it kind of feels the same."

She wrinkled up her face, shaking her head.

"More to do with Grant, then?" She asked wearily. I nodded.

"Now I know why he entrusted me to so much of the information. I was actually a part of the story and the other half of you or Emma, however you want to look at it..." She rolled her eyes, taking a deep breath. I can't imagine how hard it is to know you're in the situation you're in because someone thought you looked like their dead daughter. "...He called me the morning he fired you to tell me he was sending me the name and contact info for his attorney in charge of his will. He said that everything he has is in that will, and you're the beneficiary." She jumped up off the couch.

"I don't want it." She was swinging her arms around, shaking her head wildly.

Yep, that's the reaction I was expecting.

"I kind of thought that's what you'd say, but he wouldn't let me talk him out of it. He didn't want me to tell you until, well, the will was being read."

She looked scared and said, "What the hell is in that will? He was a hitman, a murderer. I don't want blood money or anything purchased with it. Can I refuse it? There has to be a legal way to get me out of this." I wrapped my arms around her to help her calm down. We sat back on the sofa and I handed her tea to her.

"Look, I don't know what's in that will. Honestly, I don't..." She looked at me skeptically while taking a big gulp. "...I do know that Grant wouldn't do that to you. He wouldn't connect you to any of his past life. Not on purpose, anyway. I know that what's happened recently is one big coincidence..." Or maybe not. "...that really snowballed but you're the only family that Grant acknowledges and I know he loves you like a daughter..." Her nostrils were flared and she was ready to breathe fire. "...You can always donate whatever's in that will."

***

ALEX

No more damn surprises. I don't care what Grant is leaving me. I can't accept it. I'm not his daughter. This is going a bit too far now. Standing, I pulled my arms out of his grasp. "I'm going to sleep this off. I don't know if I can take anymore of this shit." With that, I hurried down the hall and got in the bed, pulling the covers up over my head.

I'm jerked out of sleep by a loud noise that sounded an awful lot like a gunshot. I'm covered in sweat, practically hyperventilating. Roman was sound asleep. *How did he not hear that?* I gently rock his shoulder, trying to quietly wake him in case there was someone in the penthouse.

"Roman, I heard a noise." He's so groggy and having a hard time waking up.

"What's wrong?" he mumbled through a very sleepy haze.

I repeat myself, "I heard a noise. It sounded like a gunshot."

He woke suddenly and jumped out of the bed, frantically putting on clothes as he ran out to the kitchen with his phone. I followed him closely, listening to him talk on the phone to Randy. He finally hung up, walking over to me with a sympathetic smile on his face.

"I think you had a bad dream, babe."

I took a couple of deep breaths, realizing he may be right. It was the most vivid dream I've ever had, though. I saw it in flashes—the gun pointed at me as the trigger was pulled.

I put both hands on my face and began to sob. Roman put his arms around me and held me close, trying to comfort me by telling me everything was going to be alright. I don't know how to believe that right now. My dreams have been so telling of real life lately. I don't know what to think. Someone is trying to kill me and my family. What am I supposed to do? How do I not worry about this?

"I'm so scared something terrible is going to happen." I whimpered, clinging to him for dear life. Just having his arms around me was security to me. I've never needed this to feel safe, and it's terrifying.

"Nothing is going to happen..." He assured me. "...I won't let it. You will have constant protection until the end, I promise."

But how can he promise that?

"I can't live like this..." The panic was setting in again. *Will tea fix this?* I don't think it will stop a bullet, that's for sure. "...I don't want bodyguards surrounding us 24/7. This is no way to go through life."

"I know that babe, but right now we don't have a choice and I'm not willing to put you or my child at risk with this maniac on the loose."

Oh my god, we're prisoners in our own home. I cried some more and he took me back to the bedroom.

"Nothing is going to happen to this little miracle, that's all I know. We'll keep you safe." I sobbed as I stared down at my growing abdomen.

I was hoping to convince myself as well. Roman laid his forehead on my knees, wrapping his arms snug around us before ushering us back to sleep.

Chapter 38

ALEX

The morning of New Year's Eve, Roman seemed nervous and pre-occupied. I don't know what's gotten into him. He's assured me there's nothing to worry about, but he's been avoiding me most of the morning. We were having Amelia and Harrison over, but other than that, nothing exciting, so I wasn't sure what his nervousness was about.

Did he get more news about Marcus I wasn't going to like?

We went to the gym and walked to the coffee shop with Boss and Franco to get coffee and a pup cup for Tao, as well as keep some semblance of normalcy. Roman seemed unusually quiet and preoccupied still and it was making me nervous, but I didn't want to get upset in public.

"Hey. What's going on with you?" I whispered.

He smiled and said, "Nothing, sorry, just realizing that tomorrow is the year I become a dad, and you become a mom. It's sort of an overwhelming realization, I guess."

Now I was the silent one. I hadn't really thought too much about it lately and I'm the one who's having the baby.

I blew out a puff of air, sitting down with a thunk next to him as I looked down at my hands automatically splaying across my bump. "Holy Moly." I huffed. He laughed, grabbing my hand, kissing the back of it gently with a grin plastered to his face.

"Are you ready? There's no turning back now." He asked and I nodded, quickly leaning in for a very reassuring kiss.

Back at the penthouse after Amelia and Harrison arrived, Boss and Franco went home; Randy and Scott came on duty with Harrison and Amelia's bodyguards. They were staying in the apartment downstairs again and hanging out in the lobby to make sure the place was secure. There hasn't been anyone in the building for a week, since Roman told everyone the building would be closed until January second. It was a little ominous around here, but at least we felt safe.

Plus, there was no news on Marcus from anyone. He was like a ghost. The thing is, we can't just hide out until they find him. We have to go back to life as usual in a couple of days. I'm just glad I planned that vacation that's coming in two weeks. That gives me time to work on the gala details and make sure Darius and Shay have everything they needed to handle the District five project.

***

ROMAN

I'm a nervous wreck, sitting at my desk with sweaty palms, flipping the ring around in my hand, watching the sparkles bounce off the diamond with each turn, becoming hypnotized by it. Alex doesn't know I'm planning to propose. I came up with this idea when she asked me for the number of my travel agent. I called him right after telling him to charge whatever plans she made to my card on file and to get in touch with the venue and let them know we would be having a wedding there one day, but she doesn't know so not to tell her. I'm sure that was a challenge for him to maneuver around, but he worked it out. I also told him to book extra rooms and flights. That was the whole reason I put it all on my card, so she didn't find out about all the extra stuff.

I sent over the names of everyone that afternoon and their contact information to call them all and let them know this was a surprise. I only got laughed at by Edward, thinking she was going to kill me. I had a feeling after all this craziness this would be a welcome distraction, and she may even be happy that she didn't have to go through the burden of planning a wedding—*right?*

Tonight, however, I'll find out if I'm right or if Edward's right. Only Harrison and Amelia know I'm planning to propose to her at midnight.

I felt exhausted thinking about everything by the time Harrison and Amelia showed up, but they seemed in good spirits. Harrison and I went straight to the bar, pouring a couple of bourbons. I had a bottle of champagne chilling and a bottle of sparkling grape juice to ring in the new year. The girls went over to the sofa and turned on the TV to watch the start of the festivities before the ball dropped. We could see the lights of downtown all lit up through the windows. It looked like there was a lot of activity going on tonight. I'm damn glad we weren't a part of it though. I was enjoying our little bubble up here above it all.

Harrison whispered, "Are you ready, man?"

I let out a deep breath and said with a shift of my eyes in his direction, "I've done this before. Why is this freaking me out so much?" I lifted my drink to my lips and inhaled deeply before taking a rather large sip, hoping it would calm my nerves.

He laughed and said, "Because it's Alex and not Caitlin. Caitlin was a sure thing. She wanted the King lifestyle. Alex doesn't care about that and you've both gone through so much crap. I'm sure you've got some reservations that she might turn you down." He patted me sympathetically on the shoulder.

I shoved him away, annoyed. "Damn Harrison, that was the worst pep talk in history." We both laughed and poured another drink as we meandered over to sit with the girls.

It was about ten o'clock and Alex was getting sleepy. She was leaning into me, and I asked her if she wanted to go to sleep and I could wake her up at midnight. I mean, that would really suck if she slept through the new year and the proposal.

She looked up at me and assured me. "No, I'm going to have a little bit of the energizing tea. I feel like being awake for this new year. It feels really important. We have a lot to be thankful for, and I want to ring it in."

That's my girl.

"Okay, but don't put too much in. You don't want to be awake till next new year."

She giggled as she marched out to the kitchen with a little skip in her step. Amelia smiled and winked at me with a miniscule nod of her head. I had a feeling she knew more about the answer to the proposal than I did, and it felt like it was going to be the one I was looking for.

Ten seconds to go.

***

ALEX

Amelia ran in as soon as the elevator doors opened and attacked me. "Hey girl!"

"Miss me much?" I laughed as I tried to catch my breath.

"I'm just excited we get to ring in the new year with you guys."

"Me too. I wish we were going to do what we had planned, and party at Maggie's tonight, but I'm sort of glad it's going to be quaint and just the four of us and Tao."

"Aw, where is Tao, by the way?" She asked looking around for the little fur ball.

"He's back in the bedroom in the crate. He had a long morning playing with the guys, so he's probably going to sleep through the night."

We went into the kitchen, made some drinks, and headed over to the couch.

She squinted her eyes towards the guys. "Roman looks a little preoccupied tonight. What's up?"

I shrugged and said, "I have no idea. He said he's just nervous about becoming a father."

"I can see that. It's funny how Harrison is getting married before Roman. Roman was always so organized and planned things out. We never thought Harrison would actually want to get married."

"So, what brought you and Harrison together?" I was so curious. They seemed so different. I tucked my knees up under me, angling myself towards her to focus on the answer. Maybe see if there was something hidden in it.

She smiled and told me as if she'd been waiting to do this. "We hung out in the same places. I never thought I would end up with someone like Harrison. He just wasn't what I imagined for myself. I thought I would end up with someone more like Roman." I frowned for a second and she hurried up and continued, "But I was never into Roman at all. He and I...just never." She shook her head like she was trying to reassure me. Sort of made me want to laugh, or else I was a little worried she might have been interested in him. "Harrison was definitely my person, even though he had to wear me down a bit. He showed up everywhere I went and bugged me every day at work. Our first date was even a disaster. Every girl he ever dated was there and made a pass at him. I wanted nothing to do with him after that. You see how that worked out."

We both laughed. I opened up to her a little, too.

"Well, after my horrific marriage, I wasn't sure that I'd ever want to go that route again, but with a baby on the way and the father being Roman, I can't imagine my life without him. It wasn't marriage that bothered me, it was the person I was married to. I found that out during my forty-five-day vacation." One of many revelations.

She leaned in and hugged me. "I can't imagine a sweeter couple than the two of you."

I rolled my eyes slightly, thinking about how our relationship started off so rocky.

"I'm pretty sure sweet is not a valid description of this relationship."

"Well, it is to me." She patted my hand, giving it a warm squeeze.

Out on the balcony, the cold January wind whipped around us hard enough to sting my cheeks and water my eyes, but Roman's arms wrapped tightly around me created a pocket of warmth that somehow made the rest of the world disappear. The city glittered below us beneath a black velvet sky while distant fireworks occasionally burst in flashes of gold, silver, and red across the horizon. Music and laughter drifted faintly from off in the distance.

The railing beneath my fingertips felt icy as I leaned forward slightly, staring out over the city while my breath curled visibly into the night air. Somewhere below us, horns echoed through the streets while people shouted countdowns from rooftops, balconies, bars, and apartments all across the city.

Ten.

Nine.

Eight.

Roman pulled me closer against him, the wool of his sweater rough beneath my fingers while warmth radiated from his chest straight into me. The scent of his cologne mixed with the crisp smell of winter air, champagne, and smoke from fireworks beginning to fill the sky around us.

Three.

Two.

One.

Cheers erupted from every direction as fireworks exploded overhead, lighting the balcony in quick flashes of color while everyone around us clinked glasses and shouted, "Happy New Year."

Relief hit me unexpectedly hard.

This year was over.

Finally.

Roman lifted his glass against mine gently before looking down at me with an expression that immediately made my stomach flip.

"Happy New Year, baby. I wouldn't have wanted to spend this New Year with anyone else." His thumb brushed softly across my hand. "And I don't want to spend another New Year without you."

My breath caught.

Then I watched him reach into his pocket. Everything around me seemed to slow. The wind. The noise. The fireworks. My heartbeat thundered so loudly I could barely hear anything else while he pulled out a small ring box and opened it.

"Will you make my New Year's resolution come true and be my wife?"

My mouth fell open instantly. I looked at him. Then the ring.

Shock completely short-circuited my brain.

Amelia finally blurted out, "Soooo?"

Laughter broke out from Amelia and Harrison, snapping me back into reality.

"Oh my God," I choked out, tears immediately burning my eyes. "Yes, baby. Yes, I'll be your wife." I laughed through tears while shaking my head in disbelief. "I can't imagine doing another day of anything without you, Roman."

I practically launched myself at him, nearly knocking the ring from his hand in the process.

"Whoa—" he laughed, tightening his arms around me. "Here, put this on before it goes flying off the balcony."

I took the ring carefully this time, hands trembling while I slid it onto my finger beneath the glow of city lights and fireworks. It was beautiful in the simplest, most perfect way. A gold band with a perfectly round solitaire diamond that caught the light every time I moved my hand. Elegant. Timeless. Not oversized or flashy.

Just right. Exactly right.

Roman kissed me then, slow and warm despite the freezing wind around us, and the emotion behind it hit harder than the proposal itself. Love. Relief. Hope. Exhaustion. Survival. Everything we'd gone through seemed wrapped into that one moment.

Then my brain ruined it.

Oh my God.

Now I have to plan a wedding.

And a baby.

What the hell was I thinking getting myself into this mess?

Apparently, Roman felt the anxiety radiating off me almost immediately because he pulled back laughing softly and grabbed my hand.

"That's enough fun for tonight," he said. "It's cold, it's late, and you're spiraling. Let's go to bed."

Honestly? He took the words right out of my mouth.

Chapter 39

ROMAN

January second. Back to the office.

I went all the way down to the first floor to walk through the lobby and check things out myself. I knew the security team had already cleared everything before anyone arrived, but I still wanted to make sure people felt comfortable being back at work again. Other than a few employees still out on vacation, everyone had returned and seemed completely fine. I'm sure the paid week off for the holidays helped with that. Most of them had no idea how serious things actually became before I shut the place down for two weeks.

Alex was still getting ready when I left this morning, but she assured me she'd be coming into the office today too. She seemed more distracted than usual, though she blamed it on baby brain again. Darius and Shay were meeting with her later to go over details involving the neighborhood project, and with only a couple of weeks left before our two-week vacation slash surprise wedding in Anguilla, there was a lot happening all at once.

Of course, since this entire trip was my idea, everyone somehow decided I was the point of contact for everything related to it. Unfortunately for them, I was wildly unequipped to plan an actual wedding. Eventually, I redirected all questions involving the trip and ceremony to Amelia because I honestly had no idea what was happening beyond the fact that apparently I was getting married on a beach in a couple of weeks.

My plan was simple.

Have Amelia casually figure out what Alex wanted, pass that information along to the wedding planner at the resort, and let people who actually knew what they were doing handle the rest.

Speak of the devil.

"Good morning, Roman."

Amelia floated into my office in unusually good spirits. The new year apparently looked good on her. I wasn't entirely sure what I was hoping to figure out regarding her situation this year, but at the moment I had no intention of letting it interfere with my plans for the trip. I'd pay closer attention to all of that afterward.

"Good morning," I said. "Do you have any meetings lined up with Alex today? Maybe something involving the gala or anything where you can casually get ideas from her?"

Amelia immediately stifled a laugh before nodding and handing me a copy of my schedule for the day.

"So what exactly do you want me to ask her?" she asked. "Flowers? Colors? Music? Food? What about a dress? Do you want me to figure out what kind of dress she'd want and order it? I'm pretty good at sizing people up, and honestly, Alex doesn't seem difficult to please when it comes to fashion."

I stared at her for a second. A dress. I forgot there needed to be a dress. This entire thing was officially far beyond my capabilities. I closed my eyes briefly and nodded before opening them again slowly.

"You know what? Yes. You do whatever you think is best, and if you can coordinate everything with the planner on the island, that would be spectacular." I leaned back in my chair and exhaled heavily. "I'll even pay you some kind of planning fee for dealing with this because this whole thing is way over my head." I paused. "She's going to kill me, isn't she?"

Amelia laughed while I sat there realizing this was rapidly turning into a monumental disaster I created myself.

"It won't be a problem," she assured me. "Alex is going to love it. She'll be happy when she sees everyone there. Honestly, I don't think she's going to care nearly as much as you think about what she's wearing or planning details. She'll probably be happiest if the whole thing just materializes in front of her so she can focus on enjoying the vacation."

God, I hoped she was right.

There were so many details involved in this I never would've even considered. Flowers. Dresses. Music. Seating. Food. I just wanted to marry her before the baby came and have our friends and families there when it happened.

Right as I opened my mouth to make another comment about it, Alex came barging into the office hysterically, flailing her arms around while rambling so fast neither of us could immediately understand what she was saying.

***

ALEX

Where the hell is my white cable-knit sweater?

I stood in the middle of the closet staring at clothes like they personally offended me. Was that even what I wanted to wear today? I had meetings, and technically it was freezing outside, but I didn't actually have to go outside if I didn't want to. Did I need to look professional today? Comfortable? Somewhere in between? Why did getting dressed suddenly feel like a life decision?

I dropped down onto the bench in the closet and stared at the ring on my finger.

Okay. I've done this before. Marriage wasn't some foreign concept to me. But last time I wasn't pregnant. Last time I didn't run a foundation.

Last time I didn't have a fundraising gala to organize while trying to launch a business, maintain my sanity, and figure out how the hell motherhood fit into all of this.

I dropped my head into my hands and tried to calm myself down. It wasn't working—at all. I still needed to get dressed, though, so after another minute of spiraling internally, I decided on black. Simple. Easy.

Honestly, I felt like I was mourning my old life a little bit anyway. Or at least mourning my manageable to-do list.

UGH.

When I finally made it out of the closet, I was dressed entirely in black, including black boots, and grabbed a black jacket in case I ended up going out to lunch. By the time I made it to the kitchen, I was already mentally running through everything I probably forgot. I grabbed a banana and a bottle of water while trying to organize my thoughts.

I know I'm forgetting something. At least we lived upstairs. If I forgot something, I could just run back up and get it. Hopefully. Roman had already taken Tao out this morning, so at least that was one less thing on my list. I glanced toward the elevator and noticed my bags already sitting neatly on the chair waiting for me. He must've done that too.

I tossed my phone into my purse, grabbed everything, and headed downstairs to the office. The panic hit the second the elevator doors closed. Perfect timing. And because apparently the universe enjoyed piling on, I glanced out the glass toward the green space twenty-four floors below and immediately got dizzy. My stomach rolled hard enough I thought I might actually throw up before I even made it downstairs.

By the time the elevator doors opened, one thought repeated so loudly in my head it drowned everything else out.

I cannot do all of this today.

"Oh my God, I can't do this," I blurted the second I stormed into Roman's office. "I have no idea what meetings I even have today. Some guy just told me he'd see me at 'the meeting' and I don't even know who the hell he is." My hands flew around while words spilled out faster and faster. "On top of that, I have a baby on the way that I have no idea what to do with and a wedding to plan? When exactly am I supposed to have time to plan a wedding with all this other stuff going on?"

I barely stopped long enough to breathe.

"And what about the gala? The fundraiser for the foundation? That's the most important thing right now. I need to focus on that. Everything else is going to have to wait." My chest tightened painfully. "But babies don't wait, do they? They just come whether you're ready or not..."

The room suddenly felt too warm. Too bright. Too loud. The last thing I clearly remembered was Roman directly in front of me, his hands firmly braced on my shoulders as the panic fully took over.

"Alex, slow down. Did something happen?" he asked.

"What do you mean did something happen?" I stared at him in disbelief. "Have you not been around for the past several months? Lots of things have happened." I pointed dramatically toward my stomach. "For one, I'm pregnant."

How was he this calm?

"For another, I have to plan a gala and a wedding while preparing for a baby and taking care of a puppy that's barely old enough to be away from his mama. I don't know what I'm doing."

My chest tightened harder.

Oh God.

I really think I'm going to lose it.

"Oh, and on the way into your office some guy said hi to me and mentioned seeing me at the meeting today, and I have absolutely no idea what meeting he's talking about, but I still smiled and said 'you too' like I knew what was happening."

I threw my hands into the air before collapsing dramatically onto the sofa.

Roman carefully lowered himself beside me like I might actually start swinging again, which honestly felt fair considering recent history. He glanced toward Amelia and nodded subtly for her to give us a minute. She immediately slipped out of the office and closed the door behind her.

"Honey," he said carefully, "first off, I need you to take a deep breath. Did you bring any tea with you today?"

I paused. Because unfortunately we'd both come to the conclusion that the tea did, in fact, help. It wasn't a miracle cure, but it definitely kept the crazy at a more socially acceptable level.

"I haven't had any tea this morning," I admitted slowly while digging back through my memory. "I'm pretty sure." I frowned harder. "I was too busy trying to organize everything in my head so I could make all of this work."

I slumped sideways onto the pillow dramatically. Roman grabbed both my hands and gently pulled me upright again.

"Come on," he said softly. "Let's go get you some tea. We need to calm you down so we can organize your day."

I nodded immediately and let him help me up before guiding me down the hall toward the kitchen.

He leaned against the counter watching me while I prepared the tea and added the calming tincture. The warm herbal scent drifted upward with the steam while I wrapped both hands around the mug and held it beneath my nose, breathing deeply.

One breath.

Then another.

And slowly, little by little, I felt the panic begin loosening its grip.

"Does Shay have your schedule? I know she used to handle all of that for you," he asked while I took a few sips of tea and actually concentrated long enough to process the question.

"Yes," I said slowly. "I believe she still does my scheduling."

Roman wrapped an arm around me and walked me back toward his office, and for the first time all morning, everything felt calm again.

*Mmm...*Nice and relaxed.

"Let's find Shay and get your schedule," he said. "Do you have your phone and your bag with your computer and work stuff? I left them by the elevator for you this morning."

I looked around his office. Nothing. Immediately my stomach tightened again. I set my tea down and walked back into the hallway, scanning around for my things. Just as panic started creeping back in, Amelia's voice cut through it.

"I have your stuff back here," she said. "You dropped everything in the middle of the hallway on your way into Roman's office, so I figured I'd keep it safe for you."

She gave Roman a quick wink while he nodded appreciatively. I dropped my head as a low laugh escaped me.

"Oh my God. Thank you, Amelia. You're a lifesaver."

"What the hell just happened to me?" I asked a few minutes later while sitting behind Amelia's desk. I was completely mortified, but thankfully she was trying not to laugh. Honestly, I felt like I'd just survived some kind of prehistoric emotional extinction event.

"Honey," she said gently, "you've got a lot going on in your life right now, and we just need to get it under control. First things first, let's get Shay out here before you go into any meetings. Have you had enough tea?"

I nodded, and she immediately called Shay.

"Hey, what's up?" Shay came bouncing out of the conference room with her usual bright energy before stopping when she looked at me. Her expression shifted into immediate concern mixed with understanding.

I took a deep breath. Poor girl was probably wondering how a complete lunatic like me ever managed to mentor anyone.

"I need to know what's on my schedule today."

She smiled softly and pulled out her phone without even blinking.

Was I always like this?

She'd worked with me for at least three years now, and somehow she never seemed remotely phased when I needed help with something as simple as remembering my own schedule.

"I sent it to you this morning in your email, but I can just read off what's on the agenda for today."

My emails. Did I even check them this morning? I paused, genuinely trying to remember.

"I don't think I looked at my email at all today," I admitted. "That probably could've prevented at least some of this insanity."

Both of them laughed while Shay pulled up my schedule and started reading through the day for me.

Honestly, I'd probably always been this scatterbrained. The difference was I'd never really noticed before because there had always been people around helping me keep everything together before it had the chance to completely fall apart.

"Amelia," I said, looking over at her, "could you do me a favor whenever you have time?"

"Of course."

"Could you make me a want ad for a personal assistant?"

That earned another round of laughter while I dramatically dropped into the chair beside her desk. Amelia continued helping me organize the day while Shay filled in details about meetings, and after a few minutes, Amelia printed my schedule out in black and white so I wouldn't forget to go digging through my phone looking for it later.

Chapter 40

ROMAN

"Amelia, can you get Alex situated? I have a call in a couple of minutes about the Burrow Township project."

The tea had already worked wonders on Alex's mood, so I left her with Amelia long enough to actually get some work done. Honestly, this was exactly the kind of thing Amelia handled best. If she ever decided to quit working for us, I genuinely hoped she opened her own assistant agency and trained people to function exactly the way she did. She'd make millions.

"Of course," Amelia said easily. "We'll go find Shay and make sure Alex is all squared away. You go take your call."

I headed back into my office and shut the door behind me, finally allowing myself a long breath. She really had to learn how to delegate.

At this point, taking over the wedding planning felt less like a romantic gesture and more like a survival tactic. Anything that removed even one thing from Alex's plate was worth it.

I sat down at my desk and called Charlie, the foreman overseeing the Burrow Township project. We conference-called the police department and the insurance company together so we could figure out how long it was realistically going to take to get the project moving again.

The insurance assessment came in at over two hundred million dollars in damages. Two hundred million.

I leaned back slowly in my chair, staring out the office windows while the numbers continued getting thrown around. At this point, I honestly questioned whether it made more sense to call it a total loss and rebuild from the ground up. This project was already pushing close to a billion dollars before taking a hit like this.

"Charlie," I said finally, "in your professional opinion, what's it going to take to salvage what's there enough to continue building?"

I wanted his honest assessment, but I also hoped he saw the situation the same way I did without me having to outright say it. We'd worked together long enough over the years that he understood how I thought. A total loss wouldn't necessarily be a bad thing here. Not if insurance covered it. That was part of the reason I made sure the police stayed on the call with the insurance company instead of relying solely on written reports. They saw the damage firsthand. The destruction was extensive. Nobody could realistically deny that. Unfortunately, insurance companies had a habit of trying anyway.

"In my honest opinion, it's a total loss," Charlie said. "There really isn't enough structure left to work with. Most everything is down to the foundation, and the amount of cleanup alone could take months. At that point, the delay sets the project back more than the remaining structures are worth."

That's my guy. There's a reason I keep working with him.

"This is Richard. I'm handling your claim," another voice chimed in. "I'd like to ask the officer a couple of questions, if that's alright."

I rolled my eyes immediately.

"Officer Rogers, it says here you were the responding officer at the scene. Is that correct?"

I took a sip of coffee and leaned back in my chair while waiting for the response. Honestly, I was probably going to send the guy a thank-you card for agreeing to sit through this miserable call in the first place. I pushed back from my desk and slowly turned my chair toward the windows, staring out over the city while listening to the obligatory insurance-company questions that inevitably wouldn't mean a damn thing once we reached the actual issue.

"Yes," Officer Rogers answered calmly. "I was on scene. I completed the incident report."

Incident?

This wasn't an incident.

It was devastation.

"I reviewed your report," Richard continued, "and while it does mention extensive damage, I don't see anything indicating a total loss."

That's because determining total loss isn't his job.

I leaned my head back and dragged a hand through my hair before turning back toward the speakerphone.

"That's correct," the officer replied. "I do not assess damage in those terms. I did, however, provide photographs documenting the extent of the destruction."

God, I really did not have the patience for this call today.

"Richard," I interrupted, "what exactly is it you need from us?"

I wanted to skip ahead to whatever point he was trying to dance around.

"I'm simply trying to determine whether the property is actually a total loss or if it's salvageable."

Then maybe your ass needs to come look at it yourself.

"Okay, so I guess you'll need to schedule a time to meet us at the site then, Richard."

I kept my tone neutral even though I already knew exactly how this was going to go. Guys like him had no desire to do actual fieldwork, especially not in the middle of winter. It took us nearly an entire day to walk the property ourselves and assess the damage. There was no chance he wanted to spend hours out there climbing through destruction in the cold if he could avoid it.

He'd ask for photos. Look over reports. Make a decision from the comfort of his heated office. Probably sitting in a cubicle somewhere far away from the disaster zone.

"I don't think that'll be necessary," Richard replied.

Agreed.

"I can tell from the officer's photographs and report that the damage was extensive enough to qualify as a total loss." Papers shuffled faintly through the speaker. "My preliminary estimate, before final review, is approximately five hundred and fifty million dollars. I'll send over the initial paperwork today along with finalized numbers tomorrow. I will also need photographs from before the incident if those are available."

I glanced toward the ceiling for a second, relieved this wasn't turning into a month-long fight.

"That won't be a problem," I said.

Charlie confirmed he'd send everything over as well.

"Thank you, Mr. King," Richard said. "And we're sorry for your trouble."

Trouble. That was certainly one word for it.

I said goodbye to Charlie and Officer Rogers once the call wrapped up. As relieved as I was by the outcome, it still meant the Burrow Township project was getting pushed back significantly. Now we had to clean up the site, tear down what remained, and have the architect start almost entirely from scratch.

The investors definitely weren't going to love the delay.

Still, I was fairly certain they'd prefer delays over financial ruin. In the end, the people responsible for this mess didn't hurt us nearly as badly as they intended to.

I leaned back in my chair and rubbed a hand across my jaw before deciding I should probably call Grant and update him on how the meeting went.

Amelia had been periodically sending me updates on Alex throughout the morning so I wouldn't worry and could actually focus on work before the meeting later with Alessandro and his vintner. Between the foundation, the project, the wine business, the wedding, the baby, and everything else crashing into our lives at once, we really did have too much on our plates right now.

Worrying about each other constantly on top of it all could quickly become its own problem.

I picked up my phone and called Grant.

"Roman, Happy New Year," he answered warmly. "How's Alex?"

I blinked for a second, realizing I'd already forgotten we were in a new year and somehow already on day two of it.

JE JOHNSON

"Happy New Year," I replied. "Alex is... Alex, if that makes sense. Honestly, she might even be a little more Alex right now since she's pregnant."

Grant laughed immediately, clearly understanding exactly what I meant.

"Well, we're all looking forward to the wedding in a couple of weeks. We're very happy for both of you."

We. He always said we. I assumed he meant the Santoros, though considering this entire insane wedding idea started with them and my father, there was a decent chance he included Fitz in that statement too. At this point, I was just grateful things were unfolding this way because we wanted them to— Not because anyone was forcing us into it.

"Yeah, we're excited too." I leaned back in my chair before shifting gears. "On the other hand, I need to talk about Marcus..."

Silence met me on the other end immediately.

The atmosphere of the conversation changed instantly, warmth giving way to something heavier now that we'd stepped into darker territory. Honestly, I didn't have the patience for small talk anymore.

"What do you want to talk about, son?"

There it was. That guarded tone Grant always slipped into whenever conversations drifted toward his old life. Normally, I hated it. Right now, though, I needed that version of him. The one people used to fear.

"Marcus devastated that community and probably thinks he won some kind of battle against me," I said bluntly. "I want to make sure he understands he actually made my life easier by doing it."

An actual laugh came through the phone, and I could physically hear the tension shift in Grant's demeanor afterward.

"I think that would be a very good idea," he admitted. "And I know you're not a fan of the life I used to live. Honestly, neither was I. That's why we fought so hard to get out of it. I need you to understand that."

I stayed silent, listening.

"There's more to this story than you know," he continued carefully. "And before we start trying to flush Marcus out of hiding, there are things you need to understand."

A knot tightened immediately in my stomach.

"He's not hiding, Roman," Grant said quietly. "He's regrouping."

My grip tightened around the phone.

What the hell does that mean? Regrouping with who? I thought Marcus was the last one standing in all of this. His father was gone. His brother was gone. Every idiot involved in the attempted bombing was either dead or arrested. Who the hell was left?

"Could you maybe be a little more specific than that?" I asked, trying to keep my voice level. "Because I was under the impression we were dealing with one isolated asshole here."

Silence stretched for half a second too long. And suddenly panic started creeping in. I should've known Grant had more information. He always had more information.

Damn it.

"I can't give you this information over the phone," Grant said. "I'd like you to meet me at my house. The Santoros will be there as well." He paused briefly before adding, "I'd like Alex there too, but I understand if you want to keep her away because of the baby. The information could be a bit much for her."

I stared at the computer screen in silence, biting down on my lip while my brain tried to process what the hell I was about to walk into.

Do I bring Alex? Do I not? Part of me thought it was better to tell her now while the pregnancy was still early instead of risking something worse later when stress could affect her more physically. But another part of me immediately spiraled into worst-case scenarios. What if the information was too much? What if the stress hurt her? The baby?

Ugh.

I already knew keeping secrets from Alex wasn't the answer. We'd learned that lesson the hard way. And realistically, she was going to find out eventually no matter what I decided.

I leaned back in my chair and grabbed a handful of my hair with both hands, squeezing hard before forcing myself to calm down long enough to make a decision. The tea helped her. But honestly, we couldn't keep living like this.

"We need to have this meeting as soon as possible," I said finally. "And Alex will be there."

God, I hoped I was making the right decision. Because whatever this was, whatever Marcus was regrouping for, we needed to stop it before it got any worse.

"I'll reach out as soon as I speak with Alessandro to set a date and time," Grant replied.

We ended the call, and the second the line disconnected, I dropped my head onto the desk and closed my eyes.

***

ALEX

I glanced over the schedule again and checked the time while trying to mentally prepare myself to function like a normal professional adult for the rest of the day. Shay was still standing there beside Amelia's desk when she finally smiled and said, "Come on, I'll walk with you."

I got up and looped my arm through hers while Amelia called out, "Good luck," from behind us.

"I'll probably need it," I muttered.

As we walked down the hallway, Shay started going over the details of the meeting.

"This one is for the Jackson side of the project," she explained. "We're meeting with some of the residents to go over renovation options. The designer and project manager will be there, and Darius is going to explain what options are available to everyone. It's based on the home they purchased, how much was used for the purchase itself, and the additional funding allotted depending on need and the size of the home."

I glanced over at her, genuinely impressed.

I always knew Shay was smart, but I hadn't realized how focused and professional she'd become. For some reason, I'd always thought of her as a little flighty, but honestly, that probably came from only really knowing her during the years we partied together and when she worked as the receptionist.

I hadn't actually worked alongside her much since Grant started training her.

Clearly, I underestimated her.

She was probably the most organized person I'd ever worked with, which at this point in my life felt less like a luxury and more like a necessity. Amelia was incredible too, but I seriously doubted Roman would ever willingly let me steal her away permanently.

"I'm assuming I'm mostly just sitting in on this one to listen?" I asked.

Shay smiled and squeezed my arm against her side as we walked into the conference room.

"We love when you sit in on these meetings. You don't let anybody pull fast ones on us, and honestly, I think Darius likes having the backup. He gets a little flustered when people start questioning his decisions about spending."

I slid into my chair and started organizing my things in front of me.

"I love the way he handles the money," I admitted. "He's frugal, but quality is always the priority. That's exactly how this project should be run."

"And oh my God," Shay continued excitedly, "taking residents out with the designer to look at houses has been so much fun. She brings her laptop and does mock renovations right there in the middle of these completely rundown houses using the architect's specs. It's amazing." She grinned. "That's also how we get the base cost estimates for each project before meetings like this."

I smiled despite myself. It actually did sound exciting.

"Today is Ronda Williams," Shay explained. "Single mother of three. You'll meet her in a second."

Honestly, if I didn't already have the wine business pulling my attention in another direction, I would've completely immersed myself in this project. Watching everything come together felt incredibly rewarding.

The conference room was already set up when we walked in. Darius sat at the head of the table while several people around him worked quietly behind open laptops preparing documents and designs. I immediately spotted the guy from earlier—the one who mentioned seeing me at this meeting.

Thank God. At least now I knew he wasn't imaginary.

I carried only my notebook since I planned to mostly observe and walked around the table introducing myself before explaining that I was there simply to listen in. Ronda already knew Darius and Ella from the neighborhood, so she looked comfortable with the entire process from the beginning. She was a single mother of three who worked full-time as a receptionist at a doctor's office downtown. Between her income and the money from selling her home in Burrow Township, she'd been able to purchase one of the better fixer-upper properties available.

We'd allocated fifty thousand dollars toward renovations, and after purchasing the house, she still had another fifty thousand remaining from the sale of her previous home. The current plan was to use approximately seventy-five thousand total for renovations, leaving the remaining twenty-five thousand in escrow for unexpected expenses or incidentals. Whatever remained afterward would go back to Ronda.

That had been the agreement she signed off on from the beginning. For now, she and the kids were renting a place until construction finished.

I flipped through the paperwork quietly while everyone discussed layouts, repairs, timelines, and renovation priorities.

The meeting lasted about an hour while everyone worked through what would be fully renovated versus what would simply be repaired cosmetically for budget purposes. Once the numbers were finalized, the designer connected her laptop to the large screen at the front of the room and began pulling up the renderings. Slowly, Ronda's future home came to life in three dimensions with updated flooring, a redesigned kitchen, bedrooms for the kids, fresh paint, lighting, and furniture placement that transformed the once rundown property into something warm and beautiful.

The transformation was incredible.

I sat there staring at the screen feeling unexpectedly emotional watching a home that once looked hopeless become something safe and welcoming right in front of us. When I glanced over at Ronda, I noticed she was quietly dabbing at her eyes with tissues someone had slid across the table to her, and honestly, that nearly broke me too.

Before she left, I hugged her tightly and she thanked me for starting the foundation. That moment alone reminded me exactly why all of this mattered. The stress, the pressure, the endless meetings, the fights, and everything we'd been through somehow led to this. Deep down, I think I always knew there was something more I was supposed to be doing with my life. I just needed the right opportunity to find it. I was still angry about the road it took to get here, but without all the obstacles and heartbreak along the way, I don't think any of this would've carried the same meaning.

The next meeting Shay walked me to involved the renovations for the Santoro Winery. Roman would be joining us along with Mr. Santoro and his vintner, Giorgio. Thankfully, there were no investors involved today, just the architectural team reviewing plans they'd already discussed and giving updates on the progress so far.

We were still working through the details involving my non-alcoholic wine business, including branding, naming, and the logistics of how everything would operate. My role in this meeting was mostly to hear about the additional space Roman was having built specifically for my business as a gift. The idea still overwhelmed me a little. Technically, the space could always be converted into additional winery production if something ever happened to my business, but the fact that he was building something specifically for me and my future still didn't feel entirely real.

Roman winked at me when I walked into the meeting, but he kept his distance physically, which I appreciated. Inside the building, he was always the definition of professionalism no matter what was happening between us personally.

Alessandro, however, was not nearly as restrained.

The second he saw me, he crossed the room, wrapped me in a hug, and kissed both of my cheeks in greeting, which still caught me off guard a little considering everything I now knew about him and his past. He introduced me to his vintner, Giorgio, who immediately seemed excited about my ideas and eager to help however he could.

"So, Ms. Kennedy, what can I do for you?" Giorgio asked, his accent somehow even thicker than Alessandro's.

I smiled automatically, momentarily distracted by the smooth musical rhythm of the way he spoke before realizing he'd actually asked me a question.

"Oh, sorry," I said quickly, lowering my head with an embarrassed laugh. "I need to know if there's a way to make wine without alcohol but still have it taste the same."

I bit down lightly on my bottom lip while waiting for his response.

"Alessandro told me about your idea," Giorgio said. "I've actually been experimenting with it for a few weeks now to see if it could be done." He smiled proudly. "I attempted both a chardonnay and a cabernet. Since there's no alcohol involved, it doesn't require nearly as much fermentation time." He gestured toward the small cooler beside him. "I brought bottles of each for everyone to taste."

My stomach tightened instantly.

Giorgio removed the bottles from the cooler and started passing around wine glasses while Roman quietly watched me from across the table. I felt strangely emotional even holding the glass in my hand. Part of me still carried that lingering fear of what if there's alcohol in it?

I glanced down at my hand and noticed it trembling slightly.

Roman noticed too. He gave me a small reassuring smile and a subtle nod that somehow grounded me enough to breathe again. I inhaled slowly and tried to steady myself while Giorgio poured a small amount into each glass.

"It's been tested," he said gently, almost like he could read every thought crossing my face. "Zero percent alcohol."

I nodded, swallowing hard before finally lifting the glass to my lips. The familiar scent alone hit me first, immediately pulling memories to the surface. Nights sitting at bars. Music playing softly in the background. Drinking wine at home after long days. Pieces of my old life rushed back so vividly it almost hurt.

I closed my eyes and took the smallest sip. Cool liquid coated my tongue with crisp notes of pear and citrus followed by a smooth buttery finish that tasted remarkably close to real wine without the harsh bite of alcohol underneath it. It was beautiful. And safe. Emotion rose so quickly it caught me completely off guard. Tears slipped down my cheeks while I sat there holding the glass, overwhelmed not by what this could do for me—But by what it could have done for my mother.

"Alex, are you okay?" Roman asked softly as professionalism finally gave way to concern and he wrapped an arm around his overly emotional pregnant fiancée.

The weight of the ring on my finger suddenly felt heavier than usual as I stared down at the glass in my hand and thought about everything it represented in this moment. Recovery. Love. Family. A future I never thought I'd have.

I nodded and carefully set the glass down before wiping tears from my cheeks. A shiver moved through me while I tried to regain control of my emotions.

"I was just thinking about my mom," I admitted quietly.

I pressed my lips together tightly, trying to keep any additional tears from falling because I still needed to give my opinion on the wine.

"Giorgio," I said, looking back toward him, "there's really zero alcohol in this?"

"That is correct," he assured me gently. "How do you feel about the flavor?"

"I think it's perfect," I answered honestly. "It's so close to regular chardonnay that it would honestly be difficult to distinguish between the two." I glanced back down at the glass again. "My only concern is whether the tinctures will affect the flavor too much. They're pretty strong."

Giorgio nodded thoughtfully before asking, "Do you think there could be a way to create a concentrate that preserves the medicinal properties while removing most of the flavor?"

I blinked.

That possibility hadn't even occurred to me. But honestly, Mr. Tanjung would probably know the answer to something like that. I needed to contact him and Melati anyway about hiring the farming family she knew to help with the herbs. I quickly typed myself a reminder into my phone before answering.

"I have a phone call to make to find out," I said. "I'll do that first thing tomorrow morning and get back to you."

Afterward, we sampled the cabernet as well, which somehow tasted just as rich and full-bodied without the sharp bite alcohol normally carried. By the time the meeting wrapped up, my emotions had finally calmed enough for me to think clearly again.

We gathered our things while Roman explained he had a few things to handle before lunch, so I stayed behind with Amelia while everyone else filtered out of the conference room.

***

ROMAN

I didn't realize how hard I was tugging at my hair until I heard someone clear their throat softly from the doorway. My knuckles cracked when I finally released my grip, and I rubbed a hand over my head before looking up to find a beautiful glowing face smiling at me. She looked far more relaxed than she had during the meeting about the "non wine biz," as she called it.

"I knocked, but you didn't answer," she said quietly while lingering near the doorway. "I didn't hear a conversation, so I figured I'd come check on you. I texted you first."

She looked sweet, rested, and calm in a way that immediately eased something inside me. Her voice sounded soothing instead of frantic like it had earlier this morning when it felt like all hell was breaking loose around her, or when emotion overtook her while tasting the nonalcoholic wine and thinking about her mother.

"I was wondering if you wanted to go out for lunch," she said with a small shrug. "Or maybe just go upstairs? We could take Tao for a walk."

She tipped her head slightly to the side while patiently waiting for my answer, and honestly, I realized in that moment just how badly I needed the break.

Without another word, she walked around the desk and carefully lowered herself onto my lap before brushing the hair back from my face. Her lips pressed tenderly against my forehead and lingered there for a moment, the simple gesture somehow soothing every tense thought running through my head. I wrapped my arms around her waist immediately and rested my head against her shoulder, nuzzling into the warmth of her neck while breathing in the soft vanilla scent that always seemed to calm me down. The combination of her warmth, her softness, and the quiet affection sent chills across my skin, and for a second the thought of having her upstairs alone nearly overtook every other responsibility waiting for me downstairs.

"I would love to go to lunch with you," I said, still holding her against me. "Honestly, I think upstairs sounds perfect. Taking Tao for a walk is probably exactly what I need to recover from this unexpected morning."

She tilted her head slightly and scrunched her brow at me, clearly sensing there was more behind that statement than I was saying out loud. I gave her a weak smile and a quick wink, hoping it would keep her from asking questions I wasn't ready to answer yet.

Thankfully, it worked.

"I just need to grab my bag from Amelia's desk and we can head upstairs."

Curiosity faded from her expression as quickly as it appeared. I pulled her in for another kiss, one that immediately threatened to derail lunch entirely, but I forced myself to pull away before things escalated any further. I gently pushed her off my lap and patted her on the backside to usher her toward the door.

We could revisit that situation upstairs.

"I'll be out in just a minute," I told her as she quietly shut the office door behind her.

Once she was gone, I finished sending the last few emails waiting for me before finally pushing back from the desk. I stood and stretched as high as I could, every muscle in my back and shoulders tightening before several loud cracks echoed through the office, especially when I rolled my neck from side to side.

God. I needed this break more than I realized.

After one long breath, I closed my laptop and shut off the lights on my way out of the office.

Chapter 41

ROMAN

I didn't want to ruin lunch with the thought of more information about Marcus, so I grabbed her hand and brought her over to the couch where I sat her down on my lap bringing my hands up to her face. I brushed my lips gently over hers as her hands looped around the back of my neck. She pulled away as I sunk my face into her neck.

"What's going on with you?" She tried to lean further away, but I needed her as close as I could get her right now.

"We have to meet with Grant. At his house." I pulled my face up slowly, looking into her eyes to see if there was alarm or worry, but there was neither. She was still calm and seemed in control.

"Do you know what it's about?" She asked.

I smiled, because do I ever know what it's about? Not really, but I'm giving her what little information I do know this time.

"No. Only that it's about Marcus and he couldn't tell me over the phone." My eyes swiped back and forth, trying to get a read on her, but I was still getting nothing to worry about. I wonder if *I* was worrying her.

"I guess we'll find out. I'm looking forward to seeing his home." She smiled and leaned in for another kiss, to which I graciously accepted, coaxing my tongue gently through her lips. Our tongues danced smoothly and in sync with every soft swipe. She turned to straddle my hips, running her hands through my hair, pulling our bodies and mouths closer together. I smiled through the kiss as I felt her stomach press against my abs, and this was the first time I noticed the bump where our baby was safely growing.

"What are you smiling about?" She said with a grin of her own. I leaned her away a little to get a better look at her tiny bump.

"I was just realizing how happy I am, even in the midst of all this other stuff." I reached down and rubbed my hand over her belly. It wasn't that it was very big or even that noticeable. There was a new firmness to it. One that was smoother than the taut, defined muscles she usually has there. Then I had the sudden urge to keep her as far away from whatever this information was as possible.

"Alex, do you think it's a good idea for you to go to this meeting? What if I give you the condensed version with all the pertinent information and you can stay here with Boss?" She pushed herself up to standing with her hands on my chest and I let my arms fall to my side ready for my verbal chastising.

"Roman, the answer is no. I'm going to the meeting. What difference does it make if I hear the information from you or from them?" She lifted her eyebrow and pursed her lips as she looked me dead in the eyes. She didn't raise her voice or even get a little upset as she stood there with her arms crossed in front her.

"You're right, of course. It doesn't make a difference in the least. I just don't want you getting upset. When you heard that information at the jail from Tanner and ended up in the hospital, I thought I was going to lose my mind. Please tell me you'll be ok with whatever they have to say?"

She uncrossed her arms and sat back down on my lap, leaning her forehead against mine.

"I promise I'll be ok. We will be ok. I was fine after we heard all the information about you and Emma. What else could there be worse than that?"

That's what worried me. I can only imagine what there could be if Grant thinks Marcus is regrouping. Whatever the hell that means.

***

ALEX

"I'll get Tao so we can take him for a walk." I said.

Roman finished cleaning the dishes from lunch and I walked back to get Tao, thinking about how worried he seemed about this meeting with Grant that was putting me in a similar state of panic that I needed to keep under control. What in the world could there be to talk about now? Marcus is a lunatic, check, we've already figured that out. He tried to blow us up. We have a squadron of security watching us. Not to mention all the other information about Grant's look alike daughter Emma being betrothed to Roman. I can't imagine there's too much more that could shock me right now. I took Tao out of his crate and got his leash hooked but didn't set him down as we got in the elevator. We met Boss and Franco downstairs to take the dog for a short walk before heading back to the office for the remainder of the day.

"Roman, we leave for vacation in two weeks. Are we ready to go? Do you think everything here will be ok while we're gone? We have the gala in two months, and the baby is due shortly after that. Do you think we should be going on this vacation right now?"

I was in the closet, casually going through my clothes to see if anything even fit to take on vacation. I didn't think any of my bathing suits were going to work.

"Yes, I can't think of a better idea than to get the hell out of here." He yelled from somewhere down the hall as I rummaged through my clothes, throwing them on the floor, trying to figure out what I might pack.

"Hey."

I jumped, startled, and turned around as he stood leaning on the door opening to the closet; arms crossed over his chest and feet crossed at the ankle, smiling at me with that gorgeous white, toothy grin. My heart pitter pattered at the sight of him looking relaxed again.

"Hey. I don't know if I'll have anything to wear in two weeks."

He shrugged and pushed himself off the wall, wrapping me in his strong arms. I think I needed this as I nuzzled in and threw my arms around his back. *Ahhh*, relaxation, if only temporarily.

"Baby, it doesn't matter. If you have nothing to wear, we can just buy you all new clothes when we get there. We are 100% going on this vacation. We need it." He kissed the top of my head as I breathed in his musky scent and began to relax further.

"Ok, but what about Tao? What are we doing with him?" I almost forgot about the dog. I don't want to leave him. Who would we leave him with, anyway? Maybe one of the girls could watch him.

"We're bringing him with us. Stop worrying."

I never thought of that. *This is good, it's under control.* I started to feel anxiety creeping in, thinking that nothing is ever really under control and the dam is just about to burst.

"When are we meeting Grant?" I tipped my head up to find his eyes, catching a small smile making its way to the corner of his mouth.

"Don't know. He hasn't called with those details yet." He was trying to stay calm and nonchalant for me, but I could tell he was feeling apprehensive about this meeting, too.

With that thought, Roman's phone started ringing and he pulled it out of his pocket, then glanced at it and back to me. "Well, what do ya know?" He released me with one hand as he turned us around to sit on the large bench, then positioned me on his lap before hitting the speaker button.

"Hello Grant. Alex and I are both here."

"Hi Grant."

"Hi Roman. Hi Alex." He was quiet for a moment before he said, "How would tomorrow night work for the two of you? We need to get all this out and over with as soon as possible. It's the only way to keep you both safe."

Roman's grip on my hip tightened as he drew in a deep breath.

"Fine. Would six o'clock work?" He looked at me and then looked back at the phone for confirmation.

"Yes, we'll see you then."

He clicked the phone off and laid it down, letting out the breath he was holding.

"It's going to be fine, right?" I tried to sound confident, but I definitely was anything but.

He nodded, then kissed my cheek as he got up, removing me from his lap and left the room.

Chapter 42

ROMAN

We pulled up to the address Grant texted and to a large wrought-iron gate with an intercom system. I pushed the button and noticed there was a video camera at the top of the black box. The gate slowly opened and we entered cautiously, following the long driveway up to a massive stone house. It looked more like a fortress than a house. It had a U shape with a perfectly manicured garden in the center. I pulled in behind my father's car, not at all surprised that he was here. The driveway opened up to what could be used as a parking lot with several cars I didn't recognize, as I looked from one side of the car park to the other. I walked around the car and opened the door for Alex, taking her hand so she didn't fall again. We walked up to the ostentatious black double doors that looked heavy and imposing. We were met at the door by a large muscled up guy in all black with a bald head and an earpiece. He looked at us but said nothing, then nodded as he opened the door, ushering us inside. I stopped, gripping her hand tightly as I looked around to see monitors in a room off to the side displaying images of who knows what while people with headphones talked to whoever they had on the other line. This wasn't a house, it was the headquarters for something. This looked militaristic. No wonder he never invited her over.

Alex was silent except for the trembling and gentle squeezes she gave my hand, letting me know she was still with me. "Are you still good with this, Alex?" She nodded her head in silence, and I watched her take it all in with deep labored breaths. Three rather large men, all dressed in black, like the man at the door, walked up to direct us the rest of the way.

"Roman, Alex. Glad you could both make it." Alessandro said as we passed him in the entranceway leading into a large seating area with a welcoming, cozy feel, if that was even possible right now.

"Edward?" Alex broke her silence as she spit out, shocked, spotting her brother sitting comfortably in a chair talking to one of the security guards, I'm guessing.

"Hi Alex," he said with no emotion, and went right back to his conversation.

"Over here, you two. Come have a seat." Grant distracted the almost sibling squabble and was being rather casual about this whole thing. I tried not to react for Alex's sake since we knew this was going to be more, but I don't think either one of us knew how much more we were getting. I hope this place is the information he was planning to give us because I'm not sure we can take much *more* of this.

"Hi Grant." I reached out my hand to shake his, then turned to my dad. "Dad." I nodded as I motioned Alex to sit on the sofa and planted myself next to her, leaving my arm securely around her waist.

"Would either of you like something to drink?" A man seemed to come out of nowhere to take our drink order. Alex just nodded her head but didn't offer up any information about what she might like so I ordered for her.

"We'll take a couple of waters, please. Thank you." He quickly returned with expensive glass bottles of water.

"We don't want to keep you two here any longer than necessary, but we do need to get this out in the open, at least where you both are concerned." Now that they were comfortable with us knowing who they were, they were no longer walking on eggshells around us. I think what they didn't realize is Alex didn't seem to be comfortable with this at all, especially now, with her brother involved. She had not taken her eyes off him since we walked in.

"How long have you known Grant, Edward?" She demanded.

It was like no one else in the room existed. Her penetrative stare was blazing a hole right through him, but he seemed utterly unfazed by the whole thing.

"Alex, let me get to that, please." Grant tried to calm her down, but the look on her face was deadly.

"No, I want to know right now. I want to know everything, right now." She yelled.

Alex was rigid and I knew how she felt, but I needed her to calm down for the baby. I knew she kept her tinctures in her purse, and it was sitting next to me where she laid it. I reluctantly released her to dig into her purse while she was consumed with finding out this information and found the calming solution. As swiftly as I could, I took her water and added a few drops. Not more than a few since the doctor said the herbs wouldn't harm the baby, but we still were careful. Then I placed the bottle of water in her hand, and she took a sip. She realized immediately what I had done and mouthed, "Thank you."

"For a while, Alex. Does that work for you for now?" Edward did not seem like his normal self with Alex. This was a new version. Maybe this was his work version.

But what work is it?

"Fine, Grant, what is the rest of the story? Could you please not leave anything out this time. I want to be done with this." She seemed to be more willing to listen now and I know once we've endured another information session, Grant style, we can get the hell out of here. I placed my arm back to her waist and tugged her tight to my side. Thankfully, she didn't push me away.

"Yes, Alex." He huffed and smiled at her, but she was clearly not having any more of the niceties as she darted her eyes around the room, making sure she got a good look at everyone. "I'm guessing seeing your brother here is a shock to you, but I've known Edward since he started running my company five years ago."

***

ALEX

Am I hearing that right? My brother is in charge of Grant's security. I looked at my brother, who was stone faced, but I wanted some answers from him.

"How is that possible when you acted like you had no idea what was going on and even asked me for Grant's information?" What else is he hiding from me?

"Alex, you need to calm down. The type of security we do is private. I can't go running around telling you who and what I know. I'm sorry for keeping you in the dark, but we needed to figure some things out first."

Does that make sense? Yes. *Am I ok with it?* Probably not.

I was wringing my hands in my lap, then instinctively wrapping them around my stomach to try to protect our baby from all this craziness, like that was going to happen. I can't believe this is part of my village to raise this baby. My face fell to my stomach as tears began to sting in the back of my eyes.

"What were the things that needed to be figured out, and did you get them figured out?" I asked, looking between Edward and Grant a few times and decided Grant was going to be more apt to give me the information I required, so I pinned my glare on him.

"The truth is the Ellington's are not who you think they are. Marcus is not just a corrupt politician; Tanner was not just the brother of a corrupt politician and Marcus senior was not just an ex disgruntled employee." Here's where I take a million breaths and try not to pass out. "The Ellington's were the rival family in Italy that murdered my family..." I gasped as my hand flew up to my mouth and I could feel tears threatening to spill over. That makes more sense now with the accent Tanner was trying to hide from me at the police station. Roman wrapped his arms around me and leaned in to ask if I was alright. I nodded furiously and let Grant continue. "Their name was Toscano. Enzo Senior and Junior and Stefano. His wife's name was Darcy and there was a daughter as well, her name was Eliana."

"What do you mean was?" I interrupted, not knowing if I actually wanted to hear the rest of this story.

"Meaning, Darcy didn't want to be a part of the life anymore either. She was good friends with my wife and our daughters were friends as well. Emma was a few years older than Eliana, but they were close. The day my family was killed, Darcy decided to go with them. My wife had already picked Emma up from school, then stopped to get Darcy to head over and pick up Eliana from her school." He paused and I could read the pain all over his face. Clearly reliving this memory is something he never wanted to do. "I should've been there. I should've done a better check on the car." His head went down as he was talking to himself. I couldn't help myself. The pain was flowing into me now. I got up and walked over to Grant, kneeling in front of him. I took both of his hands in mine and looked into his eyes.

"Grant, it's just me. Pretend it's just me in here and we're sitting in the office like we used to." He squeezed my hands and shook away the thoughts as he clenched his eyes shut, nodding his head.

"Thank you, baby girl. I'm so sorry you got dragged into this mess." He blew out a breath and I took a seat next to him, holding tight to his hand. "We were too late to get to them before the car exploded. All three died instantly. I knew where Eliana was and had a security team get her and make sure no one knew she was alive. As soon as we could, we had her shipped off to the states where I later met up with her. I placed her in a loving home and ensured her well-being. She was old enough to know what happened to her. We remain in contact, and she altered her name and appearance to avoid detection. Protecting her identity is paramount until the threat is over."

"Why would there still be a threat to her? Hasn't it been fifteen years? Don't they think she's dead?"

"The Ellington's, I mean Toscano's businesses were drugs and human trafficking. People are worth a lot of money in that market and they had plans for her. That's why Darcy was trying so desperately to get her out of there. They had plans for you too, Alex, especially since you looked so much like Emma. I had not seen them in a long time and Senior kept well and good out of the spotlight by working for King Construction and instead pushing his son into the political arena as Marcus Ellington. Marcus took to the spotlight with ease and Tanner played his role as the drug pushing playboy who manipulated women into prostitution and sex slavery. He went crazy after what happened with you, and you became his favorite target, to his own detriment. That seriously backfired on them as we all know." I think my breaths were now too shallow and quick to be good for me and I got up, staggering before I felt hands around my waist as Roman pulled me to him. I pressed my hands to my face, desperately trying to banish the terrifying images of what might have been from my mind.

"Ahhhh" the scream rang loudly throughout the room; I didn't know where it came from until I realized it was coming from me.

"That's enough. Do we need to hear any more of this? Did I get this much out of it...They were trying to take Alex for their sex trade business?" I could barely hear what he said as the blood rushed through my ears. I pressed my face harder into his chest until the sobs broke free.

"Baby, sit, let me get you some more water...Could I get some more water, please?" I heard Roman yell to no one in particular, and I tried like hell to catch my breath. We worried the information could get worse, and it did. That was about the worst thing they could've ever told me.

"I'm ok...I'm ok...I'm ok!" I screeched out through gasps of breath.

"Here, drink this." Roman pushed the bottle of water into my hands and I drank because he's right, this is not only not good for me but it's not good for the baby either. I needed to calm way down. I took the bottle and drank as much as I could, gulping furiously, trying not to spit it back out. He took the bottle away from me as I swallowed the last bit in my mouth.

"Thank you." I whispered to Roman as he leaned in, pressing his lips lightly across mine. I don't know how he was doing it, but I was feeling calmer because of him.

"Grant..." my voice was hoarse from screaming. It didn't even sound like me anymore. I felt like I was outside of my body listening to all of this. "Is Marcus, or whoever he is still coming after me for what happened?" Grant looked towards my brother who's eyes shut hard and he was taking in deep slow breaths. Well, that apparently answers my question.

"Alex, we are doing everything we can right now to ensure nothing happens to you and your family. Or anyone else involved in this, directly or indirectly." My hands were shaking so badly I had to squeeze my fists to get them to stop.

"Edward, can I talk to you in private, please?" I looked up to Roman, whose expression was so pained I knew he didn't want to let me go, but I really needed to talk to my brother.

"Sure, follow me to my office." *His office? He has an office here?* Maybe this is where he works.

I nodded and followed him into a room with monitors on one wall, which he switched off upon entering, and a large desk on the other. There was a black leather sofa and in the middle of the room was a large sandbag hanging from the ceiling like the ones we use for kickboxing class at Bruce's gym. I walked over to it to read the tag and noticed it was the same tag as the ones we use at Bruce's gym. My mind went all over the place, wondering who knew who. "Do you know Bruce?"

He nodded. "Yes, I know Bruce." Of course he did. I'm sure Bruce was a part of all of this from the beginning, but how far is the beginning? "What do you want to say to me, Alex?"

"What the hell is going on? How are you involved in this? And when am I going to get my life back?" He walked over, actually smiling at me, then reached out, throwing his arms around me pulling me into his chest. He held my head firm to him, and I could feel the tremors rolling through his body. Was he crying? My brother does not cry.

He kept me at a distance, his eyes red and teary but controlled, and announced, "This project started when Grant identified them. It's been at least for the past six months. He's sure they knew who he was and zoned in on you because of how much you looked like Emma. I'm glad you threw that little wrench in their plans when you assaulted Tanner at the bar, but it did, in fact, create some serious backlash. Is it your fault? Hell no, it's not your fault, but we need to find him before he finds every thug in this city to come after us with. We're going to get them, Alex."

"Is this all just to get back at Grant? Revenge?"

"Yes, it's all been about revenge. Taking away everything he ever cared about. They were using the kickback money from the real estate to fund their little empire. When you told Grant about Marcus reversing those zoning issues, that's how we found out about the drugs and the other business and put two and two together who they really were. We followed the money and found the talkers."

"So the drugs they used on me, that was the stuff they were selling on the street? The "Designer Date Rape" drug?" I felt the bile rise in my throat as I thought about how it almost killed me and then rearranged my memory so badly I never thought I'd think straight again.

"Yes."

"Well, what do we do now?"

He actually laughed. Why is this funny?

"You are not doing anything except keeping yourself and your baby safe and having a nice vacation." How the hell does he know about my trip?

"What? How...?"

"Alex, I run the security company. Of course, I know about your trip and anywhere else you go or are going." I guess that makes sense, except I'm not sure I like my brother keeping tabs on me. "Is it safe to assume that's enough information and we can go back to the living room?" I nodded and he led me back to the room where everyone was waiting patiently for us to return.

***

ROMAN

She got up and left the room with her brother, and I focused on my father. "Dad, I get you had this deal going with Grant, but why are you so involved? What did you get involved with?" He looked irritated and uncomfortable as I asked and that only made me believe what he was doing was illegal as well.

"Roman, I already told you..." Nope, that will not be good enough for me this time.

"Stop, dad, just stop. I'm tired of all the secrets and the lies. Just tell me." I yelled in frustration as everyone stopped talking and stared at me and my father.

"Roman..." Grant boomed, no longer having that fatherly tone he reserved for Alex. I had a feeling I was going to get shut down. "In the security business, especially private security, there are things that are not to be discussed with anyone. This is one of those times. I'm sorry if you're not getting what you want, but you're not cleared for this information. I hope that's enough for you because that's all you're getting." he said it with finality, and I realized at that moment I had no desire to know what my father had gotten himself into as long as it wasn't going to affect me or my loved ones.

"Fine. Then tell me this. Will it come back to haunt me and my family? Will it come back to haunt King Construction?"

"No." was all he left me with.

Alex and Edward appeared back in the room and Edward took up his original position as Alex tentatively sat back down next to me. She leaned in slowly and I kept her close. I'd talk to her later about her conversation with her brother since I got nowhere with my father.

"From here on out, you will comply with all safety instructions and are not to get involved with anything related to this. No more trying to figure it out. You've got all the information you need to know. We will handle it from here on out. Do you both understand me?" Grant had no problem laying it all out for us. Honestly, I never wanted to be involved in the first place and definitely didn't want Alex involved. Maybe this will help her keep her nose where it needs to be; with her projects and our baby.

"Yes, as long as you think we're safe." Alex whispered, sounding so small and scared. I've never heard her like this, and it worried me. She was shaking and the lack of confidence was so unlike her and everything I loved about her. My little fighter was broken.

"Yes, Alex. You're safe." Grant said, as if it were guaranteed. She nodded her head, then stood up, taking my hand.

"I want to go home." She tugged on my hand and I stood up, not really getting all I wanted to know but enough that I never wanted them to tell me anything ever again.

Boss appeared out of a side room on the way out and ushered us to our car, then got in another car and followed us home. I never even knew he had followed us there in the first place. This meeting seemed to be to tell us to stay out of their way, and I'm more than happy to oblige. As long as they can guarantee our safety.

Chapter 43

ALEX

I sat at the kitchen island sipping tea as I stared at the clock on the microwave turn over to 3am. Another nightmare about Marcus. Didn't really surprise me after that meeting last night. *Jesus, my* brother, *is involved in this.* Does dad know? Does Bianca know? Mindlessly, I picked up my phone, scrolling through my contacts, wondering if either one would pick up if I called at this hour. I pushed the idea far from my mind and began reminiscing about my photos. Beach trips and holidays. We looked so happy in pictures, but it's all a big lie. My life and everyone in it are all one big lie. The phone slipped from my hand with a clunk as I rested my elbows on the marble countertop and placed my face reluctantly into my hands, silently crying over my bullshit life. Everything handed to me on a silver platter. I heard Tanner's vile accusations loud and clear and they were all true. Roman wasn't even supposed to be mine. He was supposed to be with Emma. If she hadn't died, none of this would be happening right now. I'm just a substitute for the real thing. Does anyone even care about me, Alex, or am I just the ghost of Emma? I picked up my tea and walked over to the couch where I sat my cup down on the table and pulled the blanket, that was draped across the back, over the top of me and cried until the darkness enveloped me into a more peaceful existence where my thoughts no longer lingered in wait to crush my dreams.

"Alex..." *Huh, what?* "Alex, honey, what are you doing out here?"

I rubbed my eyes and focused in on the gentle husky voice. The one that lulled me into a sense of security. Perhaps false security.

"Where am I?" The gentle rubbing on my shoulder eased some of the apprehension.

"You're in the living room on the couch. Come back to bed." He stood up straight, extending a hand to help hoist me up. I took the offering, and he guided me to our room.

As he tucked me in, he admitted as if he could read my thoughts, "I love you, Alex. It's always ever been you. It was always going to be you."

My heart exploded with love as he said just what I needed to hear. He was the only one who knew me so well. I never needed to say a word. Our connection was so intense it had to be real.

"I thank God for you every day, my love. I love you more than you'll ever know." I said sleepily as I tucked myself into the warmth and safety of his loving arms and drifted back to sleep, knowing he was truly mine.

***

"Roman, hurry, we're going to miss our flight." I was frantically running from room to room, making sure I didn't forget anything, and he was in complete control.

"We can't miss our flight, Alex. It's literally taking off when we get there, just for us." He laughed as if this was funny, while I lost my mind.

Oh my God, I just want to get there already and be done with the traveling part. I forget he has a private jet and all that entails. None of the headaches of waiting in the lines and getting frisked and patted down. We just get on the plane, no hassles.

"The baby is really moving today, here feel?" I moved the puppy carrier off my lap into the seat next to me after we chose our place on the plane. I took Roman's hand and placed it in the last spot the baby was active, and he or she gave him a little kick.

"Oh wow, he's strong."

He, huh?

"How do you know it's a he? It could be a she."

We had a doctor's appointment when we got back in a couple of weeks to have an ultrasound done and find out the sex of the baby. I wanted to start thinking about the nursery; designing it and getting it ready at the new house. I made Roman bring the designs for the house with us too, so I could work on some of that while we were there. I know it's supposed to be vacation, but I have too much going on back home to neglect it all for the next two weeks.

"I don't know, I just have a feeling it's a boy." He smiled with pride, and I almost hoped he got his wish.

The stewardess brought drinks and lunch, interrupting our discussion, giving me ample time to get in my head again. *Do I care if it's a boy or girl?* I haven't even thought about it. I honestly just wanted a happy, healthy baby who isn't in any danger from madmen.

After several hours and one luxurious nap, we finally landed at our destination and stepped out of the plane into complete and utter paradise.

***

ROMAN

We stopped at the top of the stairs and took a long deep inhale of the warm salty air filled with notes of floral and cocoa butter. The scent alone was enough to take the edge off everything we've been through. I took her hand and led her and our precious cargo, including Tao, in her other arm gently down the steps to the waiting SUV.

We pulled up to this exquisite massive Mediterranean style villa situated right on the beach with a private pool and private beach access as well. The guests I invited would be staying up the trail through the trees to the resort where the reception was being held after the wedding on the beach. At least that's what the email said that Amelia sent me last night.

"Would you like to have dinner on the beach tonight? There's a restaurant at the resort with beach front dining." I asked as we walked through the living room, taking a tour of the place while the staff brought our bags in straight to our room.

The floors were a whitewashed wood in a chevron pattern with pale sage walls, adorned with vibrant watercolor paintings of a tropical nature. The kitchen was state-of-the-art stainless steel appliances with a large island of gray and white swirled marble counter tops that spanned the entire length of the kitchen, easily affording the eight stools waiting for their next frequenter. An expansive wooden dining table surrounded by ten slip covered chairs engulfed the space in front of the windows with a gorgeous view of the ocean.

Alex had yet to answer me about dinner plans tonight and I knew it was because she was enchanted by the architecture and attention to detail and design, just taking it all in-in a way that seemed only reserved for her. It was one of the quirks I dearly loved about her.

"I'm sorry. What was that? Did you see this view?" She dropped my hand and hurried to the door next to the wall of windows and pushed it open, stepping out on to the immense deck with the sound of crashing waves filling the silent void. As we stood, listening to the waves roll in from the sea, all of a sudden we noticed music off in the distance coming from the direction of the resort.

"Hey, can we go up to the resort for dinner and dancing on the beach tonight? I saw a restaurant in the online brochure that looked amazing."

I laughed, not wanting to let her know I already asked her that, but happy we were on the same page.

"Sounds like a great idea, honey. Why don't we take a shower and get ready?"

***

ALEX

Two days of total relaxation. I read two books on my to be read list, soaked up all the vitamin D I could in the sun, ate amazing food and made love to my fiancé every chance we got. Tomorrow the resort is closed to the public for some big event, so we're staying at the villa. Today Roman said he wanted to have a spa day at the resort after all this sun we got, to replenish our skin—whatever that means. I'm not sure he's ever alluded to wanting to have a spa day together, but maybe since we're alone on vacation he's letting me in on a side of him he'd never let anyone else see.

Roman snuck up behind me, wrapping his arms around my waist, kissing my neck. Shivers wracked my body as his voice vibrated the words I wanted to hear.

"Hey babe, you ready for breakfast and pampering?" You don't have to ask me twice. I hopped down from the stool and put my teacup in the sink before grabbing his hand as he led us out the door and on the path to the resort.

The large double doors opened by a man dressed in a casual pair of khakis and a tropical button up and a greeting of "Good morning Mr. and Mrs. King. My name is Leo. It's nice to see you again." I went to correct him and Roman squeezed my hand, bringing it up to his lips where he kissed my ring, followed by a radiant smile.

"Thank you. Good morning to you as well, Leo." I gazed at Roman and smiled sweetly, realizing he was proud to call me his wife and there would be nothing that could change my mind from making him my husband.

Another person stepped in to lead us to the restaurant.

"Welcome back, Mr. and Mrs. King, right this way. We have your table ready for you." I know we had eaten here a few times since we got here two days ago, but I don't remember making reservations or having sat anywhere in particular. And I know they never referred to us as Mr. and Mrs. *This is weird*. I looked to Roman for a specific indicator as to what was going on, but he was stone faced, like none of this was phasing him in the least.

As soon as we walked into the restaurant, the room filled with the sound of voices screaming "Surprise!" and a crowd of people standing in front of us. My heart pounded at the revelation of the people who were standing in front of us. Not just any people; my people. All of them. My dad, my brothers and their families, my best friends and their families, my aunt and her family, Roman's family including Amelia, Grant and all the Santoros as well as my work crew; Shay, Owen, Ryan, Landon and Piper. I scanned quickly for Ella and her family and wondered if she wasn't well enough for the trip.

"Ella couldn't make it, honey. The boys stayed home with her." I nodded quickly and tried not to think about why Ella couldn't make it and held tight to the thought of seeing her when we got back.

I ran into the crowd, throwing myself at whoever was in my way and hugged my way to everyone, tears and all. They were here; safe in paradise with me. Sophia Grace, Maggie's spirited four-year-old jumped into my arms and I heaved her up onto my hip. The boys each held a piece of fabric on my skirt as we made our way to the table.

"So, hold on. I'm so excited you're all here, but what the heck are you doing here?" Everyone looked around, tight-lipped, waiting for someone to answer until Edward let out a howling noise so contagious I along with the whole table, erupted into a fit of hysterics.

"Wait, you haven't told her yet?" Edward managed to say to Roman before resuming laughing so hard he started coughing.

"Roman, is there something you need to tell me?" I asked, after gaining some semblance of composure.

"Since you've been so preoccupied and overwhelmed by everything that's been going on, I thought it would be a nice gesture to take something off your plate."

"And that would be?" My nerves were on edge. I couldn't begin to imagine what he'd done.

"I, we..." he gestured to the table, "thought it would be a good idea to get married while we're here with all our friends and family in attendance. Not worrying about anything going on back home or having to look over our shoulder. Didn't think you wanted to plan a wedding while doing all the other stuff plus growing a baby."

I was in shock. My mouth fell open. That was honestly the last thing I thought he was going to say, and he was right. I'd never have put a moment into planning a wedding with everything else happening plus a baby, but...

"Roman, I don't have a dress or anything. I haven't, we haven't, I mean..." I started getting dizzy and Roman pulled me close, brushing his lips lightly over my cheek.

"Honey, it's all taken care of. Amelia picked out a dress and made all the arrangements for the spa today and the dress fitting. Tomorrow, all the ladies get ready together and then you meet me at the altar on the beach just before sunset."

"Roman... you did all of this?" I asked, looking around in disbelief.

He nodded, smiling from ear to ear.

"As far as I'm concerned, you're already mine, but tomorrow we make it official."

The tears streamed down my face and the sounds of women swooning and cheers all around ensued from the table.

"This is perfect, thank you."

Roman placed his hands gently on either side of my face leaning in slowly but turned his head at the last second towards my brother Edward and winked with a tip of his chin, swiftly facing back to me and planting his lips possessively on mine.

***

ROMAN

After the ladies left for their spa day, the guys and I headed to the cigar bar on the other side of the resort. The bar was filled with rich, dark mahogany and distressed red leather chairs and barstools. The scent of cedar from the humidors and Cuban cigars swirled through the air. I inhaled deeply before heading to the bar to order the VIP package. We were escorted into another room with large private booths able to accommodate at least twenty each. There were no women allowed in this area, just as the spa the ladies went to did not permit gentlemen. It was my idea of a bachelor and bachelorette party without the unwanted shenanigans. The waiter brought over a few high-end bottles of bourbon and an entire humidor full of cigars, along with a tray of snacks containing mixed nuts, pretzels and an assortment of olives and cheeses. We each filled a glass and lit a cigar.

"Thank you all for coming on such short notice. Thank you, Edward, for all your faith in my decision. I'm glad to have proven you wrong."

Edward bobbed his head and tipped his glass to me in acknowledgement of our conversation about him thinking she was going to go postal on me. Alex was happy about my surprise for once.

The laughter and the bourbon lasted for a couple hours before we decided to meet back at the bar for an early dinner to soak up some of the alcohol. The bar snacks definitely wouldn't suffice.

Grant caught up to me on my way to the villa to change into some clothes better suited for the pool bar.

"Roman, how's Alex?" He asked with genuine concern.

"She's fine Grant. What else would she be after our meeting? Honestly, can we not talk about it anymore?" I was tired of walking on eggshells with Grant and my annoyance with him felt warranted. But I wanted to keep things copacetic for Alex and not disturb the peace or the reason we were all here.

"I understand. I truly am sorry for what happened, but I do care about her and want what's best for her and for you. I couldn't be more overjoyed for the both of you. If there's anything either of you ever need, don't hesitate to reach out."

"Thank you, Grant. I'll take that into consideration." I can't imagine there would ever be anything I ever need from Grant in terms of his services ever again after this whole thing is over.

***

ALEX

The Santoro's kids took Abby and Maggie's kids to play at the pool and do all the kid's activities while the ladies spent the day getting pampered with facials, massages, mani/pedis and a trip to the hair salon for whatever was necessary. Amelia said she had a dress for me at the boutique to try on and they would alter it right there if need be.

"Thank you all so much for being here. I don't know if I could've gotten married without you all by my side." Abby and Maggie threw their arms around me as we wiggled our bellies into a comfortable position while laughing to the point of almost wetting ourselves.

After the hair salon, I'd had enough, but we still needed to go to the boutique and try on the dress. It was absolutely astonishing. I don't know how she managed to do it, but Amelia picked out the exact dress I would've picked for myself. It even had a stretchy elastic waist to expand with my belly comfortably, like it was made just for me. I couldn't wait to wear it tomorrow. But right now I'm starving and need food.

"Can we get our bathing suits on and have some pool and sun time please? They have a great tiki hut restaurant. We can order food and take it into those private cabanas to eat or just to get out of the sun."

"That sounds perfect." My aunt said, snaking her arm through mine. I leaned in, giving her a quick peck on the cheek.

"I love you auntie and I'm so glad you're here."

"Me too, sweet girl. Maybe after the baby is born, you can come see me in North Carolina."

"I would love that. We'll definitely make that happen. Maybe I can sell some of my non wine down there too."

"Absolutely. There's a bar the ladies and I frequent that's run by some-one I'd love for you to meet. I have a feeling she'll love your product."

"Sounds great. I'm really looking forward to it."

I made my way, sort of dragging my feet, down the gravel path to the villa. This baby growing business is no joke. I opened the door and jumped with a squeal when my face hit a firm, naked chest.

"Hey baby." His deep voice murmured as he pulled me to him and began kissing my neck, tugging me politely into the villa, kicking the door shut with a clap.

"What the hell was I thinking, spending the day without you?" He hummed low in my ear and goosebumps peppered my skin and weakened my knees.

"Mmmhmm," was all I managed in response.

He smelled faintly of bourbon and cigars, a scent that had somehow seemed more enticing attached to him. I wrapped my arms around his neck, threading my fingers through the thick hair at the nape while holding on as the rest of the world seemed to fade away. His smile widened against my skin, and I couldn't help smiling back. With effortless strength, he lifted me into his arms, drawing a surprised laugh from me as I wrapped my legs around his waist while he carried me toward the white leather sofa overlooking the water. The setting sun painted the room in shades of gold and amber, and for a moment it felt as though time itself had slowed down.

He lowered us onto the sofa and gathered me close, his forehead resting against mine while we simply enjoyed the comfort of being together. The steady rhythm of his heartbeat beneath my cheek, the warmth of his hands at my back, and the tenderness in his eyes made everything else disappear. The world outside no longer seemed important. The chaos, the danger, the secrets, and the endless uncertainty that had consumed so much of our lives couldn't reach me here. Wrapped in his arms, all of it felt distant.

Tomorrow I would become his wife, not because of a plan someone else created, not because of circumstances beyond our control, and not because of a desperate attempt to save anyone. I was marrying him because I loved him, because he loved me, and because despite every obstacle placed in our path, we kept finding our way back to each other.

A burst of laughter escaped me when he suddenly pulled me closer, making me squeal in surprise.

"There she is," he teased, clearly pleased with himself.

I shook my head and laughed as he brushed a loose strand of hair behind my ear. His eyes softened as he looked at me, and my heart swelled at the sight of the man who would be my husband tomorrow and the father of our child soon after. Warmth spread through my chest as I thought about the future waiting for us. All the years I spent wondering if I'd ever find the right person seemed so far away now. The fear, the doubt, and the loneliness faded like storm clouds finally breaking apart after days of rain, allowing sunlight to shine through once again.

For the first time in a very long time, I knew exactly where I belonged.

Chapter 44

ALEX

Yesterday was the longest day in history. From breakfast surprises, seeing everyone, to the whole to do with having a spa day and getting fitted for the dress to an unexpected afternoon delight. Along with dinner and dancing on the beach with a live band...not sure how I'm going to make it through the day to even get married.

I got in the shower and looked down at my swollen ankles. Walking down a sandy aisle seemed like a horrible idea right now. *Oh my god, is this cold feet talking? Am I trying to make excuses to get out of this?* Something wasn't right as my chest tightened and panic set in. I threw all the shower accessories off the bench and sat down before a startled Roman came barging in fully clothed into the shower.

"Alex, what's wrong? What happened? Are you alright? Is it the baby?"

I couldn't catch my breath, and I shook my head no, not really knowing which question I was answering or how it was being perceived by him until I heard him say, "This is Roman King in Villa 7. Could you send a doctor, please. My wife is pregnant, and I think something's wrong."

His panic was making me panic more and I couldn't get a grip, until all of a sudden, I burst into tears and loud wailing, giving me the chance to at least pull air into my lungs.

"I'm...so...sorry. I didn't know this would happen." More tears and gasping sobs as he engulfed me in his arms. His clothes were sticking to the both of us. He ushered me out of the shower and wrapped me in a towel, letting go only to take the robe down off the back of the door to help me put it on. He carefully sat me on the soft bench against the wall, angling my face up to look at him.

"Baby, tell me what's wrong." He seemed calmer now and I was able to control my breathing, focusing on the sound of his voice, my safety, my security, my heart.

"I don't know what happened. One minute I was so excited and thankful, the next I was trying to sabotage everything."

"What do you mean, sabotage?" His furrowed brow and fear-filled eyes gave away his suspicions.

"I guess you could call it cold feet, maybe."

His face drooped and I heard an audible swallow, like he was trying to keep me from feeling the pain from my words by shoving it back down.

"You're having second thoughts about us or marrying me?" He looked devastated, but that wasn't what happened. He went to stand up and I grabbed his hands in mine and my fears of losing him strengthened me, gaining dominance over my anxiety.

"No, Roman, no, absolutely not. Neither of those things. I love you. I'm not going anywhere, and I can't wait to marry you today. It's just something that happens to me when big things are up front and center in my life. I have panic attacks that I can't just drink out of my life. I have to work through them. I have to give myself the grace to believe I can be happy and allow myself to love and be loved in return, genuinely. I spent 45 days learning to do just that. When I came home and you were still there, I thanked God for that second chance and I'm terrified of losing you and now that we have a baby on the way...hormones aside, I'm even more terrified."

"Alex, I'm not going anywhere either. You're not going to lose me. I love you and our growing family. I'll work on my reaction to your anxiety but right now..." there was a knock at the door indicating the doctor he had called might be here. "I'm going to get that, and I want you to let the doctor check you out for my peace of mind, alright?"

I nodded, knowing his peace of mind would in turn bring mine peace as well.

***

ROMAN

"Doctor, thank you for coming so quickly. She's right in here." I shook the man's hand and led him through the expansive living space towards the master suite where Alex was emerging.

"I'm fine, really. It was just a mild anxiety attack."

Didn't look mild to me.

The doctor introduced himself and asked Alex to have a seat in the chair next to where she was now standing. She sat down and looked up at me with tear-stained cheeks and red-rimmed eyes. I can't imagine what it feels like to go through those attacks. She looks exhausted and wrecked. I watched as the doctor took her blood pressure and listened to her heart. She took deep breaths, in and out, in and out. Just watching the rhythm of her breathing was making my breathing sync up with hers and it blanketed the room in a sense of calm and serenity.

"Hmmm, maybe we should start meditating together or something," I thought as the calming energy swirled around us.

"Do you have these episodes often?" The doctor politely asked with a genuine smile and not just robotically like in the emergency room back home.

"Not often, no. But when I do have them, they can be overwhelming at times." The doctor looked between us like he was trying to figure out what to ask next, but didn't want to upset anyone.

"What causes them, and do you do anything or take anything to treat them?" He angled his body to where his back was almost all the way to me.

Does he think I'm the reason she has these attacks? It was almost enough to piss me off, but instead I smirked and let him have his routine domestic issue questioning.

"I went through a pretty traumatic experience. I was attacked several months ago, and he committed suicide in jail. My counselor told me it was PTSD. I'm working through it naturally with some auyervedic tinctures I created over in Indonesia, where I spent some time working through my issues." She explained.

The doctor's posture loosened and became less protective as he turned back to his original position.

"How do the tinctures work for you?"

"They're wonderful. As a matter of fact, I left one on the counter before I went in to take a shower. Roman, would you mind bringing it to me, please?"

"Of course, honey, I'll be right back." I picked up the teacup that was so feminine. It was white China adorned with pink flowers and a gold leaf outline. It reminded me of Alex now; so delicate and precious. I handed her the cup and she smiled warmly, taking a breath and sipping, letting out a relieved sigh.

"Thank you." she said sweetly, like hysteria hadn't been just moments away.

I took a seat and listened as the doctor played the beat of our baby's heart through the portable ultrasound machine. My heart melted with the fluttering symphony made by my unborn child and tears threatened to make an entrance stinging the corners of my eyes. After we listened, the doctor packed up his things, handing Alex his card and asking her to contact him if she needed anything and to talk with her about her tinctures. He was a holistic doctor looking to find more natural solutions for his patients in the nutraceutical market.

"We're good, right?" I asked, knowing the answer already. She was glowing after hearing the baby's strong, healthy heartbeat. The smile on her face tamped down whatever anxiety had riddled her, making her look more vibrant and happier.

"I'm perfect. Ready to become your wife." With that, another knock sounded at the door. I looked at her and she shrugged. Raising a brow and a finger, I signified I would be right back and answered the door.

"Hello Roman. Where is she? You two can't see each other anymore today." Maggie demanded as she pushed past me along with Abby and

Amelia, who bounced in with a look of pure excitement on their faces to help their friend get ready for her and my big day.

"Hey ladies, she's right over there." I threw my arm in the direction they were already bounding and asked, "Where are you planning to get ready?"

"That's for us to know and you to not worry about." Abby crossed her arms over her seriously eight-month pregnant belly and shifted her hip, throwing me a wink.

"Take good care of her and I'll see you all this afternoon."

***

ALEX

I watched with pure desire as Roman hustled into the bedroom to change out of his wet clothes he was now adorned in because of me losing it in the shower.

"What the hell happened here? You're a mess in a bathrobe and Roman's clothes are soaking wet. Does he not know there's a washer and dryer in here? You don't have to shower with your clothes on to clean them." Maggie scrutinized before we all burst out in uncontrollable laughter.

The girls were just what I needed to get through this day and to the altar. Tao had spent all of his time with the kids or at the doggie daycare/spa. The plan was to have the kids walk him down the aisle as the official flower puppy. Harrison had the rings and no bridesmaids or groomsmen. Everyone was equally loved in this group. No sides of the aisle, just a mix of the people we loved and cared about coming together after tragedy and triumph to share in the start of our life together.

I got dressed after Roman left and followed the girls back up to the resort and into the spa, where we got our hair and makeup done. Lots of food, drinks and laughter as we got ready for the event.

"I can't believe I'm getting married!" I said through nerves of excitement and trepidation. My aunt grabbed my hand as we walked out of the resort to the limo style golf carts covered in white roses and green leafy garland that were taking us down to the beach.

"Ali girl, you look beautiful. Absolutely stunning. Roman is a lucky fella."

I hugged her tight, wishing my mother was here and she tightened her grip on me, then held me at arm's length, looked me in the eye and said knowingly, "I know you miss your mom, Ali. She's here, I know she is. She wouldn't miss it for the world."

I held in the tears as I nodded to shake the emotions out of my system.

We came to the top of the sand aisle I was to walk down to stand with the love of my life, my soulmate, my Roman, and profess my eternal love. A lump in my throat choked me up as I realized all those things were true. He is my one true love, my eternity.

I can do this.

Roman was facing the ocean with his back to the aisle, so he didn't see me before the music played. The kids hurried down the aisle, skipping and laughing to the beautiful instrumental music that was playing before it was my turn. The ladies all took their seats and my dad came over, tears trickling down his cheeks.

"Ali Marie, my sweet baby girl. You are so precious to me and your mother. I would never be ok with giving you away to someone who wasn't worthy of you. I hope you know that. You and Roman are going to have a wonderful, happy and full life together. I am honored to walk you down the aisle today."

Thank God, they put me in all kinds of waterproof makeup because that did it. Only my dad could break me like that. I threw my arms around him

"Daddy, there is no one else on this planet that could have ever been a better dad to me. I love you so much and can't wait to see what an amazing grandfather you are." While I was embracing my dad trying to get the tears under control, the music started playing to walk me down the aisle.

Oh my God, would someone please give me a break?

As more tears broke free, I closed my eyes, remembering the night Roman and I danced under the stars at Lookout Park to the song that was now playing as my wedding march. Nostalgia by Joe Hisaishi. My heart jumped to my throat. I wanted to run down the aisle to him, but my satin dress with the delicate lace overlay and all the intricate floral embroidery may not fare well at top speed. I stayed calm and treaded lightly, so to speak.

Dad walked me flawlessly, keeping me from tripping and as we got closer to Roman his nose flared with a rather aggressive inhalation, sending sparks of desire straight to my stomach lighting the butterflies on fire.

"So damn beautiful," he growled under his breath when my father placed my hand in his.

Dad quickly gave me a peck on the cheek and a pat on Roman's shoulder, then took his seat with a grin on his face. Roman nodded at my father and mouthed thank you.

***

"Good morning, Mrs. King." The low gravely tone of his voice sent shivers to my core, while the delicious memories from last night ignited a spark that would've kept us in bed all morning had it not been followed up with a growl and some rather aggressive kicks from our little soccer player, it seemed.

"Good morning to you, Mr. King. I think someone's hungry." I mumbled, while reminiscing about last night and the reception that was so incredible, with white roses in a giant arch above the entrance to the reception hall, followed by twinkling white lights strewn everywhere. Thoughts of the rehab center emerged in my mind, but not in a bad way. The hall was filled with more white roses in gorgeous arrangements centered on all the tables and an enormous dance floor being manned by an energetic DJ who played all the right music. Our first dance as a married couple was to "Until I Found You" by Stephen Sanchez. The music was all picked out by Amelia, Abby and Maggie before it was accepted by Roman—I was later told. The memories were finally reassuring that what I had done was worth it to be here, right now, in the arms of the man I love, married and pregnant with his child. I could not think of a better outcome to the tragedy that had befallen me and my entire family. This was more than I could have ever dreamed.

"I ordered room service for this morning, so we don't have to do anything other than stay in bed all day if you want. I hope you don't mind." Such a thoughtful gesture and if we didn't have all our friends and family still at the resort with us until tomorrow, I would be agreeable to those terms, but I felt like we still had to entertain so we both got up and ate breakfast before getting ready for the day and joining the others on the beach for one last day of celebration then the honeymoon begins.

Chapter 45

ROMAN

S tepping off the plane, Alex looked well rested and she was absolutely glowing. I took her hand and helped her down the flight of stairs to the waiting car as Boss and the rest of our security put all the bags in the back of the large black SUV waiting on the tarmac. I don't think I'll ever get used to this and if there is a God, we won't have to for much longer. The two weeks away was a necessity but tomorrow we have to get right back to work. If everything from now until they find Marcus is as incident free as our two-week vacation/wedding/honeymoon, then we should be done with bodyguards hopefully by the fundraising gala the end of March.

Alex leaned her head on my shoulder after situating ourselves in the car, which was quickly followed by the gentle sound of her snoring, making me smile. She seemed so at peace and content, which made wanting to wake her when we pulled into the garage of the penthouse that much more difficult. Boss seemed to relate, so I scooted away from her enough to get out of the car, then gently lifted her into my arms and carried her to the elevator. Her face was nuzzled into my chest, and I leaned down to kiss the top of my wife's head.

My wife, I thought as my heart swelled with pride at this beautiful soul carrying my child, who also happens to be the love of my life—my soulmate. The only way I will part with her again is in death. Which I am hoping is a very, very long time in the future.

The elevator stopped on the floor below the penthouse to the apartment, letting out two of the four bodyguards and one stayed downstairs to make sure the place was secured, while Boss came up with us carrying the dog carrier with a very sleepy puppy in it. Tao spent his entire vacation going to the puppy spa and doggy daycare the resort had on the premises. He was exhausted by all his tedious activities. Memories of all the scarfs they adorned him with had me rolling my eyes and Alex swooning. He looked absolutely ridiculous, just like all the sweaters she made me put him in. But seeing her laugh and smile with not a care in the world meant everything.

In our room, I laid her carefully on the bed, hoping I didn't wake her, but she seemed so far gone that she probably wouldn't wake up until tomorrow. Seven pm was what the clock said on the microwave in the kitchen when I glanced at it as I pushed through the strain seeping into my body from two weeks' vacation and travel, carrying my wife and our precious cargo in my arms. I went into my office to check my emails since I told myself I wasn't going to let work interfere with our time away, but now I have to catch up on all the emails and who knows what.

"What the hell is this?" I sneered at my computer, brows furrowed. My emails were so sparse you would think it wasn't working. Frantically, I checked through all the boxes and folders, including the deleted ones, but there was nothing. I had a few emails from contractors and foremen, but other than that, it was like time had stopped while we were away. Calling Amelia seemed like the only obvious choice.

"Hey Roman, did you all make it home safe?" Amelia sounded normal, but she's the only person with access to my emails, so there better be a good explanation for this.

"Hi, yes, we made it home a little bit ago."

"Good. What can I do for you?" I didn't know whether I should jump right in and start interrogating her or if I should try to get her to tell me what the hell is going on without the third degree. I've had such a good two weeks away I didn't want to spoil it with being a jerk, especially since she did such an amazing job setting everything up at the resort.

"Where the hell are all my emails?" I don't have time for this.

"In your inbox, where they always are. I sifted through the junk mail. Didn't think you would want to do it when you got back and now you can just concentrate on the important things instead of stressing over the little things...Is there a problem?" She said as if this was something normal. It wasn't.

Two weeks' worth of emails and there were only five emails that weren't junk. I highly doubt it.

What the hell is she hiding?

"You're going to tell me that these are the only emails that were worth keeping? Why did you empty the deleted email folder?" There was a silence on the other end of the line.

"I told you not to talk to Amelia like that ever again. I'm glad you're home safe and congratulations, but you can f..." He grunted with a pause. "Right off," Harrison vented before he disconnected the call.

If I have to make it my mission in life, I will find out what Amelia is hiding.

***

ALEX

The breeze blowing through my hair as I sipped pina colada flavored mocktails lying on the plush cushion covered loungers, inhaling the briny scented ocean air sent waves of peace through every nerve in my body. The sun was bright, and the water was crystal clear—you could see all the way to the bottom. The tropical fish in bright colors swimming all around our feet as we waded in the ocean. Roman's tanned skin glistening with water droplets as he rose out of the water, scooping me up and kissing me under the bluest sky I've ever seen. Not a cloud in sight. We danced under the stars and made love from morning until night. I never wanted this feeling to end. As we walked down the resort stairs from the restaurant back to our villa, it had gotten dark, and the stars were twinkling high in the sky. I looked around because it was so quiet and there was no one to be found, not even our security. Finally, we can be alone, all the threats are gone. No more bodyguards, no more Ellingtons. Suddenly, I found myself gasping at the sight in front of me. The dark shadow figure pointing something in our direction. Who is that? What is that? Terror gripped me tight as I was looking down the barrel of a gun. My chest locked and my breath quickened, trying to figure out how to get out of this. Where is everyone? What happened to our security? Did they know we were in danger here? Are they in on it too? Oh my God, this can't be happening. Why now? Why are you taking everything from me now? I looked up to the night sky, screaming my plea to God. The God I just spent forty-five days getting to know, telling him all of my darkest, most hideous secrets, thinking he was on my side, and my recovery was a good thing and that I was worthy of love and a family of my own. Please don't take Roman from me...Oh God, don't take my baby.

"Alex, Alex...wake up honey, it's just a dream, baby. It's just a dream."

My eyes flew open as the panic attack gripped me tight around the throat, reminding me of the moments I could remember when Tanner attacked me. The quick shallow breaths had spots interfering with my vision, but I knew Roman's voice anywhere and I instinctively reached for him, throwing my arms around his neck and pulling myself intentionally to him. His body's vibration was what I held tight to and concentrated on syncing my heartbeat with his to calm me down. I hadn't had a nightmare in so long, but I was determined to control the outcome of those damn dreams at some point. If I didn't, it was like a self-fulfilling prophecy and that was one I was not planning to wait for.

"I'm ok, honestly I am." I was getting there anyway, taking deep slow breaths, one inhale at a time.

"Here, drink this." Taking the water from Roman and sipping slowly, concentrating on the feel of the cool liquid instead of the dream before handing it back to him.

"Thank you."

"Are you sure you're, ok? Do you need me to make you a tea or anything?"

All the anxiety took its toll, and I collapsed back onto the pillow, closing my eyes and letting out a whoosh of air.

"No, I think I'm ok. It's like you said. It was just a dream."

It was a dream I planned to keep to myself, so I didn't give it any more power over me than it already had. Roman pulled the covers up over us and wrapped himself around me, and I gladly accepted the warmth and protection of his love.

***

"Alex, Alex. I need you to come quick. Grams ain't doin good." The panic I heard on the other end of the line was so strong I was starting to panic myself and I didn't even know what was going on yet.

"Darius, is that you?"

"Yes, can you get over here? Something's wrong with Grams." My eyes widened and I knew that was not a good thing and I needed to hurry. Grabbing my things, I somehow managed to keep the phone up to my ear as I fumbled all the other items.

"Ok, I'm on my way, but I want you to call 911."

"She said she didn't want me to do that."

"Darius, I'm not a doctor. I want you to call 911 right now and I'll be right there."

"Who's calling 911? What's going on?" Roman said as he came out of his office, throwing his suit coat on and flipping his phone into his jacket pocket.

"Darius. Something's wrong with Ella. I have to go right now."

"I'm going with you. Not a chance in hell I'm letting you go and take care of that on your own." He took my hand and helped me slip my arms through the jacket sleeves, handing my purse to me as we got in the elevator.

Lights from the police cars and ambulances were flashing and bright as we pulled up to the curb. No way to get in the driveway with all the emergency vehicles. I practically jumped out of the car and was getting ready to run up to the house when Roman reached out and grabbed me around the waist, holding me back.

"I know you're worried and so am I, but we need to be calm when we go in there, not only for Darius, but his younger brothers. We have to control the room no matter what's happening in there. Do you understand what I'm saying to you?" He looked calm. He seemed calm. Why the hell was he so calm and how was he doing it? Tears were building in my eyes, and then it clicked. I had to be strong for the boys. I was supposed to be their guardian if something happened to Ella. What kind of guardian would I be if I ran in there losing it? I could do that in private if I had to. Now was the time to be strong and help those boys get through whatever was happening at this moment and in the future.

***

ROMAN

My palms were sweating when I took her hand as calmly as I could and led us up the steps to the front door of the beautiful house Alex's foundation created from practically a blank slate. It was incredible from what it was previously—dilapidated and neglected. Now it was in pristine condition, with new everything. From the white vinyl siding, the dark wood-stained window shutters, the wrap-around porch and the robin's egg blue front door. It looked like it was straight out of a Better Homes and Gardens magazine, but I knew what was on the inside wasn't going to be as pretty. My worry was what it was going to do to Alex, and if she could handle seeing it and protecting our baby at the same time.

Boss followed us up to the front porch, but I instructed him to wait outside.

There were police just inside the door blocking the entry. "Excuse me, please." I tried to ease through, but they weren't letting us pass.

"Sir, you can't be in here right now. They're working on Mrs. Jackson and they need the space.

I looked over the top of the officer's head and saw Ella on the sofa as the EMTs were trying to hook her up to all kinds of gadgets. She wasn't moving, and her eyes were closed.

"Officer, my name is Alex Kennedy. We need to get in there right now. I'm the children's guardian." Alex said with an air of authority that surprised even me from the mood she was in just a few minutes earlier. The officers seemed to let us pass without questioning the validity of her statement.

"Yes, Ms Kennedy, the boys were asking for you."

"Ms. Kennedy?" I whispered in her ear. Now was not the time to discuss the slip, but I was not going to have her call herself Kennedy when she now held my last name.

"Did you want me to correct them at a time like this?" she scolded me and I smiled, knowing damn well she knew the answer to that. That's what we needed right now— strong and sassy Alex Kennedy-King.

In the kitchen were three boys, terrified for their future. Darius was pacing the floor, popping his head out to see what was going on and the other two, Isaac and Dante, were sitting at the table distraught. One with his head down on the table and the other with his face in his hands. Both trying not to cry, but the movement of their shoulders would suggest they weren't successful. Alex walked up to Dante and Isaac at the table and attended to the boys in a motherly fashion. Not trying to downplay what they were going through, just letting them know she was available to them.

I walked over to Darius, who looked tense—scared of an uncertain future. I reached out my hand to shake his. It surprised me that he took it, and he was even more surprised when I pulled him in and embraced him. Being the man of the house is hard on any man but also losing a father and now possibly the only mother you've ever known and becoming the head of the house for your two younger siblings like a father yourself, has got to be the most overwhelming experience. He needed to know he was not alone and didn't have to carry that weight right now. I felt him shake and his fingers dug into my jacket. I held him tighter, holding back my own emotion as I felt him so strongly seeping into the room.

"It's going to be alright, Darius. No matter what happens, you have us to help you."

He nodded and sniffled, loosening his grip, then wiping the sleeve of his shirt across his face before turning around and grabbing a napkin off the counter to finish the job.

"It's not fair. She's the best person I know. Why her?" His hands were propped on the counter in front of the sink as he stared down the drain.

"I don't know. God's plans are bigger than ours. That's all I do know. I know that's no consolation right now, but that's all any of us know about things like this."

"Alex, how did you get through your mom's passing?" Turning to look at Alex, who now had the reddest rim around her eyes and a tear-stained face.

"Darius. I didn't do a good job getting through my mom's death. I still struggle with it, but I'm doing a lot better. I had to do a lot more work than I think you'll need. Big Mama did the best job with you boys. You are so blessed to have been raised with her in your village. I promise you; we will get through this together. Let's go check and see what's going on out there, alright?" She led the way from the kitchen to the living room, where they were now putting Ella on a stretcher, getting ready to transport her to the hospital.

Chapter 46

ALEX

Florescent lights and beeping noises are a familiar sound to me these days and are entirely too common. I paced up and down the hallway, waiting to hear something from anyone. A nurse, a doctor, hell, I'll take a janitor that walked past the door eavesdropping at this point.

God, I hate hospitals.

I think I'm going to have this baby at home. The thought popped into my head as if the baby was the one coming up with the idea. Screw the anxiety of lights and noises and being poked and prodded at all hours with no sense of time. How could any baby or mother get any rest in a place like this.

"Alex, why don't you come have a seat?" Roman insisted as he came back from having taken the boys down to the cafeteria to get them some food.

I stayed here waiting for some word on Big Mama's condition, but it gave me all this time for my mind to wander to dark places.

"Where are the boys?" Peering around him down the hallway with faces that didn't seem familiar at all, leaving me worried that any one of them could be there to hurt us. The boys being downstairs alone seemed like the worst idea.

"They're in the cafeteria with plenty of security. Their protection and ours are all here. No need to worry. Please, let's just sit and wait for the doctor." He said calmly.

My face must have been a dead giveaway to what I was thinking.

"I'm not having this baby in the hospital." I blurted out. His surprised expression this time seemed to disappear as fast as it came.

"Alright. Where are you planning to have it, then?"

"I want to have the baby at home. Where it's peaceful and filled with love. Not filled with sickness and anxiety."

He nodded slowly, wrapping an arm around me, sighing deeply before placing a soft brush of his warm lips on my temple.

"Sounds good to me. How do we go about doing that? Which house would you like to do it?" Knowing he was on board with the idea of a home birth took all the anxiety from me, replacing it with a stillness so peaceful and filled with love, I could barely process the answer to his questions.

"Oh, um, I was reading up on doulas and midwives. I'll have to research more and ask around for the best one, but which house would you rather have the baby in?"

"Personally, I don't think that moving with a baby would be a great idea, so how about the new house? I've been expediting the renovations, using my own team. I just need you to sign off on some personal touches, but it should be finished before the baby gets here." I forgot all about the renovations on the new house. So much going on with the gala coming up and now this. The house was such a distant memory, especially since we weren't planning to move into it for months.

"I think you're right. The new house is going to be her home, so that's where I want her to be born."

I just had a feeling this was a little girl. Like I was getting a chance to have the mother daughter relationship I always wanted. A voice pulled us out of our happy little world as a nurse approached, not giving Roman the chance to protest the idea of the baby being anything other than a girl.

"Is there a Darius Jackson or an Alex Kennedy?" I swallowed hard and raised my hand slowly as I looked around to see if Darius and the boys were headed back yet.

"I'm Alex Kennedy, I mean King. I just got married." Like any of that was important to her, but it delayed the information that I once thought I wanted immediately.

"So, Mrs. King, is Mr. Jackson here as well? I have him down as the patient's grandson." I looked to Roman, who nodded and hurried without delay down the hall. The cell reception in the hospital was awful and spotty at best, so he went to get the boys himself.

I however, had no desire to hear this news alone and opted to wait until they got back.

"He is. Roman went to get him and his brothers. They're just downstairs eating. Can we wait till he gets back..." My voice trailed off with worried anticipation.

"Of course." She responded politely.

She seemed nice enough and wasn't irritated at the fact I was taking her away from other things she may have needed to do in order to wait to give me the information she was sent out her to relay.

"How are you doing? Is there anything I can get you? Some juice or water. I don't want to assume, but it looks like you could be pregnant?" She seemed hesitant about asking. I'm sure it was because so many women seemed to get hostile when asked if they're pregnant.

What's the big deal?

The smile on my face was genuine, even if I felt a little guilty about being happy because of this sweet angel growing inside of me at a time like this. I felt the pink rise to my cheeks as I looked down and saw the marginal sized bump poking out through my fitted shirt and leggings that were starting to get snug. My jacket was laying over the back of the chair in the waiting room, so I had nothing wrapped around me to hide my growing bundle. I don't think I've ever paid as much attention to the size of my stomach as I have at this moment.

"Yes, I am. I think I'm ok for now, but I wouldn't mind some juice if it wouldn't be too much trouble, just in case." I needed to delay a little longer until they got back. I didn't want the nurse to let any information slip before I was ready to hear it. Meaning I needed Roman to hang onto, so I didn't crumble.

"Alex, what did the doctor say? Is Grams going to be alright?" Darius came running down the hall, panting and out of breath, when he reached me. Roman and the boys were still a ways away.

"I wanted to wait for you and your brothers before I heard anything. The nurse went to get me some juice and then she'll be back to give us the info. Is that ok?" Placing my hand on his shoulder, I tried to comfort him without getting too emotional. He nodded as the fear seeped from his eyes. We both needed to hear this information and process it without losing hope, if that's what was coming.

"We're all here." I said as I waved to the nurse who was walking back from wherever she got the juice from. I reached out and took the cup from her. It was covered with a sealed lid, and I had a flashback to the night I was drugged, and I watched the juice ripple in the cup as I trembled. Roman noticed and took the cup from me, placing it on the table next to the chair my coat was resting on. Roman laced his fingers with mine as the nurse smiled, looking between all of us. I couldn't tell if she had good news or bad news. She seemed well practiced at this particular aspect of her job and I hate to think she was happy about whatever bad news she might have to deliver.

"Mrs. Jackson is resting with the help of some pain medication and IV fluids. The doctor will be here soon to give you the specifics of what's going on, but it would be best if you all took the time to be with her and let her know you're there."

Darius pulled both his brothers in front of him with his arms wrapped tightly around their shoulders. I don't think the younger boys knew exactly what the nurse meant, but Darius did and his grip on his brothers probably gave it away.

"Can we all go in to see her together?" My voice cracked along with my heart. The emptiness of the space where I've kept Ella all this time is consuming me with pain. I have to fight it off, at least for now. Now, I have to say goodbye to the one person who is the reason I have a purpose in life. Her friendship in a place and time where no one else would've even talked to me, including her grandson meant the world to me and is the reason I was able to help so many people. Without her, none of this would've ever been possible.

"Sure, I'll send the doctor in-in a few minutes." She walked away, proba-bly to go back to whatever it was she was doing and would probably forget about us when all of this was over, like it was just how it was. I could never do the job these nurses do. I would never be able to witness so much pain and heartache on a daily basis, or be the bearer of that news, day in and day out, and not go through a deep depression. It's admirable and I'm glad it's not me.

We walked together into Ella's room, where she was hooked up to machines and IVs. She looked peaceful and pain free. I was definitely grateful she wasn't in pain, but I knew what was coming next. I didn't know if she would even wake up for us to say goodbye, so I hoped with all my soul that she could hear us.

***

ROMAN

I wrapped my arm around Alex, maybe to comfort her, but also for myself. It never occurred to me that things were this bad. I thought maybe she would be with us at least another year.

Did anyone know the cancer was this aggressive?

I guess it doesn't matter now. All we can do now is be there for Ella's grandchildren, like we said we would.

"Hello everyone. I'm Dr. Patel. Mrs. Jackson's oncologist." He looked at Alex and smiled robotically. "I think we met in my office. What was your name again?"

"Alex. Darius and I were there with Ella when you gave her the news of her cancer diagnosis." I vaguely remember her telling me how unimpressed she was with the way he dispensed the information to them. I hope he tried harder this time. She reached out and hooked her arm through Darius' and pulled him in front of the doctor, almost like she was making sure he really saw them and wasn't just giving obligatory information to a room full of strangers.

"Ah, yes, that's right. I'm sorry we are meeting again under these circumstances. As you know, Ella was brought into the ER unconscious and after running some tests, we've found that the cancer has spread throughout her entire body now, including her brain and that could be the reason she isn't waking up. I'm very sorry, but it doesn't look good, and I would suggest getting her affairs in order and if need be, saying your goodbyes as soon as possible. The possibility that she has more than a couple of days, maybe less, is slim. I have a signed DNR in her file, so by law we have to accept her wishes. At this point, we are just keeping her comfortable. Stay as long as you'd like. If there is anything we can do for you, let us know and we'll do what we can." With that, we watched him in silence as he left the room and walked away without looking back.

Alex let go of my hand carefully and slowly made her way over to Ella, with Darius still tucked safely in her arm. I put my hands on Isaac and Dante's shoulders and encouraged them to sit on the other side of the bed and be with their grandmother to say goodbye. Backing up slowly towards the door, so I didn't alarm Alex into thinking I was leaving, I looked into the hallway and saw Boss then nodded before pulling the handle and quietly closed the door for some privacy. I leaned on the door, crossing my arms over my chest, protecting whatever was left of the energy I had to take care of Alex and the baby when this night was over. My guess is, we'd need to take the boys home with us tonight as well. I had no idea what kind of condition they'd be in, but it wasn't a time to be alone.

I took out my phone and texted Mary. She was at the house taking care of things since we got back.

ROMAN: *"Hi Mary. If you're still at the house, can you please make sure the guest rooms have clean sheets and the bathrooms are stocked? We will be having a few guests tonight. Also, could you have something made for dinner? I think a home cooked meal would be good instead of take out."*

I really didn't know what else I could do. They might not even want to eat. I just want to make sure they know our home is their home whenever they need it.

MARY: *"Of course. Is everything alright?"*

I didn't tell her we had gone to the hospital, just that we had to leave and would be back later.

ROMAN: *"Not really, but it's nothing for you to worry about. I'll let you know later."*

Mary had been with me for about five years. She'd seen me through my breakup with Caitlin and was an ear to listen when I was going through a rough time seeing my mom battle depression. I knew she would be an asset when the baby came in helping Alex.

MARY: *"I will make sure the house is clean and ready for guests. Anything in particular you would like me to make?"*

ROMAN: *"Whatever is easiest for you. Thank you, Mary."*

I slipped my phone into my pocket and looked up as the beeping on the machine next to the bed started going wild right before a long monotonous buzz filled the room and was replaced by the sound of love and loss through sobbing tears of heartfelt goodbyes.

Chapter 47

ALEX

It's been two days since we buried Ella. I still can't find the strength to get out of bed. The boys are staying with us for a week and Roman has really stepped up and made sure they've been fed and cared for while I used being pregnant as an excuse to not function. He offered to stay home with me Monday morning since the boys were staying home from school, but I just wanted to be alone. Mary cooked for everyone, bringing mine into my room and setting it on the table next to the window, which I barely touched. She was very motherly, but not intrusive at all. I saw my family and friends at the funeral and then checked out—not answering phone calls or texts.

"Honey, we're all heartbroken about Ella, but you need to get out of bed and rejoin the world," Roman said as he handed me my phone. I felt the pain of her loss as much as my own mother and I dropped the phone on the bed, sobbing into my hands.

"Baby, I'm so sorry. I don't know how to make the pain go away. All I know is that Ella is the reason this foundation exists, and without you, there is no foundation."

I almost laughed when I snorted before mumbling, "I would be in so much trouble right now. She'd probably slap me upside my head if she could."

Roman took me in his arms and held me close. I breathed him in until all the wonderful memories of the time I spent with Ella flooded my mind, giving me the strength to focus on why I became friends with her and what I promised her.

"I love you Alex. Let's get you up and dressed. I think you have a gala committee meeting this morning in a couple of hours with Amelia."

"You're right, I'm being ridiculous. I told Big Mama I'd take care of the boys and I haven't seen them in two days."

What kind of guardian am I? Geez, what kind of mother would I be if something like this happened after the baby was born?

"The boys are fine. The only person I'm worried about right now is you. Get showered. Mary will have breakfast ready and we can all eat together before security takes Isaac and Dante to school. You and I and Darius will go into the office together. I want them to see you're alright. They've been asking about you. I told them it's a lot of work growing a baby and you needed the rest. I could tell they didn't really believe that so, I want them to see for themselves that you're ok."

I nodded, grateful for his motivation and he helped me into the shower where I did my best to wash away the pain and tears of my broken heart.

***

ROMAN

"What time will you guys be home from school today?" I asked Dante and Isaac. It was strange having a conversation like this with teenagers, but it felt almost normal. I guess I was ready to become a parent, after all.

"We've both got basketball practice after school and we usually walk home." Dante didn't look up from his plate as he quickly responded. This was all so unusual for them and I didn't want to be the parent they lost, but right now, no one was walking anywhere by themselves.

As I was about to let them know the new protocol, Darius voiced his concerns and stepped into the shoes he'd been trying to fill, for what I can imagine was years in the making.

"Guys, look, I know we've been doin' things a certain way while we been with Grams, but things are different now and we gonna make some changes. We're staying with the Kings till next week until I know how my schedule gonna work with yours and that y'all are taken care of after school if I ain't home yet, ok? No more walking anywhere for now. That's why we got these bodyguards. Y'all both better get used to it anyway when y'all go pro."

They both nodded with big toothy grins on their face at their brothers' admiration for them before tucking into their breakfast. Darius was growing into a man right before my very eyes, taking on a tremendous responsibility. When I was his age, I doubt I could've done the same. Harrison would've been totally neglected.

When Alex walked into the kitchen, she almost looked like her old self. She was wearing a fitted black dress that accentuated the growing bump and black boots, looking the epitome of a professional businesswoman. She had also done her hair and makeup. You could barely tell she was in mourning except for the barely noticeable swelling around her eyes and the slight bloodshot appearance they had. Other than that, she covered her pain well. All three of Ella's grandsons got out of their seats and made their way to hug her. I watched as the three young men embraced the woman they once assumed was their enemy.

"Miss Alex, you told us you was a hugger and you didn't care if we wanted one or not, we had to live with it as long as you were a part of our lives. So, we plan to hug you every day we see you."

Oh damn, she's gonna lose it now. She pulled them all to her, tightly; squeezing her eyes shut. Her lack of tears shocked me.

"You boys, I mean young men, sure do know how to make a girl smile. Thank you so much, and I'm sorry for the past few days. I should've been there for you."

As the three of them stepped back to give her some space, Darius shook his head.

"No, Alex, you always tell me we process things differently. I took care of my brothers. That's my job. I've been doing it for years. It scared me at first but grams and I talked about it and she said if I wasn't ready to be the man I had to be, you would've never given me that opportunity. You already took care of us, now you take care of you and that baby."

Alex's eyes widened and this time she couldn't hold back the tears, they just slid right down her cheeks and she reached out, grabbing Darius into one of her unrelenting embraces and told him she loved him and would always be there for him and his brothers.

***

ALEX

I walked into the gala meeting feeling more capable than I had a few days ago.

"Alex, the following document contains the minutes of our previous meeting, outlining potential food and decoration ideas and a possible new location." Amelia handed me the notes and sat down, getting organized to take notes for this meeting in the chair next to me. We decided on the Museum Center at Union Terminal. After the museum closed early at three p.m., we would transform it into a *Spring is in Bloom* gala with champagne and chocolate fountains. Giovanni's chef would provide a gourmet three course plated dinner, followed by dessert stations. A live jazz band and several open bars strategically placed throughout the venue. The event held a hefty price tag just to attend, at $2000 per person and that didn't include the silent auction full of exquisite paintings, exclusive Santoro wines, trips and even a vintage mustang was being donated for the auction, plus so much more. I was beyond grateful for the outpouring of support from the community. This showed me their commitment to transforming our beautiful city into a place we could truly be proud of. Where neighbors cared about neighbors regardless of all the things that seemed to divide us. I

n the end, we were all in agreement we were human beings who deserved love and respect. I signed off on all the changes and Amelia took that as her cue to implement them as I hurried into my next meeting with Grant and Mr. Santoro about the winery upgrades.

Grant got up from the table cautiously, as I walked in, possibly waiting to assess my mood, but I was in business mode as Mr. Santoro embraced me and kissed both of my cheeks. I kept my composure and said, "I'm doing better, no need to talk about it. Is that going to be a problem?" My relationship with Grant had changed so much, from fatherly to stranger almost overnight; not really wanting to share anything with him anymore.

"Nope, none at all, Mrs. King." Grant said with a smirk as he pulled a chair out for me.

"So, Alex, have you come up with a name for the non-wine business yet?" I'd been thinking about it so often and made up so many names that just didn't do it justice. But I kept coming back to one phrase that stuck while trying to incorporate the herbs into the title somehow, and that was—With Wine.

"Alessandro, what was my problem *with*? I mean, the reason I needed rehab? My drink of choice, so to speak?" He smiled at me as he nodded his head, willing to play along with my questioning to get to the answer.

"*With* wine, I presume?"

"Yes, and what am I trying to infuse the herbs *with*?" His smiled widened as he was connecting the dots.

"*With* wine." I smiled back, offering one last question.

"What am I utterly obsessed *with*, for better or worse...besides Roman, that is?" Laughter filled the room. It was music to my ears after so much had happened that sucked the happy from almost every moment of my life, it seemed.

"*With* wine." He answered again and this time I joined in on the laughter, finally able to see the fruition of my pain and suffering and why it had to happen.

"Yes! I think the perfect name for this product is *With Wine*. The tinctures will be added as ordered, so the wines stay true to their flavor in the containment process. We will fill and label as they're ordered. Each tincture has its own value and will be created as..." The right way to say this was not as easy to put into words as I thought it would be. "For example: someone wants the calming wine. It will be ordered as Be Calm-With Wine or the anti-anxiety will be Less Anxious-With Wine. More energy will be Energized-With Wine, etcetera. I've already been in contact with the people who will take care of growing the herbs. They will stay at my house in the country. I really had no other plans for it and they are a family of four who are related to my herbologist professor in Indonesia. They have extensive knowledge of these particular herbs and how to grow them, along with the process for making the tinctures. I am going to need to build a much larger greenhouse with the capability of creating and containing the tinctures in large quantities on the property, but that can be budgeted into the money allocated for this project from the fundraiser."

"Alex, this is incredible, and I think it's perfect. I look forward to working alongside you to create this amazing product." Alessandro stood up and reached his hand out and I shook it without hesitation. I finally felt like my purpose in life was being fulfilled and I was being taken seriously for who I am and not who anyone else thought I was.

***

ROMAN

The day of the gala, Alex spent with Amelia getting the venue just right and preparing for all the workers. Grant made sure there was going to be plenty of security on the premises. No one knew where the gala was going to be held until the week before, so no one had time to figure the place out and plant bombs if it got out to the wrong people where the location was. The security team thoroughly vetted all the people on the invite list and looked into whether they had any affiliation to the Ellington's or Toscano's.

According to Edward, they were all cleared.

"Harrison, what's up?" I answered my phone and sat down in the leather chair in the living room, kicking my feet up on the ottoman.

"Are we riding together tonight? We definitely don't have to, but we seem to have fun and we could use more of that in our lives, don't you think?" He was right about that.

" Sounds like a plan. Alex gets home at five. Let's meet here at seven. The gala starts at 7:30 with cocktails and hors d'oeuvres."

"We'll see you then." I looked at my watch to see how much time I had before Alex returned and decided to get ready early.

***

"Hey babe, can you help me with these cufflinks?" I hated putting these starch pressed shirts on but, what else do you wear with a tux. I waited until she was out of the shower to have her help me with the finishing touches.

I've dreamed of doing this with her as my wife. Getting ready for a big event together.

"Wow, don't you look amazing."

I heard her but I couldn't respond. I was actually speechless. She was wearing a low-cut, sparkling champagne colored dress with the waist synched high over her now very noticeable baby bump. Her skin had a shimmer to it that almost looked like she'd been out in the sun all day. Hair cascading down her shoulders in long waves took my breath away and it was everything I could do not to mess it all up. I should never have gotten ready so early.

"Um.." I cleared my throat, extending my wrist to her, trying to hold it together with her touching my skin. A warmth spread through me as I caught the shimmer of her ring signifying she was my wife.

She finished with the cuffs, and I took her face in my hands, sliding them gently to the back of her head so I didn't ruin her hair, then pressing my lips to hers softly, so I didn't smear her makeup. She moaned as she leaned into the kiss, pulling away reluctantly, knowing there wasn't enough time to finish what we were starting here.

"I know, it's time to go," she said breathlessly, and we walked out to the living room as Amelia and Harrison were walking in from the elevator.

"Wow, Amelia, you look fantastic." Alex swooned over her friend, but Harrison didn't look amused.

"Excuse me, am I invisible? You've been with her all day, and she still gets all the compliments." I knew he was hiding a smirk, but it was funny because he probably wasn't joking.

"Harrison, I'm sorry. You look so handsome in your tux. In fact..." She spun around and looked between me and Harrison "...do you have any idea how much you look like your brother in these tuxes?" She looked genuinely surprised, but we do favor each other, especially when we're dressed alike.

"Great, and here I thought you were complimenting me." We had a good laugh at my expense before I held Alex's coat out and she slipped her arms in so we could leave for the gala.

***

ALEX

The driver let us out at the bottom of the large stone stairway leading up to the venue. Just looking at all those steps made me slightly queasy. At this stage of pregnancy, the thought of climbing them felt like an Olympic event.

Amelia and Harrison led the way while Roman reached for my hand, steadying me with his other hand resting at the small of my back. Being this pregnant gave gravity every opportunity to betray me, and Roman seemed determined not to let it.

Once inside, we handed our coats to the attendant, and Roman tucked our ticket stubs into his pocket to retrieve later. Now that my eyes had adjusted to the dim lighting, I could finally take in the room.

White roses and African daisies woven with tiny lights lined the entrance to the ballroom. Giant illuminated butterflies hung from nearly invisible filament wire overhead, creating the illusion that they were floating through the air. Tables draped in crisp white linens filled the space, each set with sparkling water goblets and wine glasses that caught the glow from the chandeliers.

The bars were stocked with top-shelf liquor, reserve vintage wines, and several test bottles of With Wine along with tinctures for attendees to sample throughout the evening.

For a while, we made our rounds, schmoozing with the who's who of the city, smiling through introductions and conversations. Eventually, exhaustion began creeping into my bones, and I was more than ready for a break.

I spotted Maggie and Abby across the room, and the three of us escaped to a cozy sofa tucked away from the crowd. The moment we sat down, we kicked off our shoes with matching sighs of relief.

Abby had her baby almost a month ago now, a beautiful little girl she named Evelyn Marie. She gave her my middle name because, according to Abby, she wanted her daughter to grow up strong like her godmother.

Of course, that was the worst possible thing she could have said to me.

I completely lost it at the hospital while holding that precious little girl in my arms.

Maggie's baby was due only a few weeks after mine. Since she already had a boy and a girl, they had decided to make the birth a surprise.

A few weeks ago, Roman and I met with a doula and a midwife and came to the same decision. We weren't going to find out the sex of the baby either. Instead, we planned to decorate the nursery in soft neutral tones and wait for the surprise when our child finally arrived.

"Girls I wanted to let you know that Roman and I decided to have the baby at home." Abby gasped, just like I knew she would and Maggie waited to hear more.

"Why would you do something like that? You're going to want pain meds. It hurts like a bitch." Abby said, while Maggie snickered.

"I don't like hospitals. I hate everything about the hospital environment. I feel like if I'm at home with Roman, who keeps me calm, then the baby will have a more calming experience coming into the world. I don't want her..." they both looked at me like I was keeping something from them."...I just feel like it's a girl is all—we aren't finding out—but I don't want the first thing she experiences to be all those lights and needles and strangers."

We finished our chat as soon as Roman, Jack, and Matt walked over to interrupt.

"Time for dinner then we have some speeches to give." Roman reminded me as I winced at the thought of having to talk in front of all these strangers, but if I focused on the reason for the speech, I would be alright...I think.

"I'll be right there; I have to use the restroom. I'll be quick. I heard Chef Anthony cooked the food personally." I hurried down the hall while the rest of our table all found their seats.

"Alex, wait." Someone grabbed my arm in an alarming fashion. I jerked it from their grip and cocked my hand back to defend myself.

"Woah, hold up, don't hit me, I just want to talk."

Luke!

"What are you doing here? No. Never mind. I don't care what you're doing here. What I do care about is that you're leaving right now." I pulled my phone out of my purse and pressed the first number I thought to call.

"Alex, I just need to talk. About our div..." His voice trailed off as his eyes locked on to my ring and then my stomach, going almost black in the process. When he looked back at me, he was not the same person he was just a second ago that wanted to talk.

"Edward, I'm by the restrooms. Can you come right now, please? Luke is here and I don't feel safe."

Within seconds, I could see my brother and some of the other security guards running in our direction.

"You know, I really don't give a fuck what happens to you now. You married the asshole before I even had a chance to tell you I never wanted a divorce." He sneered, obscenities rolling off his tongue like venom.

I already knew Grant broke us up and for good reason, even if it was behind my back and my wishes. Luke took off down the hall, but Edward stopped to check and see if I was ok before following the rest of the guards after him.

I brushed off the encounter, but wondered who else could be in here if Luke somehow made his way in. I finished in the bathroom and texted Boss, just in case.

ALEX: *"I'm in the restroom. Could you walk me back to the table?"* I felt so weak and helpless like this, but I wasn't taking any chances while I was pregnant.

BOSS: *"Already here."* Thank God, I thought as relief washed over me and let out the breath I was holding before pushing the door open.

"Hi. Sorry about that. I guess Edward got a hold of you?"

He nodded and led me back to the table where everyone was talking and smiling, seemingly oblivious to what had just happened in the hall.

"Thank you, Boss." I said gratefully.

Roman looked at me with concern as I sat down and I winked at him, taking his hand and giving it a slight squeeze.

"Did something happen?" Roman whispered, but I felt like it wasn't the time to get into it, so I told him I saw Boss in the hall and asked him to escort me to the table in case I tripped. I'm sure he wasn't buying it, but he let it go.

We finished dinner then Roman and I walked up on stage. Darius and his brothers were seated with us at our table and had no idea I was planning to bring them up on stage. As the music quieted down Roman grabbed the mic and began.

"Ladies and gentlemen, may I have your attention for just a moment? First, I'd like to thank each and every one of you for being here tonight and helping make this such a special event. I hope everyone gets everything they bid on, so drink up and bid high."

The room erupted with laughter and cheers.

"But seriously, we truly appreciate your generosity and your willingness to support such an important cause. Now, I'd like to turn the microphone over to the lady of the hour, my beautiful wife, Mrs. Alex Kennedy-King."

I stood as the room rose to its feet in a standing ovation. The sight was surreal. The fact that all these people were standing for me felt impossible to process, but the truth was I wasn't the lady of the hour. That honor belonged to Ella Jackson.

"Thank you," I said, blinking back emotion. "Thank you so much. Please, everyone, have a seat."

The crowd slowly settled back into their chairs.

"I am incredibly grateful for all of you and for the generosity you've shown tonight. But this evening isn't about me. It's about a woman who embodied courage, sacrifice, and unconditional love. When her son tragically died from an overdose in a neighborhood where drugs were being distributed openly and far too often, she stepped in and took on the responsibility of raising her three grandsons. While most people had given up on that neighborhood, she never gave up on those boys."

I paused, gathering myself before continuing.

"By the time I found my way there, it was almost too late. What began as an unexpected friendship quickly became something much more. Ella became family."

My eyes drifted toward the young men seated nearby.

"And now I have the tremendous honor of introducing you to the three young men she raised. Three young men who are going to leave this world better than they found it because of the woman who believed in them."

I turned toward the large screen behind me and motioned to Amelia. A beautiful photograph of Ella appeared on the screen, illuminated beneath the ballroom lights.

"Darius, would you please come up and bring Dante and Isaac with you?"

Darius rose from his chair and encouraged his younger brothers to do the same. Together, they made their way to the stage. I hugged each of them before turning back toward the audience.

"This is Darius Jackson, the CEO of the foundation. He has proven to us time and time again that he is exactly the right person for the job. Darius helped bring nearly the entire neighborhood together behind this vision and turned what once seemed impossible into reality. Quite simply, none of this would have happened without him."

The audience applauded while Darius ducked his head modestly.

"His brothers, Dante and Isaac, are both still in high school. They're standout athletes and exceptional students. Ella kept them involved in sports, clubs, and after-school activities because she wanted to make sure they always had opportunities in front of them. She created an environment where they could learn, grow, and excel instead of becoming another statistic."

My gaze swept across the room.

"Unfortunately, not every young person in that neighborhood was given the same opportunity. Some fell into the very traps Ella worked so hard to keep these boys away from. Stories like theirs are exactly why tonight matters. It's why this foundation matters. Because hope matters. We may not be able to save everyone, but for the people we can reach, we're helping create futures worth believing in and opportunities worth pursuing."

The room was completely silent. As emotional as the moment was, I couldn't help smiling.

"And now, before I let everyone get back to eating, drinking, and spending money, I have one more announcement."

A ripple of laughter moved through the crowd.

"As for the non-wine biz." I held up air quotes. "Side of things, we've finally settled on a name."

I looked toward Amelia and nodded.

She changed the slide behind me.

Large wine-colored letters appeared on the screen.

WITH WINE.

The audience erupted into applause.

"The bars throughout the venue have samples of our wines and tinctures available for you to try, so please enjoy them and let us know what you think."

I glanced around the room one last time.

"Thank you all again for being here tonight. Your generosity is helping create real change, and we are deeply grateful for every one of you. Enjoy the rest of your evening."

Darius, Dante, and Isaac each offered me an arm as we carefully made our way down the short staircase from the stage. Together, they escorted me back to my table while the room filled once more with applause, conversation, and the hopeful energy that had brought everyone there in the first place.

***

ROMAN

"May I have this dance?" I didn't give her a moment to answer. I took her hand and led her to the dance floor. I knew she was getting tired of talking and mingling and all the things that come with hosting these events, but I wanted one more dance with my wife and to find out what happened earlier.

"Of course. I think I have one more dance in me." She said warily as her eyes droop slightly but the green sparkled.

I twirled her around the dance floor with her body as tight to mine as her belly would allow.

"So, tell me what that was earlier? When Boss brought you to the table."

She stopped dancing and looked up at me with trepidation in her eyes.

"Luke was here. I called Edward and he took care of it. Nothing happened."

We were completely stopped on the dance floor, with people dancing carefree all around us.

"What did he say to you?"

He had to be here for a reason, but what the hell would that reason be?

"Nothing. He was going to tell me that Grant is the one who broke us up, but he got upset when he realized we were married and pregnant. That's when security got there. Nothing happened. I promise." She assured me.

I could see nothing happened, but if I got my hands on that guy, something would happen. That was all I was going to let interrupt our more than perfect evening before I mentioned it was time to go home.

I took my tickets out of my pocket to retrieve our jackets so we could get out of here. I needed to cuddle my wife.

She slipped her arms into her jacket, and I pulled it closed as she buttoned it up. I took the collar, pulling her to me and placing a kiss on her warm, soft lips.

"You were perfect tonight. We are so blessed everything turned out the way it did. Without a hitch." I said as I looked around for Harrison and Amelia, but neither was in sight, so I texted Harrison to find out if they were leaving with us or getting their own ride home.

ROMAN: *"We're leaving. Are you coming with us?"*

HARRISON: *"Amelia said she had to be somewhere and took off. I have no idea where she went. Maybe she's already outside."*

ROMAN: *"Everything ok?"*

HARRISON: *"No idea. She's been really weird tonight and all over the place. I know she was in charge of this event, but damn, can't she take a minute to enjoy it?"*

ROMAN: *"Maybe she's just working behind the scenes. We don't know all that goes into making sure that happens."*

HARRISON: *"Yeah, you're probably right. I'll just text her to meet us at the car."*

ROMAN: *"Sounds good, man."*

I put my phone into my pocket and grabbed my wife's hand.

"You ready to go?" The tired eyes and weak smile were all I needed as confirmation.

"So ready. Let's go home."

Many people had the same idea that we had and the three of us walked to the top of the stone staircase but waited just a second before descending to see if Amelia was coming—she was still nowhere to be found. With my hand securely on Alex's back, making sure she was steady, we started down the stairs. She stood still then I felt her breathing become heavier.

Something's not right.

"Alex, what's wrong, sweetheart?"

"I think it's time I let you in on a little secret. Remember that time I passed out in the elevator?"

I remember that day well. It scared the hell out of me I still don't know exactly what happened to her.

"How could I forget?" I insisted.

"Well...The real truth is that I'm afraid of...." She looked terrified as she stared straight ahead.

"Afraid of what, honey?" I watched as she swallowed, not looking at me still.

"Heights..." She trailed off without engaging me, but in that instant, the entire world seemed to move in slow motion. The yelling coming from behind us or to the side of us or wherever it was coming from was loud and chaotic. I glanced behind us, not wanting to take my eyes off Alex, and saw security racing towards us. Then the shaking I felt from Alex brought me back to her as I followed her line of sight to what was in front of us. Marcus looking like a shell of the man he portrayed as the politician—disheveled, unshaven and deranged. He was pointing a massive gun at us, and I could only throw myself at Alex as the gun fired; then another shot rang out almost simultaneously. I braced my arms around her so when we fell, she didn't hit the concrete. A bloodcurdling scream pierced the air from Alex as we plummeted to the ground. I cradled her head in my hand, doing my best to keep her from hitting it on the steps. The only pain I felt was a searing ache in my wrist and hand from bracing our fall; the throbbing pulse mirrored the frantic beat of my heart.

"Alex, baby, look at me. Are you alright? Baby." I called again. Her eyes were open and she looked terrified. She lifted her hand, revealing the blood covering it. "Oh God, where are you hurt? Somebody help!!" I yelled to whoever would listen. Security immediately surrounded us, as Alex was screaming and crying.

"No, oh God, noooo." She screamed in a distressed garble, scrambling away from me, and moving toward something or someone in front of her. Not just any someone, Grant.

"We need a doctor. Is there a doctor here?" I yelled.

This group of people certainly had a doctor in the bunch. A man pushed his way through the brick wall of security to get to Grant.

"I'm a doctor, what happened?" He kneeled next to Alex, who was in shock, gripping him tight. Blood covered her; she cried and shook hysterically.

"Alex, honey, let the doctor work on him." I tried to get her away, to give the doctor some space, but she refused. The man did what he could but said he was already gone. There was nothing he could have done.

While the surrounding panic seemed to have died down. I searched for Marcus—to make sure that he was gone.

That's when I saw him on the ground with a bullet hole in his forehead. He was definitely gone.

Who the hell shot him?

I looked in all the directions I could, scanning the area for the security guard that was quick enough to neutralize the threat. What I found shocked the hell out of me even more than what happened. Harrison was standing like a statue staring at the roof of the museum, caught in a trance as Amelia stared back at him, holding what looked like a high-powered rifle with a scope. I tapped Harrison on the shoulder to bring him out of it before Amelia quickly glanced at me and then disappeared.

"I don't know what's going on, but I have to get Alex out of here. Grant's dead and so is Marcus."

He nodded, with tears welling up in his eyes and his face contorted with anguish.

Now wasn't the time to figure out Amelia's secrets. Now was the time to take care of my family.

"Let's go. We can figure this out later." He shrugged my hand off his shoulder and stomped back up to the museum.

"I'll talk to you later." He yelled over his shoulder. I can't imagine what he was about to get into with her, but I had a feeling it wouldn't be good for either of them.

Chapter 48

ROMAN

With Marcus gone, the threat hanging over us, our friends, and our families had finally disappeared. We dissolved the security detail and, for the first time in what felt like forever, returned to something resembling a normal life. Alex resumed her Saturday lunches with her girlfriends and continued teaching self-defense classes at Bruce's studio twice a week. Boss helped with the demonstrations since she was far too pregnant to be throwing people around herself.

Grant's funeral was small and private, with the wake held at the Santoros' property. I expected to see Amelia at either the funeral or the wake, but she never showed up. She didn't answer texts or return calls either. At that point, I wasn't even sure if I still had an assistant, though it hardly seemed important compared to everything else that had happened.

A couple of months had passed since the gala. Alex and I were fully settled into the new house, and she was thriving being so close to her friends, exactly as I knew she would. Thank God she had them. After everything we'd been through, and after all the death we'd witnessed, she needed that support system more than ever. None of it could have been good for her recovery.

The drive into the city still felt strange after years of living closer to the office, but I had come to appreciate the extra time. It gave me a chance to clear my head and prepare for the day before walking into whatever chaos awaited me.

Only there wasn't any chaos.

The moment I stepped off the elevator onto the fifteenth floor, an uneasy feeling settled over me. Monday mornings were usually buzzing with activity. Phones rang. Conversations drifted through the hallways. People hurried from one meeting to the next.

Today, the floor felt deserted. The stillness was unsettling. Amelia's desk sat empty again, which wasn't surprising. Shay had been helping cover her responsibilities during her absence. As I walked toward my office, I noticed the door was slightly open. I slowed. For a brief moment, I wondered if Harrison had arrived early. The floor was too quiet. Even with the threat behind us, old habits died hard. I glanced around one last time before easing the door open. The sight waiting inside stopped me cold.

Amelia.

She stood behind my desk as if she had never left, calmly arranging my schedule for the day alongside a fresh cup of coffee and neatly organized notes from last week's meetings. Like she'd been there all along.

"Hello?" I asked with concern for one of our safeties, not really knowing which one it was. *W*

hose side was she really on?

"Good morning, Roman. I brought today's schedule, the meeting notes, and here is your coffee, black, just the way you like it." She seemed normal, which terrified me after what we witnessed at the gala. There was nothing normal about this, Amelia.

"Good morning. How are you?" I asked, although it was just a pleasantry. I wanted to get to the truth.

"Fine. Is there anything else?"

I turned and closed the door. I think it's time she and I had a serious conversation.

"Yes. I think there is. Have a seat." I pointed to the chair she sat in so many other times, like we were about to shoot the breeze about some crappy contractor or what I needed to do to make Alex happy. However, I knew this wasn't going to be that.

"What can I do for you, Roman?" The annoyance was obvious, and I was glad she wasn't pretending anymore. She was not my pleasant assistant—she was definitely someone else.

"Well, we can start by being honest for once?"

"Or you could look at the file on your desk. It's the emails I erased from your computer the day you came back from your honeymoon. I didn't think you were ready for the information yet."

The emails?

Ah, yes, when she wiped my emails and told me it was all junk mail. The first page had a picture of my least favorite person. Alex's ex-husband Luke. It looked like he was a little worse for wear in the picture. I wondered what happened and who I needed to thank. I flipped through the pages, seeing a picture of the woman from the restaurant along with the pictures Alex took or Rick at the restaurant.

That's where I remember her from.

My hands started to shake when I read that Tanner's suicide was not a suicide, along with a confession from Alex's ex.

"Is this what I think it is?" I looked at Amelia, wondering how she got all this information.

"Depends. Do you think it was Luke confessing he was the reason the Ellingtons went after Alex? Then the answer is yes. When Grant broke them up, he went to his bookie. Luke owed the Ellingtons a lot of money from gambling losses. His retaliation was to offer Alex up on a silver platter for their sex trade business." Her snicker about blew a gasket in me.

"You think that's funny? What the hell is wrong with you?"

"No, I don't think it's funny at all what they tried to do. I think it's funny who they tried to do it to."

I took a deep breath, trying not to remember what Alex went through and who she became during it. It was scary as hell.

"So, you know all this information. Who are you, really?"

She smiled and I thought she was going to tell me, but before she had a chance to answer, the door opened abruptly. Harrison barging in, unannounced and uninvited, with what looked to be rage in his eyes.

"I'd like to know who the hell you are as well? Clearly, you're not the woman I thought I was going to marry and start a family with. Because that woman doesn't go around shooting people." His voice laced with anger.

Hurriedly, I came around the desk and placed my hands on his shoulders to back him away from her in case this got out of control. Since I had no idea what else Amelia was capable of, I felt Harrison should watch himself.

"Calm down. " I insisted. "We're going to talk about this like adults, without yelling."

He shoved me back, and I knew better than to placate him. I had no idea what was going on, but whatever it was, it didn't look like he had seen her since that night either.

"Fine." He grabbed the chair next to her, jerking it away from her as he sat down with a scowl on his face.

"First, I would like to formally submit my two weeks' notice."

What the hell?

I wasn't expecting that, even though I thought she 'd quit. She pointed to a paper that was on my desk right on top that I hadn't seen yet. It was her two weeks' notice in writing, signed Amelia Wright.

Shit, where the hell was, I going to find an assistant that could work in this nuthouse in the next two weeks?

I pushed the thought from my mind to try to concentrate on the issue at hand.

"Don't worry, I've already hired a new girl, and I will train her before I leave."

Ok, well, I guess that answers that.

"You know you don't have to quit. I don't know what's going on, but I didn't want to talk so I could fire you or have you quit. You've been like family to us for years now. I just don't understand what's going on is all. I'd like for you to elaborate, please."

"Thank you for everything, Roman, but my assignment is done. I'll be taking on a new assignment in two weeks when I leave here."

What?

"Assignment? What do you mean by assignment?"

Was she planted in this job?

I'm pretty sure I hired her—or did I?

Was she here before my dad left?

I remember the day she was hired—the same day I started—and I thought she'd be a problem. Guess I was right about that, after all—except not in the way I'd expected.

"Let me guess, you worked for Grant? You a security guard, too?" Harrison drawled while rolling his eyes, sounding unimpressed and annoyed.

"Not exactly. I didn't work for Grant. He and I owned the security company together. I came to America after my mother died when I was ten to live with my father. My mother left me a rather large sum of money that Grant encouraged me to invest in his company while I learned all the ins and outs. When I was old enough, I asked to be a partner, and he accepted my offer." She explained.

I watched as Harrison sat up in his chair, more than curious where this was going.

"Is that it? You just own a security company with Grant?" Harrison was prodding her to give him more to torture himself with.

What I heard, however, was she lost her mother at ten and was shipped off to America, which decidedly was not her country, to live with a father she may or may not have even known.

"Harrison, give her a break and let her continue if she'd like." I turned to Amelia, who was emotionless and cold. Whatever happened to her has left a big scar.

"I own a lot of things now that Grant is gone. He left me the security company along with his home, which happens to be the headquarters."

I think she was containing her true feelings right now and that could be dangerous, especially if it manifests like Alex.

"So, you have a ton of freaking money now. Is that all this was about, money?" Harrison glared at her, white knuckled on the arms of the chair. Amelia's face turned a deep shade of red as she took a long inhale to get herself under control, closing her eyes then opening them slowly as her head turned even slower in Harrison's direction. I was worried about my brother right now.

"I didn't need Grant's money, your money or anyone else's money, Harrison. This was never about money. This was about revenge. Marcus's father killed my mother, her best friend and my best friend, among a lot of other people..."

My heart jumped when the door opened and Alex walked in, eyes wide, looking at the three of us before locking onto mine. That's when it all clicked.

"Eliana..." Alex and I hurled the name through the open space in unison as a tear finally broke free from Amelia's stone-cold persona and splashed to the floor.

***

ALEX

"Holy..." I breathed.

The confusion on Harrison's face was understandable since he was not there the night we heard the story. I walked slowly towards Amelia or Eliana, looking like a scared child.

"Whelp, you figured it out. Good for you." She quickly brushed the tears from her face and got up. She looked hurt and exhausted. I know exactly how it feels to pretend to be something you're not for so long.

"Amelia, do you want to go somewhere and talk about this?"

I knew the guys were pushing her and I also knew that going through this kind of pain isn't good for anyone. She shot and killed her brother.

"Maybe another time. I really just want to finish out the two weeks' notice and be done. Would that be alright with the three of you?" She wrapped her arms around herself in a protective stance. I'll mind my p's and q's and let her go for now. She doesn't seem the least bit interested in being friends anymore.

"Sure, but if you ever want to talk, I'm still here for you."

She left the room silently with a simple nod of her head.

"Who is Eliana?" Harrison looked between the two of us for some kind of understanding.

"Marcus and Tanner's sister." I revealed.

Watching the color drain from Harrison's face was almost painful as I reached for my brother-in-law to ease his discomfort.

"The hell she is." He backed away from me, hands up in disbelief, not seeking comfort.

I walked over to the cooler instead, removing a bottle of water to hand to him. He took it but stood there, holding it down by his side.

"Harrison, I know this is difficult information to swallow, but maybe today is not the day to be getting it out in the open. It seems the wounds are still fresh and hearing this isn't going to fix anything."

Ouch, a cramp in my side wrenched up my face. I've been having these aches lately with the baby's due date fast approaching and the midwife said I should be relaxing more and stressing less. I guess this is as good a time as any to start destressing.

"I think I'll go do that at home then." He tossed the bottle of water to Roman and stormed out of the office. Suddenly, the pain was intense, and I saw stars thinking I was going to pass out or throw up.

"Alex." I heard the concern in Roman's voice. I couldn't breathe with the next pain, but it subsided enough to let me breathe before the next one rolled in.

"Ahhh. I think I'm in labor. We...need...to...get...home."

Epilogue

NINE MONTHS LATER

"Hey, guys," I said, hugging each of the kids on my way up to Abby's front door.

Today was Evelyn's first birthday, and it was the first party where all of our children were together. Maggie's baby boy had been born early, only days after Ella, and he'd had to stay in the hospital for a couple of weeks. But now little Brayden Michael was a big, healthy eight-month-old who was already giving his mommy and daddy a run for their money.

At last, the trio of best friends who had once dreamed of raising our children in the same neighborhood had become one enormous village.

How we got here after everything that happened was a miracle in itself. From my mom's death, to my drinking, to the mafia being dragged into our lives, it had felt like we were doomed to live in constant chaos. The day I went into labor, I thought it would be the final nail in Roman's coffin.

That was the day we found out Amelia was really Eliana, the sister of Marcus and Tanner Ellington, who were actually part of a rival mafia family—the Toscanos—whose crimes reached into drugs and human trafficking. I was still shocked Roman told me about Luke's involvement with the Ellingtons trying to sell me into a life of sexual abuse, but I knew exactly who delivered his justice and when.

Edward had barely said two words to me the night of the gala before he chased Luke down the hall.

I was relieved they were all gone, but losing Grant and Big Mama in the process still hurt. In the end, though, seeing our beautiful daughter's face when she came into the world was more than enough to outweigh every evil thing we had survived.

"'Bout time you got here," Abby yelled from the front door.

A quick hug was all I was afforded before my friend pushed me aside to get to Roman, who was holding our precious little girl, Ella Rose.

We gave her the middle name Rose because no one had more patience than my brother's fiancée, Rose, and we hoped our daughter would grow up to be just as patient and kind as her namesake. Her first name was my ultimate gift to the one person who gave me purpose when I had none. Before she was born, I asked Darius and his brothers if they would be okay with me naming our daughter after their grandmother. All three men simply nodded as tears filled their eyes.

"There's my sweet Ella. Hand her over, Roman."

Roman knew better than to argue with Abby. She might actually be scarier than I was.

She ushered us into the house, leading the way with Ella tucked against her shoulder. Ella smiled and snuggled closer, trying to find some relief from the tiny teeth pushing through her swollen gums.

"Roman, hurry out back to the bar. We've got the good bourbon, and you're going to need it," Jack yelled from the back door.

Roman didn't even bother looking in my direction. He headed straight outside to join the men, where drinks, cigars, and a few hours of uninterrupted guy time were waiting for him.

He deserved it.

I had always thought he fit in naturally with them. As for me, I had finally found my place with my friends too, not as the crazy drunk aunt everyone worried about, but simply as myself.

Speaking of aunts, Roman and I were leaving in a week for North Carolina to visit mine about getting my non-wine into the bar scene down there. She said there was someone she wanted me to meet, but honestly, I was more interested in spending time with her, reminiscing about the good years with my mom, and letting her get to know sweet little Ella.

***

"Roman, hurry up, we're going to be late."

Why is he always so lackadaisical when we're traveling?

"Honey, for the millionth time, we own the damn plane. It will wait."

"We do, don't we. Why does that surprise me every time?" I laughed.

He shook his head and took Ella from my arms, cooing and coddling her out to the car waiting in the driveway to take us to the airport.

The ringing of my phone startled me, and seeing Darius's name on the screen sent a ripple of concern through me.

"Hello, Darius. Is everything okay? What's going on?"

He rarely called for no reason, and I was about to leave them for a week to run the company on their own. With Amelia gone, I worried nothing was truly in capable hands.

After everything that happened, she had hired Felicity from Grant's real estate office to replace her as Roman's assistant. Meanwhile, Ryan took over the real estate office and hired what he considered his ideal receptionist, then another, and another after that.

Felicity, however, turned out to be a great hire.

I'd had a feeling about her from the first time we met. There was something intriguing about her, something that made me want to understand what made her tick. I supposed I would have plenty of opportunities now.

I never mentioned that part to anyone. I also never admitted that I suspected she might have ties to the mafia. Roman was already suspicious enough considering Amelia had hired her and she came from Grant's office. Thankfully, our relationship with the Santoros had begun to feel normal again.

Landon and Piper welcomed a baby boy shortly after their wedding and named him Roland after Landon's grandfather. Shay and Owen got engaged a couple of weeks ago, and Roman and I would be attending their engagement party as soon as we returned from North Carolina.

For the first time in a long time, life felt less like survival and more like living.

"Hi, Alex. Yeah, everything's good. I forgot to tell you that Alissa and I got engaged."

I screamed so loudly that the baby immediately started crying.

Oops.

A few months after Ella passed, Darius met a woman named Amanda who had recently moved into the neighborhood. She spent a lot of time at the community garden—affectionately named the Ella Jackson Community Garden and Park—helping plant, cultivate, and care for the space. Before long, Darius was completely enamored with her.

The neighborhood itself was flourishing in ways I had only dreamed about. In fact, it had surpassed even my most ambitious visions of what it could become. Their old neighborhood was still rebuilding from the damage the Ellingtons had caused, but things were finally moving in the right direction, with no new complications standing in the way.

"I'm so happy for you, Darius. We'll talk more when we get back, okay? If you need anything for the wedding, let me know. Oh my God, I'm so excited."

The words came out in a high-pitched screech before I could stop them.

Roman promptly took the phone from my hand and ended the call before I traumatized our daughter any further.

"I take it things have progressed with Alissa?" he asked, already knowing the answer.

I nodded enthusiastically.

For some reason, it felt like I had fulfilled the promise Ella had entrusted me with—to look after her grandsons after she was gone. The thought brought tears to my eyes.

My gaze drifted to our daughter, and I thought about my mother. Her accident had become the catalyst for everything that followed, including the business I never imagined I would build. With Wine had become an overnight sensation, and keeping up with demand was almost impossible. We had hired employee after employee just to stay ahead of the orders, but the Santoros continually assured me they had everything under control and would help however they could.

The truth was, I had more support than the old version of me would have known what to do with.

Once upon a time, I was the girl who didn't need anyone.

Now I had the biggest village imaginable in every aspect of my life, and I couldn't have been more grateful for it.

"Yes, they're getting married."

The car pulled up to the plane, and we gathered our bags, along with the baby, before making our way on board.

"Make sure you're not interjecting yourself into the wedding plans if they don't need your help."

Roman always thought I took on too much, and I was sure he was right. Still, Darius was as close as a brother to me, and I would do whatever he needed me to do.

Speaking of brothers, Edward and Bianca welcomed a baby boy and named him Taylor. He was the sweetest little thing, which must mean he took after Bianca. Edward also became Amelia's new partner at the security company, a move that significantly increased his income and allowed them to purchase a house that looked more like a vault than a home. Modern architecture had never really been my thing, but I had to admit the views of the city were incredible.

Patrick and Rose got married a few months ago, and he was still driving her just as crazy as he always had. Thankfully, Rose's patience remained as unwavering as ever.

"I'm not. I'll only ask if they want help, I promise."

Of course, I would probably ask every day until they said yes.

I laughed to myself as I settled into my seat beside Roman. Ella was already asleep, curled comfortably in his lap, her tiny hand resting against his chest.

My perfect, sweet family.

The thought filled my heart as I rested my head against Roman's shoulder. The steady hum of the engines surrounded us while exhaustion finally caught up with me, and within moments, I drifted off to sleep.

***

"What's the name of this place?" I asked my aunt as we pulled up behind the cutest dive bar I'd ever seen.

A purposely weathered deck wrapped around the building, overlooking the lake beyond in the distance. The dark wood exterior was interrupted by patches of chipped blue and white paint that somehow added to its charm instead of taking away from it. Unfortunately, I couldn't see the name because we had parked around back, and the sign was out front.

The rear parking lot was tiny.

I had no idea how my aunt managed to squeeze us into the last available space, especially with a massive black Hummer taking up half the lot. The place was packed, which was great news for selling my product but terrible news for my aversion to crowds.

"The Rose."

I smiled.

Very fitting for the first place outside of Cincinnati that I would ever peddle my wares.

"It's a place we found within the last year," my aunt said as she grabbed my hand and dragged me up the deck toward the back entrance.

The moment we stepped inside, the scent of stale beer and Marlboros hit me. It wasn't the kind of place I was used to frequenting, but then again, the places I used to spend my time were where most of my troubles had started.

The irony wasn't lost on me.

I laughed at the thought of being the only person in the building who didn't drink.

Roman had stayed behind at the hotel with Ella. Neither of us thought bringing a baby to a bar was the best parenting decision we'd ever make.

Still, the place had character.

Lots of it.

"O.M.G., look who it is!"

The familiar voice carried over the noise of the crowded bar.

My aunt had some amazing friends, and I always enjoyed spending time with them. Ever since I was old enough to drink, one of our favorite traditions had been spending afternoons with her friends at whatever local watering hole they happened to be frequenting.

"Barb. It's so good to see you."

She was one of my aunt's oldest and dearest friends and had always felt like family.

"How are you? It's been way too long."

While I chatted with Barb, I noticed my aunt wildly waving her arm toward what appeared to be the bartender. I reached out to stop her from flailing at the poor woman, but she assured me they knew each other.

"I'm fantastic," Barb said.

We continued catching up until the woman finally made her way over to our table.

"Hi, Diana. This must be Alex. I'm Lola."

She extended her hand across the table.

As I shook it, I noticed tattoos peeking out from beneath the sleeves of her shirt. Considering how warm it was outside, I found myself wondering why she was covered up, but I quickly dismissed the thought. Maybe the staff wasn't allowed to show tattoos. Although, judging by the heavily tattooed bartender working behind the bar, that theory didn't hold much water.

Lola wasn't what I expected. She was tall, with long dark brown hair and the prettiest brown eyes. There was something professional about her, something composed and steady that didn't quite fit with the image I'd created in my head. Maybe my empath abilities weren't working anymore. Or maybe there was simply more to her than met the eye. For some reason, I got the feeling she had a story. Not that now was the time to find out.

"Hi, Lola. Nice to meet you."

"So, your aunt tells me you have a business you'd like to pitch to me."

Before I could answer, a voice shouted from across the room.

"Hey, bartender!"

Lola closed her eyes for a brief second.

"I'm sorry. I'll be right back."

She turned and headed toward the bar.

"Hey, asshole!" she yelled as she stormed across the room.

I blinked.

Then I smiled.

And that was the day With Wine took off and became a household name.

Also by

JE JOHNSON

Acknowledgements

And just like that, we've reached the end of Alex and Roman's story.

Or have we?

When I first met these characters, I never imagined the journey they would take me on. What started as a story about love, loss, forgiveness, and redemption became something much bigger than I ever expected. Alex and Roman found a permanent place in my heart, and saying goodbye to them isn't nearly as easy as I thought it would be.

With Wine Comes Wellness marks the conclusion of the With Wine trilogy, and while every story eventually reaches its final chapter, I've learned that some characters have a way of lingering. They show up in unexpected places, whisper new ideas, and remind me that sometimes endings aren't really endings at all—they're simply doorways to something new.

What comes next? Well, you'll just have to wait and see.

I have a few surprises tucked away, a few stories still waiting for the right moment, and more than a few familiar faces who may or may not decide they've got unfinished business. For now, I'll keep those secrets to myself.

As always, thank you for spending your time with these characters and trusting me with a few hours of your life. Every page read, every review left, every message sent, and every recommendation shared means more than you'll ever know. Authors live on word of mouth, and your support is what allows stories like these to continue finding their way into the world.

If you enjoyed this journey, I would be incredibly grateful if you would take a moment to leave a review. Reviews help other readers discover books they might otherwise miss, and they remain one of the greatest gifts you can give an author.

Until next time, keep believing in second chances, redemption, and the kind of love that refuses to give up.

With love,

JE Johnson

P.S. Keep an eye on future updates. You never know who might decide to make another appearance.

About the author

JE Johnson
Just a believer who loves to write about extraordinary circumstances
wrapped up in highly dramatic fashion with a hard fought for happily ever
after bow— because a love worth having is worth fighting for!
Cheers!
https://www.jejohnsonauthor.com/

www.ingramcontent.com/pod-product-compliance
Lightning Source LLC
Chambersburg PA
CBHW031142050726
47495CB00018B/354